BRIGHT HORIZON
BOOKS

www.BrightHorizonBooks.com

SECRET
DESTRUCTION

Joseph Hergott

Bright Horizon Books
520 Thorndale Drive
Waterloo, ON, N2T 2A8
www.BrightHorizonBooks.com
books@BrightHorizionBooks.com

Ordering Information:
Quantity sales. Special discounts are available on quantity purchases
by corporations, associations, and others. For details, contact the
publisher at the address above.

All hand drawn illustrations displayed in this book whether on the cover or
inside are the sole ownership and were produced by Joseph Hergott.

This is a work of fiction. Besides the Pharaohs' names, characters, places
and incidents are a product of the author's imagination or are used fictitiously.
Any resemblance to actual events or persons is entirely coincidental.

Book design, cover design, and typsetting by
Michele Holme, www.micheleholme.ccom

SECRET
DESTRUCTION

PROLOGUE

Five knuckle bones rattled in the young man's cupped hand. The dark room was lit by two oil-filled lamps that cast black, grotesque shadows on the grimy walls. He threw the bones of chance on the dirt floor. Another winner! His wife, overjoyed with his increasing fortune, leaned over his shoulder, whispering words of love and encouragement, and then snuggled against his back. He had won more money in this game than he could ever spend. *I should stop now. I'm rich*, he told himself. The young man could barely suppress his excitement as he beamed at his long-time friend. The more seasoned gambler, usually a winner, returned the glance with an inscrutable smirk. He was a rich man. Maybe losing tonight was inconsequential to him.

"Just one more roll," he said. Once more — another win!

"OK! Time to stop," he said as he gathered his debins of gold into a black bag.

"You are on a roll, my friend," said his older comrade. "You are almost as rich as Pharaoh's prime ministers. But you can't stop now. Come on! Let me win back some of my gold."

A bead of sweat formed on his temple and then rolled down his cheek. He drew in a breath of stagnant air. Uncertainty washed over him. He paused, and then picked up the bones, debating with himself. Decision made, he rattled them, kissed his hand and cast them to the ground.

"Oh no!" His luck had just run out. He saw his jackpot evaporate before his eyes. A sick feeling clenched his gut as he stared at the dismal toss. His mouth went dry as he beseeched his friend, the winner.

"Don't worry, I'll let you win it back," soothed the older man. "Just one more game! Here you go," he said as he placed a larger bag of gold in the middle of the playing area." He picked up the bones, cast them forcefully on the floor. A mediocre result.

Hope swelled in the man's heart. His prospects were good. If he could win this one, he would be back on track. He hesitantly picked up the knuckle bones. Anxiety flashed through him as he rattled the bones and threw them. It was the low score — another loss — and so much bigger than last time. The young man and his wife gasped. The winnings were gone suddenly leaving a huge debt.

The older gambler peered at them both, his lips curving in a sardonic smile. "Too bad, my friend."

DEDICATED TO STEPHANIE AND MY SON, ISAAC

AUTHOR'S NOTE:

I have always been disturbed by the treatment of Egypt's treasures, as they always seem to have been robbed in antiquity, or mistreated during modern times. The stories of ancient Egyptian mummies being ground up for "medical" salves, fertilizer or used as fire wood was, in my view, one of the greatest travesties towards Egyptian relics and its glorious history. My respect for the ancient treasures of Egypt was the reason I decided to tell Anik's story and Amenemope's vision. The idea for this book started as something I would imagine during the night as I lay down for the evening. Surprisingly the pharaoh I chose, wrote Wisdom of Amenemope to teach his son the values of life, which helped me give a back story and show his resolve for his brutal actions. After I put my hand to Egyptian tomb painting art and was unable to continue, I decided to put my dreams on paper instead of canvas. In Egypt's history we see the beginning of so many ideas we as a modern culture have today. Egyptians developed the 365 day calendar, paper, "Holy Water," through Akenaten the heretic pharaoh; they were the first though short lived, to believe in monotheism. The crook that the Bishop carries and the Mitre that the Pope wears both originated in Egypt as symbols of power. The first stone building was constructed in Egypt. They were known throughout the ancient world, and revered for their doctors and knowledge in medicine. The gouged out eye of Horus healed by Isis evolved into the medical   symbol. Egypt was the first nation in history. Many governmental ideas originated in Egypt that the Greek and Roman philosophers mirrored. The Egyptian culture was the first to embrace equal rights for women which resulted in freeing the oppressive male dominated culture of the time. An Egyptian woman could own her own land have her own business; even take her husband or anyone else to court for improper actions. As a society we can look back to these ancient times and learn from a culture that remained somewhat unchanged for three thousand years.

Many thanks go out to the people who have helped me develop and perfect this story:

I would like to send a special thank you to Judy Schmitt, for spending the time to sit with me and help this dream of mine come true. Judy was instrumental in helping me develop my story into a more readable novel. Her determination to help correct my errant writing and style was invaluable in developing me as a writer and bringing this book to life.

Other thanks:
Derek Goupil, Ken Breithaupt, Stephanie Hergott, John Schmitt

NAME PRONUNCIATIONS

PART 1

Osorkon — o-sor-kon

Ma'at — may-at

Aaru — a-ru

Amenemope — a-men-a-mope

Dalia — dal-ee-a

Zebel — zay-bel

Amaké — a-mah-kay

Wijin — wi-gin

Akila — a-key-la

Intef — in-tef

Imhotep — a-min-ho-tep

Thutmose — thut-mose

Ushabti — u-shab-tee

Ammit — ah-mit

Nephthys — nep-this

Aapep —eh-pep

Mahnudhotep — ma-nude-ho-tep

Nekht-Ankh — neck-het-awnkt

Khnum — k-newm

Nemutptah — ne-mut-pt ah

Maatkara — mat-care-a

Maatkera — mat-keyra

Theabus — thee-a-bus

Amsu — am-sue

Min-sacornamen — min-sa-corn-amen

Part 2
Dendree Yusik — den-dree-yu-sick
Anik Masri — an-nick-mas-ri
Sitaya — sit-tay-a
Sekani — sek-ani
John Tissen — jon-thee-sin
Huy — hu-e

part 1

I

PARADISE DISRUPTED

956 BC

The haunting cry of jackals pierced the evening in the Kings Valley. In between the tombs, a pair of small, fierce canines roamed. Though the air was cool in the Egyptian waste land, the sand under their paws was still warm from the previous day's blistering heat. Their sensitive noses hunted for any slight odor of carrion.

The valley was dry, yet a few small shrubs survived against all odds. It was deathly calm and silent. No wind blew that night. The only sound was the padding of the jackals' paws on the desert sand. The barren, craggy outcrops of the cliff face were a formidable barrier against the natural elements. This was a sacred place where the ancient kings of Egypt were buried; a remote location, a private place, a place accessible to scavengers and thieves.

The poor, wanting to be buried close to the pharaohs, had shallow graves in the valley, but they soon became meals for the animals.

All the land beyond the fertile coast of the great river Nile was dry and desolate.

Five kilometers south of the Kings Valley lay a small village that was likewise subject to the harsh climate. Among the small, simple homes lived a young couple whose preoccupations extended far beyond the boundaries of day to day life in the community. Wijin, the husband, was twenty years old. He was a handsome man — tall, well-built and deeply tanned. His features were smooth and attractive — sparkling blue eyes and straight white teeth. When he smiled, people around him were drawn to him like a magnet. As a boy he had been a constant favorite with the girls, even though his parents had arranged a wife for him at the age of two.

His father had been the village butcher, and Wijin had entered that trade also, although it had not brought him much prosperity or satisfaction. There wasn't a lot of opportunity and Wijin had wanted 'more'.

There were no smiles tonight. There had been many troubled nights in the last few weeks, so many nightmares disturbing his rest. Sweat poured off of him. During his dreams, he felt a chain around his legs. A familiar figure stood holding the other end, continuing to chant, "You owe me" over and over again. The more he pulled away, the tighter the chain became.

Akila, his wife, woke up, disturbed by her husband's tossing and turning in their small bed. She reached her hand out and rested it on Wijin's shoulder. He was torn out of his nightmare and back to his hot, stuffy bedroom. Their cot creaked as he sat up, but the sound was swallowed up by the mud bricked walls of the two room house. The straw and mud ceiling also quieted most of the noise. The room smelled of sweat, although it was neatly kept, with clean dishes and pots stacked in the corner on a small, low table. Wijin lay back down on his rumpled sheets and closed his eyes. *What's wrong with me?* he thought. *It's almost over*, he told himself, but he felt sick to his stomach. Akila watched her husband's labored breathing, as he attempted to fall back asleep, even though restful sleep eluded them both.

At the age of eighteen, Akila had straight, jet-black hair and fine features. She was five foot three, much shorter than her husband and always had insecurities within their relationship because of it. Though Wijin tried to put her mind at ease, saying the height difference did not matter, it mattered to her. *He calls me his doll. I know it's in fun and a term of endearment, coming from him, but it does leave a stinging pin prick in my heart.* She had grown up in the same town as Wijin and had fallen deeply in love with him. He was the tall handsome boy that never failed to be at her side gazing into her hazel eyes.

She was always nervous about the forbidden jobs Wijin was forced to do. *Things will be alright*, Akila continued to tell herself, but this time she could not shake the gnawing fear in her heart.

Wijin finally rolled off the bed and crept outside. The scent of goats and sheep was carried on the cool Egyptian night air. He rested his head against his small hut and felt unceasing worry wash over him. The landscape was covered with hard packed, dirty sand. The slightly hilly knolls where his small village nestled were strewn with stones that could twist an ankle if one was careless with his footing. The village had small, uniformly shaped homes that were painted red on the bottom half and white on the top.

The terrible burden that his foolishness had brought on his small family was agonizing. He felt embarrassed by the mistakes that he had made. There was no one else to blame. Wijin wondered what was in store for him tomorrow. *What will Amaké have me do? I have helped him rob stores, I have helped him break into tombs, even steal from friends.* The thought of it made his heart wail in pain. *One more time and I'm free from this torment to my soul. My soul, my ba bird must be quaking when I sin this way. I will never see the fields of reeds in Aaru. Osiris will never let me into paradise. I can hardly look into my sweet Akila's face without seeing my iniquities reflected in her eyes.* Wijin looked out across the street and saw a clay pot that had been left out. *That looks like a grain pot, probably something Amaké would want me to steal,* he thought with disgust. *How has my life come to this? Ammit, The Devourer of Souls, has every right to eat my heart and send me into oblivion.* Wijin sank to the ground and put his head on his knees. *Oh, how I wish I could turn back the sun, so I could start anew.*

Short palm trees, usually barren of any fruit, dotted his tiny village between the mud bricked homes. Small gaunt dogs ran along the silent streets, scavenging any scraps that were left out and not yet devoured. The town bazaar had been locked up for the night, its goods stored away and the mats on the ground folded up. The peaceful village could calm any person willing to experience it at night. The starry sky and the bright full moon looked down on this corner of ancient Egypt and bathed it with a benevolent, loving presence. The town had the feeling of safety throughout its clusters of tightly packed dwellings.

The ambience of the village at night was lost to Wijin as his disenchantment blocked out the rest of his world.

Akila peered out of their open doorway and saw Wijin sitting there, looking forlorn, and she wondered what she could say to encourage him.

"It's okay, Wijin, it will be over soon," Akila said.

"Will it?" Wijin said, in a snarky tone. "Will it? Or will Amaké demand more?"

"There is no 'more.' After this time, you are done. Amaké promised," his wife said, trying to reassure him.

"Amaké does a lot of promising with little follow-through," Wijin spat out.

He hated this feeling of pain that penetrated his soul. *What is it that I must do to appease Amaké this time? It feels like I have already handed my heart on a platter to Ammit's wicked teeth.*

Akila sat down on the ground next to her husband, put her arm around his waist and rested her head on his shoulder. She also feared for him. *How am I ever going to have him, all of him? How can we ever find true intimacy when he is so preoccupied and distracted by this oppressive circumstance? I love him so much, and yet I am barren. And then this distance between us keeps us from true happiness,* she lamented. *And after all he has been forced to do, what if he gets caught?*

As Wijin and Akila were battling their demons in their own space, the person that caused their turmoil suffered no such distress. He lived in a spacious whitewashed home, an hour's travel away, in an aristocratic village that was favored by the wealthy. The homes here were all larger, more elegant and well appointed. The watered and trimmed lawns seemed to feel important among the sand-encroaching plains of the outlying wilderness. Trees were kept in a certain state of cleanliness, no dead palm branches lying about and no weeds growing in the manicured lawns. The most beautiful and unique house felt proud, as if it were showing off to its neighbors. In spite of its loveliness, it hid a rotting open sore in the fabric of the community.

Inside, Amaké was lying on his soft white linen sheets, content with the life that he had made for himself. Living in such a gracious home, one would assume that he was a successful businessman. Upon talking with him, however, it was obvious that he was a coarse and ignorant man. He wasn't handsome — one didn't really notice his short brown hair or his straight nose — what impressed you were his piercing brown eyes that looked right into you, leaving you feeling exposed and vulnerable.

His tall and muscular frame was a result, in part, of the hard life of physical labor that he was forced to live, because of his need to look after himself from an early age. He didn't talk about being abandoned with his younger brother by his parents at the age of five, and scrambling for survival by any means available. Bitter experience taught him that to steal is to live. The disappointments and abuses he had suffered at the hands of others through the years had left him hard and cynical, and it showed in the curve of his lips when he smiled.

Sakhmet, Amaké's wife, had been attracted to him by his confidence, the gold he wore, and his sexuality. Her own seductiveness had caught them up in a passionate affair and they had married quickly. She had moved into the elegant home, but it soon became clear that Amaké's controlling ways chafed against her own strong will.

They reduced their conflicts by having separate rooms in the house. Sakhmet had definite ideas on how to run the household, and Amaké left that to her. She could be demanding of the staff — even cruel on occasion.

But she was striking to look at — long dark hair, flashing green eyes, an exquisite bosom, and shapely waist and hips, her skin tawny. Amaké delighted in her, even during their times of turmoil. She had a weakness for gold and jewels, and whenever he brought her some well-chosen jewelry from his forays, he found her enthusiastic gratitude made life all he hoped for.

Now it seemed as though Amaké's struggles had paid off. His house was a symbol of his triumph over adversity. He was twenty-five, nearing the age that most hard-working men would begin to be concerned about their mortality. He was going to be different; he was able to afford the help of doctors. He was determined to live much longer.

The soft night breeze was funnelled into his room by a wind catcher mounted on the roof. Cool fragrant-smelling puffs of air blew across his nearly-naked body. Though the scent of jasmine wafted through his house, the home reeked of inner corruption. *I'm so glad I was able to take that wind catcher from that family's home a few streets over. The breeze it creates cools me completely in this heat!* Amaké thought to himself. *Things have been going so well! No one can touch me, no one could ever touch me.* He got out of bed and slipped on his sandals and as he walked past the shuttered window, his shadow passed across the display of his favorite golden artifacts that glowed in the bright moonlight.

Amaké walked outside, onto the quiet street that bordered the front of his house. All was silent. No animals wandered about, no sounds of joyous laughter could be heard. The town ached for vitality and life. Somehow the place seemed dead, killed long ago, like a ghost.

Amaké looked across the street and saw a cracked vase leaning against the side of his neighbor's house. It was a worthless object now, but somehow he was drawn to it, as though it was calling to him. He had to have it. He had muted any call to consult his conscience long ago. Amaké walked over and picked up his "prize," temporarily calming his irresistible urge.

Tomorrow will be a good day, the best day, he told himself. It was the day that they would be cashing in on his biggest scheme ever. Amaké felt elated with his plans. His brother Intef never had a problem going along with him, but Wijin certainly would, especially this time. *Oh well, at least this is his last job with me. His debt will be paid off. Then I won't have to listen to his bellyaching about stealing any more. Besides, after I pull this off, I will be set for the rest of my life, rich beyond comprehension. No more sneaking into commoners or minor officials tombs. No more pilfering goods from the houses of the rich. I will not need to.* A cool satisfaction swept over him. The mood was short-lived, however, as it was quickly replaced with the lust for even more.

Early in the morning, Amaké and his brother Intef arrived at Wijin's door and pounded on it, waiting for an answer.

"It sounds like they are here," Wijin said with a sick feeling churning in his gut.

"Remember, this will be the last of it. I will pray to Isis for you, to give you strength," Akila reassured him, seeing his distress.

I don't think I can do it, he said to himself, deeply troubled. After he gathered his strength he opened the door and greeted the men.

Right away he felt something was wrong when he saw the donkeys and carts. Amaké and Intef smiled at him, without saying another word. They motioned for him to follow as they headed down the road. He trailed behind them for some time, but he was never able to shake the apprehension rising within him. *Where is he leading us? This does not seem to be a place we have gone before,* he thought. Wijin glanced over at Amaké who was now walking beside him. He eyes glittered with excitement and malice.

"Where are we going?" Wijin questioned.

Still smiling, Amaké pointed to a valley nestled between high cliffs and chuckled.

"This will be my biggest payday ever," he said, almost giddy. "Your share will be enough to pay off your debt, plus you'll have extra, maybe to buy something for that pretty wife of yours."

I don't want extra! I just want to be free from you, Amaké.

Wijin looked ahead and almost threw up. Before him lay the King's Valley, the sacred location where the pharaohs were buried.

"This is the worst violation ever, Amaké! We cannot do this!" Wijin said.

"Intef and I have done this before, haven't we?" Amaké replied to Wijin's concern, as if it were of no consequence. "Besides, this is what we are doing, like it or not."

"Ammit is going to eat my heart for sure," Wijin said, with a sense of dread permeating his soul.

Amaké led them into the valley and towards one of the tombs untouched by corrupt hands. Wijin looked in horror at the sealed tomb, as the door was clearly marked with the pharaoh's name. Amaké was the first to beat against the sealed door with a sense of greed, quickly followed by Intef. With every strike, Wijin could feel a part of his soul slip through his fingers, as if he were trying to hold water in his cupped hands.

In the paradise of Aaru, The Field of Reeds, lush grasses swayed in the calm, faint breeze of the clean, heavenly air. The beautiful day enfolded Thutmose IInd and his family in continuous peace. The small statues of servants which had been added to his tomb, the ushabti, were now laboring for him in the afterlife. There was one for every day, plus their forty-eight overseers, over four-hundred in total. Their names, which meant "the one who answers," went about tending to his plots of land, without question.

The plots of grain and vegetables produced an overabundance, as the heads of grain were so full the stalks bent under their weight and the vegetables so large it took two servants to carry just one. Fat oxen plowed the fields, unceasing, never tiring.

Purple and red hues which streaked across the sky during the perpetual day time, brought a constant state of bliss to the royal family in their Egyptian paradise. There were no worries or fears, just a life of perfection.

Thutmose IInd's children, who had died at childbirth, now played at the side of the great river that meandered through the land. As they played, large fattened fish would come to shore and ask to be caught. Even without fishing poles, they would swim into their outstretched hands and thank them for catching them. The hippopotami and crocodiles parted to create a path for the children to pass, but would allow them to crawl on their backs, if the little ones wanted to play on them.

The deceased family had lived in Aaru for hundreds of years as a perfect family and were waited on by the ushabti servants.

Thutmose sat on the grass surrounded by his friends and family, playing their favorite game, Sennet. As the pieces were slowly moved around the board, cheers and laughter could be heard for quite a distance. Everyone in Aaru loved the parties that Thutmose hosted, every person who had lived correctly according to the gods' laws were there.

Thousands of people gathered, eating, playing and visiting together in complete harmony. A baker, a brick layer and a pharaoh sat together chatting without caring about their station in their previous lives. Here they were all equal.

The knuckle bones were tossed in a final roll and the last piece was placed on the winning square.

"I finally beat you!" Seknaught, the baker called out.

Thutmose smiled, laughed and placed the discarded pieces back on the board.

"OK, I give up. I guess it's your turn now," he motioned to the brick layer. Laughter erupted close by as someone told a joke.

Imhotep walked casually among the joyous crowd, looking for the multitudes of friends he had made.

"Ah … Thutmose! I thought I would find you here at the sennet board. Who's winning?"

"Well, not me today," Thutmose replied with a laugh.

A wide smile spread across Seknaught's face, the latest winner.

Children encircled the older looking man and cheered as he got down on his knees to play with them. Imhotep had always loved children and made sure he spent time with as many of them as he could. He was a short, pleasant man who had definitely made his mark in Egypt's history scrolls. His dark eyes flashed with a wisdom that could not be gained by schooling, but by experience and natural understanding.

"You must come out for a visit soon, Thutmose. I miss seeing your children," Imhotep said.

Thutmose glanced over at his wife to see if she was interested in the invitation. She always was and gave her consent by nodding and smiling.

"I'm sure the children will be happy to come over. They always are."

In the distance the parents could see a group of children playing, chasing each other around between the shrubs and trees, in a game of tag. Other children were wading and cavorting in the crystal clear water of The River. A few of the older youth picked up their throwing sticks and began hunting ducks, although, for both parties it was just a game of target practice. Whenever a duck was felled from the sky, another one would materialize in the reeds and join in the game.

Thutmose IInd and his family walked along the path between the rows of corn stalks in their personal paradise. They had walked this path for hundreds of years on their way to visit Imhotep: doctor, architect, high priest, scribe and vizier of ancient Egypt. He was usually building in his palace, beside the small lake that was encircled with fruit trees. Large fish periodically jumped out of the clear water, making large splashes as they twisted and landed on their sides.

Ahead of them, the colossal temple palace stood out as a beacon of white marble in the middle of a forest of multi-green hues. Peacocks strutted along the base of the building. The live sphinxes that lined the path to the white marble structure turned their heads in unison as they passed. The children ran up to the impressive doors, that on this occasion, stood open. They didn't speak to the ushabti, who stood mute and unmoving, ready for their master to give them instruction.

"Uncle Imhotep! Uncle Imhotep!" the children called, using the term of endearment freely.

Besides the quiet peeping of quail, not a sound, not a reply came back to them. The children barged ahead through the ornate open halls, calling Imhotep's name, but the only reply was complete silence. Thutmose soon took up the search as well. They looked in the stone shop where Imhotep loved to spend his time creating master-pieces of rock, but he was not there either.

Thutmose walked the length and breadth of the heavenly estate, but Imhotep was nowhere to be found. The children were not so quick to give up their search. They rechecked the palace and temple, thinking it was a game of hide-and-seek. After they searched every room, and walked by hundreds of unresponsive ushabti, they continued to call Imhotep's name as they made their way out into the pasture. Like their father, they looked between the lowing cattle, but Imhotep was not there. Finally, the family gave up the search and headed back to their home.

Thutmose sat, propped against a trunk, beneath one of the large hanging trees that were so abundant in paradise. As he sat enjoying himself, along came Osiris and Isis through the tall stalks of wheat that were swaying in the breeze. Osiris greeted the royal family with a smile and a nod. The presence of the god and his wife made the amulets buried in Thutmose's chest tingle with a soothing peace that was indescribable whenever he was near the god.

"Greetings, Thutmose, favored of all the pharaohs," Osiris said in a deep resonant voice.

"It's good to see you again, Great One. I would wish to see you and your wife more often," Thutmose said, pleased with the fact that he had lived properly and his heart had weighed well against the feather of Ma'at.

Osiris smiled to himself and replied; "You know you can always call on me."

"I know. It is always a pleasure to visit with you," Thutmose replied, loving the relationship he had with the god.

Nephthys, Isis' sister, played with the laughing children in the sparkling clear river all afternoon, to the delight of their parents, who wanted time to converse with the gods.

Something was bothering Thutmose and his wife, that after long talks, they finally decided to ask Osiris about; "Great god Osiris, we have been unable to find the great Imhotep. He seems to be missing!" Thutmose said with concern, missing the time he spent sitting and talking with the great architect.

Osiris shook his head sadly and sighed, closing his eyes. Beside him stood his wife and their son Horus and Hathor. Hathor, the cow-headed god, was the first to speak.

"I found his body parts scattered in his fields, his ushabti servants unable to help him. It was a great loss. The amulets had been ripped from his body."

The amulets in Thutmose's body began to ache, sending chills of fear coursing through his body. He thought of his own tomb. *How safe was he, he wondered?* I'm fine! he thought. *I have a rock-cut tomb, with a stone door. No one can harm me.* As he stood in his glorious fields by the slow moving river, long-legged ibises gathered at the banks searching for crustaceans in the mud. Thoth, the ibis-headed god of writing, stood in the water by the sacred birds, with his hand resting on one of their backs. Fattened fish swam around the god's legs in peaceful swirls.

Large branches of heavily laden fruit trees swayed gently in the breeze and periodically dropped the feathers of ma'at to the ground. Then, mysteriously, the feathers would regenerate at the top of the tree and fall again. Everything was a perfect paradise in The Field of Reeds, the inhabitants of that sublime place walking and talking with the gods as friends. Though things seemed perfect, there was a danger affecting the people living there, one they could not prevent.

Back on Earth, the tombs were being robbed, obliterating the future they had thought to be secure. Families that had stored goods, wealth, games and things they held dear for use in the afterlife, suddenly discovered them to be missing, unaccounted for. This cast a great shadow on their paradise, leaving their lives diminished.

A great outcry began to rise among the people in Aaru. Paradise was faltering — people missing, their belongings gone.

A group of gods gathered together on the banks of the Great River that flowed through Aaru, to discuss the calamity that was affecting the people.

"This has gone on too long," Re, the sun god, roared, infuriated.

"What can we do? Thieves are robbing the tombs and no one is holding them accountable for their crimes!" Hathor said.

"Our brother Amenemope, the new Pharaoh, sits back and feels as though his hands are tied, but he can do something to stop the thefts of the tombs," Anubis, the god of embalming, replied.

As they were talking, a beautiful skiff floated by with a family who appeared to be in distress. Their ushabti calmly stood at the four-corners of the skiff, emotionally unaffected.

"Help us, Great Ones, help us!" the family called to the assembly of deities, who were in deep conversation.

The deities' attention shifted to the skiff that was loaded with wailing family members. They were surrounding the father of the family, who was clutching his chest in agony. He screamed out in excruciating pain. The protective ba-bird amulet in his chest chirped loudly as it was ripped out by an unknown force. A look of shock swept over the man's face. Then, it seemed as though an invisible hand reached into his body, dislodging the two-fingers amulet that protected his organs, causing it to disappear. The man began to twist around uncontrollably. The deities watched in horror as they knew the man's body was being violated on Earth, but he was feeling the effects here in Aaru. They saw his arms being ripped off and thrown into the water, making a loud splash. The man collapsed, armless and legless, on the small boat, pleading for help, but there was nothing that could be done. They watched in horror at what happened next. They focused on the djed pillar amulet on the man's spine, gleaming in pure gold, with a rising feeling of dread. The man was viciously broken in half and the djed disappeared. He was left lying on the skiff, broken in pieces, all his protective amulets taken by the thieves on Earth.

Osiris walked through The Field of Reeds, acknowledging all the people still there. Nephthys and Isis walked together with Osiris, greeting those that remained. They arrived at the doors of the gods' meeting hall. It was a grand temple in the center of Aaru, made of blue granite, with elegant white limestone pillars all across the front, topped with ferns. All the deities were there ready to discuss the problem that plagued Egypt, and consequently, their paradise.

Montu, the god of war, was the first to speak, "We should rain our vengeance down on Egypt, with no mercy and stop this pillaging once and for all!"

"No, we should show mercy!" Ptah, the creative god suggested.

"I see all manner of things up in the sky as I cross the heavens in my nightly travels. I think we need to drastically punish all who assault the resting places of people who are in Aaru. Death to all!" the moon god, Khons, ranted.

Seth, the god of disorder, sat back laughing to himself, enjoying their arguing.

"Peace, brothers, peace," Osiris spoke in a deep smooth voice.

"We know that Amenemope will not do anything. We all know his nature — lazy," Min, the fertility god said.

By now, Seth was laughing loudly.

Standing with his wife Mut, Amun, the solar king of the gods, held up his hand silencing the bickering deities.

"Amenemope sees you, Osiris, as his totem god, worshipping you every day, so it falls to you to try to change him. If he does not alter his ways, we as his jury, will feed his heart to Ammit and he will be lost forever," Amun said, glancing over in the corner.

Ammit, The Devourer of Souls lying in the corner, slowly opened her yellow eyes and snarled.

"Will there be any mercy for him?" Osiris asked.

"No, I have spoken, and it shall be done!" Amun replied.

Birds chirped and flitted about the majestic trees, swooping down to the grain fields periodically, to eat a large seed. Butterflies floated in the air, catching the slight currents that crisscrossed the land. Thutmose stood at the edge of his perfect barley field and watched his ushabti servants, bend their backs, harvesting his grain. He had a perfect life in Aaru, his crops were perfect every time, his trees bore large succulent fruit every month and his fattened cattle never needed to be fed.

Fear gripped Thutmose IInd's heart for a reason he did not know. A foreboding swept over his ba, his soul, a fear he could not explain. He questioned his eternal security, worrying about what was happening to his tomb on Earth. As he was calming himself, his ba-bird amulet started to become restless and darted around in his chest, chirping in a panic. It was only then that he called out for Osiris, who immediately materialized in front of him.

2

Destruction

For hundreds of years, his final resting place had a calm serenity that enveloped his perfectly preserved and ornate sarcophagus. No one dared interrupt the Royal's slumber and the tomb rested in complete tranquillity. Surrounded by his private store of precious mementos, Thutmose IInd lay in undisturbed peace. Golden shrines, effigies of gods, disassembled chariots, weapons, jewelry, pottery, toys, and beds cluttered the tight confines of the space.

Blackness filled every inch of every room as the sounds of hammering got louder and louder. With each strike of the hammers, the tomb quaked in pain at its apparent violation. The stagnant nine hundred-year-old air that hung in the rooms gradually filled with small amounts of fine dust, brought about by the pounding on the other side of the door. As the door began to give way, shouts of jubilation rose to a frantic pitch from the outside.

The men grew hot as they applied themselves with renewed energy to the task of knocking the door down into a pile of rubble. They were closing in on the jackpot. They scooped the rubble out of the way to make a smoother path for removing any treasures they would find. The blood rushed to Amaké's head in anticipation as he peered in. A shaft of light pierced the darkness like an arrow. The rape of the tomb was about to begin. Amaké and Intef pressed forward and gazed into the tomb, laughing and shouting. The glitter of gold could be seen everywhere, even though the haze of dust camouflaged the wealth behind its powdered curtain. Wijin hung back.

"Well, boys, we need to wait a bit until this dust settles. Let's drink a toast to our success here," Amaké exclaimed. "I was right that this was one of the best tombs left — this is the big one. This will set us up real fine. No more small time hustling and hoarding and working hard just to keep ahead of things. Now we can really live."

Intef nodded enthusiastically — a sheep following his brother's lead. Wijin sat there in total silence, his anguish gripping him like cold metal. He groaned inwardly.

They found a shady spot beside a rocky outcrop and settled there to wait for the air in the tomb to become breathable. Amaké ordered Intef, "Get those animals into the shade, too, brother. We want them strong for the loads they'll be hauling."

After a couple of hours the men rose, made their way back to the mouth of the tomb and piled into the cramped quarters, surveying the loot and deciding where to begin.

"All right, boys. What we're after is the gold and the jewels. Everything else is junk. We don't want to be toting everything that's here — just the stuff that brings the big payoff.

All the pottery is useless to us. Leave it over there. The ancient weapons won't do much damage, so put them in the first cart. We'll separate the gold from the rest of the metal and melt that down. The gold heirlooms and jewelry can go in these baskets. Most of that stuff we will melt down but we can have a look at it first and see if there's anything we want to keep. It's not just for us either. It doesn't hurt to have some shiny things to give to the women. It serves us all well in the end, right?" he ended with a roguish chuckle. *Maybe my bitch of a wife will finally be tolerable to live with,* he thought, but he doubted it.

They continued to carry out and sort the tomb's contents in a methodical way, loading the many valuables into the various carts.

The last thing that was left was the ornately carved and delicately crafted coffin. Amaké said, "All right, boys, it will take all three of us to open this beauty. There will be some fine gold amulets inside the bandaged bones. Once we get the lid off, we can pick the body clean and be on our way."

The enormous pink granite lid broke in half as it was thrown to the ground in an irreverent act of defilement.

They dragged the body of Thutmose IInd from the tomb and took it outside where there was more space for manoeuvring and more light. The final assault began. As jackals tear apart their helpless prey, they ripped apart the tightly bound linen strips, searching for the gold trinkets that had been placed between the white layers.

The perverse molestation of Thutmose IInd's defenseless tomb would turn the stomachs of most, but these men had raided tombs for the last several years, picking at Egypt's valuables like vultures circling for a meal of carrion. All in all, two of the men were pleased with their day's pillaging.

Although Amaké and Intef worked with enthusiasm as they sorted and loaded the treasures, Wijin's mind was full of regret and disdain that the childhood friendship he had shared with the brothers had led him to this predicament. Putting his right hand to his head, and running it through his short, light brown hair, Wijin closed his eyes. He needed to stop several times to gather his thoughts. He just went through the motions as quickly as possible to quell the guilt that bubbled in his veins. No one was ever there to stop them, so theft seemed like easy pickings to them, although secretly, he had hoped that there would be someone to stop them. The gambling debt owed to Amaké had been the final blow that he just hadn't been able to recover from — yet. But this should be the end of it.

Five wide carts loaded with stolen treasure stood near the tomb entrance as the donkeys that were hitched to them grazed on a few scraggly bushes nearby. As the men haphazardly piled the precious goods into the dusty carts, Wijin gritted his teeth as he forced himself to continue. He hated stealing and the way the others flaunted the profits of their crime.

His thoughts went to the gold flecked blue opal that he had bought with money he had saved. It was a beautiful stone — it glistened like the sun-kissed ripples on the Nile at days end. A friend who was a goldsmith had fashioned a unique setting and mounted the opal to create a graceful pendant for Akila for their seventh anniversary. Even though he had his choice of pendants from the tombs, Wijin would not cheapen the occasion with a stolen gift. It gave him a feeling of integrity to know that he paid for his treasure. He was not like these men.

Wijin knew the final destination for the gold they stole. It would be taken to Amaké's private smelter. Even that had been obtained by theft when they had pillaged the market. The men had made a fortune breaking into the tombs and robbing the town's vendors.

Amaké and Intef were well known among the men of the black markets of that time for the precious goods they acquired and peddled.

The treasures were unevenly divided, the greater share going to Amaké, the older brother and self-appointed leader of the crew. He always seemed to put his own trademark of "do it or else" on all his worldly guidance, typically instilling fear in his friends. He had attempted to mold Wijin and Intef to his will without a second thought. It was just his natural way. On several occasions, Wijin and Intef had challenged Amaké, but more often than not he was able to weasel his way out of the confrontation, and turn the disagreement back on them. He definitely had his good qualities though. He was extremely loyal and would protect his friends no matter what. He was the largest of the three of them — well over six feet tall and muscular, especially through the neck and shoulders. A scar sliced across his leathery pock marked face from his right ear over his nose to his left cheek — a brutal token from the years that he had spent working in the harsh Nubian gold mines. He was an imposing figure in size as well as attitude and experience. Amaké was a rough man with a wicked eye for finding ways to benefit his needs, whether they were actual or imagined.

He would have dressed like royalty if he could have. The thin, stark white linen of the upper class was unattainable to him, but even so, he was the best dressed of the three of them. He was bare-chested, wore a fresh, white kilt fastened by an ornate studded belt, and expensive black leather sandals. His greatest embellishments were the long chain and medallion of gold he wore around his neck, and the large gold rings he wore on his strong, elegant hands — trophies of his thievery. They were often in his way, but his desire to flaunt the spoils of wealth held him like a drug.

Intef was the shortest of them at five foot five inches. He was twenty-three years old, heavy set, with a head of dark curly hair complete with a full beard, flat nose with visible red veins showing — a result of his heavy drinking. He did whatever Amaké said, like a puppet, always desiring acceptance from his older "wiser" brother. He walked with a slight limp as his left leg was shorter than his right. His heavy, coarse linen kilt was firmly tied around his ample waist by a stolen green and red rope that he had found in a vizier's tomb. As his kilt frayed, he refused to mend it, opting to tear it off and buy another or steal one from a laborer that was his size. Intef loved the reed sandals he wore as they had small holes in the soles to let the sand that built up escape. He wore a copper arm band inscribed with the word, "Chief." The tight curls in his beard had been pulled together and braided into three braids that hung against his deeply tanned chest. Each braid was held by a god-shaped clamp that rattled as he walked. He had been the easiest one to convince to begin tomb robbing, as he appreciated the benefits of free money.

Intef's wife, a self-absorbed skinny girl of modest intellect, was indifferent about the idea of a thief for a husband until she got to pick through a case full of jewels that Intef brought home after his first raid. She clapped her petite hands in glee as she opened the jewel-encrusted box he handed her. Earrings, bangles, and necklaces of every color glittered before her, clouding any misgivings she might have had about the dangers of tomb robbing. She stood up from her seated position on the floor, placing the heavy chest of stolen treasures on the nearby table and started pulling out the jewels she wanted to wear. She was quick to adorn herself with as many golden trinkets as she could fit on her skinny body, making herself look ridiculous.

"Look at my rings!" she said as she held out her hands with a big smile on her face.

"In the name of Set! You have three rings on every finger. Can you even close your hand? You have so much gold around your neck that you are slouching." Intef barked, feeling ashamed of his wife. "Take some of that stuff off, woman."

"These are my pretty things!" she said with a pout, as she petulantly turned her back on Intef's command.

Akila, Wijin's wife, had bad feelings about accepting jewels from the tombs. She usually didn't want to participate in the "benefits" Amaké almost forced on Wijin. Although, several times she had been tempted beyond her strength, and picked out a few jewels she fancied.

The two of them had long discussions on how to get out from under Amaké's control. Late one night, as Akila lay resting in Wijin's strong arms, they talked about their situation and how sickened they felt about the men pillaging tombs. Profiting from the treasures that were not theirs had always repulsed them. They made up their minds that after the debt to Amaké had been paid, Wijin would never again ransack tombs. And he would definitely give up gambling.

Amaké was the first to rebuke him after Wijin told him not to expect any more help once the crippling debt was paid off. Wijin stared right back at him, saying that the dishonesty was eating at him, and he would no longer help him after this last venture.

"This is the **last time** … I'm serious," Wijin swore.

Intef had been on his brother's side, saying that Wijin would change his mind sooner or later when his money ran out.

As the destruction of the tomb was in progress, a seven year old boy crouched behind the last of a row of small bushes lining the courtyard at the entrance of the tomb. He shivered with fear and fascination. Zebel observed the methodical liquidation of the tomb's wealth. It was evident that this wasn't the first time these men had done this. Young Zebel had never seen such wealth in his life. Then he saw the men tear apart the royal mummy with great force, breaking its bones and throwing the limbs off to the side. He watched the men circle the helpless royal mummy as they cut through the bindings and pulled out the valuable amulets.

As the son of a poor farmer, Zebel had few possessions and toys and a very limited supply of clothes. He could hardly believe the grandeur of the golden artifacts that he saw being brought out of the tomb. His family got along on what his father's farm provided — vegetables, cows and chickens, as well as the income earned from crops of Kiki, the castor oil plant, and Emmer wheat. Their one room mud-brick home and land, located near the edge of the river basin by the King's Valley, was one of a few small farms clustered there that provided a simple life of honest work. Their greatest expectation was an ample inundation from the Nile each year to provide the nutrient rich silt that supported their crops and general welfare.

Watching these strangers pillage the tomb was the most amazing thing Zebel had ever seen. He was glad that he had finished helping his father clear out some of the irrigation ditches in time to come and see this unusual spectacle, and yet he also felt somewhat disturbed by the scene. He trembled as he strained to see everything that was going on. He figured his frayed brown loin cloth and dirty tanned body would camouflage him somewhat, so he crept closer. As he did, he could see their faces and hear their voices, and understood that the name of the gang's leader was Amaké, as he was the one giving all the orders. He crouched lower as the men approached his hiding spot.

I'm going to be caught! Zebel thought frantically. *Why did I get so close? I'm so stupid!* His mind raced.

Amaké walked over to the spot by the underbrush where Zebel was concealed and relieved himself, oblivious to the youth hiding not two feet away. The strong smell of urine assaulted Zebel's nose as the stream splattered on the ground next to him. As the droplets of the yellow liquid sprayed his leg, he knew he must remain motionless until Amaké finished.

Amaké went back to his work, gathering gold trinkets together and packing them up for the trip home. *I can't believe he didn't see me!* Zebel thought as his anxiety lifted like heavy fog dissipating in the sun.

The men's backs were turned as Zebel took off running to the nearby cliffs. Catching the abrupt movement, Amaké turned to see him running away from them as fast as his lanky young legs could carry him.

"Stop!" Amaké yelled, running after the boy. He turned back to the other men and said, "Get that boy!" He was thinking, *we can't leave a witness.*

Intef took up the chase, determined to track him down, grill him and find out where he came from and why he was snooping on them. Wijin's heart leapt as he thought about the devastating consequences of their actions if they were caught.

What if the boy reports us? It would be jail for sure, if not death. Wijin fought the panic as he ran.

The young boy had always run everywhere and since he was familiar with the rock strewn terrain, he was able to pick out his proper footing quickly. Zebel bounded over the ridges and crevasses leading up to the cliff side. He found a small nook in the face of the outcrop and scooted into it, hoping it would conceal him until the men passed by. The sharp edges of the small cave poked his sides and back as he tried to settle in for the long wait. As seconds turned into minutes the pain became more unbearable but he knew he must remain motionless. Zebel squeezed his eyes shut as he tried to relax and endure as long as he could. Urgency in his groin told him he too needed to relieve himself. Right now. This was always a problem, even when he played games with his friends. Now, when it really mattered, the annoying urgency demanded relief. Zebel tried desperately to hold on. He heard one of the men walking across the stone littered ground near his hiding spot. Closer and closer the man came, and it seemed as though with every step the man took, the more Zebel had to urinate. This was life and death in Zebel's mind as he hopelessly held his bladder. Finally, as his urine started to force its way out, he relinquished his struggle and let it flow. Zebel had never deliberately urinated on himself like this before, but in his mind it was worth it. As his liquid waste soaked his short brown loin cloth and flowed down his legs, Zebel found comfort at last and could stay hidden in his cave for a little longer. The man Zebel had heard walking finally stopped pacing around and appeared to be resting against the outcrop right in front of the cave's entrance.

Zebel could see legs across the entrance of his little hiding spot as if they were two massive bars holding him in the cramped quarters like a prison. Even though it had just been seconds Zebel started to panic. *Why is he standing here for so long? Why won't he leave? Does he know I'm here?* he wondered.

In the meantime Zebel's river of urine had made slow progress to the back of the cave. A rasping sound startled him. Zebel froze in fear at the menacing sound. He turned his head slowly towards the back of the small cave. He was horrified to see an Egyptian horned viper which lay curled, rubbing his coils together making an unmistakable sound. He knew that even if he tried to get out, he would never make it without the snake striking him. The venom of the horned viper was a death sentence. The man's legs still stood outside the entrance, barring his escape. As Zebel looked back at the viper, the snake's head wove back and forth, as if he was deciding where to sink his venomous fangs.

My only chance is to try to pin the snake's head against the cave wall with my sandal, but the minute I move the viper will strike, he told himself hopelessly. The previous sharp pains that Zebel had felt, being in such a cramped area, quickly disappeared as his attention was now glued to the deadly snake.

It was Wijin standing outside the cave and he too heard the rasping sound of the viper as he stood resting. He decided to move away and rejoin Amaké and Intef on the search for the young boy. The quick movement outside was enough to alter the vipers concentration from the boy, giving Zebel the chance he was waiting for. The sandaled foot slammed into the viper's head, crushing it against the stone wall at the back of the cave. As he held his foot there, the dying viper's nerves convulsed rapidly and it wrapped itself around Zebel's leg. After it had stopped twitching, Zebel finally lowered his leg and the uncomfortable pains of the sharp cave wall came back in full force.

Amaké, Wijin, and Intef spread out, calling for the boy to show himself and not to worry about retribution. The men searched all around the rocks, and every place they could with no luck. They paused to refine their search to a far more thorough grid pattern.

After waiting as long as he could stand it, Zebel emerged from his small niche of security in the stone wall. With the urine-covered viper still wrapped around his leg, he sat exhausted from the mental and physical ordeal he had just been through. After pulling the viper off his leg, he summoned up the courage to continue his journey back home.

He slowly and cautiously made his way around the boulders heading toward the Nile, but the squawking waterfowl that flourished in the vegetation along the big river noisily broke his cover. He hadn't gone far when Amaké spotted him and chased him down. Zebel tried to turn to throw Amaké off, but Intef was right there. The young lad could not get away.

Amaké came up behind him and grabbed his arm, halting any attempts to flee. Zebel stood there trembling. Wijin trotted up to join them and now they had the boy completely surrounded. Zebel stared at the men in fear, trying to figure out their next move.

Amaké grabbed him roughly by the arm and yanked him closer.

"Don't be scared, boy, we won't hurt you," Amaké said as he reached for his knife.

"What were you doing out here by the tombs?" Intef questioned, his alcoholic breath making the child want to retch. "And why were you spying on us?"

Zebel felt his heart racing, terror engulfing him.

"I, I, was just playing here," Zebel stammered.

"This was a bad day to come here," Amaké threatened as he removed the knife from its sheath.

Wijin realized what was about to happen and grabbed Amaké's arm. He whispered in his ear,

"Wait! Stop! Think about this. Tomb robbing is one thing - murder is another. Promise him something for his silence — anything. If this boy does not return home, they will search for us."

Amaké paused, considering his words. Then he loosened his grip on the boy's arm and looked in his frightened eyes and said calmly, "My friend here says that in exchange for your oath of silence you might accept a token of gold that would keep you and your family fed for a long time. What do you think of that?"

Amaké reached into his pocket and retrieved a gold ring. Zebel's mind raced, trying to determine if there was any reason to not take this seemingly merciful offer. The boy took a couple of gulps of breath, then nodded and stretched out his hand.

"Remember, not a word to anyone. If you do, I will find you, and you will regret it."

"Not a word," Zebel repeated.

Amaké placed the ring in the small hand and as soon as Zebel felt the heavy ring in his fingers, he ran off. He ran as fast as his legs would take him, until exhaustion forced him to collapse in the shade of a large palm grove. He sat there gasping for breath. His panic started to subside, but his mind was still racing.

Zebel trudged all the way home, the ring gripped tightly in his hand. He did not know what to do. *Should I share my trophy with my family? No, I think I will keep it for a while. Who knows when I might really need it? Yes, I'll keep it. Besides, I said I would keep it a secret and I will do just that. My father will never know.*

"Hey, what's that in your hand, Zebel?" the young boy said, trying to mimic his father's stern voice and scowling face.

"Oh, nothing, I just 'found' this ring in the river."

"Well, let me see this 'ring' of yours," he continued to mimic, waving his head back and forth and holding out his hand.

He pretended to hand the ring over to his imaginary father.

"This is not a river ring! You stole it."

He felt his face flush as he said those words. "You stole it." The lump in his throat returned. Yes, he could remember very well the time his father caught him eating a loaf of bread he had taken from the market. *My father was so disappointed in me. I sure paid for my crime that night. But I did not steal this ring! It is mine to do with as I please. Yes, I think I will keep it, but where should I store it in the mean time?* He spotted a decaying palm tree lying on the river bank. *Perfect! That is a safe spot. No one will ever suspect.*

Zebel walked home to his family's farm, pleased with himself. His future was secure and any worries he had were gone.

"Zebel, come and do your chores," Aapep called out to his son, hearing him arrive home.

"Coming."

The young lad fed the animals, cleaned out the stalls and collected the eggs from their few chickens. As he worked, his mind kept racing to the encounter he had had with the men. *Why had that one man stopped his friend from killing me? I'm glad he did! And what a ring! I'm rich!* The more he thought about it the more he questioned its safety. *What if someone finds it and steals it from me? I must go and retrieve it right now and hide it somewhere else. What if a crocodile moves it while it shifts along the river bank? Yes, I must go now.* His mind spun like a top, unable to rest. He quickly finished his work and tried to make his way across the fields to his newfound treasure, but Aapep saw him and called him back.

"If you are done already I need you to help me finish clearing the irrigation canals. Isis is about to cry again and the river will flood its banks."

I never thought about the coming inundation! When that happens I will lose the gold for sure in the flood, Zebel thought in a panic, looking to the far side of the field. Aapep saw his son's distress.

"What is going on in that head of yours, Zebel?"

"Oh, nothing. Well, I think I forgot to get something the last time I went out and I want to retrieve it."

"I'll tell you what son, after you do your chores tomorrow, you can go back out and recover what you lost."

Tomorrow might be too late, he thought, but knew not to question his father's decision.

The next day, Zebel's tasks seemed to take forever. Repeatedly, just as he thought he was done, his father gave him "just one more" thing to do. By the time he finally finished, it was too dark to go. *Tomorrow I will go and retrieve my ring. I must.*

As soon as the sun rose the next morning, Zebel flew full speed into his chores and completed them quickly and proficiently, giving him plenty of time to run to the river.

A weight lifted off his soul as he grasped and held his prize in his dirty hand. This treasure would buy so much food for his family. *This ring is surely stolen, though, and if I'm seen with it I will be the one in trouble!* Zebel thought. He then found himself distracted by the beautiful circle of gold in his hands. The ring was enticing, inviting him to go down the same path of greed which Amaké had taken. Avarice played with his mind, tempting him to keep it. His options churned in his mind, making him alternate his decision from one side to the other until he was mentally exhausted. *If I report the robbers, I could be killed, but it is also wrong not to tell what I saw.*

He looked closely at the ring, his eyes focused on the insignia stamped into the gold. It was the sign of a pharaoh clearly engraved on the raised flat surface, making it a crime for him just to hold it.

The squawking of the birds on the Nile brought him back to reality. Suddenly he understood what he must do. He must go to the soldier encampment and report what he had seen. Had he tried to cash in the ring for food and money, he would have been immediately arrested for theft.

The young lad made his way back to the Nile's edge. He followed it into the next town where the army barracks was located, ready to report all he had witnessed. The undeniable fact that he had the ring was solid evidence against the three men. He knew that by order of Pharaoh, anyone reporting such crimes against the tombs would be rewarded. Zebel started feeling better about his decision, because a reward would also provide support that his family so desperately needed.

The army compound on the outskirts of Thebes was bustling with soldiers coming and going and doing combat drills. Loud cheers intermittently broke out as someone in the melody of scripted confusion completed the difficult task of beating his challenger in a mock hand-to-hand fight. Like a gaggle of squawking hens at meal time, flagrant taunts and general merriment erupted on a regular basis as a soldier went in for a mock kill.

Eyes were pulled away from the small war games as Zebel walked in unannounced. The stares of the hardened warriors pierced his confidence as he walked towards what he assumed was the captain's office. The short square block building made of brown, baked mud brick looked intimidating as he moved slowly towards it.

Zebel noticed out of the corner of his eye a large soldier catching up with him. The firm ground under his feet spoke of the amount of traffic that had traveled it in order to pack the sand so densely. The soldier nearing Zebel reached out and grabbed his arm, stopping him in his tracks.

"What is your purpose for being here, young one?" the gruff warrior questioned the ragged-looking Zebel.

The startled young lad turned and looked up at the soldier. His mouth went dry.

"I, I, uh, came to tell the captain about something I saw over in the King's Valley," he stammered. "Some bad men were taking treasures from a tomb. One of the men caught me and was going to hurt me, but he then gave me this ring instead and made me promise not to tell anyone about it." Zebel handed the heavy gold band over to the soldier.

The soldier looked at the ring with curiosity, then surprise, not knowing if he should believe him or not.

"I think you had better come with me," the soldier said as he took Zebel by the arm and led him to the captain's office.

Mahnudhotep eyed Zebel as the youngster again reported all that he had seen. Zebel's brow started to sweat as Mahnud stood in front of him in the cramped, dim quarters. The captain took a close look at the ring the soldier had given him; then he looked at Zebel, taking the measure of the boy. He thought for a moment and walked out of the room, leaving Zebel with the soldier.

Fifteen minutes went by. Looking around the plain room all he could focus on was the tough-looking soldier's breathing. The raspy breath of the large man grated on his mind as he imagined the mercenary like a large crocodile ready to snap. The Egyptian fighter started to pace behind him, making Zebel wonder if he was just waiting for an excuse to pounce. Large boxes of scrolls stacked in one corner made him apprehensive. Zebel imagined that one of them held the order to arrest him.

Why is the guard here unless I'm going to go to jail? What's the captain going to do to me? Zebel's mind started working itself to a fever pitch. He heard footsteps behind the door and he began to panic.

Mahnud walked into the room and seated himself behind the desk. Zebel was obviously distraught. Waiting to hear his punishment, he squeezed his eyes shut. The captain laughed to himself watching the young boy squirm.

"What is your crime, Zebel?" the captain asked.

"I do not know, sir."

"You spied on three men as they robbed the tomb of the great Thutmose IInd. You accepted a bribe for your silence. Does that sound accurate?"

Zebel hung his head and nodded.

"That is not accurate!" Mahnud said as he got up from his chair.

"You reported these criminals, and you didn't let their bribe corrupt you. You returned to me the ring they gave you. Is that more accurate, son?"

Zebel lifted up his head, looked at the captain and slowly and cautiously broke into a smile.

"Yes, sir, I did," he said, his confidence rising.

"Yes, you did!" Mahnud replied with a chuckle as he tossed three gold coins on the desk right in front of Zebel. "Here is your reward. Zebel, Egypt could use more people like you. You have shown that your spirit is strong and honourable. Keep in touch with me. Come back to these barracks and see me from time to time. Perhaps you would consider becoming a soldier. I'm always looking for worthy men to defend our lands."

Zebel couldn't believe it. He had never seen this new type of currency before, Zebel was familiar with the age old barter system, not these copper pieces stamped with the Pharaoh's likeness. On top of his great luck, the captain had offered him a position in his army! He then turned to leave but stopped and turned around. "These three coins I have given you as payment for reporting these criminals — what will you do with them?"

Zebel looked at the shiny copper coins in his small brown hand and then looked up at him.

"I will buy food for me and my family," he said with a big grin on his face.

The captain smiled, nodded and threw him three more coins.

Mahnudhotep sat at his desk looking at the royal ring in his hand. *If they were just there ransacking the tomb, they could not have gone too far,* he thought. He pulled out a map and placed it on the table, searching until he found the location of Thutmose's tomb. He traced his finger around the markings on the map trying to plan his next move. On the chart there was nothing that indicated buildings in the near proximity to the Kings Valley. *Well,* he thought, *I will just have to track them down!* He stepped outside and called to his commander.

"Get a security detail together. We march to the Kings Valley in one hour."

Fifty soldiers stood in a compact group, ready to follow their captain's orders and march into the desert. Their polished spear tips caught the sun and glistened in the afternoon heat. Each man had a sword strapped to his left hip and he carried an oval shaped shield. At the front and rear of the detachment of soldiers, red banners tied to the tops of spears danced in the wind. A drum pounded out a curt, steady beat as the muscular captain walked over to address his troops. He raised his hand and the drum stopped.

"Today we have a responsibility to fulfil for Egypt. Today we once again hunt for an elusive prey that strikes Egypt's core. Although we are tempted we will not be their final judge. That is for Pharaoh and the gods to decide. We will go to Thutmose's tomb and track the thieves to their den and lay our trap. They will not escape."

The soldiers banged their spears against their shields in a display of agreement. They were ready for the task at hand, so they set off, the supply wagons falling in behind.

It was dark when, three abreast, the military troop marched into the valley. Since they would need light for their investigation at the tomb, they made camp and shared a meal. The moonless night was pitch black. The chill of the desert night bit into those on guard duty like needles, and the sleepers huddled, blanketed in their tents.

In the morning they assembled, had their morning rations and made their way to Thutmose's tomb. Mahnudhotep surveyed the entrance. It had been smashed in. Ornate ancient pottery was thrown on a pile along with finely detailed reed baskets. Off to one side old style weapons lay in disarray.

"Spread out and search for the thieves' trail," he ordered his men. "They surely left a sign of where they went. Find it and be quick about it."

Mahnud looked at the destroyed tomb entrance and walked towards it with eagerness and determination. Just as he got there, the captain almost tripped on something that was partially embedded in the sand. He caught himself from falling and spun around to see what had almost floored him. There lay a mummy's arm. *Sacrilege!*

Inside the tomb the coffin was empty and the lid lay cracked, upside down on the floor. The body of the pharaoh was gone. The tomb was picked clean. Captain Mahnud heard shouts coming from outside and made his way back to see what the commotion was about.

"What is it? Did you find the trail?"

"We did indeed, captain," the scout called back, out of breath. "We picked it up just a kilometer to the south."

"Show me."

The cliffs of the King's Valley blended into the desert and there was no trail to be seen in the rocky rubble. As the terrain changed to sand a slight path could be deciphered, first by indistinguishable pock marks, then regular hoof prints and wheel furrows as if a wagon train had gone by. They followed this between the dunes for about an hour until they came to another set of stone crags standing alone.

There they discovered a mud bricked building which was tucked against the outcropping. From the front it looked like a small building, but because it was up against a cliff, the cave behind it, which provided a large storage area, was not visible. The designers had expected that no one would ever realize the wealth stored within its walls. Though the hideout seemed reasonably inconspicuous, a billow of acrid smoke seeping from the short chimney revealed the fact that metal was being melted down inside, and they had found what they were looking for.

Amaké, Wijin, and Intef were finishing the task of melting down the gold into debens. They had poured the refined liquid gold into the half sphere molds and then placed them by the wall of their hideout until they had cooled. When they were ready, they took them out of the molds and stacked them in a copper safe, which could be locked for storage and transportation. Taking a few moments to relish the large amount of treasure sitting before them, Amaké was inwardly calculating the value of the gold they would be selling. He was excited. He set aside fourteen debens and looked up at Wijin.

"Well, Wijin, my friend, it looks as though by taking this much from your portion of our haul, your debt is now paid off. Perhaps we should have another game soon!" he laughed, but with a sarcastic edge. "There is so much left for the rest of us. This has been the best day."

Relief washed over Wijin.

"Finally! I wondered if this day would ever come," Wijin exclaimed, as he felt the crushing burden lifting from his heart. "As for doing any more gambling, I think I will pass."

Just outside, Mahnudhotep gave the silent signal to his men to spread out and surround the workhouse. Another signal was given and the hardened warriors crept closer and closer. As the army methodically and silently surrounded their building, Amaké and his thieving crew were oblivious to the activity outside.

Mahnud gave the final signal and the soldiers poured in with their swords ready, surrounding the three men on all sides as the men looked up, the shock evident on all of their faces. The close quarters of the room prevented any chance for escape. Amaké's eyes darted around to the various golden trophies he had saved from other tombs he had pirated. He knew he shouldn't have kept souvenirs and now those prizes would just add to his guilt. He had been caught red-handed and there was no way he could talk himself out of this.

The men were arrested on the spot, bound with leather thongs behind their backs and ushered back into their cave where they were forced into a kneeling position. Mahnud peered at the three men closely. He eyed the big man and knew right away he was their leader.

"Tell me, who do you sell these treasures to?"

"I have nothing to say," Amaké spat out.

With that Mahnud struck him on the jaw, breaking it, and sent him sprawling to the ground.

"We seem to have gotten off to a bad start. My name is Captain Mahnudhotep. And yours …?"

Amaké remained silent.

"If you don't want to talk to me, I have someone who you will love to talk to. Amasis."

Where have I heard that name before? Amaké thought. *Amasis … Amasis?*

Then the captain turned his attention to the other two men.

Wijin yelled out. "I have paid my debt!"

"Be quiet! I did not ask you to speak," Mahnud yelled out as he kicked Wijin on the shoulder, sending him toppling over on his side.

From Wijin's position he could see Intef kneeling beside his brother. Intef was trying to hold back tears but he was unsuccessful.

The three men were marched to the stockade in Thebes and taken to the cramped interrogation room. They were pushed to the floor that stank of the suffering of those who had preceded them. In the middle of the room there was a high table with leather straps attached to it. Faint moans could be heard coming from other areas of the prison. In the corner, an oil lamp sitting on a small table against the wall sputtered intermittently in the dimness. The air was hot and fetid. The door creaked open and an older man stepped in, followed by five prison guards. Before they could close the door a brown rat squeaked and scurried between their legs into the safety of the corridor.

"Hello men. My name is Amasis — Chief Interrogator," he said quietly. He was slim, not very tall, but his ravaged face had the glint of evil which struck fear in the three men.

"I have been asked to retrieve some information from you. You will tell me what I want to know, one way or another. It will not end well for you. And I am not a patient man."

I have heard about him! Amaké thought in terror. *He is known for his savage treatment of prisoners when breaking them.* Amaké shifted uncomfortably.

"Ah! I see *you* have heard of me. By the blank expressions on your friends' faces, I suppose they haven't. Well, let's start. I have two questions you will answer. What is your name?"

Amaké remained silent, his jaw painful and swollen.

"Hmmm… Maybe you would like to have a chat with a co-worker of mine," Amasis said as he took a well-worn wooden box off the small table and placed it on the floor in front of them. Except for the faint yellow painted glyphs on the lid it was the color of midnight. Fear clawed at the men's minds. *That box is too small to hold a snake,* the men thought.

"I will ask you again. What is your name?"

Still, there was no answer. Amasis bent over and removed the lid of the box. Inside, yellow and brown scorpions lay idle. With expert hands Amasis retrieved one and held it to Amaké's hip. A fraction of a second later the scorpion whipped out its tail and stung Amaké. Sharp pain surged through the side of his body and shot up to his armpit. He flopped over on his side and convulsed, writhing in agony.

"Well, you boys are next," Amasis said as he replaced the lid and walked over to Wijin and Intef.

"Tell me your names."

The replies were quick, almost as if they were competing to be the first to answer.

"My name is Wijin."

"I am Intef."

"Tell me who the treasures are sold to."

"There is a man in the market that he sells them to," Intef replied in fear, indicating his brother with a nod of his head. "But I do not know his name."

Amasis got down on his haunches in front of Wijin and stared into his eyes. Wijin had never seen such dark eyes before. They were like empty black holes he could get trapped in. They seemed inhuman.

Then he breathed the same question to Wijin, his putrid breath assaulting Wijin's nostrils, "Can you tell me the name?"

"I do not know his name," Wijin replied, almost gagging.

"Very well. I believe you two."

"Strap that man to my worktable," Amasis called out to his guards, indicating Amaké.

Three guards picked him up, cut the cords that bound him and strapped him to the table.

Amaké thought about his majestic house, his wealth and his fine clothes. Were they slipping from his grasp? *Why is this happening to me? I'm untouchable. They have made a mistake*, he thought in pride. He knew his wrongs, but any justice in response to them seemed an injustice to him. *What is happening to me?* Amaké panicked. *My whole left side is numb, but in agony!* Amaké could not move. Confusion and misery clouded his consciousness as the scorpion's venom surged through his veins.

One hour had passed before Amasis spoke to Amaké again.

"What is your name?"

"You ... You will not break me," Amaké gasped between spasms of pain.

Amasis placed the ebony box at the foot of the table. He looked at Amake for a minute, considering something.

"Captain Mahnud tells me that this fat fellow here is your brother. Is this true?"

His finger traced around the pattern on the box, his eyes fixed on Amake's face.

Amaké said nothing, but his expression betrayed him.

"Ah, yes, I can see that he is. I wonder if his pain tolerance is equal to your own," he said as he opened the box and retrieved another scorpion. As he walked towards Intef, he looked back to see Amaké wince and struggle within the restraints. Intef began to cry out in fear. Amasis held the scorpion just above Intef's lap and looked back at Amaké maliciously.

"Tell me your name!"

"Amaké. My name is Amaké."

"You see, that wasn't that hard, was it?" Amasis said as he dropped the scorpion on Intef's bare lap. It immediately stung Intef in the groin, and even as the angry scorpion raced across his leg, the stings from its feet drew a trail of pain as it ran away.

Dread and remorse gripped Amaké. He turned his head to look at his brother who was now twisting and writhing on the floor in agony. He couldn't protect Intef from the venom that constricted his brother's throat and left him gasping for breath.

He then felt Amasis' hand hold his head to the side and heard the interrogator's voice whisper in his ear.

"Tell me. Who do you sell the treasures to?"

"I don't know their names," Amaké screamed at Amasis.

Amaké felt a sharp pain on the side of his head and blood began to flow across his face. Amasis had cut his ear off and thrown it on the floor. The stream of blood trickling into his eyes did not stop him from seeing a rat scurry from his hole and grab his ear.

"Oh, I think you do."

Then in a swift fluid motion Amasis retrieved another scorpion and placed it on Amaké's face. The scorpion swiftly lashed out and stung Amaké on his head wound. The poison roared through his body and the searing pain overwhelmed him, causing him to pass out.

When he came to, his throat was tight and it was hard for him to breathe. Amaké's head throbbed as if someone were constantly punching him in the face. He opened his eyes to see where he was. Amaké noticed he was still strapped to the table and he ached all over.

"Have you had enough? Tell me the names I want and you will not have your nose cut off. That is what will happen next."

Amaké tried to form words to beg for mercy but no words escaped his lips. *Please stop! Please stop!*

"If you are not going to speak, you leave me no alternative. You have been unconscious for one day and I will wait no more."

Amasis walked over to the small side table and retrieved the knife he had used to cut off Amaké's ear and returned to his victim.

"I yield! … I yield!"

Amaké revealed all that Amasis wanted and was spared having his nose cut off.

After he relinquished his cohort's names, he was left in prison with Wijin and Intef. They were soon joined by those whose names he had revealed. The treasures that could be retrieved were collected and stored in the palace treasury, even though their assigned place in the afterlife of their owners was torn away.

Over the next few months, even the wives of the thieves were arrested and their homes stripped of valuables.

Eventually they were all delivered to the slave masters. The women, stripped of their jewels and fine clothes, were put to work in the houses and barns of numerous officials who regularly made use of prison labor.

The crimson-dyed sheath that Akila loved so much was stripped off and replaced with a coarse brown linen loin cloth. The wide pectoral necklace laced with jewels, the only thing she had kept from the tomb pillaging, was replaced by a tight leather strap that had "slave" imprinted on it.

The same fate was forced on the wives of Amaké and Intef. Besides gardening, those who were capable were trained to paint the beautiful murals in officials' houses. Bare-breasted and left only with a loin cloth like a young child would wear, the women found the work demeaning and thankless. Any mistakes they made resulted in a lashing from a guard's cruel whip.

The women who gained favor in the eyes of officials were rewarded with a man's kilt instead of the loin cloth, and perhaps a shirt.

The men fared no better, working in the mines and quarries for the various building projects of Pharaoh. Amaké, Wijin and Intef learned the new skills demanded of them. Burned dark by the sun, they toiled unrelentingly in the quarries, cutting the innumerable blocks that were needed for building projects.

Wijin's bitterness slowly gave way to introspection. He came to know himself, seeing the results of listening to Amaké. He knew he could have paid his debt to Amaké in a different way, but Amaké would accept no other means of payment. Never again would he fall prey to Amaké's influence. Even at this slave work, he was done listening. Neither Amaké, nor Intef could push him — not one inch further. *I've been a fool; gambling, losing, letting Amaké bully me into doing that wretched thieving. Look where it has got me — slavery. I am done listening to him. What will become of me? What have I done to Akila? If I keep my own counsel, I wonder if I can ever make life more bearable.*

3

CONVICTION

At the royal palace in Thebes, Amenemope, Pharaoh of the twenty-first dynasty strolled around his courtyard, which was a welcome retreat from the affairs of state even during the hottest times of the year. Between the walkways and the gardens at regular intervals stood ancient pillars on which were recorded the wisdom of the ages. These were especially dear to Amenemope's heart and he always took his time as he passed each of the eighteen monoliths to review the proverbs carved into the surfaces. They rose so high that it was difficult to read the glyphs at the top — stone books reaching into the heavens.

Special care was taken to maintain the perfection of the garden — watering, weeding, trimming — such beauty did not occur naturally in the arid climate. It took a number of gardeners working full time to coax the splendor from the soil. It was well worth it as far as Amenemope was concerned. Walking here filled him with peace and pride.

He was wearing a white leather helmet over his shaved head, the Egyptian tradition for kings of Egypt. The starched, white warrior's kilt wrapped around his waist was sewn with gold thread, making it shimmer as he walked. It was held in place by a heavily jewelled belt, studded with red carnelian, green topaz, and blue lapis lazuli, which sparkled as he walked in the sunlight. Gold arm bands engraved with the all seeing eye of Re adorned his biceps. On a long, heavy gold chain draped around his neck swung an ankh, the symbol of life. Large symbols of eternity swinging from two thick hoops hung from his pierced ears. He wore the heavy rings of his office on his fingers. Wide gold and ruby inlaid bracelets which hugged his forearms, clinked together as he walked. His sandals were overlaid with gold and images of the enemies of Egypt were carved on their leather soles so that he could step on them with every footfall.

Osorkon The Elder, the "Hawk-in-the-Nest", Amenemope's first son by his favorite wife Dalia, followed close beside his father, eager to hear his wisdom. As Dalia walked with them, she smiled at her son.

Dalia, the Great Royal Wife, was a tall and slender woman who wore her straight hair cut just to her jaw line. The sheath she wore was blue, the color of royalty. On her dainty feet she wore ornately jewelled white leather sandals. She had attractive features, especially her large brown eyes which reflected her calm and gracious manner. She bore authority well and could assert her power when necessary. Her smile lit up any room she entered, and when she spoke, it was easy to recognize her intelligence. Her beauty attracted a good deal of attention and people were drawn to her. The people of Egypt respected and adored her as queen, and her husband and the two sons she bore him, Osorkon and Siamun, loved her as wife and mother in the same way that she loved them.

She was no stranger to the throne room, as she often sat at her husband's side, offering suggestions and helping to shape policy in the great country that they ruled.

However, concerning matters of manhood and leadership, Dalia left this instruction to her husband.

"Father, tell me again why these pillars were built."

"Our ancestors built these monuments for instruction and a reminder to all who see them, to live in harmony with each other and the land."

As he spoke, butterflies that drank the nectar from the bountiful flowers floated gracefully around looking for their next sweet drink. The gardeners stopped their work and prostrated themselves before the royal family as they walked close to them, and waited for them to pass. One gardener was kneeling in submission while holding a flower towards Dalia as they rounded a corner between some short, flowering trees. She smiled and took the flower out of the old gardener's hand.

Osorkon had a very close relationship with his father and attended to his sage teachings with relish. Unlike his predecessors, Amenemope had a unique and intimate bond with his family and lavished them with his love and attention. He often took time from his royal responsibilities to pour into their lives. As Dalia walked with her royal family, she slipped her hand into Amenemope's, even though public displays of affection in upper-class Egypt were a rarity. The family stroll among the tall pylons was used as an opportunity to teach the young first son the wisdom of Egypt. Osorkon pointed to the diverse assortment of proverbs and poems that his father loved so much. He enjoyed listening to his father explaining their significance in daily life.

"My son, living by the law of Ma'at instructs us, royal blood or not, to help each other live in truth, justice and order. In other words, live in purity. We must never stray from these teachings or we might have an unfavorable result when our heart is weighed in the Judgment Hall. As you know, there is a plague against our most holy fathers who have died. The treasures they have stored up to use in the next life are slowly being taken against their will."

They approached each of the pillars and the father-son lesson continued. He instructed his son in the merits of acceptance when dealing with issues that cannot be changed. The laws of Ma'at dictate peace, love and purity of the heart.

"Never lie, even when it is easier to do so. Live and uphold justice. Live your life under the order of the gods. When we stand before the scale and our heart gets weighed against the feather of Ma'at, all our life will be held up for us to account for. You will be pharaoh one day and will be judged more harshly than the poor that work in the fields. We must do everything possible to maintain these laws, no matter what."

As he was speaking, a sense of dread overwhelmed Amenemope's mind. *Am I doing enough?* he asked himself.

Osorkon stopped short as they started toward the last pillars.

"Father, if we live by these wise sayings, why do others totally disregard them? Shouldn't everyone live by these important teachings?"

"Yes, my son. All should live by these wise and meaningful proverbs. There are those who do not, however. They corrupt the true meaning and make excuses in their minds, allowing them to do inexcusable acts. They live however they wish, robbing and stealing to meet their own selfish wants and desires. The end for them will be a swift one when they meet Osiris, and their hearts are measured by Anubis, against the feather of Ma'at. Ammit will have his way with their souls and they will be lost forever," Amenemope answered.

Silence followed the abrupt answer. The sounds of small fountains gurgling and the chirping of song birds added to the peaceful hush of the calm day. Osorkon thought about his father's words, pondering everything.

"Will you not be judged unfavorably as well for allowing this thieving to continue?" Osorkon asked with tears welling up in his eyes. "I couldn't bear the thought of you not being together with me in the afterlife. I want us to be together in the Field of Reeds."

The question and the deep emotion behind it pierced Amenemope to the core. The effect was like a sledgehammer driving a wedge into a block at the quarries and splitting it apart.

Osorkon, at the young age of five, had the insight of a much older boy. Amenemope was very proud of his Hawk in the Nest. Although his son brought up a very valid point, Amenemope was taken aback with his wisdom. He learned at a very young age from his father, that as well as being pure in his heart, he would be judged on whether he dealt with the poor the same as with the privileged.

"I cannot have my army tied up guarding our forefathers' tombs. The Libyans and Nubians would run roughshod over us and take over Egypt," Amenemope replied.

Osorkon was right, though. It was definitely possible that Amenemope's heart would be challenged in the final day. He knew that Osiris would ask why he didn't do all he could to stop the pillaging and destruction. Would he have a good enough answer to appease Osiris? Doubt cast a shadow on his soul.

Dusk gradually settled on them and even though the evening meal was peaceful, he could not shake the uncomfortable feeling that his son's questions had stirred within him.

Why must I be questioned? I am Pharaoh Living Forever. I am doing everything I can. The pressure is too great running the country to be bothered with miscreants who don't live according to Ma'at. What more am I expected to do? When they get to the scales and their hearts fail, well too bad for them. Amenemope considered these matters, trying to justify himself and calm the nattering questions swirling in his head. His mind was overcome with inner turmoil, even as the servants brought in roasted duck, bread and steamed vegetables. As always, wine from the delta was served. Plates of sweetmeats on platters of gold were offered to the family.

"Oh goodie!" Osorkon said, clapping his small hands. "My favorites are the white ones." He took five of the round white treats.

"We know, Osorkon. Just don't take any more," Dalia said, raising her eyebrows at him.

Amenemope took his leave from the family after the evening meal was over and retired to his own rooms, deciding to give his son's question more thought. The constant chirp of crickets outside below the balcony added a mild distraction.

Why am I so troubled? I'm in the right, I'm sure of it. My ka is safe. Over and over his mind justified his attitude towards his lack of action, but never convinced him. Finally, after hours of arguing with himself with no resolution, he decided to get ready for bed. His body servant, Satisankh, walked into Amenemope's room and readied him for the night. He removed Pharaoh's jewelry and carefully washed off his makeup. He led him to the gilded high cot, to sooth him with a calming massage. At last his mind settled into a state of rest.

Amenemope had a restless sleep that night, complete with a terrifying nightmare. His dreams were of his final judgment. Led by the cold hand of Anubis, the jackal-headed god, he was brought to the scales of judgment. This was where his heart would be weighed against the feather of Ma'at and it must balance evenly for him to be allowed entrance into paradise. All the deeds that he had ever done were in his heart getting ready for the final judgment. Did he live in truth? Yes! Did he provide justice? He thought so. Did he provide order? He tried to. There were too many uncertain answers. The room was cold and the noise he heard was that of the forty-two gods seated in the gallery looking on, talking amongst themselves.

"Is he worthy? I think not. Not yet!" Amenemope could hear them say.

I am worthy! he said defensively in his mind. As if they could hear his thoughts, they all stared at him with questioning looks and raised eyebrows. Quickly looking around at the dark room he became aware of a penetrating, rancid odor. The smell was that of rotting wood and decaying flesh.

Amenemope had a pang of anxiety that burned in his stomach. He looked over at Thoth, poised with brush in hand, ready to write down the results. He remembered how his son asked if he would fail the test since he was not protecting the ancient tombs to the best of his abilities. Panic set in at the sight of Osiris pointing angrily at him. The god's green face said it all. He could see his heart teetering unfavorably and finally failing the test. Thoth started to write down the unsatisfactory results.

Amenemope could hear Ammit, the crocodile-lion-hippo-bodied Swallower of the Dead growling, licking his lips and anticipating his next meal.

No! This cannot happen! I have lived in truth. I have brought forth justice where I could. I have tried to live in order, Amenemope screamed inwardly. But not a word could pass his sealed lips. The sound of rushing water, so loud he could not think, filled his head. Although there was no water to be seen, the deafening sound was like standing beside a massive waterfall. Osiris raised his hand and the sounds within stopped.

"Amenemope, my brother, who has been given all power in Egypt, you have not lived in truth! You sit idly by as your brothers before you are violated. Don't you realize your actions here on Earth have direct consequences in the afterlife? Have you not thought about that? You have not brought forth justice! You allow the criminals who rape Egypt to sit in jail or do meaningless tasks that have no real benefit."

Osiris' voice began to rise slowly as he rose to his feet and pointed his finger straight at him. "You have not brought forth Divine order in Egypt. You have not stopped the criminals who run rampant all over this great land entrusted to you. Your leadership has made you a laughing stock to other countries. Your reputation has damaged Egypt in the eyes of others. Your son will inherit a broken land and it will be you that will have to answer for it."

This information completely unnerved Amenemope. *How could I have been so blind? Will I get a second chance? Oh please!*

The next thing he knew, Anubis was gone, and was replaced by Ammit, lunging at him, sinking his wicked teeth deep into his flesh and ripping him apart. He woke in a panic, still smelling Ammit's rotten breath. Damned and defeated, he was hardly able to breathe. His sheets were wound around him, stuck to him like the mud of the Nile because of his sweat.

Amenemope lay motionless with perspiration pouring down his temples, feeling as though his soul was on the brink of disaster. It seemed as though his life force was depleted.

He heard the Hymn of Praise that heralded the start of each new dawn, as it had for all the other pharaohs for thousands of years. Though he was already awake when it began, he lay there pondering the nightmare that he recognized was given to him as a warning. As he let the Hymn play out, his mind brought back the images of the disappointment on Osiris' face when he failed the test.

Amenemope went to be bathed when he arose. Followed by his body servant, Satisankh, he stepped on the stone slab and allowed himself to be undressed. Servants carried buckets of steaming scented water into the bathing area and washed him vigorously with natron until he was purified. But the lingering impurity from his dream still clung to him.

"Wash me again," he demanded. "With fresh natron and dry me with new linen."

After that, he sat on a nearby stool where his body servants expertly shaved him and put on his leather form-fitting cap. They dressed him in a new, gold-shot white kilt and a blue and white tight-fitting top. Then they slipped on his gold sandals, and brought out a tray of jewelry for him to choose from. Amenemope pointed to a collection of rings, armbands, and necklaces that were this week's options. Satisankh picked up the pieces that held the royal insignias and placed them on the King. Every morning he would go through the same ritual, but this day, when he was dressed by his body servant, his mind was still at the Hall of Judgment in his dream, his thoughts tumbling upon each other, trying to understand. *Was it a dream or was it a vision of things to come? Surely it was a warning.* The calm morning and tranquil atmosphere of the day seemed remote compared to his internal perceptions and did nothing to alleviate his anxiety.

Before he started his routine, he went to Dalia's quarters and proceeded to reveal to her his disturbing dream. Dalia, still in her white translucent shift, got up from her cosmetic table and looked deep into Amenemope's unsettled brown eyes. Today he feared for his eternal soul, his ka. Dalia could see right away the concern troubling his face as he put his left arm around her waist and rested his head on her shoulder. She embraced him. Amenemope told Dalia about meeting his judgment and his heart failing the test. He told her about the disappointment that had washed over Osiris' face when his heart weighed heavy and he locked eyes with the god for a split second.

"It was as if Osiris was sending me a warning that if I didn't deal with the thefts in the tombs that are going on, I might be fodder for Ammit no matter how purely I have lived my life."

"My dear brother, how distressing this must be for you," Dalia replied.

"I do not know where to go from here, Dalia, my dearest sister. I put these criminals in jail or put them to death, but there are always more. Every time I turn around, there is another tomb robbery," Amenemope fretted, placing his head in his hands. "How can I protect the tombs without lowering the protection of all Egypt?" he exclaimed.

"I will come to your bed tonight, dear brother. But today the chief priest will want to cast a horoscope in regards to the dream and divine what should be done. I pray the gods will show you the answer. You always find the solution, my husband. I think Osiris will show you what is needed," Dalia spoke, as a flock of brightly-colored shrikes flew by the window and landed in a nearby tree.

Dalia tenderly held his face in her hands, her gaze knowing him and loving him. Amenemope got up, kissed Dalia on the lips and made his way to his office.

He called the high priest to cast a horoscope for his dream. Amun-Nasser gathered together his casting oils and pots, entered the royal office and made his obeisance. His stiff white kilt and leopard shoulder sash made obvious statements of his personal connections with the god.

"How may I be of service, Great One?" he inquired.

Amenemope told the high priest of the dream and his concerns for his ka at the last judgment. Amun-Nasser slowly poured the seven various oils into the large stone pot and watched the swirling oils flow around each other like many fingers laced together in a constant state of movement. He studied the dancing oil strings and waited for the god to enlighten his mind.

"The god says he alone will show you the answer today in private. If you have the patience to wait on him, he will reveal his plan."

Amenemope considered his words.

"Thank you, priest. That will do. You are dismissed."

He stood up, gathered his casting oils and jars, bowed and left.

Amenemope toiled through the daily tasks of government. He sat behind his sprawling desk, piled high with scrolls, and opened his mind and heart for the god to whisper instructions into his soul. As he poured over the reports and dispatches that arrived, his mind was never far from the previous night's vivid dream. Sifting through the government red tape was easy compared with what he would have to deal with next.

The second pile of scrolls sent Amenemope over the edge. All that filled his eyes were reports of theft and careless destruction. Tombs were being robbed and their sacred inhabitants ripped apart for the gold they held in their bindings. Whether the robbery was by foreigners or by his own people, it was deeply distressing and deplorable.

"Such a lack of respect for our holy fathers' resting place is disgusting, and it will no longer be tolerated!"

Amenemope pondered what he could do to prevent such atrocities from continuing to happen. The jails were getting fuller with these sorts of criminals. One idea after another ran through his head until one single thought became clear and absolute. He was convinced that Osiris had whispered instructions into his soul. The powerful revelation exploded within him and suddenly everything fell into place.

"Nekht-Ankh!" Amenemope called for his assistant. "Get the chief architect! I have the plan to stop the devastation."

He stood up, bowed and retreated out into the hallway to get Khnum. Amenemope smiled as plans that would ultimately cure Egypt's desecration against the gods materialized in his mind.

Osiris, in spirit form, slowly poured instructions into Amenemope's thoughts. *Only in the fulfilling of this plan will you have a favorable weighing at the scales, Amenemope. Will you complete this task I have set out for you or will you make excuses and disregard my warnings?* Osiris spoke almost audibly to his mind.

"I will do all that you instructed and will not hold back, no matter what it takes," he answered.

4

NOWHERE TO GO

Zebel made regular trips to see Mahnudhotep at the barracks over the next four years. The captain saw Zebel as a son, a young man full of promise, someone he could rescue from an existence of poverty and limitations. *I will mold him into a fine soldier, someone with a future.*

Walking along the dusty path to the barracks, Zebel kicked at the stones that littered the well-used road and made a game of trying to bounce one stone off the others all the way there. Reaching down, he picked up a stone that caught his eye. He aimed at one of the tall palm trees that lined the broad path and cast it at the tree. After an hour of kicking and throwing stones he finally arrived at the barracks.

The typical challenges rang out as he neared the secured gates and he answered them with his customary counter-challenge. The thick wooden gates creaked open, revealing soldiers practising mock hand-to-hand combat. He watched the exercises with enthusiasm and felt at home among the soldiers whose ranks he hoped to join one day. It gave him great happiness to be so favored by Mahnudhotep and made him believe that his life might actually amount to something more than digging irrigation canals.

The captain saw him across the yard and called to him, "Zebel, come here. I have a meeting at the palace with Pharaoh and I would like you to come along." Zebel's heart surged with excitement. *Can this be happening to me? Did I hear him right? The palace of Pharaoh!*

They mounted the captain's chariot and headed towards the palace. The wind in his face was a new experience for the young boy and it thrilled him. *This is so much better than digging ditches*, he thought as the horse's hooves beat the ground and the palm trees sailed past them. As they drew closer to the palace, Zebel's knees turned to jelly and his throat went dry. The security challenges and counter challenges were given and the great doors opened. Zebel's eyes opened wide with wonder at the sight of the magnificent residence beyond the courtyard. As the captain and Zebel dismounted from the chariot, he noticed a young boy about his age staring at him. He was obviously important as his head was shaved except for a braided side lock of hair that brushed his bejewelled neck and he was in the close company of a couple of household guards.

Before Mahnudhotep entered the palace, he guided Zebel over to the curious boy and said, "Good day to you, young master. I would like you to meet someone." To Zebel he said, "Zebel, this is Osorkon, the son of Pharaoh Amenemope." Turning to Osorkon, "I would like you to meet Zebel, a young man who has provided us with valuable information concerning activities around the tombs. I believe both of you boys are nine years old and perhaps you could spend some time together while I have a meeting with Pharaoh." The two boys eyed each other and then broke into smiles.

"Do you play sennet?" Osorkon asked.

"I have played it, but I am no expert," replied Zebel. "I would love to learn it better." He felt intimidated, but excited at the same time.

The fact that the captain had spoken well of him before this young prince had given him some confidence and he loved games and any competitive challenge. With that Mahnud took his leave and walked into the palace. Osorkon eyed Zebel with a critical gaze. *This boy looks to be far from his comfort zone,* he thought. *Why is he here? He does not belong here.* Then he thought about his father's words: *"You will be Pharaoh one day and will be judged in part by how you treat the poor."*

"So where do you live, Zebel?"

Zebel struggled to grasp Osorkon's thick royal accent, but soon was able to understand him.

"I live close to Medina, right by the Nile. My father is the head of the town."

"Hmmm. Well, would you like a game?" Osorkon asked as he motioned to the sennet board.

"Sure! Remember, I'm not too good, so be merciful," Zebel said tentatively.

Osorkon smiled and set up the board and the game began.

Mahnudhotep was pleased to be correct that the boys would get along well and since the first meeting had been so successful, he brought Zebel along with him whenever he had a meeting with Pharaoh. The boys began to forge a strong connection in spite of their drastic differences of class. The proper Osorkon was drawn to Zebel's animated charm, his zest for life and enthusiastic friendship. They played for hours at a time while waiting for Mahnud's business to be done.

"Have you ever been to Tanis?" Osorkon asked as he rolled the three silver sticks in between his palms and threw them to the ground and counted the points.

"Four! Just what I wanted!" the young boy cried out as he moved his pieces along the three rows of ten squares. "You had better watch out, you are dangerously close to the 'river' square."

Zebel wrinkled his lip to one side and shook his head. "Don't you count on yourself winning just yet. All I need is a roll of more than three. Then I win!"

Osorkon sat up, a little startled. He wasn't used to being challenged or losing at anything. *And he's right, too. He's actually winning. How can this be? He learns quickly. Maybe he's just lucky. Surely he can't be better than I am.*

"Tanis?" Osorkon questioned again.

"No, I can't say that I have ever been to Tanis. What is it like?"

"Well it's where my other house is! It's far away though. There are rows of palm trees beside the roads and small lakes where I go swimming! My father keeps flowers and fruit trees in the garden, like here. I'm even allowed to take my boat to the Great Green. I have to take my bodyguard though. But I don't think I need him, because I'm nine now."

"Your own boat! Wow," Zebel said in awe. It was his turn now. He threw the sticks and got five. "I win!"

After the boys had played most of the afternoon, Mahnud finally finished his business with Pharaoh and came to collect Zebel for the trip home.

"Do you know how lucky you are to be playing with Osorkon?" Mahnud asked as they traveled back to the barracks.

"He's going to be Pharaoh one day, isn't he? Did you know I can beat him at sennet sometimes?" Zebel said with great delight.

"Zebel, you must realize that even though you can win at a game, you must still remember your place. Pharaoh has all power. Remember that. It is good to guard your heart."

"Well even if that's so, I will still like him!" Zebel replied. Mahnud laughed to himself, realizing that it wasn't just Zebel's young age or his social nature, but also his pure heart that caused him to care more for the person than the position.

The captain of the barracks mused about what sort of man Zebel would turn out to be. He was definitely convinced the young man would be a great soldier without the common judgments that plagued so many of his recruits. Mahnud decided that now was the time to start training Zebel in the many disciplines of the Egyptian conscript.

The first discipline to learn was the spear and shield. He would surely find it difficult at the start to lift the heavy spear and throw it with any accuracy, but as time went on, Mahnud was certain he would become quite a marksman. The sword would be next, then the bow and finally the chariot. Mahnud expected that Zebel would excel at all of these crafts of war, and he had every confidence that through his teaching he could make this boy into the man he was meant to be.

Later that day, Khnum, the chief architect appeared before Amenemope. Khnum was named after the god Who-Sits-At-His-Potters-Wheel, a god with design and creative powers. He was dressed in his best pure white kilt. Thick black eyeliner framed his eyes. He was tall and well built, although on the slender side. He had an air of authority, although he was reserved by nature. He was a son of an important family in Egypt, his father having worked high in the Egyptian government. Khnum was a good listener and a shrewd judge of character. He had earned his position as chief architect through skill and hard work as well as finding his way through the political labyrinth with finesse. He had a good working relationship with Amenemope, respected him as Egypt's leader and he sincerely liked him as a man.

He entered Pharaoh's office, bowed low to the ground and made his obeisance to Amenemope. The office he entered had an open, inviting feel, bright and airy and accented with fresh flowers. The bright colors and floral scent blended perfectly with the murals of Amenemope's family life that covered the walls. The ceiling was painted a light sky blue, the focus being Re as the sun at the center, lighting up all aspects of Pharaoh's world. The Aten, the rays from the sun, radiated out like hands, touching the mouths of Amenemope's family displayed on the murals, giving them all life.

Amenemope motioned to him to sit and start taking notes. Khnum took a seat on a short stool and said a quick prayer to Thoth, the god of writing. He reached into his supply sack and produced eight sheets of papyrus. He proceeded to rub them swiftly with the scraper until he was satisfied with their smoothness and waited with brush poised, ready to write down everything that Pharaoh said.

A quiet stillness permeated the room. Amenemope began to outline his plan to start a building project with the help of the prisoners that were in jail or part of the forced labor crews.

Pharaoh walked back and forth between his office desk and the window, gathering his thoughts and making sure he was confident in his soul with this new undertaking. His doubts and inner conflicts gradually gave way to a stark determination to carry out his great solution. He would not let anything get in the way of changing his future and pleasing Osiris.

As Amenemope relayed his desire for the good of Egypt and the past pharaohs, a snake made its way through the door and brushed against his feet — a good omen. Amenemope saw this as a sign from the god himself.

"We can actually put to use the skills of those ransacking criminals for our own advantage," Amenemope informed Khnum. "I have also devised a plan for a subterranean pit tomb. We will build it far out in the desert, with many rooms for storage. The location will be so remote that it would be almost impossible for anyone to discover it, let alone do any digging, as it would be a death trap in such an inhospitable place. I want to make it clear that I also intend to build a pyramid in the desert as well, but far from the pit tomb. I want it as a memorial to myself and as a place to record the story of these thieving criminal's actions and the consequences they will bear."

"I am listening, my Lord," Khnum responded curiously, as he continued writing down all that Pharaoh was saying. "Tell me more."

"Nekht-Ankh and I have also been discussing the development of preparations for my final resting place."

He turned to his personal scribe and said, "Nekht-Ankh, my well-studied servant, will you share your educated proposal with our learned architect here?"

The scribe began, "I have discovered the perfect place in the eastern delta for the location of a secluded tomb. It is a place blessed by Isis. Building this project also has the advantage of being a diversion so that the other undertakings that Pharaoh has mentioned can be carried out in absolute secrecy. The people will assume that any workers, who are leaving the cities and the fields to build, are going to work on Pharaoh's tomb. To protect the future of *this* tomb, we must create ingenious and perhaps diabolical devices. In my studies of safeguards of the past, I have realized that they have all failed. That must not be allowed to happen in this case. We must create a fail-safe solution that will last for all time. All of this is subject to your approval, of course."

Khnum glanced up from his pallet and stopped his ink, as he let the information sink in.

"Oh great one," Khnum spoke up, "those ideas seem most worthy and appropriate. But getting back to the other projects in the desert that you spoke of, I have some questions."

Pharaoh replied, "I am sure you do. What are they?"

The architect stroked his temple and looked directly at Amenemope and asked carefully, "Just what is this vast subterranean tomb to be used for and why must it be so secretive?"

"Ahh!" replied Pharaoh. "You come right to the heart of the matter. I will reveal to you all that Osiris has laid upon my soul for the well-being of the land. We will use the prison laborers to extract all the wealth remaining in the tombs of our great Egypt, along with the remains of our previous fathers, whose ba's now reside with Osiris and to place it all securely in one centralized, concealed location. Can you now see why the enterprise must be shrouded in the utmost secrecy? By moving all the remaining tomb contents to one remote location, we are taking them out of harm's way and keeping them safe. For it to work, it must escape everyone's notice."

"But, my Lord, it will take many more people to complete such a huge endeavor than are numbered among the prisoners of the land. From where will you draw these workers?"

"We will gather all prisoners in this land — every prisoner. We will also gather prisoners from neighboring lands. This way we will fill our needs and be a benefit to our neighbours," he replied.

"It occurs to me that it will be difficult to maintain the secrecy that you require when the task will include such a large workforce of criminals," Khnum suggested.

"Don't let that concern you just yet. I have a plan for that as well," Pharaoh commented.

Khnum thought for a moment, trying to understand. Something seemed wrong — it did not add up.

A cool breeze lifted the shades in the windows. Amenemope walked across the room and looked out onto the court below, letting the breeze waft over his face. With his back to the scribe and the architect, he reflected on the magnitude of what he was proposing. *It is a huge undertaking, but I believe this is what it will take to fulfill Osiris' expectation of me.*

Then he gazed at his faithful scribe, who served him so well for so long.

"You are dismissed Nekht-Ankh. Get together the list of field workers who will be conscripted to build my tomb," Amenemope said. "You will also prepare lists of the names of prisoners who will work on the labor force. And now that I think of it, include the names of the prisoner's wives. I'm sure we can put many of them to work also. In addition, prepare letters to the rulers of our neighboring countries and inform them of our proposal to take their prisoners off their hands. We will need numbers and names for those as well."

Nekht-Ankh stood-up, bowed and left.

As Pharaoh watched him go, he contemplated what he had just asked him to do. *I am standing on the edge of a knife asking for criminals to be brought here. Osiris, give me strength!*

Amenemope turned back to Khnum. He held his gaze for a few moments, smiled slightly and leaned back against his desk with his arms folded across his chest.

"So, good architect. Shall we discuss the details of these projects that I wish you to incorporate into your plans?"

Within three months, Khnum had completed the preliminary drawings for the new building projects. Along with them he had estimated how many workers would be required to work at each location. He met with Nekht-Ankh and Amenemope regularly until all of Pharaoh's vision for these projects was completely implemented. At the end of it, Amenemope sat looking over all the drawings and plans. *Khnum and Nekht-Ankh have done a wonderful job on this. This is exactly what I wanted.*

"It looks as though we are ready to begin the actual building. I will

assign the additional staff you will need to manage the whole project,"
said Pharaoh. "These buildings will take priority over any other plans
that we have. I will warn you again that these projects are not to be
discussed with anyone at all except those people assigned to the task. Is
that clear?"

There would be no room for error if his plan were to work. Ideally,
the three projects would have to be started and completed at the same
time, the only noticeable change being that the jails would be empty.

With the satisfaction of this large task having begun, Amenemope
leaned back on the chair behind his desk and let his mind turn to
other matters. He observed the large volume of scrolls that lay there,
prompting a new thought to emerge. *I want to create a book of wisdom to
guide Osorkon as he grows and becomes the nation's leader after I'm gone; to
hopefully be even better than I am,* Amenemope thought.

He sent for a priest-scribe, someone who understood the search
for enlightenment, someone not familiar with the work that was
consuming him.

Soon after, Nemutptah walked into Amenemope's well-lit office,
sheets of papyrus clamped between his right arm and torso. He was
carrying an ivory box in his left hand that contained a scraper and a
variety of brushes, all in immaculate condition. He was a short slim man
with dark, discerning eyes that missed nothing.

He wore a stark white kilt and a diaphanous pale shirt that was
bordered by a black, square design. He wore a black belt across his torso
that had the title of his position tooled into it and outlined in gold. His
hair was cut short, but with two thin braids that hung to his mid-back. His
sandals were made of soft black leather that made no sound as he walked.

Nemutptah quickly placed his scribes' kit and a stack of new papyrus
sheets on the blue-tiled floor. Prostrating himself in submission, he
nosed the floor, waiting for Pharaoh to bid him rise.

Amenemope bid him rise and prepare to take dictation. Nemutptah
sat cross-legged on the floor, put his alabaster scribe palette across his lap
and smoothed out a new papyrus sheet with his scraper.

"Let's begin," Amenemope started. "I will call this: Wisdom of Amenemope."

Chapter 1

Give your ears and hear what is said,
Give your mind over to their interpretation.
It is profitable to put them in your heart,
But woe to him that neglects them.
Let them rest in the shrine of your insides,
That they may act as a lock in your heart.
Now, when it comes to a storm of words,
They will be a mooring-post on your tongue.
If you spend a lifetime with these things in your heart,
You will find good fortune.
You will discover my words to be a treasure-house of life,
your body will flourish upon the Earth. [1]

Nemutptah's smooth and efficient hieratic script flowed without stopping, as he could memorize everything that was told to him without fail, allowing him to continue to write as he received the dictation.

Amenemope stopped and placed his right hand on his brow, closed his eyes and gathered his thoughts. He looked at his scribe, drew in a breath and spoke again.

Chapter 2

Beware of stealing from a miserable man,
Or raging against a cripple.
Do not stretch out your hand to touch an old man,
Or snip at the words of an elder. [1]

Amenemope continued dictating advice that would be given to his son at a later date. He filled the pages with instructions on integrity, honesty, self-control, kindness and how to attain these goals in life by trusting in all gods.

Later that month the first crews of prisoners were assembled and started work in the rock quarry cutting the large blocks needed for the pyramid Amenemope was going to build.

Another crew of slaves was led across the blazing desert to the second designated location where they were to create a vast underground vault. There were lives lost on the journey due to dehydration and sunstroke from exposure, but many extra people were brought along.

Pharaoh provided supply depots along the way to help minimize the losses before the great work. When they arrived, they were put to work cutting into the bedrock and tunneling out the extensive planned excavation. It was punishing work and many died in the unforgiving desert, but the work continued unrelentingly, using replacements as necessary.

At the quarry, Bakuru, an Ethiopian slave, naked except for a tattered loin cloth, stumbled as he carried the heavy woven basket full of sand and stone chips away from the stone cutters.

"Pick up your feet, you slime of Set!" the guard watching him hollered as he whipped his long leather strap across his back. "Cleaning up the debris on the site is the easiest job here and you can't even do that right. We don't pay you to lie around. Hah! We don't pay you at all!"

Bakuru tried frantically to get back up as he knew another lash would be coming if he didn't. As he struggled, the guard readied his whip to deliver a second painful blow. A hand grabbed the slave's arm and helped him up. Soknue, his friend, steadied himself as he supported his co-worker and helped carry the heavy basket.

The two men heaved the baskets on their backs and rejoined the line they had strayed from. Bakuru and Soknue had been caught robbing tombs by the great pyramids and had been working in the quarries for two months.

Soknue looked at the blood trickling down Bakuru's back from the guard's lash and said sorrowfully, "My friend, we made a fortune breaking into tombs and it was good for a while, but now I would trade anything for my freedom. I think we will die here. It has not been worth it."

Bakuru thought for a little and nodded his head in agreement. They carried their full baskets over to the small mountain of debris below the ledge that had been created by the slaves emptying their baskets. They walked to the edge and poured the contents out, watching the stone chips roll down the steep hill and puff up small clouds of dust on the way down.

"Two down, a million to go," Bakuru muttered under his breath.

Legs aching, they headed back to the sound of hammers slamming wedges into the quarry wall and sharpened punches chipping off the rough edges of the large stone blocks. The sound of dolerite constantly rubbing and grinding away at the stones like a file was a never-ending song of monotony.

Amaké, Wijin and Intef began cutting blocks for the new pyramid along with the thousands of other criminals slaving in the quarries for Amenemope.

Wijin became aware of a change coming over him as he labored in the quarry. He found that the constant physical exertions gradually hardened his muscles into iron. He could tell that his strength surpassed that of the other men and it gave him joy. The rays of the sun seemed to energize him and turned his skin to a dark brown. His skill as a stone cutter improved rapidly. He realized that even in this inhospitable environment he was gaining ground within himself and he felt an inner confidence beginning to develop. He had always enjoyed the company of other people and as his attitude improved he found a sense of community evolving around him with him at the center. The men working with him looked to him for encouragement and instruction and eventually they formed into a team that could cut and dress stones more quickly and skillfully than the other workers whose incentive came from the whips of the guards.

"Come on, boys," Wijin's voice rang out over the constant din of the quarry. "Make it perfect. Let's beat the rest of them for the tenth time!"

Wijin's move to make cutting and moving blocks into a game caused the workers to labor more quickly than ever. Soon blocks were being brought out of the quarry and stacked at an increasing rate. Wijin was keeping the slaves' spirits up as the days plodded on. Amaké could see Wijin's influence growing among the men but his grudging respect was mixed with resentment.

Wijin had always found that singing had lightened his own workload and when he started singing to the rhythm of the hammer strikes, other men joined in.

He is Happy this good prince:
Death is a kindly fate.
A Generation passes, Another stays,
Since the time of the ancestors.
The gods who were before rest in their tombs,
Blessed nobles too are buried in their tombs.
(Yet) those who built tombs,
Their places are gone,
What has become of them?
I have heard the words of Imhotep and Hordjedef,
Whose sayings are recited in whole.
What of their places?
Their walls have crumbled;
Their places are gone,
As though they had never been!
None comes from there,
To tell of their needs,
To calm our hearts,
Until we go where they have gone!
Hence rejoice in your heart!
Forgetfulness profits you. (2)

The verse was repeated and soon words were changed to lewder lyrics, livening up the oppressive work. The whole group of workers, by now, had joined in the singing, even some guards adding the verses, making waves of laughter burst out when a particularly raunchy verse was invented.

The rows and rows of perfect stone blocks ready to be transported to the pyramid site were as long as the eye could see. Wijin's cutting team produced more blocks quicker and with fewer rejects than any other team, making this criminal/slave a valued foreman. Khnum, the head architect, took notice of this outstanding young man.

He moved Wijin from one quarry working crew to another so that his great skills motivating the people could be applied to increase their productivity. This moving around gave the young man a chance to understand the scope of the whole project.

Crews divided into twenty-five slaves and one guard as a foreman were formed with names like Slaves of the god, Bright Commanders of the Disk and Strong Arm of Set.

Parallel logs were buried in the desert road between the rock quarry and the pyramid site so that the sledges transporting the numbered two ton blocks of stone would not dig into the soft sand and get stuck.

Khnum was pleased with the work at the quarry. He had overseen the general plan of organization of workers, site management and stockpiling of dressed stones. Since the work at the quarry was proceeding smoothly, he delegated the task of overseer to his assistant and considered his next step.

He thought, *I can't get that young man, Wijin, out of my mind. He has shown some real talent for the work. Perhaps he has the seeds of greatness within him. And his way with the men — he seems to have an almost intoxicating magnetism which draws in all the workers on his crew. I think I would like to take him with me to the pyramid site and see if he has any aptitude for architecture.*

He identified Wijin's current location in the quarry and walked over to where he was working and said, "Wijin, come with me to my tent for a few minutes. I have some things I would like to discuss with you."

Wijin gathered his tools and followed Khnum to just beyond the edge of the quarry where a tent was situated, giving the architect a base of operations. The roof of the tent gave some shelter from the heat of the burning sun and a pleasant breeze dried the sweat on his body.

"Take a seat over there. I'll have refreshments brought to us so we can relax a bit. I can see that you are rather anxious. I want to reassure you that I am very pleased with all that I have seen you doing at the quarry. How are you finding your work here?"

"Being a slave isn't really my choice, my Lord, but I must admit that there are many things about my tasks here that I have found pleasing," Wijin replied.

"I notice that you seem to have a positive influence on the men around you. What do you say to that?" Khnum asked.

"I have always enjoyed good friendships with those around me, my Lord, and it has worked out well here also. The men need someone who can lift their spirits and help them to accomplish the tasks at hand. It seems to come naturally to me."

"Would you be interested in learning more about this great building project, Wijin?"

His eyes lit up and he sat up straighter. He looked eagerly at the architect and a smile spread across his face.

"Why, that would be amazing, my Lord. I can't think of anything that would please me more. Indeed, I would love to learn about building the pyramid."

Khnum continued, "I am thinking that if you pick things up well, you could be a valuable assistant to me. As various tasks require teams of workers to accomplish, you could oversee the crew that carries them out. You would need to master the plans and the mathematical forces that affect the success of such a project. Does this sound like something you could do?"

"It sounds like a wonderful challenge, my Lord. I have already learned to read and write and I have always desired to become more knowledgeable about the higher things of life. May I ask a question of you?"

"I'm sure you have many questions," Khnum replied. "What is on your mind?"

Wijin hesitated and then began speaking, some nervousness returning to his voice, "My Lord, I have a wife who is a prisoner also. I haven't seen her since I have been here. I don't even know where she is. May I be so bold as to ask if there is a possibility that she could be located and brought to the pyramid site also, so that I could at least be near her?"

"Ah yes. If she is not here working as a water girl or preparing meals, she will likely have been chosen to learn the craft of tomb painting. There is a great deal of artwork within the walls of these great buildings. I will find out where she is located. If she is being taught as an artist, however, you will have to wait until she finishes her training. There will be much work for her to do at the pyramid once the main chambers are finished. When that time comes, I believe I can arrange that she will be sent to your location. I can't make extravagant promises, but with your new position, you could expect a few privileges."

Wijin replied, "That sounds wonderful, my Lord. That would make me very happy."

"So, we have an arrangement, young Wijin. I would like to begin teaching you before we travel to the pyramid site. We are intending to begin there within a month. So I would like you to come to this tent every day after the noon meal and I will spend some time familiarizing you with the plans for the pyramid and with some of the projects you would be undertaking."

As arranged, Khnum moved his operations from the quarry to the pyramid site. The location was in an out of the way place in the desert not too far removed from a nearby town. He brought Wijin with him and started working with him on a full time basis. He was pleased with how quickly Wijin seemed to pick things up and with his enthusiasm.

"I think we will arrange our time here in a similar manner to what we were doing at the quarry, Wijin. In the mornings you will be a team leader for a crew who will be clearing away the sand down to the bedrock. This must be done before we can begin building.

The pyramid must be oriented so that the four sides are facing exactly on north, south, east and west. This is the way that we determine true north: We will build a smooth cylindrical room constructed of baked mud brick and erect it in the center of the site, the walls high enough to block the view of the surrounding desert. Then we will have Mecanekbit the architect priest stand in the center of the constructed circular room over the next several days watching for the appearance of a star in the east. The position of this star will be marked on the wall and a line from that mark will then be drawn to the center of the room. As the star moves in an arc during the night, a second mark will be made on the wall as it dips below the horizon on the opposite wall and another line will be drawn from there to the center of the room. A third line will then be drawn from the middle of the room to the wall exactly between the two other lines showing true north. With these measurements we will be able to position the pyramid properly."

Wijin considered this information and said, "Ah, I see, my Lord. It all makes sense. It is fascinating to think that you use the movement of the stars to guide you."

Dalia came to Amenemope's royal bedchamber as she had promised. Even though she was the Great Queen and First-Among-Women, she got down on her knees and prostrated herself before Pharaoh on the cool tile floor.

"Rise, my dearest wife," Amenemope said tenderly.

He dismissed their servants and the guards that stood in the shadows along the walls. They were alone.

"I had some thoughts to bring to you. Osorkon is approaching the age of marriage and he must marry Maatkara if he is to become king."

"They seem to have become close and even though she is two

years younger I think they are a good fit," Dalia replied, not concerned about their fit in the future. "Tell me about what has been keeping you occupied this past while."

Amenemope looked at her, judging whether or not to reveal his plans. She was his wife and he could trust her with all his secrets. *I can't reveal my total plan, but I'll give her the basic premise.*

"As you know, I had that dream from Osiris. That vision changed everything for me," he said with emotion and conviction. She nodded her head, trying to understand his heartfelt words.

"I have been collecting every criminal from this and neighboring countries to do my building work. I will be safeguarding our forefathers' treasures for all time. This will take some time — a long time."

"You plan on bringing multitudes of criminals into our borders? How is this good? We have enough criminals of our own," Dalia said.

"This project will take a long time — years in fact. We need as many as we can acquire because many of them will not survive. Do not worry my Queen, I have this under control."

Wijin's crew cleared the pyramid site down to and the bedrock, which took half the year. Hundreds of slaves formed lines and filled their baskets with sand in the burning desert sun as they cleared away the sand dunes, getting ready for the pyramid they were about to build. It was vitally important that bedrock be at the surface of the chosen site so that the pyramid would have a solid foundation to rest on.

Bakuru bent his well-muscled back as he chipped out the water channels with a copper chisel and a dolerite hammer. The grooves that he carved into the bedrock were one foot deep and six inches wide. Soknue, who followed him, carried a basket for gathering the stone chips that had flaked off and a measuring-stick depth-gage to help guide Bakuru.

"I think it's time we trade jobs again," Bakuru called over to his teammate who was scooping stone chips out of the trench.

"I don't think so, my friend," Soknue said with a laugh. "You always want the easier job!" He hoisted the stone filled basket to his shoulder and started humming.

"How can you be happy, Soknue? There is nothing to be happy about."

The humming stopped and all that was left were the sounds of the multitudes of hammers striking the chisels, each making a high-pitched "TING" when they hit.

The ten acre building site was filled with clouds of dust and the constant song of the ringing chisels as hundreds of workers bent over their trenches and hammered out the deep grooves.

"Happy? I'm not happy, but having some enjoyment beats being grumpy all day. Besides I don't have my wife constantly nagging."

Bakuru thought for a minute. "My wife never nagged me." He paused again and thought about the last time he had seen her. "I wonder where she is?" he said wistfully to himself in a low voice.

"Don't think about that for too long, or you will have a bad day," Soknue replied, knowing how much he loved his wife.

He also had not seen his wife but for a quick glimpse as she gave water to soldiers when he worked in the quarries.

After the trenches were cleaned and filled with water, its surface was used as a level.

Large, square sandstone blocks were placed to fit tightly together — almost as if they were one stone. The straight, sharp edges of the rows of blocks looked like row upon row of soldiers waiting to be commanded into place. The first blocks were set on the bedrock, giving the dull desert floor some definite character and the immense pyramid outline began to take shape.

Light winds blew up desert dust devils, making the bedrock surface seem like a ballroom floor for the spinning sand ballerinas. The first level of stone blocks were successfully slid into place on the ten acre site, giving the area the look of a raised stage in the middle of the desert.

Khnum thought, *Things are going quite well here. And Wijin is working out even better than I had hoped. He certainly deserves the favor that he had requested of me — finding his wife and bringing her here. Even though she has been trained as a painter for the interior of the tombs and from what her instructor told me, she is as talented for her work as Wijin is for his, borrowing her to surprise him will be worthwhile. She should arrive here tomorrow, but I will not tell him today.* The next day dawned hot and sunny and soon the new workers were guided to the collection area. Khnum looked over the huddled group of women. His eyes were immediately drawn to a shorter female, one with short straight hair. *It couldn't be! I must look at her more closely. The resemblance is amazing.* Khnum felt his heart beat faster. He could hardly catch his breath. A bittersweet memory of a girl from his past rose in his mind. *Could that be Wijin's wife? Surely not!* He scanned the crowd again looking for another short woman. *There were several.* Finally he walked into the cluster of female slaves. A hush stifled the chattering women.

"I'm looking for Akila."

"I'm here," a voice called out from the cluster.

The same young woman he had been drawn to walked up to him. He chuckled inwardly. *Here I wanted to surprise Wijin and I too am delightfully surprised.* For once in his life Khnum was at a loss for words. *She is beautiful, a picture of Isis embodied in front of me.*

"Um … Ah … Could, ah, you please come with me?"

She followed him through the building site, scanning the workers, wondering if she might see her husband. She saw men dragging blocks on sledges towards a massive square form built out of those same blocks that seemed to be growing out of the desert floor. Men bent their sweat glistened backs in heavy labor. Beyond the noise of the working men, she heard the men singing. Akila closed her eyes and concentrated on the song:

> To hear your voice is pomegranate wine to me:
> I draw life from hearing it.
> Could I see you with every glance,
> It would be better for me
> Than to eat or to drink. [3]

I know that song, Akila told herself. *Wijin sang that all the time. He must be here.*

They walked over to the base of the structure. In the middle of the singing workers Akila saw Wijin. She was sure of it. *Oh, my beloved — my heart's desire.* He looked different than she remembered him. He seemed more rugged and handsome than the last time she had seen him — definitely stronger and more confident. This excited her even more. She stood there trembling.

"Wijin!" Khnum called out.

Akila saw her husband stop working mid-song and turn his head towards the commanding architect. But then his gaze immediately swayed to the short woman beside him. Their eyes met. His face broke into a radiant smile. *Could it be? It has been over two years!* Wijin felt his legs weaken.

"Now there's a fine looking woman," a slave nudged Wijin as he nodded his head towards the woman.

"Yeah, a fine looking woman — a doll," Wijin replied in a daze.

He saw that she had grown slimmer over the time that they had been separated. Her black hair was cut to her jaw and of course she was unadorned. The glow from her smile shone like the sun and everything around seemed to fade into the background. He dropped his level on the ground and hurried over to where they were standing. In his haste, he stumbled over a basket, but managed to catch himself.

Khnum was delighted to see them together. He asked, "Wijin, do you know this young lady?"

Wijin didn't take his eyes off her as he replied offhandedly, "Yes, I think so." A public embrace between slaves was out of the question so he took her hands in his and squeezed them, his eyes telling her what was in his heart.

By now Khnum had regained his own composure and he introduced himself to Akila.

"My name is Khnum and I am the chief architect on this building project, as well as others in the land. Wijin, here, has been doing very well and is now working on this project as one of my assistants. Because of his fine work, I have granted him the favor he asked — to bring you to this location."

The best part of the favor was that Wijin and Akila were occasionally allowed to spend their nights together. It made all the difference in their lives over the next months.

After the long day of heavy labor was over, Wijin heaved a sigh of relief and lay down on the hard-packed floor of the desert with his wife. They lay naked. Wijin and Akila had removed the sparse amount of clothing they had and rolled it into a makeshift pillow for Wijin's head. Akila rested in the crook of his shoulder, so she would not have the hard earth pressing into the back of her head like a merciless taskmaster that had no give and no comfort. Lying close together helped to keep them warm, which was necessary even though they had been given a couple of coarsely woven blankets to help protect them from the pervasive chill of the desert night, the biting insects and the blowing sand.

"How did we ever get here?" Akila sobbed quietly. "I mean, why could we not have just sold our house to get out from under Amaké's demand for repayment? Did you even ask him about that?"

The guilt of losing their livelihoods in the stupid game of chance tore at his soul. Akila had been right beside him when it looked as though he would win, encouraging him all the way. However, the game of chance played its deceptive song and then crushed him.

"Yes, sweetheart, we did try that, remember? But Amaké would not accept payment that way. He demanded my help with his schemes. Remember how we pleaded with him, but he just refused? Look at us. We lie here naked, insects biting us and mice crawling over us, the eyes of the other male slaves on you like ogling teenage boys. We are better than this, Akila," Wijin whispered intensely. "We must continue to be the best workers here. Already, Khnum, the chief architect, looks on us with favor, allowing us these times together. I can't imagine never being allowed to be with you like the other couples sleeping apart from each other."

As they lay in each other's arms the growl of a desert lion pierced the solitude of the night, making Akila hold on to Wijin's muscular frame more closely. That evening, multitudes of falling stars streaked across the night sky in a spectacular meteor shower. Even though they needed their sleep, the two of them stared into the diamond studded black abyss and enjoyed the cosmic show.

"How breathtaking to see such a display in the skies," Akila said softly. "It makes you think that things aren't all bad here. It seems as though life has such a mixture of things that build us up and things that try to tear us down. As you say, we just have to do the best we can in the situation and hope that things will work out."

The constant snores of the men that slept close by, at one time had driven Akila mad, but now they lulled her to sleep.

In the morning, they quickly put their sparse clothes back on and tried to treat the new crop of insect bites they had suffered during the night.

"I've been watching you, Akila," Kuric, a skinny slave called over, eyeing Akila as she squatted and urinated. "How about you come and visit me next time you are here?" Kuric called over, his eyes scanning her body in lust as she pulled up her loin cloth.

Wijin stepped out between them cutting off the lascivious probing stare.

"Watch how you address my wife, Kuric!" Wijin yelled.

"Well, what are you going to do about it? You might be the crew chief, but we are all criminals here and we all have wives that we can't be with. The fact that you are allowed to have Akila some nights and we don't see our wives ever, doesn't seem right," Kuric snapped bitterly.

Akila stood behind Wijin glaring at Kuric. *What a creep. Can I not just be left alone?* She felt assaulted by his eyes and tried to cover herself better.

"I have earned the right to have her accompany me on occasion. If you want to be with your wife, then maybe you should work on earning it as well." Wijin left it at that and stood there between them until Kuric turned and walked away, mumbling.

Kuric stopped in his tracks and turned around and glared at Wijin. "You think you are so special and that I am scum. I tell you, I am somebody, too. You are just a man, not so special. I could kill you," he said with venomous lips.

After the uncomfortable confrontation, Kuric left. Wijin was taken aback and did not know how to respond. *I had better watch out for him. Maybe we should not be with each other in front of him and when she is here we should sleep at a different place.*

Wijin's knowledge and performance continued to improve and Akila excelled as well, even surpassing the teachers from whom she had learned tomb painting.

Khnum was surprised to notice Akila's growing skills in her work, even though she was no longer being instructed, but simply developing her own talents.

"I hear you have no need of lessons any more, Akila. From what your teachers tell me you have mastered the classical art styles and even mix your own paints. I think the time for practising on pot shards is over for you. I will arrange for you to help teach at the art compound a few miles away. Of course you can walk here at the end of the day to be with Wijin at night."

"Thank you, Lord Khnum. I do enjoy the painting, but I do have a question about the hieroglyphs."

"You may ask."

"What do the writings say?"

"They are the holy language and they speak about how great Pharaoh is," Khnum lied.

Khnum was attracted to her because of Akila's beauty and how she carried herself with confidence and grace. He desired her, but he realized he was so drawn to her because she reminded him of a girl from his past that he was still emotionally attached to, even though she was now dead.

He thought about how he could take Akila for himself. He was well within his rights, he being the overlord and she the slave. He had restrained himself, in spite of the constant stirring within him, as he was a spiritual man who gave sober thought to his final reward. *How would I answer the gods when they examine my heart, if I should succumb to my desires*, he thought.

Khnum loved watching Wijin and Akila together, though secretly he wished that is was he who held Akila in his arms during the nights, feeling the softness of her body, hearing her breath as she slept and enjoying the fulfilment of her love. He never acted on his desires. Whenever he met with her, the first thing she would do would be to thank him for bringing her to the pyramid site, so she could be near her husband.

I will never have her, he lamented, *but I can enjoy her presence as a friend, along with Wijin*. The hungers and longings regularly afflicted him, but he never revealed anything about his struggle to Wijin.

Khnum saw the pyramid project was well under way and that it was time to begin work at the crypt site. He thought, *I wish I could put Wijin in charge here, as I believe he is up to the task, but of course, it is unthinkable to put a slave in charge of the project*. He sent for Wijin to inform him of the changes that were about to happen.

"Ah, Wijin, my friend, please take a seat. As you may know, I have another project to begin at another location. The time has come for me to move on. I am very pleased with what we are accomplishing here and would like you to continue in your present role as building assistant. Pharaoh has selected a man named Amsu to replace me and you will report to him. He has had experience in the building of pyramids. The next phase of the work — placing the remaining courses of stone to the top — will require a corkscrew ramp to be built. Actually, it will take two spiral ramps as the additional levels are constructed and Amsu is particularly good at this phase of the work. He will start four days from now. I will visit the site regularly to make sure things are going according to plan."

Wijin considered this news. "I will miss you greatly, my Lord. I hope this new man will have half of your wisdom and kindness."

Wijin watched Amsu arrive on the fourth day early in the morning. The man walked authoritatively even though he was short in stature. He felt his insides churn as he watched this new overseer approach the work site. He wondered what the future held for him. The last couple of years had seen real progress for him. He knew that his skills with the slaves had positioned him well for further advantages. And when Khnum had taken him under his wing, his life had changed substantially. It had done wonders for him to be treated with respect and to be taught so many wonderful things — the skill of cutting stone and then so many phases of building the pyramid. Learning the principles of architecture fulfilled something within him. He realized he had a great aptitude for it and had been so grateful to Khnum for both the opportunity to learn and the chance to exercise his newfound knowledge. And then Khnum had brought Akila to be with him. He was a marvelous mentor and friend to Wijin. How unlike Amaké the architect had been. He had kept every promise — he helped lift him up, not knock him down. He understood that he felt insecure about Khnum leaving and apprehensive about being a 'slave' to some new authority.

He stood waiting in front of the tent that served as the construction office as Amsu made his way over to him.

"I wanted to introduce myself, Lord. My name is Wijin. Khnum has been instructing me on how to build this great monument. I have served as his assistant and now I am at your service."

Wijin could see Amsu pause for a moment and look him up and down.

"Wijin, you say. Ah, yes, Khnum did tell me about you," Amsu said as he placed a hand on his shoulder. "Shoulders seem strong, that is good. He says you have great potential. You are a slave, are you not?"

Wijin took in a long, deep breath and then let it out slowly. He fixed his gaze into the distance and replied, "Yes, I am. But you may find that with all I have learned I will be of great assistance to you — much more than a slave."

Amsu replied, "We shall see."

It had been months since Khnum had left Amsu in control of the pyramid project. However, he had provided Wijin with a private small hut away from the other slaves. Wijin was grateful for this refuge from the toils of the day and all that this involved. He recognized that Amsu was a master at construction and he was learning a great deal from this new authority in his life, but he was no Khnum. There was something about him that Wijin was wary of. Whereas Khnum was tall and elegant, Amsu was short and bull-like. Khnum was calm and reasonable but Amsu, although he was an introvert and rather quiet and brooding, when challenged or upset by something, lost all restraint and poured out a barrage of venom and frustration. He was not a safe person. Wijin had appreciated Khnum's consistency, especially now when faced with Amsu's volatility.

The most recent episode had occurred last week. In order to lift the great stones to the higher levels, they had built circular ramps against the side of the pyramid. To facilitate the moving of the stones up the ramp, logs were embedded perpendicular to the sides of the ramp. Wet mud from the Nile was used to lubricate the surface and the stones were hauled upwards on sledges pulled by teams of slaves. There had been difficulty moving a stone to the next level and Amsu had stormed over to see why things were going so slowly. He had determined that some of the logs were situated unevenly and the sledge was gouging into them, halting progress. He flew into a fury, cruelly berating those who had prepared the ramp and having them savagely beaten. For the rest of the day he kept shouting about how much time would be wasted in improving the incline. He was *definitely* no Khnum.

As the years passed, the construction of the pyramid moved forward and when the inner chambers had been completed, Akila and the other painters were moved from the art school to the building site. Pharaoh and Khnum had created extensive designs, pictures and messages to be painted on all the walls of the interior chambers and it was time for this task to begin. The other artists were drawn from the ranks of the wives of the robbers. They were set to the work of painting colorful murals, ornate scenes of Egyptian daily life that were extraordinary and beautiful. Depictions of animals, fish, flowers and trees gradually cascaded across the walls of the stuffy interior. Akila continued to refine her art, far surpassing all the other artists in the ranks, creating works of outstanding beauty and detail. In recognition of this, Akila had been promoted to chief artist. She discarded her tattered loin cloth and was given a yellow kilt and a shirt to cover her breasts.

Underneath the art, a running commentary of the reason for their work was written out for all to see. Though they could not read what they were painting, they were writing about the crimes that their husbands had committed.

Months passed and Akila also grew in her ability to direct and inspire the members of her team. They were well on their way, painting the halls and entrance chambers when Khnum visited the site and met with Akila.

He said, "I have a special project for you, Akila. The inner burial chamber is a particularly key room and I would like you to do all the painting in there. I have brought some new designs for you to follow. Since you have become such a skilled artist, I want you to feel at liberty to embellish these pictures however you wish."

Akila's eyes lit up.

"Do you mean I can adjust my style from the normal way? Because I do have something I would like to try."

"Yes I would like that," Khnum said biting the corner of his lip.

What will she come up with? he wondered, smiling to himself. Khnum turned to leave, but stopped short and called to her, "I will not be back here for some time." Khnum then walked out of the room.

The months passed steadily, but for Wijin time seemed to stand still. He continued to see Amsu's volatility when dealing with the workers. Amsu watched the men like a hawk hovering over them, pointing out their shortfalls with a continuous barrage of insults.

"Can't you men do anything right?" Amsu screamed, when he saw a block that had been positioned incorrectly.

On hearing the commotion at the top of the top of the pyramid, Wijin ran up the ramp to see what was happening. He walked in on Amsu beating a worker with his switch.

"What is going on here?" Wijin yelled out.

"These men are too busy singing their infernal songs and not careful laying the blocks precisely. Don't you see?" he said as he pointed to a block that was not placed tightly against the one beside it.

With a quick glance Wijin saw the problem and replied, "The block was not dressed properly, do you not see the bump jutting out from the side? It needs to be trimmed down. That is all."

"Is that all? I think they are too occupied with their songs to notice these problems."

"This is not their fault. It is clearly the fault of the quarry workers," Wijin replied trying to keep his frustration in check.

"You do not tell me whose fault it is. I am in control. You are not. I do not see Khnum here, do you?"

The men stood aghast at the confrontation exploding in front of them. All of the men inwardly cheered for Wijin as the argument continued.

"I wish he was," someone in the crowd muttered.

Amsu turned to face the men with fury in his eyes. "Who said that?" he snapped as he struck the closest man with his flail.

There was no answer to his question. Amsu shouted and cursed at the men. He turned to the guards and sputtered, "I want you to lay the lash on all these pathetic louts. They will respect me or suffer the consequences."

The guards moved through the ranks of the slaves, laying the whip among the men in a lackluster way, their sense of duty barely covering their outrage towards the overseer who was becoming more and more out of control.

"You insolent dolts. Do you call that a beating? The whole lot of you should be fed to Ammit. None of you will get any water until the noon meal. Now get that stone rotated so the rough side is facing out. And step to it!"

He stomped over to Wijin, grabbed him by the arm and pushed him down the ramp, away from the other men.

"You insubordinate fool. How dare you confront me in front of the slaves? Do not ever speak against me again. You are just a slave," Amsu said with suppressed fury. "Also you can tell them their days of incessant singing have come to an end."

Wijin caught his breath. "That helps them with their work! You can't do that to them!"

"I can and I will. You tell them if they do not follow my rule they will be put to death."

Wijin looked over his work crew, grieved at their dispirited demeanor. *How long must we tolerate this bully? Can he not see his fault in this? Oh, I wish Khnum were here.*

Over the next weeks comfortable relations between Amsu and Wijin had dissolved. Even Akila became the object of abuse. Five days after the confrontation, Wijin heard the news he dreaded to hear — Akila was now a target. Wijin walked into the hut, tired from the long day. She had taken off her clothes and was rubbing a new bruise — this time on her left shoulder. Wijin looked at her naked back. She had many bruises — some from daily life as a slave, but most by the hand of Amsu.

"Can you not do something?" Akila begged Wijin

"Why did he hit you this time, Akila?"

"No reason at all. He just struck me as he walked by."

"He was commissioned by Pharaoh and we are slaves. I am reminded of that every day. I cannot do anything about his actions, you know that."

"We need to do something, anything," she pleaded.

Wijin closed his eyes in contemplation and then opened them. "My only suggestion is to avoid him if at all possible."

"How can I evade Amsu when it seems like he searches me out?"

It was a long six months until Khnum returned to the pyramid site. He was pleased to see the progress of the building that was being made, but noticed that there was no singing among the work teams. As he made his way into the midst of the project, he was dismayed to see the obvious decline in the morale of the workers — so different from when he had left. He found Wijin with a team at the top of the ramp, preparing to place the first stone on the next level. When Wijin looked up and saw Khnum, his face brightened and he smiled as he waved to him. He spoke to the man who was working beside him, then turned and made his way down the ramp to where Khnum was standing.

As he approached him, he exclaimed "How wonderful to see you, Lord Khnum. We have missed you so much. How long will you be staying?"

"I'll be here for at least a few days," Khnum replied. "Can your crew carry on without you for a while? I would like to spend some time talking to you before I survey the work that has been done."

"That is a good idea. I have just told my assistant, Panhs to carry on without me. They are well experienced at the task by this point. Would you like to take some refreshment and have a rest by the supply shed? There is seating there and we would both appreciate a time to sit down."

They made their way over to the water station, filled their water-skins and walked over to the shaded seating area behind the shed.

Khnum noticed that Wijin seemed restrained in his manner, more subdued. *I wonder what has been going on here since my departure*, he thought. *Can it be that the difficulties I have heard about Amsu's style have followed him here to this project?*

As he leaned back in his seat he commented to Wijin, "I notice that there is no singing among the workers today. Are the men not happy?"

Wijin took a deep breath and looked directly into Khnum's eyes. "No. There is no singing today. There has been no singing for many days, my Lord. There have been many changes since you left, but it's not my place to complain."

"I have come to see you first, Wijin, because perhaps it is your place to let me know how you are faring. I would like you to tell me honestly what is on your mind."

As Wijin opened his mouth to speak he noticed from the corner of his eye that Amsu was approaching. His jaw snapped shut and he rose from his seat.

"Well, who have we here?" Amsu declared as he came into full view of both men. "Lord Khnum, I believe. How long have you been here? I am surprised that you would seek out this slave first. I am in charge of this operation now, am I not?"

Khnum also stood up, looked at Amsu and raised an eyebrow as he said, "I arrived just a few minutes ago and yes, I understand that you are 'in charge' here. However, you realize that I have been commissioned by Pharaoh, as his chief architect, to design and monitor the construction of this pyramid. And I can approach whomever I choose at my discretion."

Amsu glared at him. "Well, when you want to know how the job is really going, come and see me." Then he turned on his heel and left.

Khnum expelled his breath and turned back to Wijin. "I believe we have a great deal to talk about, my friend. But this is not the time or place. I will have my assistant prepare a meal and bring it to your hut tonight. We will eat together. We can talk more freely then.

Khnum was eager to see how Akila was faring. He was alarmed and dismayed to see how much strife was apparent among the ranks of workers and wondered if she too was affected adversely.

He made his way into the pyramid, through the passageway and towards the inner burial chamber. *The artists have done a wonderful job here. These halls are lovely. I wonder how Akila's work will compare.* When he entered the chamber, he saw that it was nearly done and the colors and beauty of the work exploded off the walls. *Magnificent!* He saw her sitting at the far side of the room, a tiny paint brush in her hand. As he drew closer he realized she was weeping. "Akila," he said quietly. She turned suddenly, saw who it was, laid down her brush and wiped her eyes with the back of her hand.

"Lord Khnum. How wonderful to see you again." A wan smile crossed her face as she rose to meet him.

He closed the distance between them, coming as close to her as he dared. *My dear Akila, what have they done to you? I should have been here to protect you.* It was all he could do, not to put his arms around her.

He reached out and put his hand on her shoulder, feeling helpless.

"Can you tell me what troubles you, Akila?" Khnum asked gently.

Akila looked up and sniffed. "Please pardon my distress. It is nothing."

"I can see that something is wrong. I see it on the faces of the workers outside also. I have spoken briefly to Wijin already and told him I will be joining you for your evening meal in your hut tonight. I intend to get the full story from both of you."

Khnum glanced around the room looking at the new style of art Akila had created. He wanted to ask her about it.

"Tell me about your art, Akila," Khnum said as he motioned to the wall with a sweep of his hand."

Akila composed herself and wiped a tear that had run down her cheek. She turned to the wall and started describing her techniques.

"I have done all this work freehand. I feel that the old way of painting is too static, too rigid. It does not flow together. I have also used a fine brush instead of the wide brush since I am better able to blend the colors that way."

As she spoke, she started to feel an overwhelming pride in her work. Like a tour guide, Akila lead Khnum around the room, stopping at each scene to describe what she had done. She could see his interest increase and a smile spread across his face.

"You are pleased?"

"Oh yes. I am pleased, Akila — very pleased."

The worries of the day seemed to fade away as she felt reassured by his presence.

"The Great god would like this to be added in an inconspicuous place," he said, handing her a piece of papyrus with four lines of writing on it.

"I shall do so," she said, accepting the small scroll. She walked over to the far wall, pulled out her brushes and sketched the lines on the wall.

As she worked, Khnum bent over to view what she had been working on. A delicate quail stood half hidden in the under-brush. *This woman amazes me constantly*, he thought as he shook his head, pushing his desire for her out of his mind.

"As I mentioned, I will have my cook prepare a special meal for us tonight and we shall eat together in your hut. I look forward to it."

As darkness fell, the workers ceased their labors and made their way to the eating area. Akila and Wijin gratefully returned to their hut where Khnum was waiting for them.

"Ah, my friends, it is a blessing that Pharaoh has provided me with a cook to travel with me. We are also provided with a better quality of food than you are used to receiving. Vegetables brought in from Thebes, meat butchered this afternoon, fresh bread and beer. Let us sit down and enjoy this evening together."

Akila clapped her hands in delight and Wijin said, "This is indeed a rare treat. Thank you so very much."

"I am feeling a connection to you two that I cannot describe," he said as he dipped the piece of bread he had ripped off into the spiced meat broth in the center of the table.

"We both have felt your tenderness as we have worked under your guidance, Lord Khnum," Wijin replied, as he glanced at Akila, smiling. "And we greatly appreciate it."

Khnum took a long look at both of them and smiled with pleasure. "You know, I would be pleased if you would call me simply by my name — Khnum, rather than by my title. That is, in private only."

He noticed a look of confusion passing across their faces, laced with hope.

Akila reached her hand over to massage a recent bruise on her shoulder.

"Will we ever be released from our labours here?" Akila inquired.

"Akila!" Wijin snapped, squinting his eyes and shaking his head.

"I can't answer that, Akila. I'm sorry. Tell me how you got here, though."

Wijin and Akila told him about how they were trapped into helping Amaké with thievery. Wijin admitted that it was because of his stupidity that they were there in the first place.

"We tried to pay him back. We were going to sell our house, but Amaké would not accept that. He wanted my help as his repayment."

Khnum scowled at the memory of seeing Amaké work on the block cutting lines.

"I think I will have a new guard 'teach him something.' How does that sound?"

Wijin shook his head.

"He is suffering like all of us. He doesn't need to be beaten, just because of his past deeds. I have come to peace with it. While we were interrogated, he suffered under Amasis' hands and cruel knife."

Khnum tilted his head in understanding, but wanted to ask more about what he had witnessed since he had arrived.

"Tell me what has happened since I was last here … Tell me honestly, what is going on?"

"When you left to do other jobs for Pharaoh and Amsu took your place, the work went well enough for a long time. I did notice the way he was treating the workers with malice. He would lash out at them and the guards for no reason. He has lost the respect of the men here — even the security force. He strikes the women for no reason and has banned the workers from singing."

Khnum looked up from the cup of beer he was drinking, his concern apparent by the scowl on his face.

"Yes, it is obvious the men's spirits are low, but how did that happen? You just said he strikes the women … for what possible reason? Too slow when filling water-skins? Or painting too slowly? And why did he ban the teams from singing?"

"Amsu seems to strike the female workers at random, but I think he strikes Akila to get back at me for confronting him in front of the men when he made an error in judgment. The singing was canceled for that same reason."

"Has he beaten you, Akila?"

"He has not beaten me, but he does hit me when we cross paths."

Akila stood in front of Khnum, removed her shirt and showed him her back — it was covered with welts. *By the gods! This cannot continue.* Khnum's mind raced.

"How long will it be until you are finished the burial chamber, Akila?"

"Two months at the most, Lord ... I mean, Khnum. Why do you ask? Will I finally be free of that man? I beg that will be so."

"Well, I am going to need your skills at a different location, away from the pyramid, but I will expect you to finish here first. You said two months? Can you hold out here for that length of time? As for you Wijin ... just don't do anything to antagonize him. Remember he has been placed here by Pharaoh so I cannot remove him without an appeal to His Majesty.

(1, 2, 3) see bibliography

5

FALLING STARS

On his return trip to the crypt site, Khnum had time to think. He traveled on the three day trip during the nights and slept during the days. Thoughts tumbled over each other in his mind. *First and foremost, I must rescue Akila from that tyrant, Amsu. Bringing her to the crypt now will be more bearable than when the project was first begun. By the gods, what a terrible site we chose for that — so remote, so deadly. It is going to be difficult for anyone to find it in the future, but the distance and the dangers have made the challenge almost insurmountable. It is terrible how many workers we lost at the beginning to the suffocating heat. The savage dryness of the summer sun must have just sucked the energy and life out of them. That first task of excavating the bedrock to create the underground chamber cost us the most lives. When Pharaoh and I made the plans, we certainly didn't appreciate how nearly impossible it would be to make it happen. It's better now, though, so Akila will be safe. She will be working inside, doing what she is so good at and enjoys, and she will be out of the clutches of that bully, Amsu. And I can see her every day.*

Khnum spent the time at the crypt readying the walls and the ceilings for painting. He instructed workers to lay a layer of plaster over the cathedral size room. As the work was being done Khnum sat at his desk and composed a letter to Amenemope.

"Behold your servant Khnum, Chief Architect, calls for your wisdom and help. The Tomb of Treasures has been dug out according to our plans and the work on the great pyramid is nearing completion. You will be pleased with the result. I am now in need of idol carvers to construct the statues that are required. They will need to be able to instruct the workers here in their skill.

I have a regrettable situation to report with respect to Amsu, your servant. He has become troublesome. He is causing stress among the workers and guards, causing the smooth completion of the task to suffer. I realize that he has knowledge of construction procedures, but his problems with the workers at past locations have arisen again. Even though he comes from an influential family, he is a hindrance to the project.

I will be moving the head artist from the pyramid to the crypt in a short while to begin painting there. I implore you to send the carvers quickly and an answer to the problem with Amsu.

Written by my hand, Khnum, Chief Architect."

Khnum dripped a puddle of wax on the scroll, pressed his ring into it, and gave it to the driver of the supply caravan to be delivered to the palace. Before it departed, Khnum took his assistant to the storage huts to evaluate the status of the paint and food inventories. He instructed him to increase the food rations to accommodate the extra workers he would be bringing in to complete the work.

The two months seemed to pass slowly as Khnum anticipated the arrival of Akila. He felt as though he was just going through the motions, overseeing progress at the crypt. By now the workers were familiar with their tasks. Khnum's mind kept flitting back to his last visit at the pyramid, especially to Amsu's belligerent ways. He looked forward to returning there and getting Akila out.

His distress over the general situation was again confirmed when he returned to the site. There was still no singing and the feeling of defeat hung over the workers like a fog. Khnum was relieved to see Wijin with a smile on his face working with the work crew at the pyramid's base. When Wijin's eyes met the architect's, Khnum could see that he was conflicted about saving his wife and losing her at the same time.

Off in the distance he could see Amsu screaming at the workers who were hauling a block up the ramp.

"Has it been two months already?" a voice asked, startling him.

Khnum turned around and saw that it was Akila. She had water skins hanging under her arms and a cup that doubled as a stopper, attached to a rope swinging from the leather canteen.

"Yes, it has. I assume that since you are doing water detail, you have completed your task in the burial chamber?"

"Yes, I finished last week."

"Very good, Akila. So, are you ready to leave? We will have a couple of days before the supply caravan returns from Thebes. I suppose it won't take you long to pack the things you would like to bring along."

Akila glanced down at her water skins and then quickly over at Amsu, who by now was walking towards them. Nervously she placed the bags down and walked to her hut.

"What is going on here?" Amsu called out as he saw Akila walk away.

Khnum raised his hand to Amsu. "Greetings. I see that the work is progressing well. I will be staying here a short while. I've been speaking with Akila and telling her to prepare to come with me to work at a separate project. We have need of her painting skills; and those of the other painters too, for that matter."

"Why was I not told about this?"

Khnum smiled wryly at Amsu and commented, "I am telling you now. They are needed at a different place."

Amsu blustered, "What do you mean? The women are required here. There is still painting that needs to be completed and water carried for the men. You cannot take the women away."

"Do not concern yourself, Amsu. I am taking just Akila this time. I will send for the rest of the artists at a later date. How long will it take for the painting here to be completed?"

"I am concerned about it! You cannot just come here and take my slaves from my work site. I will not allow it."

"You will not allow it? Who are you to not allow it? Why do want to keep them? To have someone to beat? Yes, I have heard of your ways. I have heard about how you hit the women and how you scream at the workers."

"Slaves! That is all they are — remember that. They are not only slaves, they are criminals," Amsu retorted, his face getting red.

"You will learn that if you treat your workers like slaves they will not work as well as they will if you treat them with kindness."

Amsu defiantly accused, "You treat them as if they were friends! Remember your place, Khnum. They should be groveling at your feet. They are the slaves and you their leader. I will never forget that. Why can't you realize that?"

"I do know my place. I am Lord Khnum, Chief Architect under Pharaoh. You will do well to remember that."

Amsu breathed out with a snort, turned on his heel and stomped off.

"Come back here, Amsu! You did not answer my question."

"What question was that?" Amsu asked in annoyance.

"When will the painters be finished?"

"I do not know. You will have to look yourself," his clipped tones receded as he stormed away.

By the gods! The man is completely insane, Khnum thought as he stifled the fury he felt inside. He took a couple of deep breaths to calm himself and made his way over to the pyramid.

The odor of fresh paint was strong as he walked into the colored rooms. He saw displays of Amenemope striking scores of his enemies with an uplifted mace, as well as beautiful murals and vignettes of daily life. The scenes and quality of art was not as beautiful as Akila's, but it was wonderful none the less. As Khnum walked through the rooms watching the women paint, a shocking similarity became apparent. *All of these women are scored with bruises. This goes beyond hitting a few workers. This is wide spread abuse. It must not be allowed to continue. Even Pharaoh would not put up with such cruelty.* With a growing determination, Khnum walked through the remaining rooms and figured out that the painting would take another four months to complete. *That is far too long for them to be exposed to Amsu's tyranny*, he thought. He had made a decision. It set his mind at ease.

Later that night Khnum met with Wijin and Akila in their hut to discuss the move to the crypt.

"I am concerned about Akila moving to this new location — about her being away from me again. Do you think Amsu will just turn his attention to others — making them his personal target? I do not want to be the one who damns them to that life."

"Yes, I can see that you would have care for others at the site. You are a good man, Wijin. I do need Akila's expertise at the other location. But things will work out for the women painting here. Trust me. I have one other question for you, Wijin. How long have you been the assistant overseer here? It's been quite a few years now, hasn't it?"

"Yes, counting the time I spent training with you. I've been helping with the project from the beginning. The coming of Amsu was the only thing that has tarnished my experience in this grand undertaking,"

Wijin replied.

Khnum stared at the hut wall while considering matters within his mind.

"Well, it is getting late. We will head back as soon as the supply caravan returns from Thebes. That will give me a chance to get a more detailed update on how things are progressing here as well as having a meeting with the captain of the guards. And you can be sure that Akila will be well looked after at her new location."

"How long will she be gone, Khnum?"

"It will be for some time, Wijin. I am sorry."

Wijin's head dropped down and he closed his eyes. "We knew this was coming," he said as he looked at his wife. "We will get through this."

After the long trip across the desert, Khnum and Akila approached the entrance to the crypt early in the morning. Akila saw a small village of brown huts that had large piles of stone chips evidently removed from somewhere she could not see. She could hear the bleating of goats and the sounds of other livestock that were penned up. She followed Khnum along the hot dusty paths until they came to the center of the lean-to settlement. There she saw a large square hole cut into the earth. There were two staircases built into the stone, one along each of the two opposite sides.

"Follow me," Khnum called to Akila as he motioned with his hand. He smiled and his eyes twinkled with delight.

Khnum walked down the steps. She followed him as he walked into the crypt. What she saw shocked her. The room was massive. Columns supporting the roof were situated at regular intervals in the cathedral sized rooms. She observed the workers mixing white plaster on the floor and then taking it to side rooms only to return to refill their buckets with even more. As Akila watched she saw stone carvers who were encircled by other laborers, chipping at the ceiling supports. It appeared to her as though the carvers were teaching the workers. Akila looked at the hundreds of workers, each with his own task. It was busy and loud, but everyone seemed to be focussed on his work. Khnum was never far away from her — always watching. He walked over to her.

"What do you think of this place, Akila?"

"Well, it is much louder than where I was before, but I can get used to it. I have a question. To where are those men taking the pails of plaster?" she asked, pointing at the men carrying the white buckets.

"Come with me and I will give you the tour."

Khnum led her through the underground vault, explaining to her that there were sixty-five separate rooms. He showed her the first few rooms.

"These separate rooms will house our previous pharaohs."

Akila turned back to him with a questioning look. "Are you planning to move the tombs?"

"I plan on moving the sleeping pharaohs and their treasure from the remaining undisturbed tombs and bringing them all here. Before that happens, you will be in charge of the painters that will be coming here soon. I will give you all the drawings of what is to be put on the walls of each room. Your first task will be to have the designs sketched out on the walls for the painters. This will be a long process. You will be painting in the main entrance room."

Akila looked around the room. *What a daunting task!* An expression of doubt clouded her face. *This is an impossible task.*

"Before you think you are unable to do this, remember when you first learned to paint? You thought it was impossible, but look at you now! You are better than your teachers. If anyone can do this, you can," Khnum said with a wink.

Yes, I can do this; it will be challenging, but I can do this.

"This will be beautiful when it is done," she replied, as the visions of what she would create rose in her mind's eye.

The designs on the wall are taking shape nicely, she thought. *Even though my arms and hands ache, I think Khnum is most pleased with my work. I look forward to our times of consultation on the art here. It is so much more pleasant than it was at the pyramid with that beast Amsu breathing down my neck. The cost has been high, though. I didn't realize how hard it would be to be separated from my dearest Wijin again.*

She made her way to the corner of the chamber where Khnum had his center of operations.

"Ah, Akila, have a seat. Your work is coming along beautifully. Pharaoh will be most impressed with these renderings. I have received word that the painting at the pyramid has been completed, so the other painters who were finishing that work will be coming here within the week to start working on the walls here. So that will mean a big change for you. I would like you to organize them into teams to proceed with work in the main cathedral. The art is similar to what you have done at the pyramid, so the women will be familiar with the designs. There is still much preparation of the walls to do, and we have plans for the ceiling. We have the scaffolding built so that it can be accessed. As soon as the painter has finished covering the ceiling with the dark blue of the night sky, I would like you to start painting the profusion of stars and pictures of the gods on the surface. Here are the drawings that you can use to guide you. Do you feel comfortable taking over this task on your own?"

"Let me see. It will take some figuring to position all of this on a ceiling. I haven't done that before. But I can see that it will make the room very striking. Yes, I can do it. And it will be wonderful to see the women again. I have been getting to know the workers here, but having spent so much time with the girls at the pyramid, they became my close friends."

She spent the next day considering how to manage the changes that would be happening shortly. The work had always gone better when she was in good company so she eagerly anticipated their arrival.

Just as Khnum said, the women arrived within the week.

"We have missed you so much!" Joyful exclamations filled the camp.

"The trip was terrible," one woman commented.

"Where is the building we will work on here?" another asked.

Akila replied, "Welcome, dear friends. I will show you around in a while. First, let's get you settled. You will wish to have time to refresh yourselves and have something to eat and drink. We have a fairly comfortable tent for you to stay in until we get you organized. We can take some time to catch up on what has been happening."

As they were washing up, Akila observed, "You all seem to look so good. No bruises!"

Semat, one of her closer friends said, "Of course not. Now that Wijin is in charge, we are all doing so much better."

A shock wave ran through Akila. "Wijin is in charge? Do you speak the truth? What about Amsu?"

"Amsu? Haven't you heard? Shortly after you left the pyramid, Amsu was killed. There was rejoicing in the camp that day, I can tell you."

Akila's mind was reeling. *Amsu is dead? Wijin is in charge? How can all of this have happened and no one has told me? Khnum must have known. Why didn't he say something?*

She stammered as she tried to gather her thoughts. "Who killed him? What happened?"

Semat said, "We were painting inside the pyramid, but we heard that Amsu went into one of his rages — this time against the captain of the guard — and the captain took out his sword and cut him down where he stood. They were right on the pyramid. The workers saw it all. They cheered as his severed head rolled down the ramp. They could hardly get the men back to work. Even the guards seemed happy that he was gone."

Akila could hardly take it in. "So, you said that Wijin is in charge now. How did that come about?"

"The captain went right over to Wijin after the soldiers had taken Amsu's body and dumped it in the desert. He took him to his tent and spoke with him, and when they came back, Wijin was wearing the ring with the seal of office. Rumor has it that Khnum had told the captain that if anything were to happen to Amsu, that Wijin should be made head overseer, since he has been the assistant all these years."

At this, Akila remembered the night when Khnum had come to the pyramid to get her. *He said he needed to have a meeting with the captain of the guard. That must have been what it was all about.* Outrage shook her to the core. *This was all Khnum's doing! He knew all about it. He took me away from my husband when he knew that Amsu would soon be gone. How could he do this to me? I thought he was my friend. Oh Wijin, how I miss you.*

Akila stood up. "I will be right back, girls," she turned and walked out of the tent and boldly marched towards the crypt. Before she got to the entrance, she found Khnum walking between the storage sheds.

Anguish surged through her. "You knew!" she shouted as she stomped over to him. "You brought me here when you knew that Amsu would die! I could have spent that time with Wijin, but instead you dragged me across this cursed desert and put me to work far away from my husband. You planned all this, didn't you?" Tears streamed down her face and her body shook with emotion. She wiped her face with her hands and glared at him. "I thought you were my friend ... Was that all a lie?"

Khnum stood back, arms crossed, as her verbal assault slashed him to the core. He was at a loss for words as she ranted, but Akila continued her tirade until he raised his hand.

"Calm down … calm down. I can understand why you are so upset, but I can explain. I knew that Amsu needed to be put to death when I saw what he had been doing to my workers. I could not just cut him down without plans being in order first. I knew Wijin would be a suitable replacement for Amsu.

And you are very valuable to this project. You had finished your work at the pyramid, and now your work is here at the crypt. You did beg me to deliver you from that situation. I have a job to do here and I have been entrusted to do this work by Pharaoh. I will not let him down."

He looked directly into her eyes with great tenderness, and pausing to clear his throat he whispered, "Yes, I am your friend, Akila. I am Wijin's friend as well. I hope you can appreciate how much I depend on you both."

Her sobs began to subside as she started processing his logic. The turmoil and confusion in her mind gradually ebbed away, still leaving her unsatisfied.

"Well, could you at least take me to see him for a visit? You owe me that."

Khnum was taken aback. "I owe you?" He hesitated before he spoke. "That is presumptuous of you, Akila. As much as I realize you are having difficulty in facing the current reality, you must remember that you are, in fact, a slave, and I am the chief architect in charge of these building projects. I must do what I feel is best for the overall work."

Akila stood there motionless. She was crestfallen and her head fell to her chest. *I am stymied at every turn. What's the use?*

"Nevertheless, because of the excellent work that both of you have contributed to these undertakings, I am inclined to grant your request at a later date, once your painting teams are in place," he acquiesced.

The next day she began her planning and as soon as she had arranged plans for her painting crews, she made her way up on the scaffolding and began her tedious task.

What have I got myself into? Akila thought as she lay awkwardly on her back. *This continuous reaching upward is completely exhausting. I will need to rest more often. I can still make it something special to behold, though. I will think of the times Wijin and I lay beneath the stars back at the pyramid.*

*It was so long ago. I think I would like to add a burst of shooting stars here,
like we saw that one night when there was such a spectacular display as they
streaked across the heavens. This is not in Khnum's drawings, but I'm sure
he will not object. It will comfort me to see this.* Memories of such times
continued to dance in her head and inspire her as she spent her days
painting at the crypt, never able to see her husband. *I wonder when
Khnum will take me to visit him.* The hope in her heart kept her going.

Khnum kept a close eye on Akila as she worked, both to satisfy the
yearning in his heart to see her as well as to measure her progress on the
ceiling designs. She came down from the scaffold for the noon meal,
and walked around stretching her arms and back to bring some relief
to her tortured muscles. He called her over to his desk in the corner of
the room.

"The art is starting to take shape, Akila. It is going to be stunning. I
can see that your working on the scaffolding is more troubling than we
understood it would be. Would you like to take a time away from your
labors? I am planning to travel with the supply train to the pyramid on
its next trip, and you are welcome to come with me." An enticing smile
spread across his face. "How does that sound?"

Akila stood up straight, a look of delight, pleasure and puzzlement
infusing her. "Really? Oh, I would love to come. When will we leave?"

"The day after tomorrow when the heat of the day has subsided.
It will take us three days to cross the desert." He was looking forward
to this trip as much, if not more, than she was. After having spent the
months with her being at the crypt, he had become more enamored of
her than he cared to admit. Even though he had maintained a careful
demeanor around her, within himself he was often in turmoil.

The time to leave arrived and the caravan set out across the endless
sands. The full moon cast a gentle light on the desert as they traveled
to the first rest stop, the night breezes bringing welcome relief to the
blistering heat of the day. They rode in silence, for the most part, taking
in the eerie elegance of the lonely sands.

They arrived at a modest oasis shortly before dawn of the next day. The cluster of hardy palm trees was located in a valley where they gratefully climbed down from their camels and headed for the spring of cool water that bubbled up from an underground aquifer. It felt good to stretch and walk around before the sun brought its weight of heat to bear upon the land. The small party refreshed themselves from the cache of supplies, then watered and fed the camels and horses. There was a tent to shelter the animals and, among the palms, a good sized hut which contained cots for the weary travelers' rest, a refuge from the desert day.

Since the caravan made the trek back and forth from the crypt and the pyramid to Thebes at every full moon, the two oases in between were in regular use. The essentials were all there. After a meal and some relaxed visiting, they all settled in on the cots.

Khnum found that sleep did not come easily. He was pleasantly disturbed by his close proximity to Akila in this quiet, private environment, and found that many happy thoughts collided in his mind as he tried to get more comfortable. He noticed that Akila was restless as well, and he wondered what her thoughts were. She had seemed quietly excited on the first night out, and he wondered if it was all for Wijin. He finally dozed off, letting the lingering sway from the all-night camel ride ease from the memory of his muscles.

Late in the afternoon, the small group gradually roused from their sleep and set about gathering their belongings for the night's journey. Khnum was glad to see that Akila was in a buoyant mood. *She seems to have forgiven me for concealing my plans to terminate Amsu and for taking her away from her husband. But still, she has been more reserved with me than before. It is probably better that way, though. I must maintain authority.*

"Well, Akila, how was your rest?" he asked.

"Surprisingly good," she replied. "It is a wonderful change from the work on the ceiling. And being outside during the cool of the night is most welcome also. The trip seems shorter this time than when we came to the crypt. Thank you so much for bringing me with you."

"It's my pleasure," he said. "It's good for you to have a change of routine also. I find that these sojourns between the two locations give me time to think and plan. The vast silence and solitude allows me to clear my head of all the noise and clamor at the work sites. Do you find it to be so with you?"

She considered for a moment. "Why, yes, that's right. To have time to think and let my mind wander is a luxury for me, and I must say that I am enjoying it."

They continued in easy conversation as they shared a meal together with the others in the caravan and set out on the next night's travel.

The second oasis that they reached at dawn the next day was larger than the first one, and somewhat more comfortable. Khnum was enjoying this trip more than any he had taken before. He and Akila were closer now, and he knew her better. They shared many interests and respected each other. He longed for much more, but being reserved, he found it possible to keep his actions in check. He settled for gentle teasing and laughter. *I wish we were traveling to the end of the earth together*, he thought. *Tomorrow we will arrive at the pyramid and I will have to let her go to her husband. Still, it is a pleasure and a comfort to me to spend these precious days so close to this most special woman.*

They arrived at the pyramid complex during the night of the third day of travel. Darkness still covered the earth, and Akila was eager to make her way through the silver moonlight to Wijin's hut. The drivers of the supply wagons all dispersed to their various destinations within the camp. Akila and Khnum slipped down from their camels. As Akila came close to Khnum, his heart began to race and he smiled at her with heartfelt joy.

"Will it be all right with you if I go directly to Wijin?" she whispered.

He was crestfallen, in spite of his mental preparation. *I knew it would probably come to this*, he thought. Still, it seemed a little bitter.

"Certainly. I will see that your camel is looked after. Go to your husband. Get some rest also. I will see Wijin tomorrow and find out how the work has progressed here since my last visit."

Akila hurried over to Wijin's small enclosure and slipped past the leather flap that served as a door. He was asleep on his cot. She climbed in beside him and put her arm around him as she snuggled close. He awoke with a start, ready to strike, and then he realized who it was. His sleepy eyes came fully awake and happiness filled him.

"Akila, my darling, how did you get here?" he embraced her and covered her with kisses. "It has been so long since I have seen you."

"Yes, so long … Too long."

Their passion increased during the remainder of the predawn until they were both content and fell into a relaxed sleep. They slept until the middle of the morning, when they got up and shared a small meal.

"There is so much to catch up on since you left here, Akila. A few weeks after you were gone Amsu got himself into some trouble with the captain of the guard, and the captain killed him. That was astounding enough, but after that the captain took me aside and made me head overseer because I had been the assistant all these years. It has certainly made the time since then much better for all of us."

"Yes, my love, I heard all about it from the women painters when they came to the crypt where I am working. They told me something else that you may not know. They heard that Khnum had given orders to the captain that if anything were to happen to Amsu, he was to assign you as head overseer. I spoke to him about it — why he took me away from you — and he admitted to me that it was his plan to have Amsu killed."

Wijin's eyes grew wide and he looked startled.

"What? You mean it was all planned ahead of time? And he took you away from me anyway? How could he do that?" Wijin exclaimed.

"Yes, it was entirely his plan. He has looked after us, and we have found favor with him. He has given us great opportunities and allowed us to strengthen our skills, but, my love, when all is said and done, we are still just slaves to him. He has shown special kindness to me all along, but it is not the same as what I have with you — complete trust and honesty," Akila replied.

Wijin gradually processed what his wife had said. Confusion gave way to understanding.

"Well, at least Amsu is gone. And we have each other. Perhaps the rest can be worked out. How long will you stay with me?"

Later that day they met with Khnum at his tent. Wijin reported on the work at the pyramid. Since the general completion of the construction, all that remained now was the removal of the spiral ramp around it, and the cleanup of the surface of the stones. The large statue of Amenemope still had to be erected and positioned in front of this great memorial to Pharaoh.

"You have done a wonderful job here, Wijin. I know that Pharaoh will be pleased. Now I have an unusual request. Instead of removing the ramp around the pyramid, I want you to take the crushed stone from the supply you have been using and cover the pyramid so that it is completely concealed. I have made drawings and instructions for you to follow. You will notice that there is more detail here than I have mentioned, but I am sure you can figure it out. I realize that it will take quite a while to accomplish this task, but you don't need to feel rushed to complete it."

Wijin looked at the drawings with growing consternation. "I have a question, my lord. Why would you choose to cover up this monument that we have spent all these years constructing? It just doesn't make sense."

"You don't know the whole story, Wijin. There are many mysteries known only to the mind of Pharaoh. Amenemope is a great ruler and he seeks to do the will of the gods. Even though we may not understand his reasons, what is left to us is to obey his wishes."

"Very well. I do have one more question. It concerns my wife and me. Can you tell me whether we can stay together, now that Amsu is gone, and he can no longer mistreat Akila?"

"Ah, yes. That would be something you would desire. We must, however, keep in mind the task at hand. At this time, you are required here at the pyramid, while Akila has an important role to perform at our other construction site. And it is not just her painting that is needed there. She is also a leader for all the women painters at the site and they look to her daily for her guidance." Khnum paused for a few moments. "I will tell you this much, however. When she is finished her work there, I will see to it that you are reunited on a permanent basis. That is the best I can do."

"That is something to be grateful for. It is so difficult to be away from her, but if we have that to look forward to, it does give us hope," Wijin answered.

Akila stayed with Wijin until the next full moon, at which time she traveled back to the crypt with the returning caravan. It had been such a wonderful time together. She had never known such happiness and fulfilment, and the memory of this marvelous holiday filled her mind and heart, both on the trip back and also as she began her labors again. She went back to her painting with renewed vision and enthusiasm. Each and every star and constellation was perfect and exact. Every stroke with her brush brought her closer to the time she could go back to her husband at the pyramid. Except for the one star that had a long tail making it look like a shooting star, the ceiling was a uniform smattering of white.

Glancing at the 'shooting star', she thought about that day when a beam in the scaffolding had snapped beneath her, causing her to slide backwards about a foot. Even though there had been a repair made, since that day a nagging fear gripped her for the first few minutes she was up on the scaffold.

Tucked far in the corner with her friends, Akila rested her aching back and sore arms after the long day's work. She divided her time equally between her own painting and directing the work of her painting team. She was not only their leader, but an integral part of the group. They had formed a strong connection — a real sisterhood. They worked regularly side-by-side, chatting about their lives and their dreams for the future. Though Akila was, by all intents and purposes, their boss, they respected and loved her.

"What do you plan to do after this is all finished?" Aknet, a Nubian woman, asked the group.

"After? What do you mean after? We are never going to get out of here!" replied another.

"We might! It's good to dream, though. Keeps my mind off the work," Aknet replied.

"If we are just dreaming, I think I will marry Khnum and have three children with him," another woman said.

"You have wanted him for the past three years, Semat!" Akila laughed. "How long has it been since your husband died?"

"Four years," she answered.

"I don't think Khnum wants any one of us, you know," replied Maatkera, who was sitting at the back of the huddle of women.

Akila thought to herself, *I don't think that is entirely accurate, my friend.* She had gradually come to an awareness that he was emotionally conflicted when he was around her, though it was clear he was making an effort to hide it.

"I thought we were just dreaming, ladies," Theabus said sarcastically, rolling her eyes.

"He certainly is available. He has no wife that I know of," Akila said with a wink.

Semat raised her eyebrows and a smile formed across her pale face.

"Now look what you started," Maatkera said, laughing and shaking her head.

It was quiet for a while, as they listened to the sounds of the crypt workers settling down for the night.

"What about you, Akila?"

She could not see who asked the question, so she closed her eyes in contemplation.

"I would like to have a quiet life with my husband. That is all I desire," she replied with a sigh.

The women sat for a moment, not talking.

"What does it matter anyway? I think we will all die here," Theabus said sorrowfully.

"We might, but if we let that thought control our lives, we will never be at peace. If we all change our attitudes a little bit, we can at least have some joy, no matter what we do. Maybe I will never leave here, but I have hope. I hold on to the hope that someday I will be free. Someday I will have my own place again. Someday I will be with my Wijin again. I can't let myself drown in sorrow. If I do, I am better off dead."

Not a word was said after that. The women just went to their reserved spots in the corner, curled up and lay down for the rest of the night.

Early morning in the desert was very peaceful and quiet, not a sound besides the soft breeze that blew over the ridges and lightly transported the sand, grain by grain, from one side of the dune to the other. There was a chill in the air. The sun was just at the horizon now, and began to burst forth with its rosy glow, bathing the dunes in light and shadow. The sky was clear blue and cloudless. As the burning fingers of the sun rose higher, the colors on the dunes changed from rose to gold. Small ripples in the sand were more clearly visible, like an endless washboard, adding texture to the vast landscape.

The eerie calls of a pair of jackals could be heard in the distance, yipping their haunting song, on the hunt for the next meal of carrion.

Soon the full wrath of Re, the sun, covered the land with unrelenting heat. Workers emerged from the relatively cool crypt, making sure they did not linger long outside. The contrast between the surface and the subterranean space drove them back inside to the comfort of the crypt.

Four workers quickly emerged from the underground cathedral they were creating, watered and fed the animals which were housed outside in a makeshift shelter, and gathered the supplies needed for the day's work below in the crypt. The feel of the sand, not yet scalding hot on their feet, crept in between their toes, chafing them as they walked. The men retrieved spare clay jars full of lamp oil from the supply huts. They brought them inside to refill the empty lamps that illuminated the lightless cavern.

They carried the amphora of oil down the staircase and into the now active work area. Starting at the back of the huge room, the men proceeded to refill the lamps standing in the middle of the room and trim the torches along the walls.

The progress of the ceiling's heavenly bodies was going well in the middle of the next day when Akila heard a faint snap beneath her. She turned her head to the side to see if she could see where the sound came from, but seeing nothing, she turned back to painting her stars.

Another faint snap that was hardly audible reached her ears, but she definitely felt the scaffolding shift beneath her. Panic set in, her mind racing, her face flushing and a knot clutching her stomach.

I must remain calm, she told herself. Akila looked at the full bowl of white paint she held between her large breasts and slowly placed her paint brush beside her leg.

"Theabus? ... Maatkera? ... Semat? ... Aknet? ... are you there? I need help."

She got no response. Then, another cracking sounded below her. A choking anxiety set in.

"Help me somebody, please!" she called out, but her cries were swallowed by the din far below — hammer and chisels on stone and worker's voices talking and shouting.

Her pleas unheard, alarm enveloped her. Another snap and the bowl of paint sloshed its contents onto her face, filling her mouth with the opaque glaze. Akila panicked as she turned her head to the side and spit out the white contents. A white spray shot through the air, coating those standing below. After she emptied her mouth, she took a deep breath and screamed.

The workers milling around the base of the scaffold looked up at the terrified woman crying for help.

Khnum, who was by the nearest wall about two hundred feet away, saw the collapsing scaffold and Akila with white ooze all over her chest and face, clinging to the swaying structure, shrieking in horror.

Khnum took off running towards her, yelling at the workers to help. But there was nothing that anyone could do as the framework began to completely disintegrate. Akila fell fifteen feet with the crumbling scaffold and landed on her back, snapping several vertebrae and killing her instantly.

He rushed over to her. He was alarmed to see a woman trying to take off Akila's clothing to have for herself. He jerked her by the arm and pushed her savagely to the floor, never taking his eyes off Akila.

"Akila, Akila, are you all right?" he cried out as he shook her trying to revieve her. The workers immediately backed off and gave Khnum space. He leaned close to her and listened for her breath, but there was none. He then realized that she was gone.

"No, no, it cannot be," he exclaimed, dropping to his knees in utter shock. He drew her lifeless body into his arms and embraced her as he rocked back and forth in silent inner agony. All activity ceased as everyone gathered around, inquiring murmurs receding into stillness as they all stood together in overwhelming grief.

He picked her up and carried her outside. Ascending the twenty foot staircase, he made his way from the cool depths of the crypt to the blazing windy furnace outside.

Tears welled up in his eyes as he laid her in his chariot and set off to the destination he could see in the distance — an elongated hut reserved for the sem priests, the embalmers of the dead. Pharaoh had decided that because of the number of people located at the crypt site, and the number of years that the construction would require, a settlement of sem priests was warranted to maintain the precepts of Egyptian law. They were there only for the guards or officials like himself, but Khnum decided that Akila should be given this honor, not just because she was in charge of the painters, but also because of his own regret at having set her up for this and his secret love for her. She deserved better than the rest of the criminals who not only were not mummified, but their bodies were thrown into the desert like trash — food for the vultures and hyenas.

Khnum wiped the white paint from her face with his kilt as he sat on the back of his chariot cradling her lifeless body in his left arm. He took a few moments to feel his grief.

Why did she have to die? Out of all the scum that worked below in the crypt, why her? Why has another woman I love been torn away from me? How can I bear this? As tears flowed down his cheeks, he outlined her beautiful face with his right hand.

She had brought back old memories of the girl his parents had arranged for him to marry when he was eleven. Innamun died tragically days before her marriage contract was signed. Akila always reminded the bachelor of the love that was snatched from him. He hung his head and allowed his tears to flow, now that he was away from the staring crowd.

As he approached the makeshift house of the dead, a structure in the desert, he paused, gulping deep breaths of air as he thought to himself, I've got to get a grip here. What I am about to ask is contrary to all the rules. I must be strong and authoritative with these priests. He picked her up and approached the red painted hut and knocked on the door. Khnum stood waiting for some time until the door was opened.

"Do not enter lest you become impure by accidentally touching something inside," a quiet but commanding voice announced. "What do you want of us?"

"I require your services for this woman, workers of the dead," Khnum answered forcefully.

A priest dressed in a long white robe stepped out of the hut. His face was completely covered. The only parts of his body that were visible were his gnarly fingers that appeared old and twisted. The man, covered like a phantom, cast a cursory glance at the lifeless body, looked up at Khnum, and then back at Akila, as though she were an unwanted object analyzed for sale at a market.

"We do not ready criminals for the afterlife, Great Architect. You know that. The desert is the place for her," the sem priest replied, pointing to the wind swept dunes and turning to retreat to the dark inner sanctuary of the hut.

"Stop! Do not turn your back to me, priest," Khnum thundered.

The priest halted and turned to face him, hands disappearing under his shawl of thick white material.

"What do you want of me?" the sem priest asked, perturbed.

"You will purify this woman, priest. And you will do it with the same respect and quality as you would for someone of my station," Khnum snapped. "If you do not, it will be your body that will be fed to the hyenas in the desert."

Khnum could sense that what he said had hit home. Even though he could not see his face underneath the white cloth, he assumed that instilling the fear of being lost forever was shaking the priest's confidence and making him more compliant.

"I will do as you ask," the sem priest answered reluctantly. "There are some stipulations that you must agree to."

"Name them."

"The full seventy days of mourning cannot be observed. It is the law of Osiris. Furthermore, this will cost a great deal."

"I agree to these terms, priest. I will return to transport her body to my family's tomb upon the completion of your task. Send someone to the crypt to notify me when she is ready."

The priest said, "Very well. Place her on this low platform in front of my door and leave."

Khnum laid Akila's body down, gently kissed her cheek and walked to his chariot.

From the sem priest's hut, Khnum made his way back to the crypt, gathered the necessary supplies and headed out on the long journey to the pyramid site to give Wijin the bad news.

During the long hours on his chariot, his mind was filled with painful memories that nagged his heart and tore at his soul.

Why? That was the question that always plagued him. He knew within himself that Akila was the type of woman that he had longed to marry. Even though she was married to someone else, it had brought him happiness just to be near her. Now she was gone forever. He recalled the trip to the pyramids when he had brought her with him. It was the closest he had ever been to her and it brought him comfort to remember those few days.

Even though you are gone, my precious Akila, I will always cherish that memory of being so near to you.

The first two nights of the three day trip were filled with tears, heartache and sleeplessness. He dreaded the prospect of having to bear this tragic news to Wijin. At last, on the final night, however, he was able to have a restful sleep due to a combination of exhaustion and coming to grips within himself about the inconsolable loss.

6

A HARD CHOICE

Zebel picked up his bow and headed out towards the stables. He reflected on the great changes that had occurred in his life in the past ten years. No longer a scrawny child, Zebel had grown up and filled out, although his features remained angular. He was tall and erect, deeply tanned, well developed, and toughened from the years of hard training and duty under the mentoring of Mahnudhotep, the commander of Pharaoh's army. By now he had mastered all the weapons of war, excelling at the bow. He could hit a two-inch square block of wood while driving a chariot at high gallop.

Over the years he had also grown as a leader and a commander of men. He had always had integrity and natural skill with people, so he was especially well-suited to positions of authority. He had now become not only Osorkon's closest friend, but also the head of his private security detail.

Mahnudhotep had left the barracks in Zebel's capable hands when he had died three years previously, but Zebel was reassigned to Osorkon's security detail shortly after. Pharaoh's son had also spent much time in military training in preparation for his role as the next pharaoh and was likewise suited to the disciplined life of a soldier.

Zebel and Osorkon spent their free time hunting lions or challenging each other to competitions of the bow and spear for amusement when they were at the barracks. The crowds of soldiers would gather around the arena as the two men showed off their skills with the implements of war, drawing cheers and encouragement from the onlookers. After the displays of their abilities, they left the field of combat in friendly camaraderie, followed by their guards.

The day was calm as the sun burned its fury on the desert sands. No clouds dotted the brilliant sky. As the heat of the day began to subside, and the time of refreshment following their sport was over, Osorkon and Zebel decided to drive a chariot to the pyramid site to look things over. The two men walked around the pyramid together, watching the workers hauling the capstone to the top of the structure.

The men stood back, taking in the whole scene and realized that after ten years of construction, Khnum's impressive design had taken shape and was nearing completion. It was an elegant structure which stood like a beautiful jewel against the backdrop of the desert sands.

Off in the distance, they observed Wijin, the overseer, urging the workers on as they moved in patterns of rhythmic precision. The commander, dressed slightly better than the workers, sent out orders that were obeyed without question.

"Who is that man? Isn't he one of the robbers that were caught?" Zebel asked. "I think I recognize him. He's one of the men I saw robbing that tomb so long ago. Yes, I remember!"

"His name is Wijin, I think," answered Osorkon. "Khnum tells me he was the one who was able to build this great temple to my father faster and with greater skill than all others before him. Even the architects of old took twenty years to complete a great structure, but look what this man has done — he will finish this in fourteen. Khnum says that he is an excellent man and shouldn't be here. He should be in Pharaoh's employ, building all manner of projects around Egypt — not working as a slave."

They walked around the pyramid among the many workers moving about and wove between rows of sphinxes that had yet to be placed. They paused in the shadow of a recently arrived statue of Amenemope and admired the pyramid in the sands of the desert, distinctive even though it was smaller than the great one constructed by Kufu.

The image of Pharaoh stood with his left foot forward, the stance of royal power, raising his flail towards the pyramid in a gesture of triumph. Workers stopped their tasks to pay homage to the prince as he passed by with Zebel.

As they entered the pyramid through its unique door, workers bowed with their faces pressed to the ground.

They entered the main chamber and Zebel exclaimed, "This is wonderful."

"I would like to show you something, Zebel. You think this looks good? Just wait."

Osorkon led Zebel into the burial chamber that was completed by Akila prior to her reassignment.

The murals exploded in an array of bright colors before their eyes. As amazing as the work was in the other parts of the pyramid, this was of a quality Zebel had never seen before. They skirted the room and tried to take it all in. Unlike the wider brush that was used to paint the murals Zebel had seen in the temples, this appeared to have been painted entirely with a fine scribe's brush.

How is this possible? he thought as he studied the three-dimensional image of Amenemope's sarcophagus in the middle of the floor.

"Who did this?" Zebel asked in amazement, not able to believe his eyes.

"This was all done by Wijin's wife, Akila," Osorkon answered him, understanding his admiration.

Night had fallen. A low growl came from deep in the throat of the hungry desert lion that slowly paced around the outskirts of the pyramid complex. Its yellow eyes pierced the darkness to observe vivid details that the night could not conceal from her.

The lioness could hear the soft snores of the workers who slept in their makeshift beds around the great structure of stone. Like a patient connoisseur, she looked for the perfect meal to fill her aching belly. As she walked slowly towards the pyramid's doorway, she stopped. She lowered her head and sniffed the well-worn paths on the ground. There was a shuffling close to her and the lioness turned her attention towards the noise. There, lying on his back, a slave slept comfortably on the sand floor that molded to his body, oblivious to the hungry cat approaching him.

The man had seen many things during his time at the stone structure that he had helped build. Friends had died, his wife displaced, his once large belly now tight and rippling with muscles. Many times he had thought back to what landed him here in the desert, but now he was content with his choice of labor for his crimes, instead of death.

In the haze of his slumber, the sound of slow, heavy breathing that seemed so close to him gradually invaded his consciousness. Finally, the breathing stopped.

"It's about time you be quiet," he mumbled, not wanting to wake and release the bonds of sleep.

A few seconds of peace elapsed until the heavy breathing started up again.

There you go, breathing too close to my head. Man, your breath stinks, he thought, waking slowly, but refusing to open his eyes. The man tried to ignore the annoyance, but soon he had had enough and pried his sleepy eyes open, intending to push his noisy neighbor away. At the same time, a dollop of saliva splatted down on his forehead, which made the man come alert in a flash. An inch from his face was a mouth full of dripping, hungry fangs.

Wijin woke with a start, as a scream pierced the quiet of the darkness. Screaming continued as Wijin rocketed off his cot and stumbled outside. He heard the loud roar of the lion as he ran towards the sound, wondering what had happened, but expecting to find the worst. Wijin had heard a lion's call from the desert before, but it had never come into camp. He had assumed that the noisy work site had enough commotion to dissuade any predators. He had been wrong.

Guards and workers alike watched in horror as a large brown and yellow cat carried a bloody body by the leg through the campsite. Torches had been lit and they were being flailed around to scare the lion away. It was definitely too late for this victim as the body was being tossed around like a doll, while the cat looked for a way to escape into the safety of the dunes. A spear landed close to the marauding cat, scaring it further away.

Whoops and yells from the workers mixed with the clattering of swords and shields by the guards finally had the desired effect. The lion opened her bloody jaws and dropped the tattered body to the ground and then made her escape into the dunes.

Wijin walked over to the lifeless pulp of a body and noticed the damage that had been done to him. His head lay in a rear-facing angle, his neck had a large bite out of it and the abdomen looked like the sem priests had opened him up and removed his inner organs. The stomach was still attached but was hanging outside the body. Large gashes in the arms and legs, where the lion had carried him like a toy, revealed sharp bones jutting out from the fractures. Wijin stared at the mutilated form, and even though his face was torn apart, he recognized the individual. It was Kuric.

Two men volunteered to help carry the bloodied body of the slave into the desert to dispose of him. Bakuru and Soknue piled the remains of Kuric onto a shield and quickly carried him off into the dunes for the vultures and hyenas.

"It could have been any one of us, you know," Soknue commented to Bakuru, who was holding the shield with both hands behind him.

"I heard the sound of a lion last week, but that was all," Bakuru answered.

The sun drenched the sands of the desert in scorching heat. It was a normal day. The blue sky formed a perfect dome that encompassed the horizon as if it were a large, blue, glass bowl, making everything feel motionless. As far as the eye could see, the parched sand dunes stood like vast sentries, seemingly unyielding, but subtly shifting in the desert breezes.

The next day Wijin was pleased to see Khnum arrive at the site. He assumed that it was one of the regular visits that he made to assess the progress of the construction. It did seem unusual that he was alone, rather than traveling with the supply caravan.

"Wijin," Khnum called.

The two men had developed a very comfortable friendship during the years of working together. Although Khnum was a high-ranking and valued part of Amenemope's personal staff, he didn't bear his position arrogantly. He was discerning, and appreciated people for who they were. Because of this, he had developed a strong respect for and friendship with Wijin.

Wijin came trotting over to greet him. As he neared, he could see Khnum's face. Distress and sorrow filled his reddened eyes. Apprehension immediately filled his mind.

"Greetings, Wijin. How are things with you?"

"And greetings to you as well, my friend. Progress on the site is coming along well, but we did have a frightening situation last night. A lion came into the camp and killed one of the men. It was most upsetting," replied Wijin. "I am surprised to see you here on your own. Do you have some news?"

Khnum paused and averted his gaze. Then he took a deep breath and continued. "Yes, there is some news. I came to tell you that there has been an accident."

"Yes. Accidents happen all the time," Wijin replied cautiously, waiting for further details.

How can I tell him that his wife is gone? Khnum lamented inwardly. *His wife, not mine. I know that. In a certain way she seemed like my wife; the way I felt about her, the way I longed for her. It was as though part of me died when I realized that she was gone.*

"I- I'm," he stuttered, unable to form the words he needed to say.

Wijin looked at him, puzzled.

What is he trying to say to me? he thought, perplexed. *It is unlike Khnum to stumble with his words like this.*

"Take a breath, friend, and tell me what is in your heart."

Khnum gathered his thoughts, took a breath and spoke calmly, "It's Akila, Wijin. I am distraught to say that it was she who had an accident. She was up on the scaffolding, painting stars on the ceiling. It collapsed, and she fell to the floor. I am so sorry, and I can hardly bear to tell you. She died instantly," Khnum said.

Wijin stood for a moment, unable to let Akila's death register. He was stunned. He gradually began to process this tragic information. Gravity seemed suspended. Slowly, he felt his temples throb, and a nausea like he had never felt before forced him to vomit as he collapsed on the sand. Khnum's heart went out to his friend as he sobbed on the ground calling out his wife's name over and over. The chief architect crouched down beside him to try to comfort him in the best way he could.

"No, this cannot have happened!" Wijin cried out.

Wijin felt Khnum's hand resting on his shoulder.

"My heart is with you, my friend. I feel your grief, but what words can I say to comfort you?"

"I want to see Akila and bury her. She was better than I am. She deserves more respect than just to be thrown out in the desert," Wijin said, still trying to hold himself together, but failing.

Khnum could feel Wijin's pain as the grieving husband cried, since he had done his share of weeping in solitude on the three day journey from the crypt.

"For now, go to your hut. I will take over your duties for the rest of the day. I will come to you tonight, and we will talk," Khnum replied.

Wijin slowly made his way to the hut that had been built for him and his wife. He remembered when Khnum had brought Akila for a visit recently. Akila and Wijin had not been alone in private for several months prior, and they had taken advantage of the privacy, ripping each other's clothes off as soon as they had entered the small shack. They had made love multiple times that night. In the morning, they had clung to each other, not wanting to let go, just as they had on their wedding night.

Tears streamed down Wijin's cheeks as he lay in his bed remembering Akila's face lighting up every time she saw him, wanting to spend every moment together. Hours passed. Emotionally exhausted, he fell asleep.

Wijin woke at the sound of Khnum knocking on the hut's wall to let Wijin know he was there. The dark red-and-orange glow of the evening sky told him that he had fallen asleep and slept the afternoon away.

"I'm awake, Khnum, come in."

Khnum pushed through the heavy brown leather flap that was used as a door into the tiny, dark room. Wijin lit a candle and the small space came to life.

Across the room by the bed, a mural covered the walls. One picture showed Wijin and Akila frolicking together in the reeds, depicting their younger years together. Another picture was of them holding hands in a boat floating down the Nile. Khnum was amazed at the quality of the murals that Akila had painted. Just like the ones that she had painted in the pyramid, they were better than those of the artists who had trained her. Beautiful flowers and birds filled each scene, alive with the entire spectrum of color everywhere he looked. She was truly remarkable, Khnum thought. *Every surface she painted is a tribute to her and a legacy to those who see her work.* He pulled up a stool, and sat down close to Wijin, who was sitting on his cot.

"There is so little I can do to ease your pain at this time, my friend. But I can tell you something that could alter your future. It is something very serious — something I am not allowed to reveal and I need you to understand me. I will never speak of this again, and you must never mention the words I'm about to tell you to anyone. Do you understand?"

Wijin leaned back and stared straight at him, looking into his deep brown compassion-filled eyes.

"I understand," Wijin said, trying to focus on what was about to be revealed.

"Pharaoh is planning something in the future, I'm not even sure what, but you are in danger, my friend. You need to be prepared to escape. When you feel the time is right, run, run far away from here. I have had this sense of danger since the beginning."

Wijin looked confused. He tipped his head to one side and looked at Khnum inquisitively.

"Think about it, Wijin. Pharaoh floods this country with criminals and gets them to do a building project out in the desert. After they are done, then what? Will he just set everyone free? I think not. He has a plan."

Wijin sat for a while, mulling over Khnum's words until they were absorbed into his mind. He realized that nothing more was going to be said about the matter. *I must give this some more thought when my mind is not in such confusion*, he thought. His grief and despair rose to the surface again.

"Where is Akila? Can I see her?" Wijin implored. "She hasn't been thrown to the jackals, has she?"

"Akila has been taken to the House of the Dead and is with the sem priests as we speak. She is being embalmed. However, the seventy days for mourning will not be observed, because no criminal is granted that," Khnum said quietly.

Wijin was grateful for this favor, but a question sprang to mind.

"How can this be possible? I don't have money to pay for any of this!" Wijin exclaimed.

"I paid for the sem priests myself. She will be buried with dignity in my family's tomb," Khnum replied calmly.

"So, when can I see her?"

"That is a problem. You realize that I have undertaken this task in secret, because she was a slave. So there must be no evidence of her remains being taken from the crypt to my family's tomb. I regret that this is the way it must be. You must take comfort that you will see her in the afterlife. That is my best suggestion."

Relief and puzzlement settled on him. Wijin looked at Khnum with gratitude. He was speechless, not knowing how to respond to this new information. *Why would he pay for a burial for my wife, a lowly slave? How much gold does this man have? I will be in this man's debt forever. How can I bear it not to see her ever again in the land of the living?*

Khnum said, "I can see that you have questions, my friend. But do not concern yourself with many thoughts. It is an honor to do you both this service. You have served Pharaoh well. Let your heart be at peace. When all is said and done, things will work out for you."

It gave Wijin cold comfort. *How could anything work out for me with Akila gone?* There was small solace in being surrounded by the walls that his beloved had painted. He looked thoughtfully at the architect. *He is a good man. He has supported us and helped us to prosper in our servitude. Even though this terrible thing has happened, he has arranged to preserve my wife for the afterlife. The friendship that I share with this important man is one of the few good things left to me. What else has any worth?*

"Can you resume your work tomorrow, Wijin?" Khnum said as he prepared to leave.

"I think so," he replied.

Wijin sat gazing at the flame rising steadily from the candle burning on a side-table, illuminating his tiny world. The impact of the immense loss settled heavily on his heart, as he lay back on his cot and wept.

The south eastern side of Thebes was barren — just a cluster of small hills that were essential to the workers of the dead, the sem priests. No crops grew there, just tufts of scrub grass that lined the paths to two buildings; an embalmers house, the House of the Dead and a metal working shop that fashioned the beautiful anthropoid coffins for the pharaohs under the direct supervision of the priests of the dead.

The House of the Dead sat at the summit of a hill so the prevailing winds would carry the strong smells of their work far away into the desert through their large open windows. Though not a large building, and made of plain mud brick, it had a prominence due to its color. It was painted entirely red. It waited for Egypt's deceased — the wealthy and the important. Death was a joyous occasion that every well-to-do Egyptian looked forward to, and hopefully planned for, well in advance. They wanted to be prepared when, in death, they were called to the scales of judgment.

Pharaoh Amenemope started preparing for his trip to the afterlife to meet Osiris, gathering the possessions he planned to take with him, and talking with the sem priests to make sure everything was in order.

As Amenemope was making these arrangements, another building project was taking place. His own royal tomb was being dug deep into the cliffs by the Eastern Delta. His personal scribe Nekht-Ankh, having studied secret devices, had invented a devious trap for the tomb. It was designed to endure for all time, and to kill anyone who tried to enter. In his mind, Amenemope finally felt the loosening of Ammit's teeth, but they were still there, waiting for him to make a mistake.

He had been storing up his own personal treasures even before he had thought about protecting pharaohs who had come before him and their treasures. His favorite childhood things were all stored away, ready to be retrieved when the time was right. Altars of gold for the worship of Osiris were constructed so that they could be taken along to the afterlife with him. A solid gold inner coffin was created to hold the remains of his earthly body. His facial likeness was fashioned on the surface at the top, the expression calm and stern. Two other outer nesting coffins were constructed of carved wood.

Amenemope made one his regular visits to the House of the Dead and surveyed the construction of his sarcophagus with great interest. The shop was very organized with all the necessary tools hanging above the work benches. The spacious open windows on all sides of the building allowed lots of bright light into the interior, creating an ideal environment for the work.

The hammering of thin sheets of gold, one on top of the other, produced the constant tap-tap-tap that filled the foundry's air. Canopic jars of alabaster, with the heads of gods fashioned on the stoppers by the best artisans, were given to the sem priests for the four main body organs.

The falcon-headed Horus would guard the intestines; the ape-headed Hapy would contain the lungs; the jackal-headed Anubis would hold the stomach and the human-headed Imsety would hold the liver. Amenemope's heart would be placed back in his chest. His brain would be liquefied by inserting a steel rod through his nose and stirring it as though with a whisk. His brain would be poured out through the hole made in his nasal cavity.

"Things are progressing well. I am pleased with the gold sarcophagus. The likeness is accurate," Pharaoh commented.

Then he said aloud, "My book! I haven't completed my book. When we return to the palace I will spend some time on it today."

Amenemope's Book of Wisdom that he was writing for his son had been partially completed, but because of the demands of his schedule had not been added to for some time.

Surrounded by his guards, he walked outside and lowered himself on his litter for the two hour trek into the heart of Thebes and the protected confines of the palace. Four litter-bearers hoisted the gold litter and set off at a swift walk. Amenemope leaned back on his cushions and as they reached the edge of the city, he could not help overhearing the comments of the townsfolk as they trotted by.

"It's Pharaoh! It's Pharaoh!" he heard them calling above the padding feet of the soldiers that surrounded his litter. He also heard the soldier's demands ring out for the people to step back and get on their knees and show homage.

An hour into their travel, hearing the river and the water fowl, Amenemope called for the carriers and the soldiers to stop and find some shade for them. It was time to rest and refresh themselves with the beer and food supplies that they had brought along. The smell of wet mud on the side of the brown banks of the river brought a reminder to all as to how generous the great Nile was to everyone it nourished. The inundation of the river was good this year, covering the land with a rich layer of silt. Pharaoh was pleased to realize that the harvests would be generous — the people well supplied.

The litter-carriers lowered the golden, pillow-filled frame when Wepsawat, the chief guard of Pharaoh's security force, selected a tree-lined area by the side of the road for the rest stop.

Amenemope drew back the curtain, allowing the fragrance of the trees and the Nile air to blow through the litter and refresh him.

Servants held plates of fresh red grapes and sweetmeats for his choosing. An ornate cup of wine from the royal cellar of his father, Osiris-Psusennes' IVth, was offered after it was tasted.

As he took a sip, Amenemope let the wine linger in his mouth and remembered the time of his father's rule. *I am not going to be like my tyrannical father — overly tough, unapproachable, and blind to his own behavior as well as the needs and desires of others. His fatherly guidance was sparse, and I have had to develop my own strategies from a better perspective. I shall not be as neglectful in the training of my own son, Osorkon.*

After resting for half an hour, they continued on the trek into

Thebes. As he neared the central part of the city where the population was greater, the curtains were closed again to block the view from the stares of onlookers.

When they reached the large gates of the inner compound, the litter stopped and the soldiers that surrounded it slammed the butts of their spears to the ground in unison, making a sound like a thunder clap. Amenemope heard the challenges and counter challenges between the guards. The litter was soon moving through the heavy gates, past the gardens and fountains, where it slowed to a stop and was lowered to the ground. After the guards stepped back Amenemope opened the curtains and climbed out. As he stood up the litter bearers and soldiers prostrated themselves on the ground. Stretching himself from the long journey, he walked sedately into the palace and called for Nemutptah to meet him in his office.

The tall, slim scribe walked silently through Pharaoh's office door and bowed with head to the floor. Then he sat with his legs crossed, laid out his scribe's kit and readied himself for dictation. After placing his palette across his lap and taking the stopper out of his ink pot, he prepared his brushes and said a prayer to Thoth, god of writing: *O Thoth, god of the holy word, make my pen exact and my hand steady and swift. Let me please your brother, Amenemope, god on earth, as I take this dictation.* Nemutptah dipped his brush and looked up at Amenemope.

"Nemutptah, we will continue the book of wisdom that I am writing."

Chapter 7

Do not set your heart upon seeking riches,
For there is no one who can ignore Destiny and Fortune
Do not set your heart on external matters,
For every man there is his appointed time.
Do not exert yourself upon seeking excess,
And your wealth will prosper for you,
If riches come to you by theft,
They will not spend the night with you.
As soon as day breaks, they will not be in your household;
Although their places can be seen, they are not there
When the Earth opens its mouth it levels him and swallows him up,
And it drowns in the deep.

They have made for themselves a great hole which serves them.
To one who has done this on Earth, pay attention,
For he is a weak enemy.
He is an enemy overturned inside himself,
Life is taken from his eye.
His household is hostile to the community.
His storerooms are toppled over,
His property taken from his children,
And to someone else, his possessions are given. [1]

Amenemope stopped his dictation and looked at Nemutptah.

"That is all for now. You can go and put a good copy in with the others tonight," the scribe was advised.

Nemutptah put the stopper on the pot of ink, gathered up his supplies, bowed and returned to his small office

Khnum approached the palace for one of his regular meetings with Pharaoh concerning the progress of the building projects that the architect was supervising.

"So, what do you have to report?" Pharaoh inquired.

"I think you will be pleased, my Lord. Both the pyramid and the pit tomb are nearing completion. It has taken just a bit longer than the ten years we had allowed, and even with the set-backs, the progress has been consistent. You will also be impressed with the quality of the work. Even though we have used slave labor, the leadership of one supervisor in particular has raised the standard of the whole enterprise. I believe I mentioned him to you before. His name is Wijin. He showed skill as a stone-cutter and has distinguished himself as a leader of men. He brought things along much better than did that unfortunate man, Amsu. Some of the artwork is likewise superior. I would say that up until now, we have achieved great success with the plan you conceived so long ago. We are now ready for the next stage," Khnum stated.

"You deliver good news, Architect. As the years pass, I become more aware of my responsibilities to fulfil the instructions of Osiris. And these things take time. But it seems as though we can expect to complete our mission within the years I have left to me. I will set out the next part of the plan to preserve the treasures and remains of my predecessors for time and eternity. As you know, there are still many tombs which have remained undisturbed. We have identified the location of each of them. Here is the list. What we must do next is assemble these thieving slaves into teams which will be dispatched to each of these locations, and, under guard, they will be required to open the tombs, collect the contents, and transport them to the crypt site. I believe you have arranged a schedule of which rooms the various collections will be stored in. We will want to keep each pharaoh's treasures close to his own sarcophagus. Nekht-Ankh can work with you on this to prepare records so that all of these transfers can be properly documented. You won't need to send all of the slaves on this business, however. I spoke to you of the means we will use to keep the location of these building projects concealed from the prying eyes of greedy men. Use the rest of the workers to create the sand coverings which will appear to cause the crypt to be swallowed up by the earth, and obscure the pyramid. There will be vast wealth hidden in the crypt and it is imperative that it never be found. The pharaohs and their belongings will be safe and they will have secure access to all the things that they need in the next world. Anyone who attempts to steal from the tombs of our forefathers, will figure that they have already been ransacked, and our secret destruction of these monuments to their lives will serve to discourage treasure hunters."

"Your plan has merit," commented Khnum. "How much time do you anticipate this part of the endeavor will require?"

"I expect it will take more than one year, but less than two," replied Amenemope. "When all of this is complete, my heart will be at rest, knowing I have fulfilled all that Osiris has instructed me to do."

The worst of the day's heat had passed as the sun began its descent to the western horizon. There was still a great deal of activity as the team of twelve men hauled the last load of artifacts from the tomb. The gold and jewel-encrusted weapons, jewelry and furniture glowed in the softer afternoon light. Six vigilant guards kept a close eye on the former felons as they delivered the relics to a waiting wagon.

"When you have finished emptying the vault and loading the cart, you can stop for some food and beer, you scoundrels," shouted the head guard. "You will have a time to rest, and then we will head out. We can make several miles on our journey towards the drop-off point tonight. If you are quick about it, we might even make it to the oasis, and you can have all the water you want, not just your ration of beer. And you can forget about going anywhere with some of these trinkets," he said, holding up an ancient sword with a golden hilt and a gold shield. "You know there is nowhere to run and nowhere to hide in this empty wilderness. Anyone found trying to escape will be flogged, and the whole gang will be shackled. So resolve right now to do what you're told and it will be better for you. The great Pharaoh doesn't care whether you live or die, and by Seth's fetid breath, neither do I." He laughed coarsely at his own joke.

The weary workers plodded on in single file, their arms filled with items from the royal tomb, hungry, thirsty and tired from the long day's labor. The promise of a break spurred them on a little, as they realized they were almost finished. The years of working as slaves had hardened them, but the meager rations and rigorous demands had kept them manageable. Hope was in short supply.

"I am more than ready for a rest, I can tell you," said Bakuru. "These long days on the move are harder to bear than those spent at the pyramid. It seems strange to be robbing these tombs as punishment for robbing tombs. I can't understand why this is happening. It seems so strange."

"It's not like they will tell us anything," replied Soknue as the two men headed towards the supply cart. "They did give us a job that we are good at this time, though." He managed a smile as they collected their rations of beer, bread, and cheese then sat down gratefully on a small knoll where they could lean back while they ate.

"My feet are giving me so much pain today. The ground here is gritty and sharp. I thought my feet were tough enough to bear anything, but they are getting cut up. I'm not looking forward to tonight's trek along that barren road" Bakuru complained.

"Mine are hurting too," replied Soknue. "But at least it will be cool to walk in the night. We have survived this long. It's not much of a life, though, that's for sure.

The small party made their way along the desert trail, their precious cargo filling several mule-drawn wagons. The contents were covered with heavy blankets and if any traveler were to venture that far into the wilderness, they would have no idea of the value of the contents. A few drifters did disappear in those days, however, and no one ever knew why. No one saw anything.

As dawn approached on the second night of travel, the group all caught site of an oasis in the distance. At first it looked like a dark patch against the paleness of the horizon. But as they got closer, they could see there were people there, some beginning to move about, others still asleep on the ground. There were quite a number of soldiers there as well. Some camels and mules were tied to the palm trees that clustered together by the water supply.

"All right, you mangy bunch of loafers, it looks as though you are at the end of this journey. We will stop here and you can say good-bye to your wagon-loads of 'supplies'. These fine folks will take them somewhere else." The guard found his comments amusing, and enjoyed taunting the disconsolate men.

"I wonder where all this treasure will be taken from here," Soknue questioned quietly. "It seems hard to believe that all this wealth of merchandise is being shifted around in the desert like so much baggage. And the sarcophagus of some pharaoh is going with it. If we ever get out of this cursed bondage, I will want to find out where it is."

"So you think you might have an advantage if you ever get free, do you? I think you would not be the only person in this group that had that idea," said a man with a scar across his face. He was older and gaunter and his eyes glittered with malice.

"It's just talk, Amaké. What chance do we have of escape? We have been more heavily guarded during this task than we ever were before. It's just that holding all that treasure in my hands brought back memories of the past. That's all."

"Stop that talking," a guard shouted at the men. "You will wait here while the wagons are hitched to the mules over there. You are not to speak to any of those people or go near them at all. If you do, they will be the last words you ever say. They will be leaving shortly, and when they are gone, you can refresh yourselves and have a meal. We will rest here for the day. Tonight you will find out where you go next."

It was the middle of the night when the party transporting the treasure arrived at the crypt. It was a day's travel from the oasis to the pit-tomb, but they had to travel during the day this time. Even though it was the fall of the year and the day-time temperatures were more bearable, the soldiers had taken the group and the wagons off the road to a rocky outcropping where they had erected a makeshift shelter. After a meal, they had spent the heat-of-the-day hours resting. Progress was always slow and energy-draining during this time and even the guards had a hard time keeping to the gruelling schedule. So having an afternoon rest strengthened them all for the remainder of the trip. The slaves were returned to their sleeping places inside the crypt and the shipment was secured in the storage compound and heavily guarded.

Shortly after dawn everyone arose, had a meal and prepared for their day's work. The women who had done the interior painting reported to their new leader, Semat.

"Good morning, ladies. We received another shipment of treasures last night, so storing that will be our work for the next while. The men will lower the goods on the pulley lift to the opening and they will carry the sarcophagi and other heavy items into the room which is allocated for this shipment. As usual, you will be carrying the other objects, and arranging them in the room. You know best how to do that now, so that the space can be used most efficiently. It will be floor to ceiling with this lot also. And handle things carefully. We don't want any damage. Check with Kemosiri as you take each item in and he will make a note of it. Do you have any questions?"

"Will we need to help load the goods on to the pulley lift at the surface this time, or will we all be working inside, down below?" asked Theabus.

"You can all work inside this time. There are many smaller articles, and it will take more arranging in the room, so the men will do all the work on the surface," replied Semat.

The women headed down the steps to the entrance of the crypt and waited for the first load to come down.

"I wonder how many shipments of treasures we will be putting into storage," asked Theabus. "This whole thing seems so strange. I wish I knew what was going on with Pharaoh for him to make all these changes.

I can't see how anything is going to be more protected here than it was in the tombs. There are so many people that know about what has been going on."

"It does seem like we are going to a great deal of effort. But if it isn't one thing, it's another," said Aknet. "By the way, do you know if Lord Khnum is back? I haven't seen him around for quite a while."

"Yes, he's been here for more than a week. I think he's been busy organizing things for all this storage of treasures. He seems to stay away from the people more than he used to, though. It was nice to see him around quite often back when we were doing the painting. If you ask me, ever since Akila died, he has been a different person," said Theabus.

"That's for sure. I mean, we all miss Akila, but it seems obvious that she was far more than just the team leader for the painters as far as he was concerned. The day she died, I was shocked at the way he went to her and took her away. Anukri was working on the surface that day, and he said he saw Lord Khnum put her in his chariot and take her to the sem priests. Nobody knows what happened to her after that."

"I guess the calm and cool architect has some heat in him, after all," Theabus chuckled. "It seems such a waste for him to be taken with someone who already had a wonderful husband. I wonder what it would take to get him interested."

"You're not the only one!" exclaimed Aknet. "He's certainly much better than the men from the work crews that we end up with. But I suppose we should be grateful that the guards can't keep us from having a little fun in this dreadful place. And to be honest, some of the guards get plenty lonely too."

"Well, here comes the lift. Let's get our baskets and load them up."

As they brought the baskets into the main cathedral, they cautiously skirted the supporting pillars that were spaced evenly around the area. They had been carved into the likenesses of the main gods of the land. At the doorway stood the most imposing pillar, representing Osiris, god of the dead. His steady gaze observed everyone in the room, guarding the space and its contents. As they moved towards the storage rooms, they passed the others: Amun-Re, Thoth, Anubis, Horus, Ptah, Isis, Hathor, and Nephthys. The merriment of the women was subdued as they moved past these silent symbols of power. As they continued to bring the loads of items into the storage room, they were in awe as they handled each item, beautiful precious gold artifacts, idols and jewels. As the pile grew, they were amazed at the casual way in which the stunning treasures were stacked up as if they were simply ordinary household objects. The oil lamps on the walls cast a dim light which glowed on the surfaces, giving the merest hint of the exceptional value of a room filled with gold.

At the same time as the treasures of Egypt were being gathered and stored in the crypt, work was done on creating doors to secure the entrance. A large recessed ridge was created around the entire rectangular opening on the surface, and thick stone doors, accurately measured, were quarried from the bedrock nearby. After they were dressed, they were transported to the opening and positioned at the edges of the shaft, and rigged with ropes and pulleys so that they could be set into place with an economy of effort.

As reports of progress from the crypt and the pyramid were brought to Pharaoh Amenemope, they continued to give encouragement to the great king that the plans given by Osiris were being completed. Finally, as he could see that his future and the future of his forefathers were being secured, his confidence was restored.

(1) see bibliography

7

THIEVES PLAN

Khnum made his way to the royal palace for his regular meeting with Pharaoh. He had been here many times before, but this time he realized that things would change. After nearly thirteen years, the work at both the pyramid and the crypt was coming to completion. The architect wondered what the future would bring for the country, and what lay ahead for him also. Having heard about and worked on the ruler's plan for so long, this point in time had always seemed to be in the distant future, but now it was at his doorstep. The projects he had planned and supervised had challenged and satisfied him, and for the most part he had kept his questions and concerns about the conclusion out of his mind. Now it must be faced.

Amenemope entered the royal office and smiled at the architect. "Greetings, Lord Khnum. I trust you had a pleasant journey to the capital."

"It was quite satisfactory. It looks as though I will not be making that trip much longer."

"Yes, tell me how things stand with these two projects," Pharaoh inquired.

"I believe we are able to say that they are finished. The pyramid has been completed for some time, and the workers have covered and concealed it, along with the statue of yourself and the other statuary surrounding the site. I have inspected it, and if you didn't know it was there, you would have no idea of what lies beneath the great mound of gravel.

As far as the crypt is concerned, that has been finished for many months as well. The emptying of the tombs of the forefathers is completed, and the contents have all been transferred to the storage rooms at the pit tomb. The doors for both locations have been fashioned and put in place. I wish to show you the drawings which explain how the ropes and pulleys work to close the doors with a minimum of effort. I think you will find that everything is in good order," Khnum said. "I know you want to personally close the doors to seal in the treasures, but what will happen to the criminals that are still alive?"

"Your report pleases me. I have been giving great thought as to how to proceed from here. It is my intention to have a great feast at both locations to celebrate the completion of these projects. There is one difficulty, however. The number of people left working at the pyramid is quite substantial, and there isn't enough room in the pyramid to accommodate them all inside for the meal. And there aren't that many left working at the crypt. I wondered about the feasibility of moving the slaves from each location and switching them so that the pyramid slaves would celebrate at the crypt, which has a much larger central space, and sending the crypt slaves to the pyramid, which could handle the smaller number. It is preferable that the festivities be held inside the structures. What do you think?" asked Amenemope.

"That could be done. It will take a while to move the people across the desert. The supply wagons take three days, but they are not traveling on foot as the slaves will be. The number of slaves left is now only in the hundreds, but it would still take some planning to move that number so far. We can manage it though. If they travel during the nights, we can erect shelters for them to sleep under during the days. Traveling at night greatly reduces the amount of drinking water needed. There are only the two main rest stops available on the way, but the path is well established. Those coming in the other direction could be handled more easily. There are less than one hundred of them. May I ask why you wish to have these celebrations inside?" replied Khnum.

"We will need extra guards for the travel time," continued Pharoah, skirting Khnum's question. "We have kept track of which soldiers have had any contact with either one of these operations, so they will be recruited for this duty. I will leave it up to you to see that the slaves are transferred to the other locations, and I will see to the rest of the arrangements. Let us have it finished within the month."

The notice came to the pyramid and was given to Wijin. He gathered the workers together for the announcement.

"You have all worked long and hard. Your efforts have not gone unnoticed by Pharaoh. Now that we have completed all that Pharaoh has required, I can let you know that we are all invited to a wonderful banquet to celebrate the conclusion of our labors. We will travel across the desert on the route of the supply wagons to another location which is much larger and can hold us all for a wonderful dinner. Pharaoh himself will be there. You will no longer be working here. So gather up anything you wish to take with you and be ready to leave the day after tomorrow at dusk."

The next day, soldiers arrived, and preparations were made for the trip into the desert. There was jubilation among the slaves as they anticipated the trip and the banquet, as well as seeing Pharaoh upon completion of their duties.

Everything was ready. The last meal was eaten and everyone was organized for the trek. The sun was low in the western sky as they headed out. Supply wagons carried away all the useable goods from the transient work site as well as food and water for the trip. This part of the desert was not so sandy — more gritty and rough, so the trail they followed was hard-packed and fairly easy to follow as the darkness closed upon them. It was the spring of the year, and the night air had a definite chill to it. It was an unusual experience for them to be cold, having been in close quarters for such a long time. Many people were glad to have even old, worn-out blankets to wrap around themselves as they trudged along. Wijin was one of the fortunate few who had earned the right to wear a proper kilt and a cloak to shield him from the desert wind. His heart was with the people though, and he walked among them. He knew them all by name and by nature. They had spent many years working to build the marvelous monument, now hidden, and they shared a secret sense of accomplishment that bonded them together.

Wijin reflected on how many had been lost to the work, to the weather, to illness, starvation and to the cruelty of the whip. *It has been a strange time of contrasts: to be made a slave, but to have become a leader; to have been confined and controlled, but to have learned so much; to have been brutalized by Amsu, but blessed by Khnum; and to have faced the devastation of losing my wonderful Akila.*

As he walked along, Amaké and Intef came alongside him.

"Well, if it isn't our beloved leader," smirked Amaké. "I see that even though you are well dressed for this trip, you still have to walk, just like us."

"Is it well with you, Amaké? I haven't seen too much of you. You have been moved around quite a bit. Where have you been?" asked Wijin.

"We spent much of our time at the quarry, cutting blocks, and then crushing stone. That seemed as pointless as building a pyramid and then concealing it. But we do as we are told, do we not? The last year and a half has been much more interesting. We were taken out in a small group to empty tombs that were still undisturbed. Those treasures were all delivered to an oasis in the desert, and turned over to another group of slaves. There were too many soldiers for us to take advantage of the situation, unfortunately. We don't know where everything was taken, but if I ever get out of this bondage, I intend to find out. Do you know where we are going on this trip and to what purpose?" asked Amaké.

"I understand we are going to a place for a great feast to celebrate the completion of our work as slaves" replied Wijin.

"I think we have certainly paid for our 'crimes,' don't you?" Amaké prodded Wijin. "It is fitting that we should be rewarded in some way for all we have done."

"Amaké, I think we are lucky to be alive. Isn't that enough?" Wijin responded.

Soknue and Bakuru, many years older now, the hair on their heads graying and thinning, walked side-by-side in the middle of the river of slaves snaking its way between the dunes on the way to the final destination.

"It's good to see you with a smile on your face, Bakuru," Soknue said, with good humor.

Bakuru's grin widened, revealing a number of missing teeth.

"Well, our work is done. We are being treated to a banquet by Pharaoh. What more could you want? I also hear rumors of us being freed," Bakuru replied, continuing to smile.

"What will you do if we are freed?" his friend asked.

"I, Bakuru, will grow the best crops in all Egypt!" he said, raising his hands and bowing.

"I think you need land for that, dreamer," Soknue said doubtfully.

"Dreams are almost all that I have. What about you? What are you going to do?"

"Well, first thing I'm going to find my wife, if she's still alive, beg her forgiveness for letting my greed take control of me, and then hire myself out to an architect."

"You would be good at that, my friend," Bakuru replied, believing that Soknue might indeed do everything he had just mentioned.

The large group of workers continued to file across the desert on a fast-paced march. The enthusiasm of the beginning of the excursion began to wane by the fourth day. There had been few rest stops during the night, as they had a long way to go. The temporary shelters set up for them to rest under during the day were barely adequate. The rations were small, and far short of what they required for the demanding journey. The soldiers fared somewhat better.

When the sun began to set each day, it was clear that some of the slaves were not going to continue with the rest. Some slipped into a stupor, unable to rise and go on. Rather than giving them extra care, the soldiers simply dispatched them with a spear on the spot. It made Amaké and Intef remember what Wijin had said to them so recently about appreciating the life they still had. It brought grief to those who watched, but then they all realized that it was the merciful thing to do. They had to be left behind, and a quick death was far more preferable to a slow baking in the sun. Their bodies would be dehydrated into mummification, and buried in the blowing sand if no wild animals found them. As the days passed, those who survived realized that the available rations might go a little further with fewer people to feed. Somehow the prospect of a celebration seemed less worth the struggle, but in each heart, hope's flame still flickered dimly. *Maybe we will soon be free!*

Wijin spent time talking with the people for the first couple of nights. He did a lot of thinking, too. *How long will we be expected to keep up this demanding march? It is becoming increasingly difficult to encourage the others. I'm finding it hard to keep going myself and so many are less able than I am. This does not seem like Pharaoh is showing appreciation for our accomplishments. Still, I must do my best to be strong and supportive for the others.*

Dawn of the tenth day finally came, and they arrived at the pit tomb. As they drew near, all they could see were the two massive stone doors standing up on each side of a deep hole, a few shacks situated nearby and huge piles of stone chips.

Intef said, "We must be here. Praise to the gods. I don't think I could have lasted another day. I have never been so hungry in my life."

"You always have your stomach on your mind, brother, but this time

I am in agreement with you. It is a great relief to be done that terrible walk," Amaké replied.

The head soldier was also obviously glad to be at the end of the trek.

"Alright, people, we have arrived at our destination. We will have a meal and then you can rest for the day. Let's have those shelters raised over there, men, beyond the piles of stones and have the remaining food and water distributed. I believe the cistern here has some water for washing. After you have rested, you will have a chance to clean yourselves up a little. You will have to stay away from these huts. The banquet that you have been promised is being prepared there for tonight's meal and I know we are all looking forward to that."

As the afternoon wore on, the prisoners started stirring from their rest. They could smell the food being cooked for them in the huts that circled the entrance. They had been turned into make-shift kitchens for that night. Open fires cooked the many dishes that would be served at the banquet. Wooden pens that held ducks, goats and cows, littered the area. Close to the pens, the slaughtering corral was red with blood as the animals were led in one at a time. The screams from the dying animals could be heard all over the compound. The aroma of baking bread filled the air with the familiar and delicious scent that the slaves had long forgotten. The odor of cooked vegetables, steamed with fragrant spices and served on trays ready to be brought into the crypt, drove the slaves mad with hunger.

"All right, you sorry bunch," announced a soldier. "Pharaoh Amenemope will be arriving shortly. You will have some time to go to the cistern over there. Do your best to clean up your unwashed bodies. When you are finished, come back here and line up in this open area. Do your best before the ruler of Egypt.

Bakuru and Soknue stepped up towards the towering blocks on each side of the entrance to the pit, feeling that at last they had come to the end of their labor. Their muscles were now hard and taut, as veins protruded from their biceps.

The past thirteen years had been tough on their bodies. All abdominal fat was gone, replaced with sinewy muscle. They had seen friends die, crushed by massive stone blocks being slid into place. Some friends had succumbed to the heat and just dropped over dead in their tracks. They were forced to step over them like trash with no pause to reflect on the suddenly ended life. Still others died at the taskmaster's hand as they were beaten to a pulp for being unable to continue doing a task.

Hunger pains that caused their stomachs to growl intensified as they saw the cooks carrying platters into the deep entrance. The two men stood near the top of the impressive shaft, so that the cooking aromas would reach their nostrils in a marriage of fragrant smells blended together.

"Will this be it? Is our debt paid?" Bakuru asked out loud to no one in particular, feeling doubt, as it seemed too good to be true.

On hearing his friend's rhetorical question, Soknue wondered the same thing.

"All I know is that this will be the best meal that I have ever eaten!" Soknue replied, not needing to answer.

Horns blared as a chariot, flanked by sweaty guards, rolled up into the large group of slaves. Everyone prostrated themselves on the ground as Pharaoh's golden chariot rolled towards the crypt. As soon as the horses stopped, a soldier dismounted and a second held them steady.

Amenemope stepped off the back platform with grace. He wore his blue and gold war crown and clutched the crook and flail tightly to his chest. His titles were called as he made his way into the crypt.

Amenemope was seated in the place of honor as he watched the criminals file into the cool, underground tomb. Decked out in his royal regalia, he was a sight to behold. The gold pectoral draped around his neck, rings on his fingers, and bracelets covering his arms, made a stunning impression on the impoverished slaves. They couldn't take their eyes off him. He projected an aura of power, wealth and dignity.

The people crowded into the large central room and walked all around, looking at the paintings on the walls and ceiling. They were especially interested in the pillars that supported the ceiling, which had been carved into the likeness of the most important gods of the land. It had been a long time since the slaves had seen anything like this, and they wove in and out among the idols, saying prayers and thanking them for their good fortune.

The meal was served and the people crowded closely together to see all the food that was laid out, and to fill their plates in undisguised desperation. A great amount of wine was served, and all they wanted was provided. The meal of sweet meats, roasted duck, fish, steaks, lamb, vegetables, bread, and beer was like nothing they had ever seen.

Many husbands and wives were reunited for this occasion. It seemed as though a nightmare of many years had come to an end. Relief and joy mingled in their midst.

A small area was cleared and the entertainment began. A number of naked dancing girls emerged from behind a screen and they began a slow series of undulations to the beat of the music provided by a few instruments. The slaves were used to naked bodies, but the beauty and the sensual movements of the dancers were something they hadn't seen for a very long time, and they were spellbound.

After the meal was finished and the people started becoming restless, Amenemope stood up from his seat of honor, and held up his hands.

"I, Amenemope, Pharaoh Living Forever, do hereby thank you for your hard work these past many years. After this night, I will personally blot out all your crimes from the records as my thanks to you. You have served your Pharaoh well, building monuments of security and safety for our past fathers."

The prisoners that had been caught pillaging the tombs raised a cheer.

"Furthermore, I have directed some of this crew to remove all the treasures from the remaining tombs, and have stored all the previous kings' valuables here, in this location, for their safekeeping in these sixty-five, separate rooms."

Amaké sat totally still, although his mind was racing. *That man is a fool to tell us all this. I can't believe it. He is setting us free and telling us where all the treasure of Egypt is. All the gold is here, right here! All I need to do is wait until the party is over, then come back for the greatest payday of my life.* Even with the prospect of freedom and an expunged criminal record, Amaké and Intef still could think of nothing else but the gold and jewels that were so close.

Amaké turned away from his wife and whispered to Intef, "It looks as though we may have a successful future after all, my brother. Can you believe what this Pharaoh has said to us — a pack of criminals? We must act swiftly, as there will be others with the same idea as us."

Wijin looked across at his two former cohorts and saw them conversing quietly and thought, *those two are conspiring again. They haven't learned a thing from all they have suffered. That treasure holds no grip on me. That is not where real treasure lies — it is altogether deceitful.*

"Let's go outside for some fresh air and conversation," Amaké suggested. The press of bodies was worse than the busiest day at the market, and they were glad for the change. The three men painstakingly edged through the crowd and made their way outside. Amaké and Intef weren't about to be dissuaded from their plan to raid the crypt after the party was over, having heard about the wealth that was beneath them.

Wijin grabbed his cloak as he left. When they stepped out of the doorway into the large pit that led to the surface, they stretched and took deep breaths of the cool night air.

Amenemope, happy with how the evening was progressing, looked out at all the felons that had worked on the ventures he had set them to. He felt a loss for their souls as he witnessed them enjoying the celebration in total abandon. Husbands and wives clung to each other as if it were their wedding day. The sense of relief on their faces showed that the jubilation of the evening washed clean their memories of hard labor and dirt. So many had died during the past thirteen years, that Amenemope questioned his resolve to complete the task he had set out to do. Sitting in his place he felt the god's eyes on his, burrowing into his soul like hot pokers burning a dead reed. Amenemope needed to leave soon to make the long trip back, but decided to wait for just a little while longer. He felt the warm hands of Osiris on his shoulders keeping him there as if he must wait for something. Only when he felt released would he get up and move.

Osiris, in spirit form, looked on at the three men who had walked out of the crypt and watched their souls intently. The god had, unbeknownst to Wijin, become interested in judging him and decided to see how true his nature was. To test him, Osiris planted a seed of avarice and greed in him to see how strong his ka, his very soul, was.

"I can't believe Amenemope is going to give us our freedom," Amaké whispered in amazement. "I thought we would have been put to death the moment we were caught. I think Amenemope is going soft. It won't be much longer until he is overthrown."

Wijin ran his fingers through his hair, wondering whether he was so sure about not going along with Amaké and Intef's plan to come back and raid the crypt right after they were freed.

Wijin's mind started to needle his soul, but he couldn't grasp the meaning of it. A slow desire for easy wealth filled his mind. *Perhaps I should reconsider. No one is better at tomb robbing than Amaké. If anyone could pull it off, it would be him. It could make my life so much easier. I could* *live as I wished — no worries about making my way in life, paying for the* *things I need. All these years of faithful service — such a treasure would be* *no less than I am owed. And what payment could possibly reimburse me for* *the loss of my wife?* He shook his head to dislodge these corrupt thoughts. *What is the matter with me? Here I am, freedom given to me on a silver platter* *— but something is wrong.* He suppressed the kernel of greed that Osiris had been testing him with.

Suddenly his mind became clear and he thought back to Khnum's words to him just after he had come to tell him that Akila was dead. *Khnum told me that he knew something was going to happen, but he didn't* *know what. He had said I was in danger.* "Run, run far away from here when *the time is right." This is that time!* Wijin looked up at the stone doors that stood precariously at the pit entrance and heard the boisterous criminals laughing inside. Waves of panic rolled over him. He knew what was going to happen. *Khnum, you were wrong. We are all in danger!*

"I think I will take this gift of freedom and live right. Somehow I will make an honest living," Wijin whispered so the nearby guard could not hear. "Look at us. Our actions got us years of bondage, and robbed us of the prime of our lives. How can we possibly consider repeating the same foolish mistakes? I will never rob anyone again. Will you two never learn your lesson?"

Off in the distance Osiris smiled to himself as Wijin's true nature shone through. The god knew he had truly changed in his heart.

Wijin turned on his heel and walked across to the other side of the pit, staring at the wall, disgusted at the others.

Amaké went after him, trying to persuade him. "Are you sure you won't change your mind? Your wife has died. We have been friends our whole lives. We have had good times together. You can't just turn your back on us now. Come on. Let's go back inside and have some more beer."

"I have had my fill for now. I will stay out here and get some more fresh air. You go on back in. I will join you shortly," Wijin lied.

Amaké lifted up his hands in resignation and turned around, joining his brother to go back inside. Wijin watched as Amaké and Intef made their way back to the small entrance and waited until they slipped inside.

Wijin stood quietly in the darkness at the bottom of the pit. The guards at the entrance were distracted in conversation with someone from inside.

This is my chance, Wijin thought, and he silently made his way up the staircase that was carved into the wall. *I will never see you again, Amaké. I am counting on your warning, my friend Khnum. May the gods smile upon me.*

Amaké and Intef edged into the crowd, and sat down in the middle of the throng of people looking for more food and beer.

"He wouldn't come in, Intef, and I don't think we will ever get him to help us anymore. His mind seems made up."

"You pushed him too much, Amaké. That's your problem. You expect everyone to see things your way, no matter what."

The pretty dancers had settled into a more informal swaying to and fro around the tired press of bodies, much to the delight of the festive mob.

Body servants swarmed around Amenemope, meeting all his needs.

Now is the time. But wait — there is Kamun-Min, my wine taster, who has served me faithfully. And Huy-Amon, my sandal bearer, who served my father and has known me since I was still wearing my youth lock. Look, the priests that chant prayers for me. They have secluded themselves in the corner. The food tasters I bring along with me, here they sit at my feet testing everything on my plate for poison. They have all served me well. Can I really do this? Amenemope's resolve wavered, but he steeled himself against the feelings of compassion. *I must do all that I set out to do, all I have been commanded to do.*

The music changed tempo, and a livelier beat brought most of them to their feet. More wine was opened and passed around until most of the underground merrymakers were fully intoxicated and stumbling over each other.

During the height of the revellers' drunkenness, Amenemope felt a release in his spirit, allowing himself the freedom to be excused. He stole away through the entrance, making sure the guards were still inside keeping order over the intoxicated crowd. Amenemope said a prayer to Osiris, who was watching the party-goers just inside the door. He made his way up the staircase to the surface, and found the rope and pulley device that Khnum had described to him.

The rope was secured more tightly than he had anticipated, and he fumbled with the knot in the dim light. Then it was loose and he began to pull on it. The stone blocks resisted his efforts briefly, but then they began to move from their upright position and close together horizontally with a "thud", lying against the ledge that had been carved around the entire opening of the pit, totally covering the shaft, and sealing everyone inside — the pyramid slaves, dancers, priests, servants, and guards. Pharaoh stood there motionless for a couple of minutes. *I have done it. No one here will ever be able to reveal the secrets of the pyramid or the crypt to anyone. This is amazing. These stone doors are completely flush with the surrounding stone. Khnum really knew what he was doing when he built this crypt. The desert sands will drift over it and remove any trace of its existence in no time.*

He sat down and took several deep breaths to try to still his racing heart. He waited a few more minutes. Then, gazing around, Amenemope looked for anyone who might have been left outside. All he heard was the sound of the wind lightly blowing across the barren desert sands. Satisfied that he was alone, he stripped off his crown and royal regalia, placed them in a storage compartment on his chariot, and closed his eyes, still waiting to hear any sound. He walked slowly over to the wooden shacks that had been built for the workers during their many years of labor. Picking up a torch, he peered into each of the structures and set them on fire as he went along. He watched the fires burn for a while, many thoughts tumbling around in his mind and gradually subsiding as the flames licked away all traces of habitation. A calmness came to him, and an intoxicating lull caused his eyes to glaze over.

The snorting of horses snapped him out of his trance and brought him back to reality. Revived in spirit, Amenemope made his way over to his golden chariot that was secured nearby. *This part of the plan is finally complete*, Pharaoh thought as he climbed onto the platform and took the reins in hand. With a sense of relief and accomplishment, he rode off into the desert.

Inside the crypt, the people felt the tremors as the heavy stone doors fell shut at the top of the shaft. When they sealed against the ledge with a "thud," a great cloud of dust poured through the doorway into the central room. It billowed behind the statue of Osiris. Everyone stopped what they were doing and stood motionless, wondering what had happened. The soldiers were the first to move, making their way through the doorway into the base of the pit.

"Stay calm, everyone," one of them said. "We'll go up and see what has happened." As he grabbed a torch and ran across to the stairway cut into the wall, he thought, *surely those great doors have not been closed with us inside. How can this be?* But as he got near the top of the staircase, he came against the stone ceiling. He held the torch out to increase its span of light. *Perhaps there is an access to the surface at the top of the staircase on the adjacent wall.*

"Nebtawi, take a torch up that other staircase. Check for an opening."

He did as he was ordered, while people made their way out of the great room and into the pit. The air was full of questions.

"What happened?"

"How can we get out?"

"Who closed those stone doors?"

Nebtawi hastily climbed the steps to the top where he, too, came against the cold, heavy stone above him.

"There's no opening over here, sir."

People started climbing the stairs. The realization of what had just happened began to sink in. The shock was overwhelming. Murmurs began rising to shouts and shrieks.

"Where is Pharaoh?"

"He's gone."

"No, no… this can't be happening!"

"Are we going to die?"

"I thought we were going to be freed."

"Is there any other way out of here?"

Many of the frantic partygoers pushed back into the crypt to discuss the next move they needed to make. As they shouted back and forth an ominous grating sound echoed through the pit and a second stone door slid shut, closing the entrance to the crypt. Everyone heard this door close. Some of them ran back to see this second door and were shocked to see Ammit, the Swallower of the Dead, carved in the door, glaring at them.

Sobs and wailing rose as the desperate rabble ran back and forth in a futile attempt at deliverance.

"I knew it! I had a bad feeling about this," said Bakuru, hanging his head and turning away from the door.

Soknue just stood there, his face blank and lost.

Amaké took a torch and stood on one of the tables.

"Listen to me, people. Listen to me. The more commotion you make, the faster you will use up the air. Maybe the soldiers can break through the stone somehow. Stay calm."

His pleas went unheard and the clamor increased. Amaké and Intef sat with their sobbing wives, contemplating their fate. They would never be free. The punishment was death, and had been since the very beginning.

"Wijin was right. We should have listened and not been so bull-headed," Amaké shouted to his brother over the din. He leaned back against the wall and closed his eyes. "So, this is it."

The shocking turn of events brought many to a state of sobriety as they sought for a means of escape. They frantically checked out any new spot and direction to see if, just maybe, there was some secret passage to the surface. People were shouting and pressing against each other as the level of panic rose.

The young, naked dancers became objects of the mob's violence. Groping hands and gripping arms struck terror in them and they screamed in fear and pain.

The head soldier shouted, "Get in there and protect those innocent girls. Let's get this mob under control. Use your blades as necessary."

A new guard spoke to the commander.

"What shall I do, sir? This is my first assignment outside the palace."

"Stay with me, lad. We must use force to maintain some kind of order. Follow my lead," answered the commander.

"Forgive me for asking, sir, but what is your name?" Nebtawi asked.

"I am Zebel, commander of Osorkon's private security detail. Take courage, lad. Our time here is short. Make it count. Do your duty."

The minutes seemed like hours as the soldiers pressed back against the panicked mob. Fear was palpable. Doom began to settle. Injuries inflicted by the guards restrained the most objectionable resistors. As the oxygen was being used up, the torch lights began to flicker and dim, until the whole cavern subsided into total darkness.

Zebel, still on alert, realized that the end was near. As the people stopped stirring, he sat down and waited. The only sounds were crying and moaning.

My work is done, he said to himself. *All hope is lost.*

Two days later, the last ones to succumb to the lack of oxygen were Amaké and Intef. They were still sitting, facing each other with their dead wives between them.

There is no pain, thought Amaké. *I just want to sleep. So this is death.*

He drifted in and out of sleep, until finally he slumped over, never to open his eyes again.

8

NEW LIFE

It was two days past the full moon, and the pale light reflected off the sand.

Amenemope jumped off his chariot just in time as it toppled over the edge of a sand dune that he had misjudged because of the darkness of the night. The horses screamed as the chariot tumbled down the bank, dragging the horses with it.

At the bottom of the dune, the four horses lay still amidst the mangled chariot and tangled reins. They were the best horses in the kingdom, and they remained reasonably calm, as they had been trained. Amenemope made his way down the steep bank to the distraught mares. Reaching the twisted pile of the crippled chariot, he knew that it was a lost cause. The horses whinnied as he circled the disfigured, once-glorious machine built of wood and overlaid with gold. The chariot itself was encrusted with gems of every size and color.

He moved in close to get a good look at the horses. *Oh no*, he thought. *Star has the chariot tongue piercing her abdomen, and Nuru obviously has a broken leg. Iset and Dawn seem like they may be reasonably unharmed. My excellent beauties, what have I done to you?* He carefully unhitched all the horses and led the uninjured ones to the back of the chariot, where he tied them. Then he went back to the injured mares and stroked their flanks. Star nickered in response to her master's touch.

"You are breaking my heart, my beauties. We have had many adventures together. What I must do now grieves me greatly, but I cannot let you suffer. And here we are out in the middle of nowhere. There is no help for us here."

"Hello?" a voice called out from the top of the dune.

Amenemope slowly drew his sword and pointed it toward the figure coming down the bank. As the man got closer Amenemope could see he was not young. He was strong, reasonably well dressed, wearing a decent kilt, and wrapped in a sturdy cloak. *Surely he can't be one of the criminals from the pyramid at the crypt. Did the doors not close correctly? If so, all my work is undone*, Amenemope thought in a fearful rage. *Thirteen years I planned for this to save my ba from the torment of Ammit, and now this. Will I ever achieve security for my existence in the next world? It seems as though life with my family in paradise is constantly at risk. Getting back to Thebes without my chariot is bad enough, and now I have to deal with this stranger and who knows what else!*

"Where did you come from?" Amenemope snapped in a fury, still pointing his sword.

Wijin could see a man marching towards him, and suddenly realized it was Pharaoh Amenemope, Supreme Ruler, the most powerful man in Egypt — staring at him with anger in his eyes and sword drawn, ready to cut him down where he stood.

He dropped to the ground, arms outstretched, pressing his face against the sand in obeisance. Wijin could hear Amenemope walking over to him and felt the blade of his sharp sword pressing against the back of his neck.

"My great king, I am Wijin. I have been working at the pyramid that you, Lord of Life, created. I arrived for the banquet at the crypt this very morning. During the banquet, my friends and I went outside for some fresh air. My friends were plotting to go back there days after the feast was over and ransack it, but I would have no part of it. I decided to take advantage of your promise of freedom right away, not wanting to be caught up in another one of their schemes."

The blade's pressure lessened on Wijin's neck. *This man speaks the truth. The regret in his demeanor is unmistakable.* Amenemope pulled back his blade, sheathed it and ordered him to stand.

"Did you see your friends return to the crypt?" he asked.

Wijin kept his head bowed, feeling the weight of Amenemope's authority.

"Yes, Lord of Life, I glanced back and saw them enter."

"If I find that you speak untruths to me in this, or ever, you will lose your life immediately, do you know that?"

"I understand, great Pharaoh. I speak the truth. I swear on my life," Wijin said, maintaining his position.

Relief spread through Amenemope when he heard his words.

What shall I do with this man? Was he the reason Osiris held me back? I must question him further. I can't afford to make a mistake here.

"Do you know why I ask these things, Wijin? ... Wijin ... Wijin. I have heard that name. Let me think. Ah, yes. Lord Khnum spoke of Wijin. Now I remember. He said he had placed Wijin as overseer at the pyramid. Are you that Wijin?"

"I am that man, Great One," he replied.

"Well, Wijin, that explains why you are not dressed in rags like the others and perhaps other things as well. So I say again, do you know why I ask these things?"

"I do not know why you ask, Great One."

"All of you were condemned to death the minute you dishonored the resting places of our sleeping fathers, the very minute you walked into their tombs," Amenemope answered evenly. "The penalty is being carried out as we speak. Your friends are granted freedom, but they will never enjoy it."

Wijin fidgeted slightly as he started to understand what Pharaoh was saying.

"Do you really think I would just let all the criminals against this very Egypt go free? Your friends and all the other pestilence of Egypt will be enjoying their freedom in that crypt for all time. They will never again see the sun, moon or stars. Look at me, Wijin. What do you say for yourself, now that you know what the outcome truly is for this desecration?"

Wijin looked into Pharaoh's face with tears welling up in his eyes.

"I have no words. I ... I am guilty and should die like the rest of them."

He sank to his knees and offered his neck.

"Get up. I can still use you," Amenemope said, impressed by Wijin's willingness to die. "Do you know how to butcher a horse? Two of my prize mares are badly injured and need finishing."

"Yes, I do," he answered with confidence.

Amenemope walked over to the two wounded horses and slit their throats. He handed the dagger to Wijin and said, "You can use this to cut up some meat for the trip back."

Wijin couldn't believe what had just happened. He was about to die, and should have, but he didn't. And Amenemope had just asked him to do something he was very good at, having been a butcher by trade many years ago.

Wijin took the dagger and skinned the beautiful horses, then carved the meat into slabs.

"I am thinking that if we wish to cook this horse meat while we are still in the desert, we will need wood for a fire. We could use the poles to which the horses were harnessed to make a pole-drag to carry all that we need to take with us. Can I have your permission to disassemble your chariot to create such a device?"

"That is a good idea. I will never drive that chariot again, it is so damaged. Do whatever you see fit with it," answered Pharaoh. *This man is most resourceful.*

Wijin ran over to the damaged chariot and removed all the gold and gems, putting them into separate piles. Amenemope noticed the expertise with which Wijin stripped the chariot and commented, "It is clear that butchering is not your only skill."

"I have always done my best at any task that comes to my hand," he smiled sheepishly. "And I was taught this skill by an expert."

Wijin broke the poles away from the body of the chariot and set them aside. As he continued tearing down the chariot, he came across the compartment which held all of Pharaoh's golden jewelry. He took the bag that held the items and gave it to Amenemope.

"These are yours, my Lord. I give them to you so you can see that I have no designs on them," said Wijin.

"You are an honorable man, Wijin. You will notice there are also some tools in that storage box. They are suited for repairing the chariot, and will probably serve for taking it apart."

Wijin took the tools and disassembled the damaged vehicle. He then took the poles and crossed them part way from one end, assembled a basket-shaped carrier and secured it to the crossed poles with reins from the dead horses. He attached the box which held the tools and jewelry, then gathered up some wood from the chariot and put it in the basket.

"The water skins for the horses fell off the chariot when it tumbled down. We must retrieve them or the horses won't be able to go the distance. Hopefully they are not damaged," said Amenemope.

Wijin found them nearby. One was torn, the water spilled, but the others were intact. He fitted all but two of them in the basket.

"We could each carry one of these," Wijin said. "The basket is quite full. I also found a water skin and some extra bread in one of the huts before I left the crypt."

"Good," replied Pharaoh. "This first ride will be the hardest. There are supplies at the oasis which we must reach before we can stop."

"I can also save space by compacting the gold plating which was on the chariot." Wijin said as he selected a broken wheel hub, and using it as a hammer, molded the thin gold sheets into small blocks.

Amenemope strolled around watching Wijin as he deftly hammered the thin gold strips. Reaching into the folds of his white linen kilt, he pulled out a small pouch. He walked over to the pile of gems that Wijin had pried from the chariot and put them in the pouch. Wijin gave the gold blocks to Pharaoh, who added them to the bag that held his gold jewelry. Then he gathered the tools and put them in the compartment. Pharaoh added the bag of gold. And thus all was secured.

"It looks as though we are finished here," said Amenemope. "Do you ride?"

"I have not had occasion to ride a horse, Great One," replied Wijin.

"You shall learn tonight. I think I would like the pole-drag hooked up to Iset, whom I will ride. You can ride Dawn. She has a gentle disposition. When it comes to horses, I suppose I am the expert. We must keep up a steady pace to reach the first oasis by morning. We will find supplies there. I hope you ate your fill tonight. It has to last until the morning.

They finished breaking camp, mounted up and headed towards the pyramid. They made good progress along the established trail. The pale light was adequate for them to see their way. Wijin found riding a horse to be a wonderful experience for the first couple of hours, but then his backside began to complain. There was nothing to be done about it, however. It had to be endured.

The night seemed long. The road was unfamiliar to both the men and the beasts, and in the dimness it seemed as though they were traveling endlessly to nowhere. They spaced their rest stops as far apart as the horses could bear, and conservatively dispersed the drinking water. Even then, it was an hour past dawn when they finally saw the small cluster of trees and buildings that promised their destination.

The men dismounted the weary steeds and walked around to stretch and relieve stiffness. Between the two light brown buildings was a water trough for the horses. Wijin went to the well and drew water for the horses, filling the trough. The horses began to drink noisily. Pharaoh went into one of the huts and found a container of feed grain which he brought outside for them.

Small lizards scurried away from doors and walls as Wijin walked around the meagre, but well-built huts. Inside were numerous containers which held an assortment of dried foods.

I remember this place from our trip to the crypt, thought Wijin, *but the supplies have been replenished since we were here: figs and dates and even several kinds of nuts. How welcome. I am as ready for a meal and a rest as those horses. They did well, considering the tumble they took last night. I would like to check out the other hut. This one seems smaller. Maybe the larger one is more interesting.*

Entering the larger hut, he noticed a shield and spear propped up for easy access on the way out. In one corner was a small shrine to Osiris, and next to that, a sleeping cot which was more substantial and of better quality than a number of other cots that were piled up in the far corner. *This must be where Pharaoh will sleep. That is a better cot than I have ever slept in. I could sleep anywhere today though, I am so spent.*

He surveyed the rest of the space and returned to where Amenemope was sitting in the shade. *I wonder why he keeps looking at me*, thought Wijin. *I don't think he distrusts me as much as he did at first, but he is still skeptical. All I can do is be myself, and hope that is enough. I know he finds me useful. I like him and I think he is fair. Perhaps I can win him over yet.*

He smiled. "This place seems well suited for our needs."

Pharaoh said, "It will do. Let's have something to eat and then we can rest now before the next part of our trip toward the pyramid. You can take one of the cots piled up in that hut, and take it to the other shed. I'll sleep here."

He got up, unhitched the pole-drag, curried the horses, and tethered them while Wijin assembled food from the cache and cooked some of the horse meat. He even found some beer there, and that would go down especially well, he reckoned.

Sleep came quickly to the sojourners. Several hours had gone by when, for reasons he could not fathom, Wijin awoke with a deathly sick feeling in his gut. He got up and, brushing away the sand that had accumulated on his face, he walked outside into the searing heat of the desert. He let his eyes adjust to the bright sunlight, and looked towards the horses, which nickered in restless apprehension. He began moving in their direction to calm them, and then stopped short as he saw the tracks of a desert lion going back and forth between the two shelters. Panic gripped Wijin as he remembered the lion that visited the pyramid and killed Kuric. He looked around, waiting for it to attack at any second. He scanned the ground to see if he could figure out where the lion was at that moment. The tracks were quite a jumble, but as he glanced over at the entrance to Amenemope's hut, he could clearly see tracks entering, but not exiting. A wave of dread engulfed him. Slowly he crept over to the hut and peeked in through the crack between the door flap and the wall.

As his eyes adjusted to the dim interior light, his worst fears were realized. Amenemope lay sleeping on his cot with his feet towards the door, but the lion stood at the head of his bed, staring intently at the helpless ruler with cruel, hungry, yellow eyes. Beside the cot was a large storage box which held extra clothes for Pharaoh. The massive lion silently hopped up on the black wooden box and perched like a living gargoyle, ready to make a feast of the Pharaoh with her frightening teeth. She stared down at Amenemope and then up at the door flap that Wijin had moved as he began to enter.

The desert lioness seemed unable to decide what to do. She nodded her head, looking back and forth between the two men. *Come in and meet me. I dare you! Yes, yes, come in*, the desert warrior seemed to be saying. Her piercing yellow eyes were enough to make Wijin want to retreat quickly. Making up her mind, the cat placed her huge clawed paw on the cot's headboard and readied herself to lunge down and attack the sleeping Pharaoh.

Wijin fought down the panic that surged through him trying to dungeon his will. He remembered the spear that stood leaning against the wall just inside the door, and swiftly reached for it. The noise woke Amenemope. Peering through clouded eyes, he saw Wijin standing at the foot of his bed, spear in hand, with a frantic, hateful look on his face. The haziness of sleep immediately disappeared, replaced by the horror of an impending spear thrust. He opened his mouth to let out a tirade of curses aimed at his perceived aggressor, when Wijin suddenly held up his finger as if to tell him to keep quiet. Wijin hurled the spear with such force that it would have killed any living thing. The spear flew by, missing Amenemope completely. Enraged by his assailant, he lit into him verbally with such force, that he didn't even notice the drops of blood speckling his shoulders. He reached for his sword, ready to attack Wijin, when the dirty, yellow lion collapsed on the bed, pinning him to his cot. He shouted in alarm. Wijin rushed in, snatched the sword out of Pharaoh's hand, and slit the twitching lion's throat. After dropping the blade to the ground, he grabbed the lion that was now lying across one side of Amenemope's shoulder and pulled the three hundred pound beast to the floor. Blood pooled beside the cot, making a large red puddle that slowly seeped into the packed sand floor.

Amenemope was soaked with blood, and the shock of what had just happened to him took a few minutes to dissipate. He had seen battles before, but this was the first time he had been surprised so ferociously, and he sat on his cot, trembling uncontrollably. He was unable to speak as Wijin dragged the lion outside. Wijin re-entered the hut with exclamations of nervous laughter.

"By the gods, that was close! Did you see that? Are you all right? It is a good thing that spear was there. And I got her on the first throw! I never did anything like that before! I'm shaking like a leaf!"

"You had better sit down, too. Let us have some beer to calm us. It was truly fearful, having that wild animal right in the hut."

They sat together, covered in blood and dirt, letting time and beer settle their nerves, as they relived the attack and considered other possible outcomes.

"You fought well for a butcher, Wijin," said Amenemope, smiling. "I thank you for saving my life. You have shown yourself worthy — more than worthy. This is a sign from Osiris. The first thing that I must ask you now, is that you must not reveal what has just happened here. Can you do that?" He waited and watched Wijin considering whether or not he could keep such a triumph to himself.

"Yes, Majesty, if that is what you wish, I can promise to keep it a secret," said Wijin. Once the matter was decided in his mind, his thoughts quickly shifted to the realization that he really didn't consider himself to be a butcher any more.

"You continue to please me, Wijin. I can see why Lord Khnum spoke so highly of you. Tell me, how long did you work as overseer for the pyramid?"

"For the first few years, I worked as the architect's assistant. He taught me much — reading, writing, figuring plans, construction. It was most exciting. Then after Amsu was gone, I directed operations for about five years. I learned much during that time too. Even though I was a slave, that work pleased me more than any other," Wijin replied.

"I see. I consider myself a fair judge of character, and everything I have seen and heard from you confirms to me that you are a capable and trustworthy man," said Amenemope. "As you can realize, I have lost a number of staff recently, and I would like you to join me as my personal assistant. This can be a small role, or if you develop enough skills and are loyal, you could find yourself becoming an important man in Egypt. What do you think of that? Does that sound like something you could 'do your best' at?"

Wijin sank to his knees and bowed his head.

"It would be my great honor to serve you, Lord of Life," Wijin replied, realizing that Pharaoh also thought of him as much more than a butcher. "I am your humble servant."

"There is something else. As a member of my staff, you will be well-compensated during my life. But I will require you to fulfil Osiris' command to me — when my life is ended, you must also end yours. Could you do that?"

"From now on, my life exists to serve you, Great One, and I believe I can fulfill this demand," he answered, thinking, *And then I will be reunited with my beloved Akila.*

"Rise, Wijin, and take this token as proof of your pledge to me." He retrieved one of the golden cubes from the bag and held it out to Wijin.

Wijin accepted the block of gold, held it to his heart and bowed.

"I promise you my faithful service" he said wholeheartedly.

"Well now, let us get cleaned up, have a meal and get packed and ready to leave. I don't think there will be any more sleeping today. The horses also must be fed, watered and prepared to go."

Before they left, they set fire to the huts which had served their purposes, mounted the horses and rode off towards the pyramid.

9

GOLDEN CHARIOT

It had been a week since the slaves arrived at the pyramid. Khnum was relieved to see the supply wagons coming from the capital with all the food and drink for the banquet. He thought to himself, *at last they are here. Keeping these people busy has been difficult. It's been nearly two weeks since the supply train made its way past here for the celebration at the crypt. I haven't heard anything. There are less than one hundred of them, but if I don't keep them busy, they will get into trouble. Moving sand is an unsatisfying task, but it gives them something to do. The statue of Amenemope is well covered now, and the device to hold back the sand from the pyramid door is well filled. So this will be the last day or so for this make-work project.*

The weary workers saw the wagons pull in at the work site and stopped what they were doing. They began to gather in groups and talk about the new arrivals.

They are as glad to get on with this as I am, thought Khnum. He went to show the visitors where they could set up, and explain the arrangements for the meal in the pyramid. The banquet was set for tomorrow evening.

The next afternoon, Khnum was shuttling between the slave overseers and the workers for the banquet, making sure things were progressing on both fronts. He heard a commotion on the trail, and when he looked up he was delighted to see Amenemope riding in a golden chariot, entering the pyramid compound. Even more surprising was the sight of Wijin, dressed in a dark green top and a bright white, pleated kilt, driving the chariot.

Well, look at that, he smiled inwardly. *It looks as though Wijin didn't run away as I told him, but befriended Egypt's most powerful man. And he's even driving Pharaoh's chariot. I wonder how he managed to ingratiate himself so quickly. Hopefully I will get to hear the story. Wijin has many wonderful qualities, but it usually takes Pharaoh some time before he trusts anyone. He's always on guard, wary of sabotage. But he has obviously discovered the potential of this diamond-in-the-rough as I have. Good for him.*

As the chariot drew to a halt in front of him, he reached out and took the reins to steady the winded mares. After engaging the wheel brake, Amenemope stepped off the chariot's platform. Khnum immediately bowed to the ground, showing his submission.

"Rise, Khnum."

Khnum stood but kept his eyes on the ground.

"It is good to see you again," began Pharoah. "It looks as though all is in readiness for the banquet tonight. It that so?"

"Yes, Majesty. All is prepared for the celebration. Would you like to come to my tent so that you can refresh yourself before it begins? They will be ready to start in a while, and that will give you time to relax."

"That sounds like an excellent suggestion. Wijin, take the horses over to the animal shed. Someone there can look after them. I would like the horses brushed, fed and watered. Make sure they have them hitched to the chariot again and ready to return to Thebes tonight after the festivities. You know what supplies we want on board. When you are finished there, come back to Khnum's tent to wait with us for the meal," said Amenemope.

"Yes, my lord," answered Wijin, and off he went, driving the chariot.

After a servant had washed Pharaoh's feet, and cool drinks were delivered, the two men sat down and relaxed.

Amenemope leaned back and eyed Khnum for several seconds. Khnum shifted uncomfortably in his seat. He guessed what was coming.

"It appears that you have been busy revealing secrets. Isn't that so?"

A sickening feeling welled up within him, dispelling the joy of seeing his friend again.

"Who else have you warned, my impertinent one?" Pharaoh asked, determined to know the whole truth. "Be careful how you answer this question. Your life may depend upon it."

Khnum hung his head and sank to his knees, recalling the time that the king had told him to gather the criminals for the work project.

"Great One, I assumed that something was going to happen to the workers after I asked about it and you did not answer. I told Wijin to escape when the time was right. Wijin was the only one I warned of my suspicions. I swear on my life that this is true. I have never lied to you."

"No, you have not, but it is not your place to be freeing my slaves. If I had found Wijin to be of a different character, we would be having a much different conversation right now," Amenemope said as his finger tapped the hilt of his sword.

Wijin approached the tent door, and looked in on this scene of power and submission. He turned to leave when Pharaoh bid him enter.

"Come in, Wijin, we were just talking about you. I have asked the good architect, here, what information he has been sharing. I want you to tell me exactly what he said to you."

Wijin looked uncertainly at Pharaoh, then at Khnum, and back to Pharaoh again.

"He came to tell me that my wife had been killed in an accident. To assuage my grief, he told me this — 'When you feel the time is right, run, run far away from here. I have had this sense of danger since the beginning.' That is all he said to me, and only once. I didn't understand it at the time, but then when the celebration was held at the crypt, suddenly it came back to me, and I risked everything at his word. I just walked away into the desert."

Amenemope sipped his wine, looked at the two men, and considered Wijin's words.

"This matter troubles me. Such well-developed plans for such noble reasons. It takes only a small error to undo many years of hard work. I must judge whether or not I can continue on my course, depending solely on the strength of your word. If both of you have spoken the truth, then the plan may succeed, but if you have spoken falsely, the results could prove grievous, indeed.

He turned the cup in his hand and watched the wine swirling. He took another sip.

"I have been giving this a great deal of thought. As it turns out, it was most advantageous that Wijin was available at the crypt. There were some difficulties, and he assisted me most ably."

He paused and fixed his gaze on them. "I have decided. I will take you at your word. Khnum, you have never let me down before, and Wijin, you are proving to be a welcome addition to my staff. I wish to keep you both close to me, however. I trust it will serve us all well."

Relief and gratitude were evident on the faces of the men, but they didn't speak, noting that Pharoah had more to say.

"I have made a decision regarding your future as well, architect. I'm sure you have wondered what your fate would be at the end of this day. In spite of your error in judgment, I find that you are a most valuable resource and an important confidant. You will also prove useful in training Wijin in matters of service and government. Rather than join the ranks within the pyramid, I want you to remain outside with Wijin and my chariot. You will return with us to Thebes, and continue in your current role as architect and general adviser. Do not become complacent, however. I must remain vigilant towards all who serve me. Any lapses in loyalty will not be tolerated. Do I make myself clear?"

I am saved, thought Khnum. *A close call, though.*

"Yes, Great One, I understand completely. I am your servant," he replied.

"Good. Now please leave me. I would like to have some time to myself to rest before this next 'celebration.' Come and get me after everyone is assembled in the pyramid. We will talk some more regarding your future in my kingdom, but this will do for now."

Wijin and Khnum bowed and retreated outside the tent. Khnum took a deep breath as they made their way to the shaded seating area behind the supply tent. Both men looked relieved that they would live to see another day.

"It is so good to see you, Wijin. I'm glad you are here. In the midst of all this turbulence, it seems as though we are survivors. It pleases me that we will have years together for living and working. And look at you — not only alive, but rising to the highest rank. You are to be congratulated."

"Thank you — and many thanks also for your warning so long ago. I had no idea of the value of your words. My life has changed completely. I used to be a poor butcher with no prospects, and now I will live in a great house. Pharaoh has given me his signet ring as a symbol of the authority he has invested me with, this gold chain to wear around my neck, and these wonderful clothes."

He spread his arms wide for Khnum to see.

"It suits you, my friend. It suits you."

The time had come for the pit crew to enter the pyramid for their banquet. At first glance it seemed as though they were entering a doorway at the base of a great sand dune. They had been here for a couple of weeks, however, and knew what was hidden beneath the contours of the land. The women who had been painters were much more familiar with what had been covered, and all of them were puzzled as to why all the grandeur of the pyramid, the statue of Amenemope and the sphinxes that bordered the perimeter had been concealed. They had no knowledge that all the hieroglyphs they had applied to the walls revealed detailed explanations of the thefts and desecration of the forefathers' tombs. They could not guess what other secrets were recorded in cryptic messages at places within the site.

They knew only hard labor, the heat of the day, the overseer's oppression, hunger and want.

But on this day, hunger would be satisfied. They lined up and filed into the pyramid like sheep to the slaughter. They were oblivious to everything but the banquet they had been promised.

Esanithn and his wife, Dendrith-Amon, made their way through the pyramid entrance. The cramped doorway forced them to crouch and go in single file until they got inside. The first room they came to was modest in size. They followed those ahead of them, drawn by the savory mingling of food aromas. Roast lamb, beef, rice, steamed vegetables, various kinds of bread, as well as various sweetmeats tantalized their taste buds as they moved past the heavily laden tables.

"We'll never be able to try all of these things," said Dendrith-Amon. "It's been so long since we've had much to eat. Our stomachs can't bear it. What a wonderful feast. And look … they have beer and wine, too. What a special way to celebrate the end of our labors."

"Come along, my dear," said her husband. "It looks as though we have to find a place to sit in one of these other rooms along the hallway. It isn't very suitable to have such a meal in here. I wonder why they didn't just have the festivities outside. We could all be together that way. And if Pharaoh comes, how will he be able to talk to us when we're all separated into groups like this?"

"Oh, don't worry about that," replied Dendrith-Amon. "It seems as though we can look around in here freely. I would love to see as many rooms as I can. The art work on the walls is so beautiful."

They found a spot and settled down with their plates and cups. As others gathered, the rooms filled up, becoming crowded, and the temperature rose. The air became stuffy.

Still, there was an atmosphere of joyfulness. Even though their clothes were tattered, they did their best to look good. The women used black carbon of burnt wood to highlight their eyes and deepen the color of their nipples to appear more alluring. Some had found smooth little sticks which they inserted in their ear piercings to add style. There was chatting and laughter as they made their way into the rooms that lined the hall.

Soldiers and servers circulated among the people. Then the musicians and dancing girls arrived, increasing the merriment with music and dancing.

Esanithn reflected on the journey that had been forced on him and his wife. They had been in love all their lives, it seemed. Their parents had signed their marriage contract when they were both twelve. It had been a good union. The problem had arisen when his wife's brother, leader of a band of thieves, had hidden in their home from the authorities, along with the spoils of his thieving. *I knew that would get us into trouble*, he had thought at the time. *Dendri is so easy going. She never thought of the possible consequences. Then we were all sentenced to this terrible life. I love her dearly, but I wonder how it will end. Can we finally break free of this servitude and go back to living our lives? I hope so.*

Night had fallen a couple of hours before, and in the darkness, the sounds of music and voices echoed into the void around them. Wijin and Khnum were now the lone occupants of the outdoors at the pyramid. Everyone else had crowded inside to feast and celebrate. Pharaoh had decided to have a light meal outside with the two men who now waited for the evening's activities to conclude.

"Pharaoh seemed reluctant to go into the pyramid," said Khnum. "And he was so quiet while we ate. I wonder if he is all right."

"I expect he is not all right at all. I can't imagine what it takes to send all those people to their deaths. I don't understand what has prompted him to do what he is doing. It seems quite extreme to me," replied Wijin.

"He is doing this for the welfare of Egypt, Wijin. He is a good man, and the decisions he has made have been required of him by the gods. It is not up to us to question his motives," said Khnum.

"I have much to learn. It pleases me that you will be my instructor.

I can hardly fathom what has happened to me in this short time. Two weeks ago I was a criminal, destined for death, and now I am the assistant to the king of the whole land," said Wijin.

They had brought Amenemope's and Khnum's chariots, ready to go, to the supply shed and tethered the horses. They brushed the mares' copper colored coats while they waited. The grateful horses leaned into the brush strokes, relishing the extra attention.

"We have a while to wait. Would you like to sit and have some wine?" said Khnum.

They sat down and sipped the excellent vintage. They chatted some, and also spent time in silence, each with their own thoughts.

Wijin suppressed the anxiety that welled up within him. He remembered only too well the similar scene he had experienced at the crypt just a couple of weeks previously. Hearing the music, he remembered the naked dancers at the crypt, their athletic bodies moving sensuously to the slow beat of the musicians' drums. There had been happiness and pleasure that night, but it had ended so horribly for everyone else. Dread washed over him.

He leaned back in his seat and looked at the night sky. *This reminds me of the time when Akila was here with me and we saw that beautiful display of shooting stars. I was fully content that night. And now she is gone. It's been so long since she died in that fall, and the pain in my heart is still almost more than I can bear sometimes. I can't see her as clearly in my mind's eye anymore, and I wonder if I will ever be happy again. Life is strange. I have more favor now than I have ever had before, and yet without her by my side, everything else falls short for me. But I must go on. What else can I do?*

Tears filled his eyes.

In the flickering torchlight, Khnum glanced at Wijin, and saw that his friend was in distress. He put his hand on his shoulder.

"Take comfort, my friend. You have had a rocky ride. And you have suffered a great loss. I know no one can replace Akila. I, too, have lost a woman I loved. It changes our lives, does it not? But at least we both have a future, and that can give us hope."

Khnum had been right. Pharaoh had been reluctant to enter the pyramid. He had been surprised at what a toll it had taken on him to close the crypt and walk away. *I drank too much that night*, he thought. *It was as though their voices cried out to me as they perished, pleading for mercy. The burden of their deaths weighs heavily on my heart. And now I must do it again. I must be more deliberate tonight. If I had had my wits about me at the crypt, I wouldn't have driven my horses off the road and down the hill. At least I have someone to drive the chariot tonight, and the support of those two good men.*

He bent low as he crossed the threshold in all his royal regalia — golden pectoral, rings, arm bracelets, and gold edged white kilt. He stood up straight when space permitted and strode into the first room. This serving area was crowded with people who were chatting and laughing. When they saw him, they all turned towards him and bowed. Conversation ceased.

He smiled and nodded his head to them.

"I trust you are enjoying yourselves tonight. I have come to thank you for your hard work all these years in building these important monuments. You have served me well, and I am pleased with the results. Many of you have been forced into slavery because of your crimes against the crown of Egypt, and tonight I am announcing that your debt is paid. All records of your wrongdoing have been expunged."

The people cheered and clapped in gratitude.

This time Amenemope did something different. He lingered in their midst, much to their surprise. A few people were so bold as to express their appreciation and adoration.

Then he moved on to the other rooms, made the same announcement and spent some time in each place, observing and listening to the eager throng. Esanithn and Dendrith-Amon spoke to him, telling him how much they enjoyed the dinner and what a thrill it was to meet him in person.

These are my people, he thought. *How can I do this terrible thing to all these individuals? It is not only the thieves that are doomed. There are also many staff members, cooks, guards, the pretty young dancers, all those who have any knowledge of these two building projects. And there are many others as well, such as this gentle couple. What possible harm could they have done? Is it right to condemn the innocent along with the guilty?*

The more he circulated among the crowd, the more he became distracted by his own doubts. Within his mind he called out to Osiris — *why must my heart bleed for these people? Please give me a sign. Am I truly doing the right thing?*

Osiris was there, listening to the pleas of his soul. He saw the anguish Amenemope was experiencing and considered the lengths he had gone to in atoning for his sins against Ma'at. The god reached into Pharaoh's being and relieved his mind of the despair he felt for all the lost souls that were about to meet their end. Amenemope watched members of his staff chatting and dancing, and observed happy reunited couples, and many friends enjoying each other's company. Slowly the heavy weight of sadness for the impending loss of workers and acquaintances lifted, and he felt a quiet detachment come over him. He had no feeling of guilt holding him back.

Now is the time, he thought. He retreated from the celebration and made his way outside.

Nekht-Ankh, his chief scribe and assistant, hurried behind him and bowed.

"Great Pharaoh, Living Forever, is it time? Are you going to close the pyramid now?"

Amenemope turned suddenly in surprise and stared at the scribe.

"This is the culmination of all our plans," said Nekht-Ankh. "All these years of building the monument to your greatness, and your own tomb, and punishing those criminals who robbed the resting places of the forefathers — it is all coming together on this very night."

Pharaoh backed away from him, taking steps further from the pyramid.

"You are presumptuous, Nekht-Ankh. These plans that you mention are not your plans. They do not involve you, except for the contribution you made to the designs. You do not understand why I have decided to do what has been done," replied Pharaoh.

"But we have worked together so closely. You have had every confidence in me. I thought your trust was because of your affection for me. You know that I serve you with all the love in my heart," said the scribe, looking into Amenemope's eyes with heartfelt sincerity.

Pharaoh paused and returned his gaze. *Why did I reveal my plans to him? What a mistake that was. I need to be cautious how I handle this now.* He chose his words carefully.

"It is true that you have served me well. You are a talented man. I have greatly appreciated the contribution you have made to the building projects. Do not concern yourself at this time. I have simply come outside to get some air and to pray by myself. I want to be left alone. Now go back to the celebrations inside. I will let you know if I require anything."

"As you wish, Majesty. I am your servant," replied the scribe. He bowed, turned back and entered the pyramid.

Across the way, Wijin and Khnum saw Pharaoh coming out of the doorway, followed by Nekht-Ankh. A short conversation ensued, and the scribe retreated into the pyramid. Wijin watched as Amenemope dropped to his knees and bowed his head.

"It's nearly time," said Wijin, getting up, suddenly alert.

Pharaoh said a prayer to Osiris, asking if there was anything left for him to do before closing the door. Peace surrounded him as if Osiris himself were wrapping his arms around him, telling him that he was pleased, and that everything was ready for the door to be closed.

Amenemope rose to his feet, found the rope which would close the door, and pulled it hard. A loud grating sound rumbled as the thick stone door slammed into place, sealing the pyramid's entrance.

Wijin could feel a lump in his throat and the shivers that ran down his spine. He could almost taste the panic that would soon escalate inside the pyramid. He reached inside his tunic and held the small cube of gold which Pharaoh had given him after he had saved him from the desert lion. While those unfortunate people would suffocate and die, the gold in his hand represented his escape to freedom and friendship with the most powerful man in Egypt.

Pharaoh then found the lever to release the sand which would completely conceal the doorway of the pyramid, and cause the appearance of the entire monument to fade into the surrounding landscape. He watched as the sand flowed and settled into place.

Inside the pyramid a loud scraping thud thundered throughout the entire structure, silencing all voices. Nekht-Ankh was closest to the door as it slid into place. Shock and alarm struck the scribe as he realized what had happened. He sank to his knees, looking at the large stone slab that blocked access to the outside. *How can this be happening? He cannot have shut me in here to die with all the others! How could he? Have I not served him better than any other? Have I not loved him more than any other?* He began to weep and wail. Although he knew his fate was sealed and the door would not open, he waited. The people came out of the rooms and gathered in the hallway, looking toward the door, questioning what had happened. A troop of guards muscled their way through the press of bodies, trying to escape the death trap. The soldiers surrounded the lone figure kneeling in front of the closed stone door.

"He said he was coming right back. I just have to wait," Nekht-Ankh sobbed hopelessly.

There was a rush to the exit as the priests started chanting spells of salvation to Amun. The rest of the people began to press towards the sealed door. The soldiers unsheathed their swords and demanded that everyone back up and return to where they had been. A few panicked men kept pushing and the soldiers cut them down.

Blood spattered on those who stood nearby. Esanithn and his wife Dendrith-Amon backed away from the horror. He put his arms around her to protect her from the violence — a tiny island of calm in a sea of chaos. She trembled as she tried to hold back her sobs of anguish. Then he picked her up and moved to a quieter room where there was a small open area on the floor. He sank to his knees and then lay on the floor, embracing her.

"It's all right, my dear. No matter what happens, we are together, now and always. I love you. It's all right," he whispered.

This time the oxygen was used up more quickly. The torches flickered and died, sending the pyramid into utter darkness.

Nekht-Ankh still sat in front of the great stone door waiting for his master like a heartsick lover until he finally succumbed to suffocation and breathed his last.

Eventually everyone entered the sleep of death. The pyramid was now as silent as the stones with which it was built.

Amenemope made his way to where Wijin and Khnum were waiting by the chariots.

"The deed is done," said Pharaoh. "I had thought we could return to Thebes tonight, but I have changed my mind. There is not enough moonlight to see the way, and after the mishap at the crypt, I would prefer to wait until we have daylight for the return trip. We have good accommodations here. Let's spend the night and head back in the morning. Could you see that the horses are unhitched and settled in?"

"Certainly," replied Khnum. You have already had a long day. I think that is a good idea. Is there anything else you require?"

"Could you bring some wine to my tent?" asked Amenemope. "The plan that Osiris revealed to me seemed a noble enough idea, but having to make it so by my own hand has not been so easy. In fact, I would be pleased if you would both join me for a while. Sleep will not come quickly, and some easy conversation would be welcome."

The next morning they had a small meal, fed the horses and hitched them to the chariots again. Khnum and Wijin inspected all the tents and huts, gathering things that were useful or valuable and placed them in a supply wagon. They hitched the wagon to a team of mules and waited while Amenemope surveyed the whole site and set fire to all the buildings. It was almost noon when he was satisfied that the ruin would be complete, counting on wind and weather to finish the job.

They headed back along the dusty path through the dunes — Khnum and Amenemope in the lead, and Wijin driving the wagon.

Wijin commented, "I'm getting lots of experience with animals here. It greatly improves the traveling — much faster and less tiring than walking."

Khnum replied, "I'm glad you like it. I think I could probably walk as fast as those mules. But you are right: it's worth the care that the beasts require."

As they ambled along, Pharaoh was lost in his own thoughts. A restlessness came over him, and as they drew near the outskirts of Thebes and he could see the towers of his palace in the distance, he thought, *I grow weary of this old place. We have lived here for too long and the refurbishing still seems to leave it dreary and unsatisfying. It's time for a change.*

When they arrived at the palace, Khnum showed Wijin where to take the wagon and they left Pharaoh. A servant led his horses and chariot to the barn while Pharaoh made his way into the palace to see Dalia. She was anxiously awaiting his return.

"I thought you were going to come back last night," she whispered as she entered his fervent embrace. "Did something happen?"

He continued to hold her close to himself, long and tender, and then he kissed her.

"My wonderful Dalia, what would I ever do without you? No matter what I must face in this life, you are always my comfort and my life. I decided to stay there for the night. Everything went according to plan but it was still a very long day. Let us walk in the garden and sit. I could use some food and refreshments also. The trip back was long and filled with hardships to my ka and I am depleted."

Dalia arranged for a meal to be brought to them in the garden and then followed him to the delightful shaded area among the trees and flowers.

"All the plans that have been made to appease Osiris have now been fulfilled. It has sometimes been difficult to see it through, but now it feels as though a great weight has been lifted from my shoulders," said

Pharaoh. "On the way back today, I was thinking that a change would be welcome. Tanis is where the center of commerce has shifted. It's right on the main trade route, as you know. Also the navy headquarters has relocated there, in the delta. And the palace there is much newer and more convenient. With some modifications, it could be made larger and more elegant than this one here. I believe I would like to shift the capital of the land permanently to Tanis, and leave Thebes behind. Tanis is much more modern and we could build a whole new center of operations there, which would be much better suited to the needs of running the country. There is better space for new temples, and lots of room for housing.

"I have spent too long on these matters of thieves and crypts. It's time for a fresh start and a new focus on the future of the land. What do you think?"

"It pleases me to hear you speak of new ventures, my love. I have seen the toll it has taken on you to do the will of Osiris. You have the devotion of the people, and it would be an ideal time to launch into new areas of growth. The land has prospered during your rule, and the people are grateful. They will surely support such an endeavor." Dalia got up and walked behind her husband. She put her arms around his shoulders and pressed her cheek against his. "My precious husband. You are the light of Egypt."

Tanis was located in the delta, much closer to the main trade routes along the great sea. It had been growing from a more modest recreational center to a hub of commerce. It was defended from aggressors by the navy, the best in that part of the world. The waterways in the delta made it awkward for armies to cross, but the rivers, blessed by the alluvial deposits from the yearly inundation of the Nile, made the land ideal for growing crops — many kinds of grain, vegetables, and fruits.

Tanis was built on higher ground, and wasn't subject to the consequences of the yearly flood. The climate was more pleasant than in Thebes, with lots of sunshine and cool breezes blowing in from the sea. Amenemope had always loved being there and he drew energy from the task of planning and overseeing the building of new temples and monuments as well as expanding his palace.

The city core contained a central square with a fountain, and a marketplace where shops of all kinds and beer halls did a brisk business. The smell of baked goods permeated the air. It was a vibrant community — bustling and busy. Outside of the commercial area, smaller homes were clustered along narrow streets, and further along, there were increasingly larger homes with gardens and trees, belonging to the wealthy and the influential. The roadways became wider and more spacious.

One walled area was the temple complex, the main focus of which was the great temple of Osiris. Eight lotus-flowered stone columns stood out in dazzling white, holding up the black painted roof of the cult's main entrance. Two large statues of Osiris, carved of black granite, stood in front of the temple at the edge of a large colonnaded courtyard. Fragrant myrrh trees filled the air with the holy perfume that was used in the daily ceremonies.

The other walled compound housed the royal palace. There had been a generous allowance of space for further development when it had first been built. The enlargement had begun as soon as Khnum's designs were ready. It was elegant and luxurious — a graceful vision in pale white marble. Within a year, Amenemope brought his entire household to Tanis and moved them into the expanding palace. Dalia was especially thrilled with the results. In addition, a large reflecting pool in the center of the grounds became a favorite place to spend time. The riot of colors in the gardens conveyed a sense of joy and well-being to everyone who entered there.

In the main courtyard by the front entrance stood two large alabaster statues of Amenemope, looking dignified and authoritative. On the base of the statues were written the wise proverbs of old. Inside, the high ceilings boasted ornate drawings of vines loaded with grapes, against a starry background. On the walls, scenes of daily life decorated much of the space. Along the halls were a number of niches which were small shrines, containing idols that were part of their religious heritage. The highly polished floors of blue slate echoed faintly as residents and staff made their way from room to room. Two guards, spears in hand, were positioned at the end of the first main hall that boasted double gold doors which led into the throne room. Perched on a dais at the far end of the room was Pharaoh's golden throne. High windows let in the brightness of the day's light and sea's breeze, and lining the walls were torches which provided a constant, comfortable glow when darkness had fallen. Incense burners, constantly charged, filled the immense room with a pleasant aroma. This was the heart of the palace, used both for government activities and for ceremonies and celebrations. Beyond this were the offices from which the business of running the country was conducted. The royal family's quarters occupied almost as much room again, and every convenience was included in the new décor.

This move has given us all a new start, thought Amenemope. *Now I can get on with the business of the future. I must also finish my book of wisdom for my son, Osorkon.*

Nemutptah sat ready for dictation, preparing to complete Amenemope's Book of Wisdom.

Chapter 25

Do not jeer a blind man nor tease a dwarf,
Neither interfere with the condition of a cripple.
Do not taunt a man who is in the hand of the gods,
Nor scowl at him if he errs.
Man is clay and straw,
And the god is the potter;
He overthrows and builds daily,
He impoverishes a thousand if He wishes.
He makes a thousand into examiners,
When He is in His hour of life.
How fortunate is he who reaches the West,
When he is in the hand of the gods.

Chapter 26

Do not stay in a tavern
And join someone greater than you,
Whether he be high or low in his station,
An old man or a youth:
But take as a friend for yourself someone compatible:
Re is helpful though he is far away. [1]

Amenemope continued dictating until late into the night, stopping only to let Nemutptah fill his ink-well. Words of instruction and wisdom poured out of Pharaoh's mouth like an unstoppable waterfall. When he finally stopped, he had composed a total of 29 chapters. Amenemope finished with chapter 30.

Chapter 30

Mark yourself these thirty chapters:
They please, they instruct,
They are the foremost of all books;
They teach the ignorant.
If they are read to an ignorant man,
He will be purified through them.
Seize them; put them in your mind
And have men interpret them, explaining as a teacher.
As to a scribe who is experienced in his position,
He will find himself worthy of being a courtier.
It is finished. [1]

Amenemope sat back, and closed his eyes, feeling content that he had poured his heart into this book for his son, the future pharaoh of Egypt.

[1] see bibliography

10

BA BIRD

Large ostrich feather fans held by young female slaves who methodically swished them back and forth created a tall, brightly-colored, dancing kaleidoscope that sent cool air tumbling over the royal bed.

It had been three weeks since Pharaoh had contracted the fever that now confined him to his personal quarters. They weren't sure what had caused it, but all the physicians' ministrations, and all the incantations of the priests had not helped. In fact, he was getting worse. As the days wore on and he had not been able to attend to the affairs of state, he had been meeting with his advisers and with his son, Osorkon, with the intention of turning over to him the double crown, making him the next Pharaoh. Amenemope was in his mid-fifties now, no longer a young man. It had been twelve years since they had moved to Tanis and created fresh visions for the country.

I must gather my thoughts and focus, thought the king. *It looks as though my time might be coming to an end. My son is in his thirties now, and well able to take over the reins of power. Each day it becomes more difficult for me to face the future. Things are good in the land now. I have loved my people and done my best to lead them. These last years have been particularly satisfying, with prosperity, growth and safety well established. With Wijin by my side, all that I have planned has been made easier to put into motion, as he has served me with distinction and excellence. The darkness is closing in on me again. I must sleep.*

He slipped into unconsciousness once more. Dalia sat by his side, and tenderly laid a cool moist cloth on his forehead.

"Rest now, my love," she said. "I will be here when you awake."

She had stayed by his side throughout the recent ordeal. As first wife, she had been far more than his spouse. They shared a deep and reciprocal love, a rare and precious partnership that extended far beyond what was deemed to be culturally normal, even into the area of ruling the great land of Egypt. As his strength began to fail, it had given Pharaoh confidence to know that Dalia would do all she could to see that things were attended to properly.

He roused again, struggling for breath.

"My beloved wife, embrace me. Give me the comfort of your arms," he said.

Dalia dismissed the attendants and lay close beside her husband. She put her arms around him and as she felt the shallowness of his breathing, tears filled her eyes and ran onto his cheek.

"Know this, my dearest, that I love you more than I can say. If love could restore you, you would always be well and strong," she said.

He replied, "I also love you more than life itself, my dearest sister, but I believe that it is my time to go to the scales. I cannot seem to come back from this affliction. I think I am ready. But it grieves me greatly that I may be separated from you, if only until you join me in paradise." He held her close.

The fever in his body soon drenched Dalia's light gown. She looked at the face she had loved through all the years, and took a little time to imprint on herself the familiar feel of his body against hers, realizing their time together was soon coming to an end. He drifted into unconsciousness again, and she extricated herself from his embrace.

The slave girls with the fans returned, and Dalia continued to cool him the best she could with wet towels.

After most of the morning had passed, he came around again, and drank a little wine mixed with poppy to relieve his misery.

The priests gathered around his bed, saying prayers. He also became aware of Osiris drawing near to him. He formed his own prayer in his mind. *I pray to you, Osiris, god of the dead, totem god of my life. Look upon me this day with favor. I believe I will soon be drawn to your bosom. Will you invite me to live in the Field of Reeds forever with you?*

As the day wore on, Dalia could see him slipping into the quicksand of death, as his breathing became even more labored.

"Go get Osorkon and Maatkara," she told her servant, "and also Wijin and Khnum. The end is near for the King. My husband will want to have these dear ones near as he finishes his earthly journey."

They had all been waiting to be summoned, even though they dreaded the coming moment. They gathered close around his bed, waiting for him to recognize them so they could say their good-byes.

The drug in the wine wore off, and he regained consciousness, opening his eyes. He was comforted to see his wife, children and the two men to whom he had been closest, all there together. No longer able to speak, he looked at each one, trying to convey with his eyes what was in his heart, and to bid each one, "farewell."

Maatkara wept openly. The men suppressed their emotion. As each of them spoke fondly to the dying man, the face of Osiris appeared above them and said to Amenemope, "Are you ready yet? Do you want to stop struggling? Are you ready for your deeds to be weighed?"

The high priest of the cult of Osiris stepped forward in a cloud of incense, and the low droning prayers of his under-priests filled the space. Amenemope lay back and let the prayers of the priests fill his mind and heart. He felt truly at peace. Eyes still open, he could see the wisps of incense making their way to the ceiling, slowly filling the entire room with its sharp scent. Finally, he breathed his last, and he was gone.

He awoke. The fever, the physical distress was gone. Everything was quiet and a soft blackness enfolded him. Amenemope turned around and reached out his arms, trying to find his way.

So this is death, he thought. *Guide me, Osiris, to your place of judgment. I have done all that you required of me, and I am ready to stand before you.*

His hands gently touched a wall and he proceeded forward into the absolute darkness. Keeping one hand on the wall he reached out in the opposite direction. His other hand touched another wall as if he were in a corridor. Again he started walking, the tips of his out-stretched fingers brushing lightly on each side of the black hallway. Amenemope hadn't walked more than a few steps when suddenly a circle of lamps surrounded him, illuminating everything. He was no longer in what he thought to be a hallway, but now he was in the middle of a slowly widening tunnel. The sides and ceiling were blue and white silk, the color of royalty. He continued forward and in a flash it opened into a room with no walls and no ceiling. A door frame was standing in front of him, blocking entrance to the remainder of the room.

"I will not permit you to enter through me," the jam of the door said, "unless you tell me my name."

"Plumb-Bob-in-the-Place-of-Truth is your name," Amenemope replied.

"Welcome," replied the door frame, which then vanished.

Amenemope cautiously entered the room, where he noticed that he was surrounded with the fluttering blue and white banners of kingship. Above the flags he saw stars everywhere as if he were floating in space. Questions were posed to him, as though the room itself was interrogating him. The room revolved slowly around him, and vertigo threatened to disorient him. He stood his ground, and the insistent questions came into focus.

I am well acquainted with all these matters, he thought, *and can easily answer all that is asked. I have a voice, I can speak out loud.*

One by one, he answered every one of the forty-two questions they asked him. Then everything was quiet.

Off in the distance he thought he could hear music playing. The celestial room slowed in its turning and began to elongate into an endless corridor. The sound of women crying was added to the music that filtered into the room. Amenemope was drawn toward the sounds of music and women weeping. The hallway burst upon a brightly lit room. He was suspended in the corner, close to the ceiling.

This is my bed-chamber, he realized. *The priests are standing around my bed. My wives and my precious Dalia are weeping. Why, I am the one they are mourning. I wish I could let them know that now I am free — no more fever, no more struggling. There are Wijin and Khnum, comforting Dalia. I am glad that they can be there for each other. I would not have expected less.*

Great sobs of grief came from his beautiful wives as they were ushered out of the room. The priest spoke to Dalia. It was time to leave and let the embalmers remove Pharaoh's body. Dalia turned aside from them and threw herself across her husband's body.

"How can I go on without you, my beloved?" she cried.

Amenemope's spirit looked at her fondly, a deep understanding filling him: *We will be together again, and it will be for all time.*

He knew that his ba, his spirit, had now crossed over into Osiris' world. He wanted to reach over and sooth Dalia's distress, as was his usual way, but he couldn't reach her.

Khnum put his hand on her shoulder. She rose and turned towards him, looking bereft. He put his arms around her awkwardly, intending to console her. Then his own grief rose within him. His face crumpled into a mask of sorrow, and he burst into sobs, burying his face in Dalia's hair.

From his point of observation, Amenemope looked on the scene below with some surprise.

The architect, for all his calm nature, has a depth of emotion after all, thought Pharaoh. *It is reassuring to know that those closest to me were not only loyal, but deeply committed.*

As Khnum sought to regain his composure, Wijin moved towards the bed of the deceased Pharaoh. He reached into his tunic and retrieved a small cube of gold. Tears welled up in his eyes as he placed it on the chest of the body, took one last long look at the man who had rewarded him so well for his act of bravery, and left the room.

Khnum took a deep breath. *I must get hold of myself.* Such a display in public is shameful, he thought. He straightened his shoulders and backed away from Dalia.

"Forgive me, my queen. I was out of line with such an outburst. I don't know what came over me."

"Don't be concerned, Lord Khnum. If ever there was a time for tears, it is today. My husband was a wonderful man and a great Pharaoh, and it is a consolation to know that others feel the pain of his loss. Thank you for your comfort," replied Dalia. "It is probably good to say our private good-byes now. There will be a great deal of public activity for the burial rites and then installing Osorkon as Pharaoh. The next while will place great demands on us."

You don't know how true those words are, thought Khnum as he bowed to her, walked over to the cosmetic counter, and removed two vials that he had previously placed there.

He followed Wijin to a room down the hall, entered, and closed the door behind him. The two men sank to the floor, facing each other. Wijin pulled the stopper that was holding in the venomous liquid. He was ready. He had been prepared since the minute Amenemope had held his blade to the back of his neck in the desert. He had pledged to take his own life when Pharaoh died and now the time had come. The cost did not seem too high, as he believed that the sooner he drank the poison, the sooner he would see Akila in the afterlife. No one had ever filled her place in his heart, and his longing for her subdued any misgivings. Khnum held the vial with trembling hands. He opened it and swirled the opaque liquid in the small vessel. He looked into Wijin's eyes, saying nothing. Dread churned in his stomach and bowels.

I am not ready for this, he thought. *Even though I realized this time was coming when I saw Pharaoh's health failing, I'm not sure I can actually go through with it. Perhaps I could just walk away, and live out the rest of my life quietly in some remote place: a small farm, an unimposing house. Who would be the wiser? I have no one waiting for me in the afterlife as Wijin does. It grieves me that I have never married. My family had arranged for me to marry my dear friend, Innamun, but we were just children then, and hardly knew what love was. Even so, she died two days before our marriage contract was sealed, and I was left with nothing. So unfair!*

Wijin looks at me, waiting for me to drink this wretched potion. Look at him. He will soon be reunited with his wife, Akila. Why couldn't I have found someone like her? It was all I could do to restrain myself from revealing my love to this man's wife. What will happen when I reach Aaru? Will I be forced to watch them be happy together for all time? How can I bear such a situation?

Perhaps I can pretend to drink the poison, and after Wijin drinks and dies, I could just walk away.

The unseen presence of Osiris stood between the two men. He knew Wijin would follow through with his promise, as his desire to be with Akila was paramount. He would not be disappointed.

The god looked intently at Khnum. He felt the architect's bitterness, and saw the intensity of his inner conflict. He waited impassively for Khnum to decide.

Without speaking, Wijin raised his vial and drank it. The poisonous liquid numbed his throat as it trickled down to his stomach. He looked up to see Khnum, still holding his vial with trembling hands. Though he tried to reach out to comfort him and give him strength, his arm froze and the bottle slipped out of his hand, smashing on the tiles. He collapsed on the floor, and almost instantly, he was gone.

Khnum looked at his friend lying there, hesitated, and then a sense of duty to his promise swept over him. His decision made, he shut his mind, tipped the contents of the vial into his throat, and waited. In a few moments, he too was gone.

As Wijin's ba left his body, he found himself enveloped in the soft darkness. As his consciousness arose, he felt uncertain about what to expect, as he did not know the ways of the gods. He reached out to get his bearings, and touched a wall.

I guess I will follow this wall and see where it goes, thought Wijin. *I hope I don't need to know anything special to find my way to Aaru, if, in fact, that is where I am headed. Being reunited with Akila is all I am counting on.*

As he moved forward, he heard a sound in front of him.

"Who is that?" he asked.

"I am Ma'at, goddess of truth and justice," a soothing voice called back. "I will take you to the scales of judgment. Come with me."

The pungent scent of jasmine filled his nostrils as he continued along the corridor.

"Do we have far to go?" Wijin asked. "Does everyone come this way?" He was wondering, *Where is Khnum?*

Amenemope had not moved, but his surroundings changed again. Someone took hold of his hand. He turned to see the jackal-headed god Anubis — the gatekeeper of the underworld — beckoning him to follow. The music and weeping that had drawn him here had ceased, replaced by absolute silence: the bedroom, the priests, his wives — all gone. Anubis pointed straight ahead, and in the distance, Amenemope could see a large room — the seat of judgment. As he stood there, the room rushed to meet him. As he looked about, he saw a large balancing scale with the feather of Ma'at on one side. There before him, a man was being judged at the scales. He heard a low growling coming from Ammit. She was a more fearful goddess than Amenemope had imagined — the head of a crocodile, the body of a lion, and the backside of a hippopotamus. She showed enthusiasm for the new arrival.

The man's fear was palpable. Anubis walked up to the man and removed his heart, then placed it on the other side of the scale. They all watched as the scale tipped immediately as if the heart were solid lead — a bad result. Ammit's yipping and growling increased frantically until Thoth picked the heart off the scales and threw it to her. The demon bit into the man's heart with great relish, devouring it and thus ending any chance for the man to have an afterlife. The man vaporized before their eyes, ceasing to exist.

Panic struck Amenemope like a shock. *My turn next! That wretched creature has turned her eyes upon me, licking her lips just like in my dream. Have I done enough? Will I pass safely? This is the moment of truth.*

Before Anubis reached into Amenemope's chest, the dead king turned and looked behind him, and there, next in line, were Wijin and Khnum. He took courage from their presence.

As with the previous man, Anubis reached in and plucked Amenemope's heart from his chest and placed it on the scale. A loud snarling and yelping arose from the crocodile-lion-hippo monster, anticipating another morsel.

Thoth silenced the demon Ammit, and poised his brush to record on the scroll the result of weighing Pharaoh's heart. The scale teetered back and forth briefly as Pharaoh held his breath and then — such delight — the two sides balanced perfectly — the heart and the feather.

Beyond the scales he saw Horus and Ma'at, who gazed at him approvingly, and bid him come. As he drew near to the god, Horus turned back to observe Wijin and Khnum, and Amenemope understood that he was being allowed to watch their judgments.

Wijin stepped forward.

Khnum stood back, uncertainty rising within him. *What will become of this man?* he thought. *He has been guilty of the very crimes that Pharaoh spent all those years eradicating. Wijin has never served the gods. His only redeeming act was to save and serve Pharaoh. All he cares about is seeing his beloved Akila. I wonder if his hope will be realized or if all his efforts will fall short.*

Just as these thoughts were swirling in Khnum's mind, Anubis suddenly stepped in front of Wijin, barring his way.

"Who are you? Why have you come here? You have no standing in this place. When have you ever served the gods?"

Wijin was speechless. He looked across at Amenemope, his expression pleading for his ruler to speak up on his behalf. Then he looked back at Khnum, his eyes wide with alarm.

"What shall I say, Khnum? What shall I do?" He backed away from the gatekeeper of the underworld, uncertain as to how to proceed.

Then Ma'at stepped forward, drawing Anubis aside and whispered something to him. He stood back, looking at her incredulously.

"How can this be? It seems highly unlikely. I must deny him access until I hear the words from Osiris himself. You must all wait here until I return."

With that, he turned and passed the scale, Amenemope and Horus, and passed into another room, the throne room of Osiris.

Wijin stood there helplessly. Ever since Akila had died, his whole expectation was focused on this moment when he would be reunited with her. All his hopes began to falter and dread grasped him with icy fingers.

Look at him now, thought Khnum. *All he ever thought about was Akila, but that wasn't enough. And there's nothing he can do about it now. How could he expect to enter paradise when he never knew the gods, he never worshiped the gods, he never served the gods. It's out of his hands.*

They waited. Time slowed to a crawl. No one spoke.

Wijin's gaze turned towards Ammit, whose sulfurous yellow eyes consumed him with hunger. She yelped and growled as she waited for Anubis to return. As Wijin's anxiety threatened to consume him, Ma'at caught his eye and smiled at him with calm assurance. It did little to console him.

After what seemed like a lifetime, Anubis returned and stood before Wijin.

Without a word, he grasped Wijin's heart and placed it on the scale. Wijin trembled as he waited for the result. No need to fear. Perfect balance! Thoth recorded the positive result in his scroll.

Wijin raised his hands to his face and shouted with relief as Horus motioned him forward to join Amenemope.

Khnum was confused. *He is safe. Was it his good attitude that made the difference? Do the gods know my attitude, my motives? I have tried to serve with excellence, but the thoughts of my heart have often been wrong. What if they are saved and I am doomed? No more time!*

As his mind was racing, Anubis stepped up to him and reached into his chest. He removed Khnum's heart as the architect marvelled at the strangeness of the experience. He watched intently as the heart was placed on the scale. As Anubis' hand was withdrawn, he saw the scale tip back and forth and then it seemed to settle into an even balance.

Khnum let out a breath that he hadn't realized he had been holding. *It looks as though I am safe*, he thought, his tension beginning to ease, but then, *oh no! It's starting to wobble again.* Alarm shot through him. *No, no, please — this can't be happening. I am powerless to do anything about it.* He stood there rigid, immobilized as the scale continued to teeter back and forth. He glanced up to see Wijin and Amenemope looking at him with startled expressions. All the gods were watching, their gaze going between the wavering scale and the deceased architect, his uncertain future exposed for all to see. Everything around him faded into nothingness — all the onlookers, the howling demon — and time seemed to stand still again. Then he noticed that Ma'at, the goddess of truth and justice, was glancing his way with an enigmatic smile. He turned his eyes back to the scales. *Is my future slipping away? Am I lost?*

As everyone's eyes were fastened on the scale, all were amazed as it gradually slowed in its action and then — oh bliss! — perfect balance.

Khnum collapsed on the floor, relief washing over him in great waves. As he rose to his feet, a powerful lightness suffused his entire being, and a marvelous peace burst forth within him, washing away all his inner distress. *I am safe too.* Horus came to receive him and led him, along with Wijin and Amenemope into a large throne room. The air was filled with the fragrance of flowers and the strains of beautiful calming music.

Khnum felt transformed and he was filled with the delight of his surroundings. Seated at the far end of the room, in complete Royal regalia, holding the Crook and Flail, was Osiris, smiling broadly and welcoming them with a nod. Behind him stood Isis and her sister Nephthis.

The counsel of forty-two gods sat next to them, looking on. They spoke in unison.

"We find no sin or guilt in these three before us! Join us in Aaru; let them dwell with us and the other souls in The Field of Reeds."

"I, also, find no fault in the three of you. You have all heeded my voice when I spoke to you in the land of the living. Welcome to paradise," Osiris said.

Akila stood waiting for them in a breath-taking golden sheath. She held out her arms as Wijin walked into her embrace. The years of separation vanished like a mist as Wijin clasped her close to him. At last — hope fulfilled. He held her at arm's length and looked into her face.

"My beloved, I have waited so long to see you again. I have so much to tell you. Even though I have not had you by my side, the last years of my life have been so amazing. And now I have all the time in the world to tell you about it, and to hear what has been happening in this beautiful place."

"My wonderful Wijin," said Akila. It seems like no time at all since I have been here, and everything is better than I could have imagined. Having you here with me now makes my joy complete. Come with me and let us begin this new adventure."

A young girl stepped forward from behind Akila and reached out her hand to Khnum. Taken aback, he accepted the little girl's hand. She wasn't more than twelve, decked out in a shimmering green sheath, wearing beautiful necklaces with large, heavy earrings.

"I have been waiting for you, Khnum. I have been watching you as well," the girl said. Khnum stared at her, not sure if his eyes were deceiving him. Then certainty came rushing to him like a horse at a full gallop.

"Innamun?" he asked.

The girl just smiled and giggled as she opened her arms for an embrace. The young girl was indeed Innamun. Khnum remembered being told how she had been killed by a hyena as she tended her father's sheep. She was eleven, as was Khnum — the normal age for marriage in their culture. Khnum reached out and touched her face, remembering all the details of her features as he recalled the distress and disappointment he had felt when she had been snatched from his young life. Something stirred within him. He looked deep into her brown eyes as she held out her arms to him. He drew her against himself, enfolding her and resting his cheek on her head. They stood in a quiet, comforting embrace for some time. It had been so long ago that they were promised to each other.

Khnum finally opened his eyes and stood back. He saw with wonder and amazement that Innamun had now transformed into a stunningly beautiful mature woman.

He was shaken to the core of his being.

I have not been denied in paradise. My earthly journey was not my real life. I have found peace here, and now the emptiness within me is gone.

He smiled radiantly at Innamun, moved towards her and wrapped one arm around her shoulder. The other arm he thrust into the air and laughed with delight.

Amenemope observed the reunions of his friends and thought of Dalia. Osiris held out his hand to Pharaoh.

"All the best things that you have imagined about the Field of Reeds will be fulfilled for you and Dalia, my brother. You have come home to paradise, and now you will await the arrival of your beloved wife. I invite you to stand here, so that yours will be the first face she sees when she arrives. You will find time and space are vastly different here. Although it will take many years for Dalia to finish out her life on the earth, to you, waiting here, it will seem like only a moment. You will be together here for all time, all your sorrows gone. Be at peace."

I I

BITTER REST

Osorkon and Dalia stared at the motionless body of Amenemope. Even in death he bore the aura of power and authority. Dalia sank to her knees and wept as the priests ushered the other royal wives from the room. Princess Maatkara moved towards her father's body, placing her hand on his and through her tears she said, "Journey well, father. Find peace in Aaru and wait for us".

Osorkon stepped forward and put his arm around his sister who was now also his wife.

"His ba is gone. He was a wonderful father and a great Pharaoh. We mourn his loss. You know that this will mean great change for us, my dearest. We must be strong for each other during this time of transition."

Osorkon's mind swirled with thoughts and emotions as he considered what lay before him. He had been married to his sister for many years now, in the time honored tradition. To become Pharaoh, he must be married to a royal daughter.

We share all things, he thought. *The loss of our father, the seventy days of mourning, my being crowned Lord of Two Lands with Maatkara as my queen. My time is here. My father has been preparing me for this day for a long time, but the prospects of the future are dimmed somewhat because of his being gone. May the gods help me as I rise to the occasion.*

Maatkara left the room, returning to her chambers so she could be alone with her grief. Osorkon watched Khnum attempting to comfort Dalia as best he could. He also noticed that Wijin moved up to the bed of the deceased ruler and placed a small cube of gold on his chest, and then left the room, followed by Khnum. He drew near to his mother and spoke softly to her, then embraced her as they both gave themselves to their shared distress.

The sem priests waited quietly while the two of them communed in their loss and let the separation from the departed ruler take hold. When Dalia was ready to resume her walk among the living, she let go of her son, and he directed the priests to take the Pharaoh's body to the House of the Dead for the final preparations.

I must see to many things now, he realized. *I am not yet crowned ruler, but all will look to me for direction. I know what is happening with Khnum and Wijin. I must find them before I do anything else. My father confided in me that they had pledged themselves to live for him and to die with him when the time came.*

Osorkon walked down the long, brightly-lit corridor. Statues of serene-looking gods and large pots of flourishing, green plants and trees along the wide hall made one feel like an intruder at a god's reunion in the forest. The alternating myrrh trees and thin sugar-cane plants made the whole area around the royal bedroom smell like sweet passion of honey mixed with the confident bite of authority. All doors were wide open, revealing the beautifully crafted interiors that boasted delicate tables of inlaid gold and wall decorations painted with scenes of family life. The only closed door was between the tall statues of Osiris and his wife Isis. Osorkon's sandals slowed and quieted on the blue-tiled floor as he approached the door, apprehension clouding his mind. He opened the door, and there they were — Khnum and Wijin lying on the floor, their faces contorted in a mask of pain that the poison had inflicted in their last moments of life. He knelt beside the two men who had been so loyal to his father, and reached out to feel for a pulse on their necks. Even though they were still warm, he realized that they were gone. A new wave of sadness washed over him — more loss to bear on this difficult day.

Standing up, he retraced his steps back to the sem priests that were caring for Amenemope's body. They had covered it with a white linen sheet and were carrying it down the hall, followed by more priests who continued to chant blessings over it. As Osorkon walked towards the procession, the sem priest that led the group bowed with his face to the floor and waited for permission to rise.

"Get up, priest. Your job is not done here today," Osorkon stated. "Two more faithful servants await you down the hall. See that they also are afforded funerary care. They will all be buried together."

During the seventy days of mourning, work in the country ceased as three of the most important men in Egypt were being readied for burial. Preparations were made for the journey down the Nile to the sea, to the tomb prepared for Amenemope in the cliffs. Even though Egypt's trade and commerce was suspended, Osorkon maintained a firm grip on the citizenry as commander of the army.

Although he had not yet been crowned Pharaoh, Osorkon The Elder took up residence in his father's old room and his wife, Maatkara, moved into an adjoining room.

He made regular trips to the sem priests to observe the embalming. After the lengthy and intricate process of preserving the body, one-hundred gold amulets were placed on specified parts of the body for protection in the afterlife. Each body was wrapped with over seventy yards of new linen. Between the layers, hot resin was poured over the fabric to preserve it. The mummified forms were then placed in their sarcophagi. All was finally in readiness for the burial.

Blue and white flags fluttered in the breeze by the water steps as the procession of anthropoid coffins and mourners drew near. The luxurious royal boat, along with two other ceremonial rafts, was moored at the water's edge. The king's coffin was carried aboard first, followed by Dalia, Osorkon, Maatkara and then the priests and the other royal wives. They were followed by the carriers of the sarcophagi of Khnum and Wijin, who were each placed on one of the other two rafts. A service raft carrying soldiers, servants, cooks, the carriers and supplies followed behind them.

Women with bared breasts scooped up dust from the shore and covered their heads and chests with the brown dirt and mourned loudly. Officials, soldiers, farmers and slaves lined the banks of the Nile as the rowers made their way along the vast river, assisted by the gentle current. They reached the great sea, and veered right along the shoreline until the funeral procession neared its destination. At Ufur the boats docked and the sarcophagi were carried up the roadway to the top of the cliff. The army had put up barriers to stop anyone but the family and priests from following the funeral procession.

The waves thundered at the bottom of the cliff as the funeral party approached the location that Amenemope had chosen as his final resting place. Seagulls screamed at the intimate group as they prepared for one last meal with the three most prominent men in Egypt.

A large wooden frame had been set up at the edge of the cliff and the three sarcophagi were leaned against it, as if they were participants at the feast.

Dishes of roasted duck, dried fish, beef and tender spiced vegetables were prepared for the living and the dead. Platters of food were set out for the family and around the feet of the coffins, so the "honored guests" could partake in spirit.

The crash of the waves at the base of the cliff made one feel as if the gods were present and welcoming the three men with their drums.

When the banqueters were finished, they left the rest of the food to the gulls as an offering to appease Horus, the falcon-headed god.

Osorkon stood in front of his father's sarcophagus with the new high priest, Min-sacornamen, who began the ceremony by approaching the Royal coffin. As he spoke the proper incantations, he placed his right hand on the lid.

"May you regain your strength as you pass from here to Osiris' side. Let your feet be firm as you walk through the Field of Reeds. Let your eyes see the glories the gods provide. Let Isis and Nephthys hold your hands as they lead you through paradise."

Min-sacornamen passed the magical implement, the adze, to Osorkon so that he could touch the different parts of the body as they started the Opening of the Mouth ceremony.

"Open your mouth so that you can speak and eat. Open your mouth so that you may breathe," the high priest chanted. "Open your arms, son of Amun, so that you can be embraced and enjoy the Field of Reeds."

The ceremony came to an end as Min-sacornamen lit an incense burner and let the sharp blue scent flow over and around the sarcophagi. Tears filled the eyes of Amenemope's wives as they knew this was the last time they would be close to him. Dalia stood stoically and with dignity beside the coffin.

"Oh my darling, now you are at peace in Osiris' bosom," she whispered. "Although we are apart, I look forward to the day when we will be reunited in Aaru."

The caskets were laid flat on the wooden platform that protruded from the side of the cliff, and two groups of soldiers grabbed the lowering ropes and slowly, through a series of pulleys, lowered the frame down the cliff. The bulky supporting structure came to rest on an outcrop that protruded from the tomb's entrance. Large amounts of fresh manure were hauled by basket into the tomb and the vents that supplied air to the workers during the excavation of the tomb were plugged.

One week after they had first brought the men to their resting place, the tomb was sealed. The carts that moved the sarcophagi into place were pulled up on the large wooden frame, and the structure was burned, as was the stairway which had led down to the opening. All trace of their presence there was removed, and all access to the tomb destroyed.

Back in Tanis, Osorkon approached the temple of Horus, followed by his wife, Maatkara, and his mother, Dalia. He was here to seek the blessing of the god for him as the prospective leader of the great land of Egypt. Ahead of them, at the first tall pylon, Min-sacornamen, a leopard skin draped over his shoulder, extended his arms in invitation to Osorkon.

The royal ladies followed Osorkon as far as the third pillar before the entrance to the Holy Place, the abode of the god. Min-sacornamen pointed to two benches where the women could sit and wait.

The tall, heavy doors of the temple were made of electrum, a gold-silver alloy, and studded with jasper and turquoise. They creaked open and the high priest led the prince inside the temple. It was dark, and eerily quiet except for the echo of their sandals on the tiled floor. In the middle of the first room was a large pool, filled with holy water, shimmering and smooth as glass. On the far wall was another door — the entrance into the holy place of the god.

"Step into the god's pool, cleanse yourself and come out purified to meet the holy one. Let his waters fill your mouth so that you may speak with his words," chanted the priest.

Osorkon stood at the edge of the sacred water and removed his clothes. Then he stepped into the tepid water and submerged himself, lying flat on his stomach and letting the water flow into his mouth. He took a handful of natron that had been provided and vigorously scrubbed every inch of his body.

Min-sacornamen stood at the end of the god's pool and waited for Osorkon to finish cleansing himself. He emerged from the water, dripping wet, and the priest led him to the small door of the holiest place.

He said, "You must now prostrate yourself, crawl into the god's presence, and stay there until the god speaks to your heart."

Crawling naked on his hands and knees, he approached the golden image of Horus and lay flat on his stomach, his forehead pressed against the cool black tiles. The only sound he heard was the slap, slap, slap of the priest's retreating sandals.

All was silent as Osorkon lay before the god, his own breath the only sign of life in the room.

Time seemed to stand still. He grew chilled and restless, and his back ached. Osorkon lay with his head against the tiled floor. *How long must I stay like this? How can I summon the god? Why can't I hear the god's words?* he asked himself. *It is my birthright! I must rule. Never again will Egypt, My Egypt, be at the mercy of thieves! My father made this land great, but because of his hesitation, he almost let it slip through his fingers. But not me! I will rule this land with no excuses — with the courage of my convictions. Where is the god? Does he not care?*

All his life he had been trained and prepared to succeed his father as Pharaoh, but right then a lack of tenderness birthed rose in him. Since he had become a man, he had focused on developing his leadership skills and his knowledge of the land in preparation for this time. An impatient feeling prickled at his skin. But then … a voice.

"That feeling you are experiencing right now is what I have been waiting for — impatience for right to be done. Egypt needs to have a strong ruler — a King that does not waver. A King that will not stand for the rules of Ma'at to be broken. Why have you come into my son's temple?" the deep voice continued echoing in his mind.

"I have come to seek your blessing to rule this land," Osorkon declared, unsure if it was really Osiris' voice he had heard.

"Stand up and meet my gaze. Look into my eyes if you dare."

Osorkon rose quickly, his joints stiff from maintaining a prostrate position. The smell of death mixed with jasmine filled his nostrils. There before him stood Osiris, swathed in burial linens, a double plumed crown atop his green head and the crook and flail firmly gripped in his bandaged hands. Appearing to have the consistency of a cloud, Osiris stood in front of the golden, hawk-headed statue of his son Horus.

Osorkon could see through him, but his shape and features were obvious and powerful.

"Why should I bless you, son of Amenemope? Will you disappoint me as your father did? Will you become lazy and let evil be done to your forefathers' monuments?" bellowed Osiris.

"No — no I will never do that!" Osorkon replied with force. "I warned my father against such things, but it was only after he had a dream given by you that he changed. I am strong and I will make this land stronger than it has ever been and I will have no regrets."

His face reddened as anger rose, resistance and resentment stirring within him. *How dare the god chastise me for my father's actions!*

"Well said, young one. I see greatness in you. Prove your promise to me and I will bless your days on MY THRONE. That's right, My Throne. You are only borrowing the privilege to sit there," Osiris said with authority and arrogance.

Osiris reached into the folds of his linen bandages and produced a dagger which he threw at Osorkon's feet.

"Sprinkle your blood as a promise and an offering at my son's feet," he said as he motioned towards Horus' golden foundation.

Osorkon picked up the dagger, the black blade severely nicked and rusty, the handle made from a human forearm with rotting skin attached and crawling with maggots. He stepped to the base of Horus' statue and with his right hand on the festering, putrid handle, drew the wicked blade across his left palm. Intense pain seared through his entire body the moment the blade sliced his skin. Osorkon collapsed from the agony, as if the blade had been laced with poison.

"I have forgiven your father, Osiris-Amenemope Glorified, and he is now with me in Aaru waiting for Dalia to join us. Do not forget your promise to me this day. I will not be as forgiving with you as I was with your father."

With that, Osiris was gone and Osorkon was left with a scar on his left hand and a small ache that traveled up his arm as a constant reminder.

There was no blood left on the floor, the cruel knife was gone and the calm, resolute gaze of Horus still pierced the very depths of his soul.

When Osorkon emerged from the god's presence two hours later, Min-sacornamen could see that the god had spoken to the son of Amenemope. The confident assurance that Osorkon projected clearly reflected the blessing of the god, and the priest said, "Now we can proceed with the coronation. You are ready."

A great celebration to crown Osorkon Pharaoh of the Two Lands was planned. In ten days he would officially assume power.

In preparation for the ceremony, he was dressed in a white and blue kilt, bordered with gold. A lapis and gold collar, gold arm bands and electrum bracelets were slid onto his arms, rings with his name engraved on them were placed on every finger. Gold dust was sprinkled on Osorkon's face, making his countenance appear as pure gold. Osorkon's earring was replaced by a large, dangling ankh that brushed his shoulder. Bright red henna was painted on his palms and the soles of his feet, the sign of supreme royalty. Golden sandals were slipped on his feet.

When his dressing was complete, he was joined by his wife, the priests and the top officials of the land.

Osorkon and Maatkara, along with Dalia, were ushered into the royal litters, and the procession made its way to the Temple of Osiris. A sacred ritual was held before the god, where Osorkon was pledged to the service of Osiris in leading his people in the ways of Ma'at.

Then the priest led the royal party back to the palace and into the throne room for the actual crowning of the Pharaoh. Fanfares and high honors were extended as the entourage filled the room. The highlight of the ceremony came when Min-sacornamen took the red crown of Lower Egypt and placed it on Osorkon's head. Then he took the white crown of Upper Egypt and set it inside the red crown, showing the unity of the two lands.

Following this, the high priest led the new Pharaoh on to the dais and seated him on the golden throne. Min-sacornamen opened a large jewel-encrusted box from which he produced the Crook and Flail and placed them in Osorkon's hands.

Turning to face the crowd, the priest proclaimed, "Hail Aakheperre Setepenre, Osorkon II, Lord of Two Ladies, Son of Horus, Son of Re, Son of Amun, Ruler of Upper and Lower Egypt. We ask for your mercy; do with us as you will!" Min-sacornamen shouted out.

A loud cheer went up from the crowd that had gathered and everyone fell on their faces in submission.

"Hail, Pharaoh Osorkon The Elder, Hail Pharaoh, Hail Pharaoh," the crowd shouted.

Osorkon stretched his hand towards Maatkara. She stood up, walked over to the King and knelt at his feet.

"Rise, and be honored, my Queen, First-Among-Women," Osorkon announced to her.

As she stood up, Min-sacornamen placed the Queen's crown on her head and bowed with his head touching the floor. The crowd did likewise. When they had all risen, they raised a great cheer.

The office was well lit, but Pharaoh Osorkon's demeanor was far from cheery. He sat behind his cedar desk drumming his fingers one at a time in a quick impatient tempo. In front of him the Wisdom of Amenemope lay in tightly rolled scrolls, yellowed and slightly frayed. He knew every word that they contained. *Why should I listen to that wisdom? My father was deficient in ways that I will never be. I have my own wisdom to follow.* A new era had begun.

PART 2

12

FUMES

2006 AD

The rumble of heavy machinery, mixed with the tangy smell of diesel fumes, permeated the Luxor construction site. Multiple heavy machines, all with the Sekani & Son emblem embossed on their sides, worked like unrelenting ants, digging at the ground, preparing it for a new high-rise apartment building. Large excavators scooped away the hard-packed earth, increasing the depth and breadth of the hole they had dug, readying it for the cement foundation they were about to lay. A pay loader, with a bucket so large that a small car could comfortably fit inside it, scooped away the mounds of earth piled high by the excavators, and moved them away to a different location. The massive bucket was manipulated with precision by the small joystick control in the air-conditioned cab.

The young man controlling the large Komatsu loader was very careful with the placement of the gigantic machine, knowing one small mistake could lead to disaster. The cigar-smoking construction workers had all helped train the son of the owner, who planned to take over his father's business when he was old enough. The hardened construction laborers, who had worked loyally for Sekani for years, directed the large machines as if in a choreographed dance routine. Sekani had hired the men more than ten years ago when he was just building lean-tos for the light industrial shops in town. The crew had guided the twenty-year-old man in all aspects of the construction business, including how each of the machines were to be operated and the proper techniques of building.

Sekani, strong physically as well as in depth of character, had at one time been a large equipment mechanic for a big construction business in Shibin El Kom. That northern city was known for the central and local government offices that were built in the ancient style of short, stubby, sand colored stone. Shibin El Kom was now also known as an internet hub for Egypt — a prosperous place. However, the construction job opportunities dried up, forcing him to move. Sekani packed up his family and relocated in Luxor thirteen years ago. He had started out with a gravel truck, making deliveries to local construction sites, but soon bought a pay loader and hired himself out to do private work.

After a few years he had purchased three other dump trucks and a second loader. When the boy was not in school, Sekani regularly brought his young son with him to the construction sites, letting him ride on the lap of a worker in the huge machines. During the building of his business, Sekani divorced, retaining custody of his son, and was now living with him in a quaint home in Malkarta on the outskirts of Luxor.

A few nice houses dotted the poor area where they lived. Numerous rundown homes squatted along the roughly-paved streets, punctuated by a few short, scrubby trees that had been there for eons. The houses were unfinished on the upper floors, like many buildings in the vast city of Luxor. Re-bar jutted from the tops of the walls — declaring the building unfinished and thus not yet taxable. Broken-down vehicles seemed to be parked by every house, as if it were a forgotten scrap-yard. In between the discarded wooden boxes and empty skids dogs and cats freely roamed the streets, on the hunt for their next meal.

At the end of a particular side-street, one house stood out in contrast to the others. It too had a broken-down car, but this one, a '72 BMW, was kept behind the house and Sekani was restoring it. The house was well kept and completed, without boards falling off the outside walls. Sekani took pride in his little home and manicured his lawn as if he were expecting company. The trees he had planted in front of the house were not the usual variety. Though gnarly on the trunk, they exploded into an array of colorful shades of greens and yellows. Once a year they would seed and blossom with splashes of light and dark purple. Always trimmed and well-watered, these trees were the envy of the neighborhood.

Sekani's seven-year-old son, Anik, was expected to do his share of chores, though his father was not a taskmaster. As well as being a father, Sekani was a mentor to Anik, guiding him through the lessons of life. "Dad, I'm going outside to play," Anik called over to his father, who was in the kitchen cleaning up after lunch.

"Ok, Anik, just stay close," Sekani answered, but before he finished his sentence, he heard the screen door slam shut.

Anik ran out into the street, ready to explore. He walked up and down, crawling inside many of the abandoned vehicles littering the roadsides. Anik had already gone farther than he knew he should have, when his eyes focused on an old rusted pickup truck with its hood opened. The truck had flames painted on its side, making it look to Anik like a rocket ship ready to blast off. Anik climbed aboard and seated himself in the "cockpit," checked the flaps, and blasted off to the Moon, making sounds all the way.

"10-20 roger that," he excitedly called back to his base using the gearshift as a microphone.

A multitude of rocket sounds, mixed with beeps and gun shots emanated from his mouth.

"You're silly," a young girl's voice called out, jarring him out of his imaginary world.

Anik, looked out the driver-side window and saw a skinny black-haired girl looking up at him.

"What's your name?" the little girl asked.

"Anik. What's yours?" he asked.

"Sitaya," the girl answered, "I'm five," she replied with her hand on her hip and cocking her head, as if he should have known.

Aha, I'm older than she is, so I have the upper hand here! he thought.

"This is my rocket ship," Anik announced, staking his claim.

"Oh! Can I come on your rocket ship, Anik?" the girl's high little voice asked.

That was something that made Anik very wary. After all, he was at the age where girls were "yucky," and he did not want to get infected by her girl germs.

"Permission denied!" Anik answered in a strong voice, hoping to be rid of her, as a good captain would, protecting his ship from invasion. "Besides, I'm seven and you have to do what I say."

"Well, this is my dad's truck, so let me come aboard or I'm telling," Sitaya answered back quickly.

She's got me there, but I can still save the situation by deploying my force field! he thought.

"Permission granted, as long as you stay on your side," he countered.

Sitaya climbed into the passenger seat and strapped herself in. Anik could feel the infectious girl cooties start to creep over to his side of the rocket ship, so using his hand he drew an invisible line of protection, stopping the disease from spreading.

Later that afternoon, Anik ran back home and was greeted by the angry stares of his father, who had been looking for him.

"Where have you been, young man?" Sekani asked, in an angry but worried tone.

"I … I was just over one street, playing space ship with Sitaya!" Anik said hesitantly, hoping he wouldn't get in too much trouble.

"Sitaya? Who's Sitaya," Sekani questioned, still irritated.

"She's just a little girl I met, but don't worry, I used my force field so I didn't get her cooties," he said, showing his dad how he drew the invisible line beside him.

To Anik's relief and amazement, Sekani burst out laughing and shook his head. After he wiped the tears from his eyes, he cleared his throat.

"Tell you what, Anik. Tomorrow is Sunday, so how about we both walk over to her house so I can meet her parents," he said with a smile.

Abdullah Singh sat on his comfortable green La-Z-Boy sofa, half-listening to Sitaya natter on about this new friend she had found and had played with. His mind was far from the young child who was talking his ear off. A small home covered with yellowed vinyl siding, a lawn of brown grass that was choked with weeds, and an old pickup truck parked out front was all he owned.

Abdullah worked long hours at a factory in Malkarta, a place he could walk to. He was able to provide a living for his family of three, and was able to keep his debt lower than most. At the age of five, his daughter already had a quick mouth, but a lovable smile. Abdullah thought about his daughter starting school shortly. *At least the school is close enough for her to walk to. That, at least, is a stress I am free of*, he thought to himself.

"Dad … Helloooo," Sitaya called over to him, jarring him into the present. "Is it okay if I play with that boy?"

"What boy is this that you are talking about?" her father asked, now paying close attention.

"Anik, the boy who lives just a street over. He was here yesterday!" she said impatiently.

Just as she finished her sentence, there was a knock at the door. Abdullah answered, and found a man and a young boy standing on his brown dilapidated porch, looking as though they were there for a business meeting.

"Whatever you are selling, I don't want it," Abdullah said, holding up his hand and shaking his head.

"No, no, I'm not selling anything. I just came by with my son, Anik, to see where he ran off to yesterday," Sekani replied, seeing the petite, black-haired girl standing behind her father and holding on to his leg.

On seeing Anik, Sitaya rushed out past the two men and threw her arms around the boy, much to his dismay.

"I'm glad you came back, Anik!" she shrieked.

"Sitaya!" Abdullah yelled.

The father grabbed Sitaya's arm and pulled her off the young boy, who now looked like he had been mauled by a lion. Anik quickly ducked behind his dad for protection and held on to his waist.

"You can't do that, Sitaya! What have I told you before?" Abdullah scolded the tiny girl. "Sorry about that," Abdullah said apologetically to Sekani. "I didn't catch your name yet."

"It's OK, it's OK." Sekani replied, letting his strong arm rest on Anik's shoulder. "Sorry I didn't introduce myself yet. My name is Sekani, and I guess you now know my son, Anik."

"My name is Abdullah, and *this*," he said, motioning to the girl, "is Sitaya. Sorry, but my wife is working at the hospital right now. She would love to have met you."

The two men talked over beers for the rest of the afternoon and it was soon decided, that since their children would be going to the same school, Anik and Sitaya would walk together in the morning. Of course, Anik was *not* pleased and argued about getting girl germs, but Sitaya was on cloud nine.

Anik, now seventeen and his school years behind him, had begun to learn his dad's construction business. Although he was very good at it, he didn't feel it was something he would want as a life-long career. He didn't know what he actually did want to do, but the nagging desire for "something else" was always in the back of his mind. Until he knew what that something was, he excelled at the jobs he was working at.

A steady stream of dump trucks drove into the construction site to pick up loads of dirt and carry them away. A few times in the past they had found artifacts and twice they found destroyed tombs that had been completely plundered long ago. That small encounter with ancient history piqued his interest in archaeology, and Anik wondered if this could be his calling in life. Although he applied himself to the task at hand while he was at work, in his spare time he dabbled in exploring the mysteries of the past.

As the afternoon wore on, the Egyptian air current slowed to a halt, resulting in a stifling stillness that bore down on the workers, and the choking dust clouds that hung in the air aggravated their lungs and clogged the air filters.

A lone truck was lined up, ready to be filled with another load, but everyone appeared to be busy. As Anik saw the impatient trucker, he transferred to a size-appropriate loader, an old Volvo that he hated. The hydraulic pump leaked terribly, causing the arms on the bucket to constantly lower. This was a never-ending battle. The radio could receive only two stations and both of them were awful. One was an old-time country music station and the other was "All News, All Day". Anik reluctantly chose "All News, All Day" and proceeded to fill the truck's box, fighting against the leaking loader arms, all the while being serenaded by the News. As he filled the truck, the bucket caught the dust screen that covered the truck's box and tore it slightly.

"What are you doing?" the trucker ranted, in a heavy accent.

His truck was a metallic blue color, with SIG printed on the side.

"Sorry about that!" Anik replied, getting flushed with embarrassment.

"Well, sorry doesn't replace what you have wrecked!" the trucker fumed.

"I'm sorry, sir," Anik replied again.

The trucker shook his head, muttering curses as he got back into his vehicle and slammed the door closed. *I didn't even see it*, Anik thought, feeling terrible. *Yeah, SIG probably stands for stupid, ignorant guy.*

He remembered this trucker. This guy had an awful time properly backing his truck up to the piles of dirt. It was as if he had never been taught how to drive. At one point the foreman had to back up the truck himself, to the obvious irritation of the foreign trucker.

After he finished loading the dump truck, he carefully started towards the next one in line. The man in that truck quickly flagged him down and walked up to the machine, motioning that he wanted to speak to him. *Oh brother, what did I do now?* Anik thought, frustrated.

"I saw what happened to the last truck. That guy is cranky about everything, so don't worry about him, just slow down around him," the man said, with a smile and a wink.

In the late afternoon, Anik's day got much worse. Back in the big loader, he was filling a large dump truck when a careless driver parked his vehicle behind the loader. He had just finished emptying the bucket and began backing up when he heard and felt a loud crunch behind him. A sick feeling swept over him as he hopped down and discovered a partially flattened red Jaguar.

"Oh no," he shouted as he ran to see if anyone was trapped inside. "Is anyone there?" He looked all around the totaled luxury car and saw that it was empty, but even though he was relieved that no one was injured, his innards churned with guilt.

"That's just great!" Anik exclaimed as the workers gathered around. He was badly shaken up as his dad came along and he explained what had happened.

"I think you had better call it a day, son. Go on home and I will look after this. The car was parked in a clearly marked 'No Parking' zone," his father said.

That evening they discussed the situation again, and Sekani could see that Anik was still very distressed by the day's misfortunes.

"Why don't you take tomorrow off?" Sekani suggested. "It's a Friday, and we can get along without you for the day. After all that, you would do well to take some time to calm down and settle yourself. Things like this happen from time to time. You do the best you can, but you have to learn to deal with them. This time you will need a couple of days, though."

"Thanks, Dad," said Anik. "I'd like to take you up on your offer. Just getting away from things for a while would be a great help. I feel just awful about what happened."

He headed to bed, hoping to make his day off a means to wash away the guilt that stuck to him like a leech.

13

MISSING PAWN

The next morning Anik slept in a bit, and when he got up, he was glad to have the day off. He was still rather shaken up about the fiascos of yesterday. After a relaxed breakfast of coffee, pineapple, eggs and pita bread, he considered how he would spend the day.

I think I want to spend it alone, and I'm thinking about a trek into the desert.

Before his parents had separated, there had been a great deal of arguing in the home, and he had often been dragged into their fights by his mother, who used him as a pawn in their squabbles. Through that, he had discovered that when he could get away to the desert, the big sky and wide open places helped him calm down. The sands were a place of tranquility for him.

Searching through his clothes drawer, he decided he wouldn't wear one of the outfits that he wore to work, as he could never totally rid his wardrobe of the smells of the construction site. He generally opted for sports shorts and a T-shirt, preferably one with a funny slogan. He wasn't up for that today though, so he wore a new Coca-Cola shirt he had picked up in Jerusalem on a recent trip there. A hat and sneakers finished off the outfit.

He packed some leftover lamb, a couple of pitas, some bananas and oranges, a plentiful supply of water and some juice in his backpack and then set off in his Jeep for the west side of town.

As he neared the edge of town, he spotted a convenience store with a good sized parking lot, so he pulled in there, figuring he could walk the rest of the way.

The road he was on headed directly into the desert. It always amazed him how the green space along the Nile stopped abruptly, immediately replaced by dry ground. Along the road were small homes on each side, struggling for survival in a place of quickly diminishing resources. Observing them made Anik feel as though he wasn't so badly-off after all.

The last place on the right was one of the most dilapidated, and in the back yard, Anik noticed an old man sitting under a sparse grove of trees, smoking a pipe and bent over a small table. As Anik slowed down to have a look, he noticed that the man was dressed in old gray work pants and a yellow shirt that was stained and missing some of its black buttons. He was shaved except for a white mustache that was trimmed short. His face was traced with deep wrinkle lines that reflected his years of experience and time in the sun. On his almost bald head he wore a straw hat with a frayed brim. His shoes were badly worn with the seams barely holding together.

Anik could now see that on the small table was a chess set, and the old man seemed to be playing a game with himself. When he noticed Anik looking his way, he put down the chess piece he was contemplating and gazed inquisitively at the tall stranger that was looking back at him.

"Can I help you?" the old man asked as he lowered his pipe and blew out a cloud of smoke.

"No thanks. I'm just going through on my way out into the desert for a hike."

Waiting for the man's reply, he noticed an old woman chopping vegetables on the porch of the house and smiled over at her.

"That could be quite a hike," the old man said. "It's a pretty big desert. I hope you've got enough food and water in that pack of yours. We don't see many hikers pass by here."

"No, I haven't come this way before, either. But I do enjoy getting out in the wide open spaces. I like the heat."

"Well, that's good. There's plenty of that out there."

The old woman came over and joined her husband. She was slender and a bit stooped over, wearing a blue floral print dress. A red bandanna kept her long white hair away from her wrinkled face. Her brown eyes sparkled with alertness and the wisdom of her years.

"What's your name, young fella?" the old man asked.

"Anik. Anik Masri. What are your names?"

"My name is Huy, and this here is my wife, Sarin. We're pleased to meet you."

"Pleased to meet you as well. I had better get going. I'll see you later," said Anik as he turned to leave.

The old man nodded, stuck his pipe back in his mouth and re-lit the tobacco. He turned back to study the chess board that was laid out in front of him and made a move against an imaginary foe.

As Anik began to walk away he thought about the old couple he had just met. *I wonder if these folks know anything about this part of the desert.* Anik turned on his heel and walked back to the rundown property. Huy was still contemplating his next move when Anik walked into their yard, which was no more than hard packed sand and a few trees. Huy looked up from his chess game as soon as Anik walked in.

"Sorry to bother you again, but do you know where this road leads?" Anik asked as he pointed to the dirt path in front of the house.

The old man grabbed his pipe, took it out of his mouth and motioned to a chair that was on the far side of the small table. Anik took the hint and sat down on the side of the chess board that was playing black.

Anik quickly scanned the board and noticed that it was set to start a game. The chess pieces were well worn and some of the men were badly damaged — the white king had the top broken off, one of the white pawns was missing, and a stone was used as a replacement for a black pawn.

Huy moved his king pawn then took his pipe and placed it in the ash tray.

"The road goes into the desert as you can see," he said with a raspy voice. "That's pretty much all there is. Your move," he said as he coughed and motioned to the board.

Anik moved the stone that replaced a pawn to meet Huy's pawn.

Huy brought out another pawn to protect his center pawn.

"Have you ever walked the road?" Anik said as he moved out his king knight.

"I did once, but all I found was sand dunes," the man said as he moved his black bishop, attacking Anik's knight.

"Your move."

Anik moved his black bishop out and immediately Huy moved his queen's rook pawn up one.

"How far out there did you walk?" Anik asked as he brought out his other knight.

By now Sarin had walked over and was watching the game.

"I walked until the road disappeared," he said, placing his hand to his temple and attacking Anik's bishop with a pawn.

Sarin came to stand behind her husband and began to massage his shoulders. Anik took his knight, which was blocking Huy's bishop skewer-attack on his queen and took the king's pawn, sacrificing his queen.

"I thought that living here all your life, you would have explored as far as you could. Oh, your move."

Huy started smiling as he saw what he thought was a massive mistake on Anik's part and took his queen.

"I guess I never had the desire to explore."

Anik inwardly smiled to himself, as he had snared the old man into "Legal's Mate".

"Well, I would like to go into the desert and stretch my legs. Thank you for the game, Huy," Anik said as he got up and prepared to leave.

"Where are you going?" Huy asked, not seeing that defeat would come in two simple moves.

"Okay, I'll move," Anik replied, as he slid his bishop across the table and declared "check."

Huy moved his king to the only available "safe" spot and shook his head. Anik advanced his other knight and declared "checkmate." Huy sat back in his chair and studied the board, and then raised his hands in submission.

"Very good, very good." A beaming smile crossed his face. "You must promise to come back and play me again."

"I will do that," Anik said as he stood up from the table.

He walked away from Huy and Sarin's simple home, pleased with himself that he was able to beat the old man so easily. As he thought about it, he started to feel guilty about his savage playing style with the old-timer. *I shouldn't have been so merciless against him with my moves. He can't have much of a life, living in that decrepit old place. And that poor excuse for a chess board, how can he stand to play on that thing?*

Anik decided right then and there to bring him a better chess set and visit him. After he made up his mind to visit Huy on a regular basis, he felt much better about himself and looked forward to the next time he would see him.

As soon as he crossed into the desert, he became more aware of the brilliance of the sun shining overhead, and the hot, dry breeze blowing from the sands which expanded before him in an endless spectrum. The severe beauty of the Western Desert started to work its magic on him, the warmth of the sand beneath his feet radiating comfort and peace. A few sparse ficus trees endured along the path into the desert and soon the hard packed dirt path gave way to the sand, and the trail ended. Beyond him, the plain of sand gradually merged with the encroaching dunes. As he continued to hike along, the dunes increased in size and number, eventually creating an ocean of yellow waves. Between the dunes, small black flakes of dried up organic material skirted the dune bases.

Anik always liked to think of the mountains of sand as fat, flouncy old-fashioned dresses with a tattered hem. Sometimes the ridge of small black flakes from the ficus shrubs would form a band around one side and would disappear on the other, due to the wind, as if Mother Nature would continue her sewing after a short hiatus.

After a two-hour trek into the desert, Anik saw an unusually large dune. *Now there's a dune I would like to climb. It's huge!* thought Anik. *I had better stop for a break and get something to eat and drink before I start up.*

After a few minutes, he started to make the slow, arduous journey to its grand zenith. He wanted to have a look around and a great slide down. Climbing up, he could see a little lizard and sand viper scurrying to find shelter under some little ledge in the sand. It was going to be a hot, punishing day — just what he liked. The heat seemed to energize him.

At the summit he gazed around in every direction. Visibility was so much better out here than in the city. He saw the horizon far in the distance, fading into a hazy mauve. He felt like he was at the top of the world and observed the curvature of the earth all around him. Sitting down in the burning sand and catching his breath, he let the sun's warmth bathe him in its healing rays, releasing all stress. This was what he needed. The hot, arid wind dried his sweat. He closed his eyes and gave himself to the moment.

After a brief rest, Anik took a cautious look down the treacherous slope and mentally visualized the wild ride he hoped to have. He could see a small grove of date palms growing on the desert floor at the dune's base off to the right. It was a long way down, he thought with excitement, laced with a trace of fear.

He let himself start out slow and easy, holding himself back with his hands, using them as brakes. Slowly he let his weight take over and was soon sliding faster and faster down the massive dune. Close to the bottom he started applying his "brakes" so he would not end his fun by being totally out of control and hurting himself. His hands dug deeper and deeper in the hot sand, slowing his descent considerably. His fingers painfully grazed a hard surface for an instant, but he was too enthralled at the sheer pleasure to take notice.

Finally he reached the bottom and stood up, pleased that he was able to find so much enjoyment with this new "sport." That was even better than I expected, he thought. Anik turned around and scanned the trench he carved in the side of the monster dune, and noticed the tip of a rock that was totally out of place about thirty feet up from where he was standing. I wonder what that is. The granular sand was still flowing into the trench from the sides and soon the rock and trench were again covered over and smooth. Just as he raised his hand to wipe the dust from his face, Anik noticed his fingers were bleeding. He turned his hand over and saw two scrapes on his 3rd and 4th fingers.

"Well, I guess I know what I hit," Anik said out loud, talking to the wind.

He suddenly noticed the sand on this dune was very different from the other yellow dunes. This sand was coarser, drier and flowed into any trench that was made, more readily than the sand of other dunes, which tended to be firmer and damper the deeper you dug into them. Anik's curiosity got the best of him and he was determined to find that rock again.

He started back up the now smoothed trench to where he thought it was and began to dig by hand. As he was digging, he was thinking how much faster it would go with one of his dad's loaders from back home.

Sweat beaded down his temples as he dug by hand for several minutes until he found it, but the sand just kept covering it again. He persevered through his frustration, and in so doing, he was able to reveal more of the rock. He discovered that it was more than just an average stone. The rock looked like it was carved and shaped.

How did it get here and what is it? Anik wondered. *Rocks don't just show up in a sand dune! Dunes move and flow in the wind. That rock is definitely rigid. Very intriguing.*

Time is getting on. Maybe I had better start heading home. I'd like to take a closer look at this, but I can't go get the tools I need and still come back today. I had better make a mental note of where to find this "rock" again. This dune is way bigger than any of the others around here, so if I time how long I need to walk here from the edge of the town, I should be able to find it again. And when I find the dune, I'll count the number of steps between that little outcrop of date palms over there and the base of the dune, and then I'll count the number of steps between here and up where the "rock" is. I think I can find the spot again now.

Anik was curiously drawn to this larger-than-life hill in the barren and parched wasteland.

The trek back home took another two hours, although the time seemed to fly by. Anik was full of wonder and speculation about what he had found. *Maybe it's a lost civilization. Maybe I found a temple, or the remains of a palace.* He could just see in his mind's eye, hundreds of priests emerging from a golden temple, bringing offerings to someone of great importance. People would have come from miles around to pay homage. *Yes, that's what it was!* As Anik's mind started creating a whole culture from one rock, he started laughing at the absurdity of it. *Settle down Anik, settle down,* he told himself as he brought his thoughts back to reality.

The shrubs at the edge of the desert formed a stark contrast to the yellow-beige of the dry blowing sand that coated everything. He was always amazed at the endurance of the plant life that survived in such a hostile place.

Sitaya would love this place, he thought. *I've got to bring her here,* Anik decided. *This has been a great day.*

As he came alongside Huy's place, a feeling of familiarity enveloped him. He realized that he was tired and thirsty.

There was Huy standing on the side of the dirt path leaning on an old cane. His pipe was clenched between his teeth and a small wisp of smoke continued to bleed its way out of the bowl and into the air. Anik raised his hand in greeting and Huy returned the greeting.

"You made it back!" Huy said, obviously happy to see him.

"Sure," Anik replied with a smile and a nod. "Were you expecting me to vanish?"

"No — at least I hoped not," Huy smiled back, showing his nearly toothless grin.

"It was a long trek. Do you mind if I come and have a little rest?" Anik asked, looking for a chair.

Huy motioned with his hand to a chair beside the small table under the cluster of trees. Anik collapsed in the seat and felt his legs almost breathe a sigh of relief. The chess board was set up again. This time, however, the white side was facing him, complete with the king that was missing his cross. Anik sat back on the chair and closed his eyes.

"Would you like a drink, Anik?" he heard Sarin ask.

Anik opened his eyes to see her holding an old cracked and chipped mug full of water.

"Yes, I would. Thank you," Anik answered.

He picked up the battered mug and took a drink of the water. Anik peered into the rough looking mug and noticed small grains of sand swirling around the bottom of the cup. He felt pity for this extremely poor couple who had so little, yet shared what they had.

"So Anik, did you see all the dunes you wanted to see?" the old man asked.

"Pretty much." Anik shared how he had traveled a good distance and found an especially large dune near a group of date palms. He didn't mention the mysterious rock that was embedded in the dune, in case it was indeed something of importance.

"That's good," Huy said as he filled his pipe.

Motioning to the chess board, he grinned. "Your move."

When Anik arrived back home, he gathered the tools he would need for the next day — a shovel, hammer, stakes, and a deflector tarp. He decided he could put together some food and water in the morning. Thinking of his promise to himself to bring Huy a chess set, he took a look at his extra sets and chose one with the men made to resemble ancient Egyptians. He was sure Huy would love that one.

The next morning Anik got up early, gathered together the things that he needed and started to head out, but his dad flagged him down before he could go anywhere.

"Where are you off to in such a hurry?" Sekani called after him.

Anik's dad was always interested in his son's activities and was, for the most part, a great father. Sekani was a man who, in spite of the hardships life had handed him, consistently put a high value on honesty and integrity. Though the failure of his marriage hurt him greatly, his son Anik was a great compensation and he was proud of him.

Sekani had not wanted the breakup of the family, but his wife Neema was never happy with what he could provide. Her name meant "born to wealthy parents," and she was a spend-thrift, with no regard for how much debt she created.It was a no-win situation.

"Well Dad, I had a great time on my little trip into the desert yesterday. I met an older couple on the way and I had fun surfing down a gigantic sand dune, but I did cut my hand on a rock that was embedded in it," he said as he showed his father his "war wound." "I'm going back again today to investigate that further. You never know ..."

"Perhaps it's something to look into, but don't let your mind get the best of you. Remember the time we were convinced we had found an 'ancient pillar' and it turned out to be an old sewer tile? I'll never forget the look on your face, or the pungent smell when it broke as we tried to lift it out!" Sekani said with a chuckle. "Why don't you take the satellite phone and the three-wheeler as well? And call me if you find it again. Okay?"

"Okay, Dad. Do you think I should bring a change of clothes as well?" Anik added with a laugh. "Actually, the ATV is a great idea. It will get me there a lot quicker."

"I won't be close by today. I'll be in town, so be careful when you're out there, Anik," Sekani cautioned as he left.

"Oh, I will," laughed Anik.

He topped up the fuel, hitched the trailer to the Jeep, and loaded the three-wheeler on the trailer. The supplies and food he put in the back of the Jeep, and then he headed over to Sitaya's house to invite her along.

The front door to Sitaya's house opened and she stepped outside raising her hand in greeting.

At eighteen years old she was beautiful, and wore her usual short-cut T-shirt that exposed her pierced navel, which sported a delicate silver chain. She wore ripped jean shorts and white Nike Air runners and ankle socks. Today she had taken her hair out the twin braid she commonly wore and let her straight black hair fall to her mid back. A white heart "tattooed" her stomach. She had worn a heart sticker on the side of her abdomen so as she tanned, the skin stayed white under the sticker and when it was removed a white heart was revealed.

"What's up?" she asked, seeing the ATV.

"I'm heading out into the desert to investigate a mystery. Want to come?"

"Sounds like fun. If we're going to ride on that, I'd better put my hair up. Back in a minute"

Anik drove to the same spot that he had parked the day before. He maneuvered the ATV off the trailer and then loaded it with the supplies, food and water. Sitaya hopped on the back of the three-wheeler, wrapped her arms around Anik's waist and jokingly yelled out, "Giddy up."

Anik pulled the ATV over to Huy's yard and came to a halt. Huy got up from his seat with the help of his cane, his pipe still in his mouth, and hobbled over to Anik and Sitaya.

"I didn't expect to see you this soon. Are you here to play another game?" he said as he pointed to the chess table, smiling hopefully.

"Actually, no. We are heading out into the desert again today. I just came to drop off a gift for you and we'll be on our way," Anik said as he presented Huy with the wrapped package.

Sarin came out of the house, wiping her hands on a towel.

"Well, hello Anik. It's nice to see you again so soon. And who do you have with you today?"

"Hello, Sarin, this is my friend Sitaya. Sitaya, this is Sarin and Huy."

"Hello," Sitaya replied, waving her hand.

During the introductions, Huy was opening the gift.

"Will you look at this now!" he exclaimed. "Anik, what a beautiful chess set. I've never seen anything like it. You didn't need to do this. Thank you."

"I wanted to. I hope you like it. It will make our games more interesting. We'll probably see you on our way back. "

Anik casually mounted the three-wheeler and started it up. Anik and Sitaya waved to the older couple and sped down the road.

Off they went, bouncing along the hard-packed trail and then into the desert. Anik decided to take the scenic route, swerving between the small hills and rocketing down the steeper embankments. The wilder the ride was, the tighter Sitaya's arms got around his waist and the more he felt her breasts push into his back. Anik loved the feel of her arms gripping his body for protection. Even though they didn't take the most direct path, it took them only thirty minutes to get back to the dune.

He surveyed the huge, sandy incline and filled her in on the mysterious hidden treasure he hoped to find again. Before they did anything, they rested their legs, which felt cramped from the jarring trip.

Anik and Sitaya sat under the date palms and shared a bottle of water. They helped themselves to the ripe treats that were there for the taking. They bantered back and forth as they had always done in their casual times together. Sitaya filled Anik in on her new babysitting job in Luxor.

"I want to get some money to buy a car, you know," she commented.

"Hey, you could be my sitter if you wanted," Anik said with a big smile and a wink.

"You don't want me as a sitter 'cause I would make you go to bed without any snack," Sitaya said with a laugh.

"And just what kind of a snack would you deny me?" Anik teased.

Sitaya rolled her eyes and laughed and punched him playfully in the arm.

After their short rest, Anik began to count out the steps to the precise location of the "carved rock." After he was satisfied with his measuring and re-measuring, he hammered stakes into the sand at the base of the dune to mark the location.

Anik grabbed the shovel and proceeded to climb the steep dune bank until he was satisfied with the height to which he had climbed. He started methodically probing with the shovel. Even though sand trickled in the tops of his shoes, he continued to try to find the tip of the trophy he searched for.

Sitaya stood at the bottom of the dune watching Anik work, making light conversation and joking about the sand filling his shoes. They reminisced about all the years they were friends and the trouble they got into together. They were always together going off on adventures without telling their parents.

"Remember the time we walked across the city in search of the Discman you were sure you left at that park and then we got lost and couldn't find our way home?" Anik asked between shovelfuls. "We got in so much trouble we couldn't visit each other for a month."

"I think that was because the police had to bring us home. I'll never forget the look on your dad's face as we pulled up in the back of the police cruiser."

"I felt so stupid after I found it in my room the next day," Sitaya recalled sheepishly.

"Come on! Where are you?" Anik spoke out to the hiding stone as if it could answer him.

After some time he felt a definite "clink" through his shovel handle. He proceeded to use the spade as a marker, sticking it in as deep as he could. After retrieving the deflector tarps and stakes from the ATV, Anik draped the tarp into an inverted V-shape above a stake to deflect the flowing sand.

Later in the afternoon, Sitaya and Anik had shovelled deep into the dune's face and had uncovered the top of his prize. As he stared at the unique "rock," he realized that what he had found was the head of a statue, and the part he uncovered was just the crown. His elation and glee overtook him like a sand devil swirling around an unsuspecting lizard. Anik remembered the phone he had brought and thought, *now is the time for that call!*

Retrieving his shovel, he removed some more sand just to make sure he was correct in what he was seeing. Then he slid down the bank to make the call to his dad.

"Dad?" he asked, after he dialled the number and Sekani picked up.

"You will never guess what I found in the dunes and no, it's not a sewer pipe!"

As he was talking, the stake holding back his deflector tarps gave way with a loud snap and their hours of work disappeared before their eyes.

"I'm going to need some more help with this, that's for sure," Anik said with annoyance. "It had better be more than a fragment."

"Don't get too worked up. It looks like you have found something worthwhile," Sitaya said, putting her hands on her hips and cocking her head to the side.

14

STATUE

Huy sat in his chair, puffing on his pipe, the chess board set up on the table in front of him. The pieces gleamed in the sun, casting sunbeam reflections across his face. His gnarled old fingers slowly caressed the smooth sides of the new pieces. He had never owned a new chess set before in his life. *There are no scratches, no nicks, no fading. And the pieces are so Egyptian. It's perfect*, he thought as he admired the set that Anik had given him.

"Are you still fussing with that chess set, Huy? It's been a whole week, you know," Sarin called out.

"But my dear, this is the first time I have owned something so beautiful like this," Huy called back.

As they were talking, Sarin looked up and said, "There's a truck coming down the road." Huy gazed up, wondering if it might be Anik coming to visit him again. The red truck that approached didn't stop; it just drove past them along the road into the desert. He did see Anik in the passenger seat. *Maybe he will stop by on his way back*, Huy thought wistfully. It had certainly added to the activity of his life to have met Anik, and he looked forward to every meeting. He did wonder why they were traveling into the desert again, but perhaps the young man would tell him about it some time. He was a very busy fellow.

Anik, Sitaya, and his father strolled around the base of the dune. Sand swirling around their feet reminded them of the instability of the weather in the Western Desert. Without warning it could change from beautiful and tranquil to ferocious and deadly.

Sitaya walked over to the date grove they had previously eaten from and plopped herself down against the tree trunk, calling them over for a snack. They munched on some dates they found in the branches of the trees that cast a welcome shade for the three of them. Anik sat cross legged holding a fistful of the tasty treats against his T-shirt that read: What's Up?

Like a new paint job, the barren dunes showed no disturbance as the wind continuously erased all signs of human activity. The surface of the desert sands was a sea of ripples that expanded rhythmically into the distance on every side.

Sekani walked up to the dune, scooped up a handful of sand and let it run through his fingers.

"So your special stone is somewhere in here, is it? This sand is altogether different from the sand of the other dunes around here, don't you think? It's like small pea gravel," Sekani said. "Well, let's have a look at your statue head and see what we can see."

Anik counted the steps from the small grove of date palms across and up to the spot where he had discovered the rock the last time. The two men shovelled steadily, with occasional breaks when Sitaya brought them water. Before they knew it, three hours had gone by and still, much to Anik's dismay, his prize was nowhere to be seen. Frustration began to build in his mind. *Why can't I find it? It was right here a week ago. I wasn't just seeing things!*

"This is starting to tick me off," Anik ranted. "It was here. Even Sitaya saw it."

"Maybe the measurements are slightly different. You know how the dunes change with the wind," Sitaya added her two cents worth.

"You could be right. Let me measure it again and see if I am off. I'm glad I brought my GPS this time because when I find it, it will stay found."

Anik got to the bottom of the dune and jogged over to the date grove where he had begun his original measurements. He recalled the exact placing of his foot by the first palm and started counting. Sure enough, the dune had moved from his first measurement, covering the original stake he had driven in, and he hadn't taken that into account. The final spot was six feet to the left. Anik grabbed his spade and once again started digging with new determination. Within two feet his shovel hit something solid with a familiar "thunk" and he realized that he had found the right place. Another hour passed, and they had uncovered a fair amount of the shaped rock. The wind started to pick up, but they continued digging. Anik's excitement grew as they realized what they had discovered was a statue which appeared to be a pharaoh.

"This is amazing," Anik exclaimed. "What is it doing here in the middle of the desert?"

"I've got to say that it looks as though you found something very special here, son."

"Let's shore up the sides so there won't be any more cave-ins. And I want to get some photos. But first I want to enter the exact location on the GPS. I sure don't want to let this beauty disappear on me again," Anik said.

"I wonder which pharaoh this is," Sitaya mused. "And why is it way out here?"

"Why is it the same color as this bizarre looking sand?" Anik added. "You know what? If you didn't know exactly where to look, you wouldn't even see it at a distance. It blends in so well, it's invisible."

"Yes it's the same stone as the statue and that's why it looks invisible," Sekani added. "It looks like they crushed the stone chips of the same rock to make an invisible covering for it, but why?"

They inspected the shoulders and saw hieroglyphs on the left side. Then Anik got a pencil and paper and copied them down as well as taking close up pictures. The wind increased and blowing sand made their efforts increasingly difficult.

"Well, if we are going to get anywhere with this we will need the 600 Komatsu loader back at home," Sekani yelled to Anik over the wind. "We had better head back while we can still see where we're going."

They packed up as the wind drove swirling sand into their hair and clothes, hopped into the truck and headed back home. As they entered the house Anik said, "I have been thinking about who we should contact about our discovery. We want to make sure they are reputable and official. In the courses I've taken to learn hieroglyphics they often mention the Egyptian Archaeological Society. I think that's who I should contact. What do you think?"

"Sounds good to me," replied Sekani.

"Their office is right here in Luxor," said Anik. He looked up the number and entered it on the phone. He made his way through the maze of "please hold" and "I will put you through to…" until he spoke with someone who listened to what he had to say and asked lots of questions. After a lengthy discussion, Anik hung up the phone, and turned to

Sitaya and Sekani, his face beaming.

"So, what did they say?" asked Sitaya.

"They want me to come to their headquarters tomorrow morning, first thing. They are interested in what I have found and want to see my photos. I'll have to fill out some paperwork and then I have a meeting with Mr. Yusik, the head of the society," Anik responded. "Can you both come with me?"

"This is something that I don't want to miss," replied his father.

"Oh, I have to work tomorrow," said Sitaya, with disappointment showing on her face.

The office in downtown Luxor was a black and gray brick structure four storeys high. A warehouse with its overhead doors set into the gray bulk, sat expansively to one side of the main office. Anik and Sekani pushed through the double glass doors into the brightly-colored office.

Anik approached the reception desk and gave his name to the receptionist.

"Oh yes, we are expecting you. Please have a seat and I'll let Mr. Thissen know you are here."

Anik and his father sat in the upholstered wooden chairs and waited with suppressed excitement. Within a few minutes John Thissen appeared. He was short and slight in stature, stooped in posture and with a demeanor of outward curiosity, but inward weariness.

"Good morning. Mr. Yusik, my supervisor, has asked me to speak with you and get the details of your discovery, along with your information. It was me that you spoke with yesterday. I'd like to make notes, so if you could tell me again the location of your find, and everything you can remember about the statue, I'll include it all in this file."

After they repeated the facts of their venture, Mr. Thissen finished making notes. He closed the file and said, "Thank you. This sounds like an authentic discovery. Please wait here. I'll just take this to Mr. Yusik and I'll be back shortly."

With that, he disappeared down the hall. When he came back, he invited them to join him in Mr. Yusik's office.

He led them down the hallway adorned with many authentic paintings on papyrus sheets in pressed glass that dotted the pale brown walls. On the right side a complete Book of the Dead filled the space. The end of the hall came to an abrupt end with a black wooden statue of Anubis. John Thissen led them left and into a large, well-lit office. A man sat at an elegant, old hand-crafted mahogany desk which stood in front of the only window in the room. Besides the filing cabinets, there were a number of tables and display cases. These were crowded with files, papers and relics.

A tall, slender man rose from the desk and approached them. He had thinning straight gray hair, a hawk-like nose, and glasses covering brown eyes that sparkled with intelligence.

"Ah, yes. Good morning. You must be the young man who called yesterday."

"Anik, this is Mr. Dendree Yusik, the head of the Egyptian Archaeological Society. And Dendree, this is Anik Masri and his father, Sekani."

"Hello, Mr. Yusik. I'm very pleased to meet you."

"I understand you have found something of great interest. I would like to hear all about it," replied the archaeologist. "Just where did you find this statue?"

"It's in the desert. I followed a road which leads into the desert on the outskirts at the west side of Luxor. I walked for two hours before I spotted an especially high dune. The statue is buried in that dune. I've got to say that I have a powerful interest in the history of ancient Egypt. We have found a few artifacts during excavations with my father's construction company. I have taken a number of courses in archaeology and hieroglyphics and I'm quite excited about finding this large statue. I put the pictures I took on this flash drive. If I could plug in to a computer you can see for yourself. I also noticed hieroglyphics down the left side. They don't show up particularly well on the pictures, but I have copied them down on paper here."

"You can use this computer for the pictures. This sounds quite promising, young man."

Anik plugged the flash drive into the laptop and set it up for Dendree to have a look.

"Why, this is most intriguing, Anik," said Dendree as he carefully observed each picture, scrolling through them a couple of times. "Hmm, this looks as though it might be something created around 1000BC. Yes … yes, this does look like a statue of a pharaoh. I believe you have found something very valuable — something that will need to be retrieved and studied."

He stood up, removed his glasses, then turned and looked intently into Anik's face.

"And what involvement would you like to have in this venture, young man? What is your interest in the matter? "

Anik's face lit up and he smiled at Dendree, enthusiasm and conviction in his voice, "I want to dig it up, study it, and donate it to the Museum's collection of Egyptian treasures. What do I need so I can do this?"

"We usually prefer to have such digs handled by trained archaeologists. There are important protocols for unearthing precious objects which amateurs can damage by carelessness. You mentioned taking some courses, however. Tell me about that," said Dendree.

Anik explained his own journey, both in the construction business, and his own studies.

"It sounds as though we have a budding seeker of relics here," commented Dendree. "I'll tell you what I'll do. I can provide you with the proper license and documentation to give you permission for this exploration. I would like to include your father in this matter, as his excavation expertise will be useful in the project. As well, I would like to come with you to the location and have a look for myself at this statue in the sand. You have done well to contact us first, and we can monitor your progress. This is an exciting day. It looks as though this might be a significant discovery in a unique location."

During the next week they assembled the tools and supplies that they needed for the task of digging the statue from the sand. Soon they were rumbling out into the desert. Dendree and Sekani led the way in the Society's SUV, using the GPS, and Anik followed in the big Komatsu loader to the vacant desert landscape, hiding its royal treasure. Sitaya comfortably fit beside Anik as they both bounced across the uneven surface of the desert. A vulture flew off in the distance, suspended in the air, catching an up-draft. Anik thought about his "find". *Was he going to be famous? Probably not. Dendree might look at it and say "This is not particularly special."* Anik started to second guess himself, and Sitaya could feel a drop in his usual joyful demeanor.

"Hey grumpy, what's your problem?" Sitaya needled him.

"I'm just nervous about dragging Dendree out here. What if this is just no big deal? Then I will have brought this important man out here for nothing. You know, Murphy's Law seems to love me for some reason," Anik said, scowling.

"You've got to be kidding, Anik. Where were you when the statue head was uncovered? I know what I saw. It is the best preserved statue in all Egypt — at least the best that I have ever seen. You know that."

"Could be a partial statue, a fragment," Anik argued.

Sitaya stared at Anik and shook her head.

"If that thing is a fragment I'm going to kiss you right on the mouth," she threatened, trying to snap him out of his self-abasing attitude.

Anik returned her gaze, a smile spreading across his face.

"In that case, I guess I'll come out a winner either way," Anik said, his positive outlook restored.

The site was as stark as ever. The sand storm the previous week had totally filled in any progress they had made. Anik was at the controls of the loader, working more carefully than he ever had before. The bucket began biting into the bank of the dune, taking bucket after bucket of coarse, granular sand and piling it out of the way. As soon as he had dug away enough of the side of the dune to access the statue, he shut down the big machine and joined the group of eager archiologists manned with shovels and brushes, ready for the next step of the the excavation.

As they worked, the statue gradually came into view until it was totally uncovered. The four of them looked in amazement at the image. The majestic likeness of the long-deceased pharaoh looked as if it were made yesterday. Being buried in such a dry location and out of the elements had preserved it perfectly. The statue was twenty-five feet high, including the base of black granite.

"This is a marvelous find!" Dendree exclaimed.

Looking at the fourteen-foot wide granite base that shone with a mirror-like finish, Dendree started pointing out the names of the many pharaohs engraved in the different cartouches: Narmer, Snefru, Kufu, Khaffre, Shepseskare Ist, Amenemhet, Sesostris, Amose, Horemheb, Neferefre, Amenhotep Ist, Seti Ist, Rameses Ist , IInd, and IIIrd, fifteen names in total.

"This is incredible!" marvelled Dendree as little wisps of his hair were caught by the warm breeze. "You never see the other pharaohs' names on a statue together like this. The cartouche on his shoulder bears the name of the figure. Ah, it's Amenemope! He was a less important Pharaoh from 956 BC or so. There is not a great deal about him in the historical documents, but he did write some literature."

Anik gazed up at the imposing figure that looked straight into the dune with a calm, yet piercing gaze. Amenemope's confident stare held Anik spellbound. His face displayed determination and authority. He held the flail in his right hand, his arm extended out toward the dune as if he were waiting to severely punish whoever emerged. The statue of Amenemope seemed to be backwards, facing into the dune from which he had materialized. Anik walked back toward the road a little way to get a good view of their work and take a picture, but he was shocked at what he saw.

"Wow ... you've got to come here and check this out," he hollered to his dad and Dendree.

Soon they were all standing side-by-side looking back at the sand dune to where the pharaoh's stone image was standing. Other than the black base, they could hardly see the statue they had uncovered. The colors blended into the face of the dune, making it almost invisible again.

"I've got to say, that is an awe inspiring sight if I've ever seen one," Anik said, not being able to adequately express his excitement.

Dendree looked over at him, adjusted his glasses, looped his thumbs in his pockets and nodded.

"It's actually hidden in plain sight. It's amazing," he replied.

Sitaya leaned close to Anik and whispered how proud she was of him.

Dendree brought out his high resolution camera and took a series of photos of the pharaoh's image that seemed to be so mysteriously out of place this deep in the desert so far from any ancient town.

"These are for the record. I know this discovery will reveal quite a bit of knowledge about this particular pharaoh. I don't know why his time of rule was so lacking in the historical record. Perhaps the information written in these hieroglyphics will fill in some gaps."

On their way back, Anik and Sitaya stopped by Huy's house to fill the older couple in on their discovery before they drove home. Anik revealed how he discovered the statue as he was sliding down the dune, when his hand scraped against the top of it.

"Let me get this straight," Huy said as he took another puff from his pipe and let the smoke curl out through his mouth and nose. "You found the statue by accident while you were playing?"

Anik nodded, a smile lighting up his face. As they were talking, they saw Dendree's SUV approaching, and they waved to him. He waved back, pulled his vehicle up to the front of the home and parked. Then he and Sekani walked over to join them.

"Huy, I'd like you to meet Mr. Dendree Yusik. He is the head of the Archeological Society. And this is my dad, Sekani. This is Huy. I met him the first time I went out in the desert," Anik introduced them to each other.

"I'm pleased to meet you, Mr. Yusik and Sekani. It sounds as though you have found something very special out in the sands. By the way, Anik, after you were here before, I remembered that my grandfather had told me a little bit about this road. Did you know that it's called The Road to Death?"

Dendree spoke up, "Do you know why it has such a name?"

"Can't say that I do," replied Huy.

"I would be interested to know why it is so named," commented Dendree. "I wonder if the statue we found has something to do with it. We must look into it."

Anik, Sitaya, and Dendree said their goodbyes, walked to the vehicles and drove back to the city, filled with enthusiasm and anticipation.

Anik's mind reeled. *The Road to Death — what does this mean? So many unanswered questions!*

15

SELF-WORTH

A haze of air pollution hung over Luxor in the early morning, waiting for the sun to break free from the horizon and burn it off. The smog that permeated the large Egyptian city made it smell filthy, as if it were an unclean automotive shop. Horns beeped as cars and trucks crisscrossed the congested streets, each jockeying for position to lead them around the maze of city roads.

Along with the older vehicles in various states of disrepair, hundreds of horse or donkey drawn carriages and carts timidly walked the garbage-strewn streets and alleys. Older buildings and newer buildings with re-bar jutting from the roofs filled the once majestic city.

The beautiful temple of Luxor sat nestled in the chaotic town, seeming to wish that one day the city would return to its glorious past when it was called Thebes. Here, the black markets sold their wares: knock-off clothing brands, ancient relics and weapons.

The cataloguing of the statue and official photos took several weeks, during which Anik could spend much-needed time alone with Sitaya. As a long-time friend, Anik had always had a complicated affection for her. She had attended the same school as he did, although two grades behind him.

She had a higher voice than the other girls, and he loved that about her. She had high cheek bones and slightly uneven teeth. Her aqua-colored eyes highlighted her permanently tanned complexion.

Sitaya's long jet-black hair only enhanced her slender five-foot-six-inch frame. Anik had known her for most of his life and in some ways she felt like a sister to him, but in other ways he was definitely glad she was not his sister. Anik valued the private times spent with her and he wanted more.

"We have been together as friends for some time, Sitaya," Anik said, taking some initiative as they were out strolling among the tiny shops on the outskirts of Luxor.

Goats, cows, and small dogs also crowded the streets and walked around freely. Anik and Sitaya picked their way through the noisy streets. The pleasant smells from the shops and restaurants enabled them to put up with the occasional harsh scent of animal feces as they window shopped.

Stores also displayed their butchered animals for sale by hanging them on hooks in the windows, inviting the various insects to land and have their fill, unchallenged.

The tightly packed stores had every possible enticing trinket imaginable, but Anik's mind was far from being tempted to shop and buy something he would discard within a week.

"You're right, Anik. Probably since you were seven. That is a long time. So, what have you got to say?" Sitaya answered coyly. She smiled slowly and looked directly into his eyes.

"We, uh," Anik stammered. "Uh, that is, you mean a great deal to me, and I — I was wondering how you felt?"

A quirky look washed across Sitaya's face, as she maintained a steady gaze.

"You mean a great deal to me, too," she mimicked in a low voice. "What's all this about?" Anik paused uncertainly, thoughts swirling, before he said any more. He knew Sitaya's sarcastic humor was just in fun, but he was still nervous about rejection.

"I was thinking that maybe we should consider taking the next step in our friendship."

"Meaning?" Sitaya said, staring straight at him.

She couldn't help but smile looking at his shirt that read: STAND BACK! PROFESSIONAL THINKER AT WORK.

"I want to go out with you, Sitaya, on a real date — not just hanging out. I'm starting to have some really strong feelings for you."

"Really! It's about damn time you asked me about this. I've been wondering how long it would take you to ask," she laughed. "I've loved you for a long time, Anik — ever since you proudly showed me around your father's construction vehicles, bragging that 'one day I'll be better than my dad at using these.'" She smiled as the memories flooded back.

"I suspected it for a while, but I was still dealing with things in my life, as you know, so I wanted to go slow and make sure," he answered.

"Of course I want to go out with you. I love you," Sitaya purred.

Anik felt a massive weight lift off his heart and all he could do was smile. He couldn't even speak. This was the happiest day in his life, and no words could describe it.

After he gathered himself together, he looked deep into her beautiful aqua eyes that matched her lapis nose ring, and replied, "I love you too."

They linked their fingers together and walked off towards Anik's home. Feelings of passion, newly ignited, permeated their hearts. As they walked down the dusty road, thoughts of future possibilities swept into Anik and Sitaya's minds.

Anik's mind wandered to the times he had thought about her in a purely sexual nature. He had imagined her sneaking into his room while he was sleeping and asking to spend the night with him. Of course he would agree.

Anik could feel his temperature rise, beginning in his neck and across his face. Embarrassment swept over him, forcing him to stuff his hands in his pockets to conceal the growing tightness in his shorts. He forced his mind back to reality, though he didn't want to leave the daytime fantasy that often washed over him.

Sitaya's mind was also wandering, imagining Anik as her future husband. She knew their life together wouldn't be free of hardships though. He still struggled at being satisfied with his current job and the abandonment of his mother.

He had said he felt there was something more for him, but he didn't know what. His desire to make his life better every day was what had always made him so desirable to her. *He would make a good husband to me as well as a great father*, she thought to herself. She wondered if he had ever thought about marriage or children.

As they walked, careful not to stumble into animal waste that littered the road, Sitaya glanced over at him, realizing he had become very silent over the last while. Anik's face had become a deep red color as he seemingly was concentrating on something else. Sitaya looked down and noticed a bulge in the front of his shorts.

Oh! I know what he's thinking about, she said to herself with a smile, and she deliberately walked closer to him allowing her breast to brush against him.

Anik's home made Sitaya feel welcome. Sekani, Anik's dad, had always treated her as a daughter.

"Dad? We're home," Anik called out as they opened the creaky screen door and stepped in.

The smell of freshly dried clothes filled the air, making the house feel welcoming and safe for any visitors that might stop by.

From the rear yard, Sekani called a greeting back to them both. Anik walked over to the fridge and with a yank, opened the door and took out some Cokes for the three of them.

Working outside on his car, Sekani looked up in appreciation as Sitaya walked over and handed him a pre-opened drink.

"Just a second, Taya," Sekani replied, using the pet name he had adopted for her.

He reached over and looked around for the shop rag he had been using and wiped his oil-coated hands before grasping the icy cold Coke Classic that had been offered.

"So how's the car, Dad?" Anik asked.

"Well, I think I finally got it fixed this time," Sekani replied as he looked over at the '72 BMW he was working on. With several large gulps, he finished the cold drink.

A triumphant smile washed over his face as he walked over to the car's glossy metallic green driver's side door and hopped in. He reached for the key that sported a discharged 30-6 bullet hanging from its chain and inserted it into the ignition. Without another thought, he confidently turned the key.

The engine roared to life and stayed primed and ready to go. Sekani stepped on the accelerator, revving the engine several times to test his hard work. The engine seemed fine, but the excitement was short lived — the motor lost power. It was then followed by a couple of spats of backfiring, coughing, then sputtering to death.

"Come on!" Sekani yelled.

"Looks like you will be here for a while, Dad."

"Yeah, looks like it," Sekani replied with a sigh of resignation.

"Sitaya and I are going to go for a walk to the dunes. OK, Dad? We'll take a picnic lunch to the statue so don't worry about saving food for us."

Sekani looked over at them and smiled, knowing all too well what it was like to be in love.

"Maybe I'll have the car fixed when you come back. Then you can take it for a spin."

"Dad, I think you should just get a new engine and stop being so stubborn," Anik said, shaking his head.

Sekani had tried, time and time again, to repair the BMW's motor, never able to successfully find the problem that plagued it. Anik repeatedly suggested to his dad that he replace the old lemon. Sekani was just as determined to repair it, though.

"Have fun, Anik, and look after him for me, will you, Taya?"

"I promise," Sitaya called back as they went to the kitchen and gathered food for their picnic.

Anik and Sitaya walked together, hand in hand along the dusty path that led into the desert. They passed small shacks and palm trees that lined the road. As they walked further from Luxor, the pungent smell of the polluted city no longer hung in the air, but was replaced by the clean, dry smell of desert sand.

Up ahead, Anik saw Huy's house. Right then, spending time with Sarin and Huy was the last thing he wanted to do. As they approached the tiny house, Anik could see Huy sitting at the chess board and Sarin pulling weeds out of their meager garden.

"You don't want to be here, right?" Sitaya stated, seeing his demeanor change.

"No, not really."

It was too late to turn back, as Sarin spotted them and started waving her dirt covered hands. Anik returned the wave out of courtesy, but begrudged the impending "meet and greet."

"Hello, Anik!" Sarin called over excitedly.

Anik quietly let out a sigh of annoyance. They slowly walked over to the enthused couple. Anik greeted Huy as he saw him look up from his table — a chess game ready to play.

"Would you two like to have an iced tea?" Sarin asked, wanting some company.

"Thank you Sarin, but we were just heading to our favorite dune to have a picnic. We'll stop in on our way back, OK?" Sitaya called to Anik's relief.

The trail they were traveling soon gave way to the desert sands, forming small, rippling waves that made them almost expect to see the ocean and the beach filled with sunbathers. Off in the distance, a small dark-colored creature skittered between the dunes. The tiny big-eared and wide-eyed desert fox stopped in its tracks, gazed at the two people, and then turned and ran into the desert.

Anik and Sitaya stuck to the narrow track that the previous trucks and loader had left imprinted in the sand. After a couple of hours of walking along the track that was disappearing into the blowing sand, they came to the site they were looking for.

In the distance they saw what appeared to be a large, glorious lake, but they were not fooled by the mirage. They just kept walking.

The tall image of Amenemope looked odd, standing in the sea of dunes like a tower in the middle of a heaving sea.

Off to one side the small grove of date palms flourished against all odds, the dry sand seeming to have no effect on them. Anik assumed that the trees' roots had burrowed into cracks in the bedrock and were being fed water from a small aquifer below the arid desert. They walked around the perimeter of the statue and the dunes.

The discovery still seemed fresh in their minds even though it had been a while. Observing the statue again flooded both of their minds with the events that had followed their discovery and the subsequent fame and attention that came to them. The statue was as timeless as ever, whereas their lives had changed a great deal during the brief interval. Their new celebrity status meant being in the public eye, answering the same questions in numerous interviews — except for the exact location of the statue — and being recognized frequently as they went about their daily lives. It was both exciting and annoying. But here in the desert, being alone with the statue made all the hype fade and they once again took in the beauty and splendor of their find.

Anik and Sitaya strolled around the dunes until they found themselves at the top of the mountain of sand that had hidden its treasure from view for so many centuries.

They circled the peak and began to appreciate the majesty of the location itself. A soft, hot wind blew their hair from side to side, making today a particularly gorgeous day for being together.

"Let's have our picnic lunch right here and enjoy this incredible view," Anik suggested.

"That sounds great. Besides, I'm starving!"

Luxor could be seen far in the distance. A brownish haze covered the bustling, choked city. Individual buildings could not be deciphered because of the distance and the smog, but the startling difference between the clean crisp air of the desert and Luxor was shockingly obvious from this vantage point. They opened the container of rice and vegetables mixed with a meat sauce and folded several flat-breads to dip into the soupy mixture. They sat with the dish between them and alternately dipped their bread in and bit off chunks, savoring every morsel. Anik opened a bag of fruit, nibbled on some of the dates they brought, and sipped their refreshing mango drinks. After they were finished, Anik stretched out on his back and looked into the sky, feeling content. Sitaya scooted over and lay beside him, resting her head on his shoulder and her hand on his stomach. They both dozed on top of the sand dune for an hour or so. After the rest, Sitaya sat up, and reaching out, stroked his cheek with the back of her hand. *He has such a beautiful face,* she thought. *Model material for sure.*

The breeze began blowing the grit around and soon it really started to dampen Anik's enjoyment of the otherwise perfect day. As he sat up, his foot smacked into a hard object. What was that? He got to his feet and proceeded to kick at what he had just bumped into. He dug at the surface and brushed away a layer of sand to reveal a huge stone, a dressed block with a rounded top and a smooth finish. As he whisked it off more carefully, he sent showers of sand to the left side and sprinkled Sitaya. There on the top of the rock was a name engraved. It said "Wijin."

"I think we need the shovels again," Anik said as he glanced at Sitaya with an excited expression. Inside, his mind began to swirl and rush with new anticipation.

Just then Anik heard the rumble of trucks approaching from the direction of the city. He saw them a long way off from their position at the summit of the dune and was curious as to how anyone could find their way to this location. Sitaya leaned over to Anik and he slipped his arm around her waist.

"I have a bad feeling about this," she said just as the exact same thought entered his mind.

They quickly covered the hole he had dug and scooted down to the base of the dune to wait for the visitors. After a few minutes, three trucks pulled up and five men got out of the orange SUVs.

"Can I help you?" Anik questioned.

"Not really," replied one of the older men, who appeared to be in command.

"We just came by to get some rubbings of the statue for research," the older man added.

They marched past the couple dismissively and went right to the statue where they took out the necessary equipment and went to work. Anik and Sitaya moved over to the palm grove and sat watching the men, listening to everything they said while feeling incredulous and alarmed. They picked up on the older man's name: Bill Landing. He seemed to lead the other men, but was apparently the head of their research organization. Egyptian Artifacts and Studies was the name printed on the side of their orange SUVs, but Anik and Sitaya had never heard about them before, and they'd lived in Egypt all their lives.

After they finished making the rubbings, the older man, Bill Landing, came over to where Anik and Sitaya were sitting while the others headed back to the vehicles.

"So," he said "this is a pretty impressive find. You're the young fellow who found it, am I right? I recognize you from the newspaper. Have you found anything else around here?

"No. I can't say that I have. The actual location of the statue was never mentioned. I'm kind of surprised that you managed to find it," Anik answered back as pleasantly as possible.

"We like to keep up on things," Bill replied vaguely as he took a look around. "Well, we'll be on our way, but let me know if you find anything else, and we will be glad to help you," Bill said, tossing a business card in Anik's lap.

"Who is this pretty girl?" Bill said, his eyes settling on Sitaya for the first time.

"She's my girlfriend. Why?" he said forcefully, realizing that it was the first time he had referred to her in that way.

"You should keep a leash on her. This is a big desert, and you wouldn't want her to get lost out here, you know what I mean?" Bill said nonchalantly, with a wink at Sitaya.

They got into their vehicles and motored off back down the road.

"I doubt it, pal," Anik retorted when they were out of earshot. "Something's not right with those guys, Sitaya. They pissed me off the way they talked to us and how he looked at you. I'll tell you one thing. I'm not saying anything to them about what we found at the top of the dune."

"That guy gave me the creeps. Let's get on our way back to your house," Sitaya urged.

Anik nodded and reached for her hand, and they made their way down the long path home. As they walked back, he said, "I don't know whether or not that guy is dangerous, but I think we had better not come out here alone with no phone and no transportation any more. We might find ourselves in a real predicament. Dendree thought that keeping the location of the statue out of the news would provide some safety for it, but it looks as though the secret is out."

The journey back gave them a chance to discuss their reactions and worries and by the time they reached the outskirts of town, they had calmed down considerably.

They were plenty thirsty when they came to Huy and Sarin's place, so they stopped in as promised and gratefully accepted the sun-warmed "iced" tea that had been offered previously. Anik sat down to a game with Huy as Sitaya chatted with Sarin, filling her in on the unexpected meeting with Bill Landing.

"I'm sorry to hear about your troubles. It must have been very upsetting," she said, truly concerned.

There was a pause in the conversation as Sarin seemed to be searching for the next words to say.

"On another topic, Anik seems to really care about you," she blurted out. "You can see it all over him."

Sitaya glanced over at her, blushing, and a smile crept onto her face.

"We have been friends for many years. Actually, just this morning he told me he cared about me and wants to pursue a relationship. I've been waiting for it for some time," Sitaya revealed.

"He seems like a really nice boy. Did you say yes?" Sarin asked, sure of the answer.

"Of course. I'm not about to play hard to get," Sitaya answered, her eyes sparkling.

Sarin just nodded and smiled, remembering her times of young love. Over at Anik and Huy's game, Anik had Huy's king in his clutches. He slowly made meaningless moves to prolong the game and not totally crush Huy.

"Alright, Anik, I see what you are doing. You are not going to make me mad if you beat me!" Huy said with a smile of surrender on his face.

"Checkmate," Anik said as he moved his rook into place.

"That was a great game, Anik. I really appreciate it when you stop by and play with me. Thank you," Huy said gratefully.

"We had better be on our way," said Anik as he and Sitaya stood up and took their leave.

On their way back in the Jeep, Anik said, "I want to call Dendree before his office closes and tell him about Bill Landing coming to the desert. It's getting sort of late and I'm anxious to hear what he has to say."

"I've never heard about 'Egyptian Artifacts and Studies.' It's not a company that is associated in any way with us," Dendree replied immediately. "Why don't you come by the lab in the morning and we'll talk further?" he suggested.

"Okay! I'll see you then," Anik replied.

Anik thought about what Dendree had said about Bill Landing, and considered being more careful if he ran into him again. He could be just a nosy person, but he might be someone with ulterior motives. Anik decided there was nothing he could do right now.

At the well-lit, dull, gray lab, Dendree was sitting with John Thissen before Anik arrived, discussing a broken statue that stood in the middle of the warehouse. The talk went from work to their personal lives.

"How are your mother and sister?" Dendree asked John, deeply concerned.

Dendree knew that John's family was suffering from long-term injuries sustained in an automobile accident in which they had been struck by a drunk driver.

"Well, to tell you the truth, the medical expenses are killing me, and I don't know what to do," sighed John.

Dendree and John had become acquainted years ago at an antiquities convention they both attended. Their friendship had developed over time and eventually Dendree had asked John to come to work for him at the lab as his primary assistant. John had agreed and began working at the Egyptian Archaeological Society in Luxor.

"It's a most difficult situation, John. I think I can change around some schedules and find you some more hours to work if that would help," Dendree said, feeling John's pain. "I wish I could do more."

The bland interior and slight echo of the lab mirrored John's feelings of despair at his situation. After their accident, his mother and sister could no longer work and needed a great deal of home health care. John had taken them into his home so that his wife could help out with their care. It was the only solution that they could manage, but it was difficult. Although his intentions were the best, John didn't realize the full impact it would have on him, and especially his wife. It was taking all they had in terms of energy, time and support.

"Yes, that would help, Dendree. Thank you.

"How would you like to get together on Friday for dinner?" asked Dendree. "I can ask my wife to assemble a meal that we can carry over to your place. I know she is eager to do something to help out, and she would enjoy the visit with the ladies."

"That would be wonderful," replied John. "I know we would all look forward to that."

Over the years, John and Dendree's families often got together for dinners during the weekends. Dendree's wife had become acquainted with John's mother and sister a few years previously when she had broken her leg at work. During her recovery, these women had been a godsend to her, helping with cooking, cleaning, and laundry, as well as visiting with her, and keeping her spirits up while she convalesced and got back on her feet. They had shown themselves to be very giving and caring friends, and now they themselves needed the care that they had given to others. They looked towards a good recovery, but it would be a long road back. Dendree understood some of the pressures that build up in the home when there are those who require special care, and the value of joining together with others to help share the load.

"Say, how is the deck at your place, Dendree?" John questioned. "Because I can help again, if you want."

For the previous two years, Dendree and John had been slowly replacing Dendree's dilapidated back deck. While the men worked on the deck, the women sat in the shade and visited. After the day's work, they would all share a picnic supper that the ladies had prepared.

"Yes I would like to get that finished, John. Could you bring the girls over on Sunday, say 11:00?"

"I'll do that. Should I bring the nail gun again?"

"Absolutely," Dendree said with a smile. "We could get a few hours of work in. And probably the wives could be coaxed into making a supper for us all."

"It looks like a great weekend, then," said John. "I should get busy. I have a report to prepare, and it needs to be finished this afternoon."

The trip to the lab in Anik's Jeep had been quiet as Anik and Sitaya mulled over the previous day's events out in the desert. *Who is Bill Landing? What does he want?* They stewed over possible answers to the questions in their minds, and looked forward to learning something from Dendree.

Anik and Sitaya opened the big front doors of the now familiar building and approached Dendree with a smile.

"Good morning, Dendree. I'm so glad to see you. Did you find out anything about that Bill Landing and his 'Egyptian Artifacts and Studies'?"

Dendree said, "No, I haven't found out anything about him. There is no 'Egyptian Artifacts and Studies' organization registered. I suspect he's simply another relic hunter who's trying to get away with fraudulent credentials. I'd like to talk with him."

"I have something else to tell you," said Anik with enthusiasm. "I was so concerned about meeting up with Bill Landing yesterday that I forgot to tell you something really exciting that we found. You won't believe this. I think there is a pyramid hidden under that huge sand dune in front of the statue. Sitaya and I spent a while at the top of the mound, and I found what looks like a cover stone. It's dressed and shaped like one. There is an inscription on it. I was just starting to dig around to have a better look when Bill Landing and his crew drove up. I did enter it on my GPS. And I covered it before we slid down."

"That sounds extremely promising, young man," replied Dendree. "It would be quite possible that there would be some other building in the area of the statue, and I must say that I don't like the idea of that Bill Landing sniffing around the statue location. If, in fact, you have discovered a new pyramid, we want to discourage him from interfering with the explorations there. It is very exciting that there may be a pyramid there. Yes, very exciting indeed. I must take another trip out there with you and see for myself."

Dendree stared at Anik and started to laugh and shake his head.

"Anik, my boy, I haven't told you this because I was going to surprise you next week when everything had gone through the proper channels. Did you know the Egyptian government pays people like yourself, who make a significant discovery and turn their findings over to the government, rather than trying to steal them away to profit?"

"No, I didn't know that at all. That sounds wonderful," Anik answered, his pulse beginning to race. "How much are you talking about?"

"A statue of a pharaoh like the one you found? Well, because of the tourists it will bring in … let me think. Probably, you would receive 58,000 EGP at least," Dendree replied. "They will let us know in the near future."

Anik's mouth gaped open. He couldn't believe it. That was more money than he had ever had. *I must have heard wrong*, he thought, unable to grasp it.

"Don't tease me, Dendree," Anik said with a laugh.

"I'm not joking, Anik. I'm serious, very serious." Dendree sat back, really enjoying Anik's reaction.

Anik's heart started to beat so loudly he thought he could almost hear it. He could feel Sitaya's hand tighten in his. *I will be able to marry Sitaya, rent a house, and look after all those dear to me, all with no debt.* Anik slowly looked over at her, his face beaming. She returned his gaze with a curious mixture of anticipation and reluctance. *What does that look mean?* Anik asked himself, unable to discern what was going on in her mind.

"Well, put me down for maybe one more discovery!" Anik said to Dendree, not being able to hold back the joy rising within him.

Dendree looked up from his computer, tipped his glasses down, and smiled. "Already done."

Dendree picked up the phone in the lab, entered the number of the office of the government agency responsible for tourism and antiquities, and asked for the director. After a lengthy conversation, he looked up at Anik.

"Where's your dad today? We want to hire him to do some work for us. We'd like him to haul away the sand from that big dune so we can see what is concealed beneath it. He's welcome to sell the sand, or handle it however he wishes."

As they left the building, Anik and Sitaya began talking about the new developments that were taking shape — the reward from the government, the new discovery.

Then Anik said, "I noticed a really odd expression on your face when Dendree mentioned the reward. What was that all about?"

Sitaya paused and then looked down at her hands.

"Well, it's great that they will pay you a finder's fee for the statue. I mean, it will make you quite well off. And, uh, I know that your mother really wasted your dad's money, and that it broke up your family. I just hope that you don't think that I would be like that."

"Sitaya, no. I never even considered …" Anik reacted, and then drew her into the circle of his arms.

"I will never do that, Anik, never. Please believe me," Sitaya cut in, as she returned his embrace with fervent sincerity.

"I don't believe you would do that to me, sweetie. Just like I wouldn't do that to you."

Within two weeks the work was under way. Anik, Sitaya, Sekani, and Dendree climbed to the summit of the dune and peered out over the loaders and dump trucks lining up, ready to move the sand away from the base. Anik dug the surface sand away where the GPS indicated the capstone was. As he uncovered the smooth surface of the tip of the pyramid, Dendree moved in and brushed away some more sand for a better look. As he peered down at the solid rock, he said, "It looks as though you are right, Anik. This is fantastic. Well, Sekani, tell your men to go ahead with the excavation. Let's head down."

As they neared the base of the dune, they looked up at the statue of Amenemope, who seemed to be monitoring the whole operation from his black granite platform with his right arm stretched out toward them. As if in a warning, Amenemope's flail pointing at them sent an uneasy feeling down Anik's spine. Then he looked up, and there in the distance Anik could see an orange SUV screaming down the road to the site.

"It looks as though we are getting some visitors again, Dendree," Anik groaned. "You see the writing on the side of the trucks? Can you see?"

Sitaya's hand slid into Anik's, and she looked intently into his eyes, her expression reflecting fear. Dendree spoke into his walkie talkie and immediately Anik could see army vehicles materialize behind Mr.

Landing's truck. A short while later Bill's truck rumbled into the site in an enveloping dust cloud. Within minutes, Bill was spouting off to Dendree in a rage.

"What do you people think you are doing here? And what's the meaning of these army Jeeps and all this building equipment? This is my site. You have no right to be here!" Bill shouted. "I have the license to do digging here and remove any valuables I deem fit."

"Bill, is it? First of all, I don't see any valuables here, just sand. Second, who gave you that license?" Dendree replied mildly, playing his cards just right.

Bill Landing stepped boldly up to Dendree, as if he had all the authority in the world, leveled his gaze on him and replied, "I got my license from Dendree Yusik, if you must know. So get off my site."

Dendree looked at Bill, and then at Anik and Sitaya.

"Well, I guess Bill here is correct, isn't that right, Anik? Dendree Yusik is the only one who can issue a license like that. You see, Bill, I'm Dendree Yusik, and I'm the head of the Egyptian Archeological Society which oversees all discoveries of antiquities within Egypt. I alone have the authority to grant or deny any digs in the country. How strange that I don't remember ever giving you a license."

Shock swept over Bill's face as though he were caught with his hand in the cookie jar. His eyes grew large and he sputtered incoherently as he turned bright red. He stormed off to his truck and sped away in the same dust cloud in which he had arrived.

"I enjoyed that," chuckled Dendree. "But I find him quite worrisome. Tell me, Anik, what was he doing when you saw him here last time?"

"Well," Anik replied "he took rubbings of the statue's hieroglyphs."

"I would like to transport the statue back to our lab and do some further examinations," Dendree said. "I think it would be wise to remove it from such ready access for this Bill Landing. There is a cryptic poem written on the sides of the base that I'd like to look at it in the lab. What's written is very odd, and I need time to decipher it, and to understand what it means," Dendree commented, his thoughts far away.

"Yes, I translated it as well, and it does seem puzzling to me," Anik agreed.

"Three and four mares
Forever deeper than sleep
Amenemope stands in protection."

He recited from memory.

Dendree looked at Anik, his eyes open wide with surprise.

"I believe that is the very translation that I had come up with," Dendree exclaimed. "And how did you figure that out so quickly?"

"I have spent quite a bit of time studying the ancient writing. I mentioned to you that I had taken courses in reading and translating hieroglyphics. It fascinates me and it just seems to come quite easily to me somehow. It just feels sort of intuitive," Anik smiled. "I always wondered what was written on the ancient shrines and temples. Every free moment I could spare I spent learning everything I could. This is the first time I have seen the ancient writing on an actual artifact, and I was really eager to translate it myself. What do you think it means? I've thought about it ever since we uncovered it. I honestly think it has a deep meaning, but there are some lines missing or hidden. It's like a riddle."

There was a big uproar at the dune. Anik and Dendree turned their attention to the activity close by the loaders, and were surprised to notice that although the machines had stopped working, the people were shouting with excitement and clustering at the base of the dune. Dendree's walkie talkie went off, calling him in a garbled voice to come over immediately. Dendree and Anik took off running the short distance to join the rest of the crew to see what the commotion was about. As they were running, they could see the sand flowing like a river down the 45-degree angle of the dune. A perfectly smooth triangular form emerged from the flowing sand. Several minutes passed until the river of sand stopped pouring down the grade. Dendree was the first to arrive at the emerging pyramid, mounting the settling sand. He put his hands on the smooth surface.

"It's stone just like the statue," he exclaimed. "This is amazing! It's an entirely new pyramid — hidden in plain sight! In all my years in the field with the Society, I've never been first on the scene at such a marvelous discovery. By the gods, this is absolutely intoxicating!"

Dumbfounded, Anik walked over to the smooth, inclined plane, and rested his right palm on it. He could barely grasp the enormity of this find — his find, actually. Tears began to well up in his eyes as he was overcome with emotion. Anik heard Sitaya walking up behind him. She slowly reached her arms around his waist and rested her head against his back.

"I'm so proud of you, Anik," she whispered in his ear.

Anik didn't know how to respond, so he remained speechless. He stood with all the others as they backed up and drank in the sight, savoring the moment.

16

PUZZLE

One month later, they were still loading the sand around the pyramid into dump trucks and clearing away the surrounding area. In addition to the statue, two smaller alabaster sphinxes were uncovered on either side of Amenemope, facing out with their backs against the base, guarding the edifice. A small community of mobile homes and work trailers had been situated around the elegant structure to house the workers and security so that there would be a constant presence to monitor the site.

The statue had been moved into the air-conditioned warehouse at the Egyptian Archeological Society in Luxor. Anik and Dendree spent many hours trying to understand the hieroglyphics. Anik spent a great deal of time looking at the shiny black granite base that Amenemope stood on, gazing at the mysterious message it declared. Anik's eyes took in the whole statue — the smug expression on the pharaoh's face, his piercing gaze revealing nothing, his arm raised authoritatively. Looking up at Amenemope, Anik shook his head and swore at the calm but indignant face that stared back, daring him to solve the riddle. The cryptic poem gave no hints of its meaning, just an underlying challenge that could not be deciphered. Anik went over the poem repeatedly, but something was missing.

"I think we are overlooking something here, but damned if I know what it is," Anik said in frustration. "There must be a key verse that unlocks this whole thing, and it has got to be here somewhere; we just can't see it. Did we check the statue completely? Everywhere?"

"I think we did Anik," Dendree replied.

"Maybe there is something written underneath the base," Anik suggested. "The poem does say 'Amenemope stands in protection'."

They jacked up the statue so they could look underneath the black granite platform, but there was nothing there.

"Dendree, how about this? Look at the way the feet of the statue are sunk into the granite base. I've never seen that before. Usually they are flush with the top of the platform, not partially submerged in it. Isn't that right?" Anik said contemplatively.

"There's got to be a reason for it, Anik. I think maybe you've got something there."

Anik gave it some more thought and then an idea surfaced in his mind.

"I want to try something, Dendree. Bear with me, if you don't mind. What if Amenemope is actually standing on the clue. How 'bout we try to try to lift him off the base?"

"I was just wondering the same thing, Anik. Let's lash those ropes around Amenemope's chest, and see if we can lift him up," Dendree called to the workers assisting them.

John Thissen, along with Alex Jins, another one of Dendree's assistants, placed ropes tightly around Amenemope's chest. Max Reeves, yet another assistant, tied the lead rope to them. Once they were securely fastened around the chest, making sure that the statue would stay upright if the base did happen to fall off, a hydraulic winch was set up to lift the statue gradually. They turned it on and the statue slowly rose off the floor. Then they stopped the winch and applied pressure to the base. At first nothing happened, but then there was a snapping sound and the base suddenly detached from the feet of the statue and dropped back onto the protective padding on the floor. The gleam of gold flashed from the feet of the statue, attracting everyone's attention. Golden sandals strapped on its feet were now exposed. A closer inspection revealed engraved pictures of his enemies being trampled and crushed on the soles.

"Look at this! This is marvelous," exclaimed Dendree. The others all crowded around so that they could see the golden treasures themselves.

"I think this is what we are looking for," said Anik. "And look in the hole left in the base where the feet were! There is some more writing. I bet that's the missing piece of the puzzle."

Anik and Dendree quickly peered into the hole left in the base by the feet.

"Let's copy this down and see what it says," said Anik. He took pen and paper and carefully copied the hieroglyphs. Then he and Dendree set about deciphering the message.

"There seem to be two passages here — one beneath each foot. What do you think it means, Anik? It looks to me like: 'The Aten's arm hides' and 'When he sleeps'. That's almost as bad as the rest of the verse," Dendree exclaimed.

Anik repeated the whole verse from memory.

> "The Aten's arm hides, when he sleeps
> Three and four mares
> Forever deeper than sleep
> Amenemope stands in protection"

Anik and Dendree looked around at his assistants. Their fascination was palpable although they didn't have too much to say. Dendree looked at Anik and then turned to the other men.

"Well, men, it looks as though we have found what we're looking for. We've got the message we were looking for, so you can replace the statue in the base. Make sure it is reattached firmly. We wouldn't want it to tip over on us, now, would we? Once you have finished that, you can call it a day. Thanks for your help. Good work."

It was the end of a long day, but the new discovery made it all worthwhile. Anik wasn't ready to go home yet, though. He wanted to have time alone with Dendree to share his thoughts on the newer, more complete message, so he waited until the others packed up, and left.

Dendree was obviously of the same mind. Even though he was weary, he was too excited to leave a discussion about the riddle to another day.

"Let's go to my office," he said. "Perhaps we can figure out what Pharaoh Amenemope is saying to us now."

After they were settled in Dendree's office, Anik laid on Dendree's desk all the papers on which he had copied and translated the poem.

"I've been thinking about this for a long time and I really felt that this poem was sort of a map to another location, but without the direction given. That was what was missing. But now that we have these other lines, I think I might have an idea what the riddle is saying."

"That's wonderful, Anik," replied Dendree. "Tell me what you think it means."

"Okay. As I said, I think the lines we found in the base, under Amenemope's feet are the beginning of the message. 'The Aten's arm hides when he sleeps' may refer to the direction, west, since the Aten is represented by the sun's rays, and the sun 'sleeps' in the west.

"The line that says 'three and four mares' could refer to distance. In those days they traveled by chariot, right? So maybe that line means how far a four horse chariot could travel in three days. What do you think?"

"Could be," agreed Dendree.

"Next, it says 'forever deeper than sleep'. To me that tells me that there may be something buried underground, the same as people are buried in the sleep of death. Then the last line says 'Amenemope stands in protection.' That was the clue as to where to find the rest of the poem. It was the key to finding out exactly what direction to take, because he was literally standing on the key. Without the direction you would never figure out where to look."

"Hmmm," began Dendree. "Let me look at this some more. A map, you say. Curious. What an exciting thought that Amenemope might be referring to something else buried at another location. That raises a whole lot of other questions, but you know, I think you might be on to something. It's rather obscure, but it does seem to make some sense, given the style of the language of that day. And what do you suppose might be the thing that is buried at the destination he is suggesting?"

"I can't really be sure. But if there is something to be found, I'd sure like to find it before Bill Landing gets wind of it and tries to horn in on us," said Anik. "Speaking of Bill Landing, I would sure be interested in finding out where he is getting his information. His timing seems too good to be coincidence. What about your workers here, Dendree? Maybe it's one of them. Do you trust them all?"

"I don't think that is likely, Anik. They have all been with me for at least five to ten years. I have complete trust in all of them. They have all shown total dedication to the preservation of Egyptian treasures. John Thissen, especially, has been a dear friend to me. I really can't see that any of them would have anything to do with that dreadful man," replied Dendree earnestly. "It is a puzzle though, I'll grant you that. He does seem to pop up at the most inconvenient times."

Then Anik spoke up again. "I know this might seem farfetched, but I was also thinking about the names of the other pharaohs that appeared on the base of the statue. Do you remember?"

Dendree thought for a while, mentally recalling the names. *Narmer, Snefru, Kufu, Khaffre, Shepseskare Ist, Amenemhet, Sesostris, Amose, Horemheb, Neferefre, Amenhotep Ist, Seti Ist, Rameses Ist, IInd, and IIIrd.* Dendree then recited them perfectly.

"Their tombs were all robbed a long time ago. I can see where you're going with this, Anik, but you're right, it does sound pretty far-fetched. Do you really think Amenemope would raid the other tombs?"

"If the last line also refers to standing in protection of the treasures on behalf of the other pharaohs, it would stand to reason that Amenemope was doing them a great service," Anik answered thoughtfully.

Dendree looked at Anik for a while, considering his suggestion. Then a smile spread slowly across his face. He couldn't believe it. They were possibly on the brink of the greatest discovery of all time.

"Well, you know, my boy, I wonder if perhaps you are on the right track after all. I think we need to find out the distance four mares can travel in three days. Is it worth a try?" Dendree inquired.

"I think so," Anik agreed. "Do you know where we could get a team of horses and a chariot to do the test?"

"My cousin Mik has horses, and my brother has a replica chariot that I think he would lend me," Dendree said. "Let me put in a call to them, and if we can assemble all the resources we will need, we can check it out tomorrow and make definite plans to conduct our experiment. I think we ought to head home now and get some rest. It sounds as though we have some busy times ahead."

An orange SUV drove up the dirt path in a cloud dust and diesel fumes. Huy was not expecting visitors but guests were always welcome. A tall, heavy-set man with muscular arms eased himself out of the driver's seat and boldly walked over to Huy and addressed him in a pleasant manner.

"Hello there, old timer."

Huy nodded at him and raised his pipe with his left hand in greeting.

"It looks like you've lived here a long time. Have you had visitors out here, maybe about the statue that was unearthed out there?" the man asked, using his thumb to point down the road into the desert.

Anik and Dendree made their way over to Mik's stables to talk to him about borrowing some mares to help put their theory to the test. Mik was a tall lanky man with a ready smile permanently creasing his suntanned face, and he was wearing a leather cowboy hat and worn-out blue jeans — a real cowboy from the Middle East. He sauntered lazily up to the SUV.

"Dendree! Long time since I saw you, Buddy!" Mik cheerfully greeted him. "What can I do you for?"

Dendree smiled as Mik adjusted his treasured crinkled leather hat.

"Last week's dinner at my house wasn't that long ago, Mik," Dendree replied with amusement.

"Mik, I'd like you to meet Anik. He's the young man I told you about who found the statue of Amenemope."

Mik reached out his right hand to offer Anik a greeting.

"So you're into old Egyptian stuff like my cousin here, eh?" Mik prodded nonchalantly.

"Well, I just sort of bumped into it actually, but I do find it interesting," Anik answered, shaking Mik's calloused hand.

"It's all the same to me. I was never into that stuff like Dendree here. Even though Dendree would try to get me excited about some little pharaoh statue as a child, I stuck to riding every chance I got. I just like my horses. I even moved to Australia thinking I could be a horse rancher. Turns out I could have horses in Egypt too, so I'm back. So, Dendree, you still haven't told me what you want."

"I would have, but you've been too busy giving my friend Anik here the story of your life," Dendree shot back, trying not to laugh.

"I want to borrow four of your best mares if I could, for a distance test."

Mik cocked his head, and adjusted his hat again. "Stop the presses! Anik, what have you done with my cousin here?"

Anik could hear Dendree trying unsuccessfully to hold back a chuckle, and soon he could see that this was just how they were together.

Anik imagined them growing up, Mik with little pop guns strapped to his pajamas, and Dendree in full Sherlock Holmes getup, running through the house on some pretend adventure.

Mik, I need to find out how far a team of horses could travel across the desert in three days."

"Three days in the desert? That's a pretty punishing test for my beauties. This sounds like it has something to do with your Egyptian research. Am I right?"

"That's exactly right, Mik. We have a theory concerning a puzzle we are trying to solve, and we think this experiment with your mares will help us figure out something very important. Do you think I could borrow them as well as your trailer?"

"Ok, I'll bite. Maybe we can work something out. I have just the mares for the job, but the trailer is a no go. However, come with me. Maybe I have something even better."

Mik led them to an old shed just down from the stables, reached in his pocket and produced a key chain so full that Anık was amazed that even Mik could find the correct one. In short order, though, Mik was opening one of the double doors and ushering them inside the dusty, dark room. They passed the horse trailer that looked like it had been up on blocks for some time.

They followed behind Mik as he made his way to the back of the room. He turned on the light, and through the dust motes filling the air they all looked at a large mound covered with a green canvass which dominated the space. Mik turned and looked at Dendree with a broad grin of delight. He hesitated, arousing their curiosity even further, then grabbed one side of the covering and pulled it off with a flourish. There, before their eyes, gleamed a golden-colored chariot. The detail was astonishing. Beautifully shaped curves on the sides showed images of the defeat of armies in stark realism. The platform, made of dried and woven reeds, was painted a deep crimson. Plumes of peacock feathers embellished the blue and white flags that hung lazily on poles jutting out the back.

"What do you think of this, cousin? From the way your jaw is hanging open I can tell what you're thinking. Yes, this is the chariot that your brother restored. He sold it to me three months ago because he said it was just getting in the way," Mik explained. "Go figure, right? Do you want to try it out?"

"Of course I do! Why didn't you tell me that you had it before this?" Dendree asked, excitedly eying the beautiful work of art.

"Well, I thought I'd surprise you on your birthday, but seeing as how you are practically asking for it here and now, this as good a time as any, don't you think?" Mik added.

"Why, thank you, cousin. This is indeed a most generous gift. Most astonishing! Look at the workmanship! I've never seen anything that compares to this. Just looking at it takes me back in time. What a wonderful way to conduct our experiment. What do you think, Anik? Will this fit the bill for calculating the distance we are looking for?" asked Dendree.

"It will probably give us the best result we can find, Dendree. Horses and chariots — what could be better?"

"I can hitch my beauties up to this chariot, and we can take the works out to the track, and see if we can get you what you are looking for. Shall I get one of the boys to do the driving for you?" Mik asked.

"That would probably be best," replied Dendree. "But can you take me around for a couple of laps before we start timing this run? It's not my birthday today, but I could scarcely be expected to wait until then to take this ride, now, could I?"

Mik turned to Anik. "You look as though you would like to have a go as well, mate. There's room for all of us. Just let me get things organized here. You can wait outside."

As they waited for the horses to be hitched to the chariot, Dendree was as giddy as a child.   "I've got to say, Anik, I never thought that I would have such exciting times at this point in my life. Things just keep getting more incredible and amazing. Mik has always been lots of fun, and here at my age I will have a chariot ride for the first time. Ever since you showed up, life has certainly changed for me."

"It's changed for me a lot since I met you, too. It's because of the statue, of course," replied Anik. "And if this next project works out, I think there might be a whole lot more to look forward to. I can hardly wait."

They started to clock the horses pulling two men around the track, added in breaks for water and rest, and by the end of the afternoon, they figured that they could probably travel one hundred and fifty kilometers in the 3-day limit.

"You've kept the ladies on the run for the whole afternoon, lads, and I think that even though we've only got a slice of the pie on this one, that your calculation is pretty good — one hundred and fifty kilometers. In the desert, of course, you would need to take a supply wagon to haul the water and food, and have a decent place to spend the night. Actually, I've heard that the old-timers would often ride into the night when the moon was full. Much easier on the horses, you know, and then resting during the heat of the day. So do you think you can take your trip in the desert to the right distance with what you have learned today?" asked Mik.

"Yes, I think we've got what we need," replied Dendree. "We've got some more plans to make, but I think you might see more of me, especially if I can keep the chariot here. That ride was the biggest thrill I've had in a long time, and I'd love to come by for a ride on a regular basis, if that suits you."

"Well, it looks like we might make a horse lover out of this old archeologist yet, wouldn't you say so, Anik?" teased Mik as he clapped Dendree on the shoulder. "Sure. You're welcome here anytime."

Later that evening Anik went over to Sitaya's place, and caught her up on the day's activities.

"You should have seen them, Sitaya! Mik had these four white Arabian horses hitched up to this incredible chariot. They pranced around as though they were royalty. And riding in the chariot, it was exhilarating, the wind blowing in my hair. I even got a chance to drive the horses for a while. It was definitely a rush," Anik chattered on.

He was so elated about the events of the day and the possibilities the future held, that she let him talk on and on, not interrupting him once. After his excitement subsided, Sitaya asked the question that had been floating around in her mind since he first told her about the hieroglyphics on the statue.

"How did you come to figure out the riddle, Anik?"

"I don't know, Sitaya. I've been thinking about it ever since we discovered the first writing on the base of the statue. I memorized it, and over time I started to think about what message Pharaoh Amenemope might be telling us. And after we had our picnic at the top of the dune and we were resting, it just came to me that even though this pharaoh went to all the trouble of concealing the statue and the pyramid, that he put a message on the statue — he wanted to keep what he had done concealed, but something in him made him want to reveal what he had done. He made the poem obscure so that it would be difficult to understand and would probably remain a secret. At that point I knew there was an important message to be discovered, and I knew it would come to me. Then it all came together when I read what was written under Amenemope's feet. I hope we can complete the venture successfully," Anik confessed. "And I want you to be with me when I go on the journey to look for what Amenemope hid. I love you so much,

Sitaya; I hope you know that," he blurted out.

"I do know that you love me, Anik. I love you too — more than you could know."

She leaned in and kissed him tenderly. Sitting on his lap and facing him, she wrapped her arms and legs around him. They stayed in the embrace for what seemed like hours, enjoying each other's warmth and touch. He was glad to be resting in Sitaya's arms, revealing his heart and sharing his plans.

Sitaya looked at Anik with a new-found appreciation and respect. Just being with him made her feel emotionally secure and completely safe.

17

PAST MEMORIES

Anik, Sitaya, and Dendree walked onto the pyramid site, greeting Sekani, who was hard at work directing his staff. Sekani greeted them, his face beaming, which was so typical of him.

"What brings you here? Checking up on me?" he said with a big grin. The dry air was clean and hot, the only smells that could be detected were the diesel exhaust fumes expelled from the loaders and dump trucks going about their routines loading and shipping the valuable material to construction sites around Egypt.

"I see you are getting along well with the progress of clearing away the sand from the pyramid. It's really taking shape. Being buried like it was has preserved it perfectly. It looks great!" Dendree said with enthusiasm.

"Yes. And this sand is so clean and coarse I have companies out-bidding each other to get their hands on it, so I'm making a nice fortune from it. I even had to buy a second loader to keep up with the demand." Sekani said, his eyes sparkling.

Dendree and Anik walked around the exposed part of the pyramid with Sekani and Sitaya trailing behind. The sloping sides were absolutely smooth and uniform.

Sekani pulled Sitaya aside as the other two men walked around the pyramid.

"Anik tells me you two have been getting more serious in your relationship," Sekani stated. "Is this true?"

"It seems to be the case," replied Sitaya. "So much has happened since Anik found the statue. He has been changing in many ways, and I think he is becoming more sure of himself and what he wants his future to look like. It has made us both very happy. And I'm glad he's not so taken up with all the discoveries that he doesn't have time for me. He seems eager to share all of these new experiences with me and I'm excited to share them with him, that's for sure."

"Well, I think it's wonderful, too. You have always been a special friend to Anik, and I could think of no one better suited to be with him than you."

"Thank you, Sekani. That means a lot to me. He's a terrific guy, and I want to be there for him. I think we make a pretty incredible couple, even if I do say so myself," Sitaya said with a broad smile.

"Well, your name does mean 'Lady' so I have every confidence that you will do right by my son," Sekani said with a wink.

He excused himself from Sitaya's company and told her that he had to fetch something to give to Dendree and off he went, jogging to his trailer.

Just because my name means Lady doesn't mean I always have to act like it, especially when I get him alone, Sitaya reflected, her thoughts conjuring up various scenarios with Anik that brought her delight.

Anik took a few minutes to simply stand back and admire the pyramid. He took in the details of the perfectly polished sandstone that glistened a warm golden color in the sunshine. It wasn't a huge pyramid, but its graceful proportions and its perfect state of preservation gave it a special elegance. He could hardly believe that if it hadn't been for him, it might never have been discovered. *I discovered this — amazing,* he thought, shaking his head. He could still hardly grasp the enormity of it all.

His trance was broken by the movement of his father as he hustled over to Dendree with an indistinct mass in his arms.

"Take a look at this, Dendree," said Sekani, holding out a coil of ancient-looking rope that he had retrieved from his trailer. "I found it under the sand. Do you think it has any special significance?"

Dendree held the large coil and fingered the bronze spike through the one end.

"This is what they used to trigger a trap door. I've seen one before. They are extremely rare," Dendree said, without having to deliberate.

"Trap door? For what?" Sitaya questioned.

"Trap doors were used at that time to seal a room where you didn't want to be when they closed. Once they were closed, they stayed closed," Dendree said calmly.

They all looked at each other for a moment until it registered, and then in unison they all turned to look at the pyramid.

"You have to be kidding. Are you saying they buried people alive?" Sitaya asked, astounded.

"They did indeed, when they believed it was necessary, such as when some wealthy or important person had their servants buried with them."

"I wonder what we would find inside, behind this door," Anik said. "It seems hard to believe that such a beautiful structure would be used as a death trap."

"That's pretty creepy," Sitaya replied with distaste.

Dendree led the others close to the smooth stone side of the pyramid. They gazed up at the structure built so many thousands of years ago. There was a slight rectangular depression in the blocks at ground level, and lines cut in the blocks, hinting that there was a door hidden there.

"I wouldn't mind having a look inside," Anik said. "My curiosity is killing me. Can we get inside?"

"Anik, I think we will have to open that door with jack hammers," Dendree said, amused as he looked at Anik's shirt that read: WARNING! I'M COMING IN.

The workers made their way to the truck which held all the necessary supplies and hauled out two jackhammers. They set to work chipping away at the thick door, chunks of stone flying away as they made steady progress. It was dusty work, requiring many dust mask changes and lots of patience. Halfway through the next day, the jackhammers broke through the last of the stone and they gained access into a dark passageway.

Stagnant, foul air escaped from the bowels of the pyramid as if the pyramid itself was letting out a breath it had been holding for thousands of years. They spent a couple of hours clearing away the debris from the stone door and letting the air escape from the interior. Then Dendree knelt down to examine the perfect sliding track that had once held the impressive stone door.

"Incredible!" Dendree said as he tried to bend his mind around how this door worked.

"See this, Anik. This track is sloped so that when the rope was pulled, the door would slide into place by gravity. It wouldn't take too much effort to close it, even though it was so huge and heavy. Let's get the generator and the exhaust fans over here. I want to get the interior well ventilated before we go in. We can set up some lights as well, so that we can see where we're going and get a better look at what's inside."

While they were waiting for the extra equipment to be set up, Dendree shone his flashlight into the mouth of the pyramid, as Anik peered over his shoulder. Right away they spotted a body sitting just beyond the opening where the door had been. Anik recoiled in alarm, as it was the first dead body he had ever seen. He took a deep breath to replace the air he had suddenly expelled, then turned back to have a closer look. The withered flesh on its face and body was black and grotesque, and it sat on the floor in a humble position, its head resting against the wall, arms lying on its crossed legs. The clothes had deteriorated, but looked as though they had been quite ornate, a man's tunic. He appeared to have been waiting for the door to open so long ago. What was his story? A feeling of sadness engulfed them, as each of them considered how they would have felt in this unknown man's place.

They carefully moved the body to the outside of the pyramid to clear the way for entry.

The workers set up the fans and started running some strings of lights to the interior as Dendree and Anik peered into the darkness and reluctantly backed out to give them room to maneuver.

"I wonder what else we will find inside," said Anik. "I guess one thinks there will always be treasure inside such a grand structure. It's quite upsetting to realize that maybe it was just used as a place to annihilate people."

"There's only one way to find out what's inside, my boy," replied Dendree. "Hopefully there will be messages recorded within the walls that will explain why this pyramid was built. Without a communication from the past, this place would remain shrouded in mystery. We shall soon see, though."

When the lights had been strung as far as the first large opening, the workers came back and invited Dendree and Anik to go ahead and take the first look.

They made their way down the short sloping corridor, and halted in shocked horror as they gazed across the floor area of the spacious dark cavern — the floor was cluttered with dozens of dead bodies.

Dendree drew back, and covered his face with his hands.

"My god, what a horrible devastation!" he exclaimed. "All these people. This was not a proper burial, this was a massacre. Oh, Anik, what have we uncovered here?"

Anik stepped around Dendree as he crumpled to the ground. Shock coursed through him as he took in the sight. Bile rose in his throat and he thought he would be sick. He turned away, and looked back to the entrance of the sepulcher. His head grew dizzy and he leaned against the wall of the chamber to maintain his balance. He made his way back outside and took several deep gulps of air and then slid to the ground. He began to tremble uncontrollably and hot tears stung his eyes.

That is the most horrible sight I have ever seen, he thought. *What is this? Who were all those people?*

Sitaya came and sat down beside Anik.

"What did you find, Anik? What's the matter?"

Anik just held his head in his hands with his eyes shut.

"Give me a minute. Just give me a minute," he whispered.

After a few minutes the men had composed themselves. Anik explained somberly to Sitaya what they had seen. Dendree and Anik conferred in hushed tones, and after they talked things over Dendree said, "Well, we've come this far. I believe we must press on. Do you think you are up to continuing, my boy?"

"I guess so. They've got the spot lights positioned inside, so we can see better. Dendree, this is not what I signed up for. It's no wonder this whole place was concealed underneath the sand. What a terrible destruction."

Having an idea of what lay within the pyramid, Dendree and Anik fortified themselves and re-entered the corridor with Sitaya trailing behind. Anik had tried to talk Sitaya out of entering the horrific scene, but she assured him she would be fine. They slowly approached the well-lit chamber, and again the gruesome sight assaulted their senses. This time they looked around more thoroughly in order to observe the details.

Despite the thousands of years since their burial, the lack of oxygen had, to some extent, mummified the remains. Ragged clothes partially covered the black, rotted and withered bodies. The expressions of fear and grief frozen on the faces of the corpses, though exaggerated from the partial decomposition, surely told a tale of terror and torment. Some of them looked like they had been trampled to death, some were missing arms and legs but others actually looked peaceful, curled up in a ball or in calm repose.

The bodies of a couple, evidently husband and wife who clung to each other in an embrace, were the most heart-rending to see. Sitaya and Anik could sense their obvious tenderness, as the husband appeared to be holding his wife, attempting to shield her from the inevitable. Anik's hand found Sitaya's as they stared at the two bodies that looked astoundingly calm and serene.

"I can't imagine how they managed that," said Sitaya. "It looks like a circle of quiet in a clamor of evil."

"A much better choice than what some of the others did," commented Anik.

Dendree moved forward, picking his way carefully over the bodies.

"I've got my flashlight. Let's have a look in those other rooms."

As he shone the light against the wall to see where the other openings were, he said, "Look at that, Anik. There are painted scenes all over the walls. And look, on the ceiling too. Why, the workmanship is beautiful. What a contrast to the devastation of humanity."

All three of them strained to see the artwork that covered all the inner surfaces of the cavern.

"Once we get the room cleared, we will be able to take a closer look at the walls," said Dendree.

The other rooms off the main area told the same story of agony and terror on the decomposed faces of other bodies. There was no evidence of prosperity in the tattered rags that hung limply over the skeletal remains. Every room was the same. No escape.

The walls of all the side rooms were also a riot of color — scene upon scene with all sorts of animals and people depicting many facets of everyday life and activities. Other pictures displayed scenes of war, smacking of glory and prestige, and boasting of Amenemope's importance.

The three observers made their way outside into the light again.

"This was a place of great tragedy," said Dendree. "I can't imagine what prompted such a dreadful massacre. And Pharaoh Amenemope is probably responsible for this. There is not much detail about his reign in the history, and if this is his legacy, I can see why no mention is made of this. However, we shall sort this out. Perhaps when we are able to examine the pyramid more closely, we can learn why all this happened."

"It does seem very strange," said Anik. "The pyramid is so beautiful inside and out. I certainly hope we can unravel the mystery. I can tell you, I will never forget what I have seen here today."

Sitaya had no words. Anik turned to look at her and he could tell by her expression that she was in shock. He walked over to her and put his arms around her. She laid her head against his chest and quietly wept.

Dendree arranged for his workers to help with the recovery of bodies. After an inspection was done at the lab in Luxor, they were stored in a secluded mausoleum where they could be retrieved for future study.

A fence was installed around the perimeter of the pyramid and round the clock security was set in place. Then lighting was set up throughout the interior. When the lights were turned on, the brightly colored murals sprang to life. The rooms, seventeen in total, were covered floor to ceiling with exceptionally detailed and colorful murals. The ceiling was covered with stars and outlined constellations. The floor was a map of the Nile with depictions of boats, fish, hippopotami and fields that skirted the river.

At the base of the murals, in perfect Egyptian script, was the story that the archeologists were eager to know. It told of the grievous crime of tomb robberies committed by the thieves and their greedy women. It described how the criminals and their wives were forced to build their own death trap, played out with no apologies.

The murals spoke of Amenemope rescuing several previous Pharaohs' sarcophagi from hideous demons that were dancing and chopping up the king's spirits in Aaru. Private family scenes showed Amenemope's wife and children enjoying boating trips, hunting and fishing. There were scenes of them sitting down at banquets with tables piled high with food. One room was totally covered with a painting of Amenemope's burial scenes. The room itself stood out with a quality that surpassed all of the other rooms, filling all that saw it with amazement. A sarcophagus was painted on the floor, as well as the book of the dead painted on the walls. Both projected the illusion of three dimensions in their rendering. There was no body though, just another cryptic poem that made no sense, painted on the wall hidden in the corner. This burial chamber seemed as though it had been painted separately, possibly by one or more highly skilled artists.

All paintings were completely photographed, and all hieroglyphs translated for later study. All that was visible within the pyramid was captured in photos and in written records with measurements and notations. The beautiful structure had displayed a great deal, but were all its secrets revealed? Anik didn't think so.

Back at the edge of town where the vegetation gave way to the sands of the desert, an irritated Bill Landing marched onto Huy and Sarin's sandy front lawn and confronted Huy who had come out to see who was approaching.

"Do you remember me? I was here a while ago, talking to you about that statue out in the desert. You are friends with that young guy and his girlfriend, right? Have they been here lately? I was just on my way out to the site, and there is a whole lot of commotion going on there. What do you know about what is happening just down the road from you?" Bill paused for a minute, getting no response from the startled man. "Well, let me tell you, they are digging on my site. My site! It wasn't enough that they have taken the statue: now they have found a pyramid. That should have been my find! The treasure should be mine! So tell me what you know," he said as he grabbed Huy's arm and violently shook him.

"We don't see what they are doing back there. No one has been here recently, and we have no idea what is going on. It's not our business, and we can't get there to see for ourselves," Huy managed to croak out in fear as Bill shook him. "Please let me go. I don't know anything about it."

Bill released the man's frail arm and Huy collapsed to the earth.

"What's going on out here? Oh Huy, are you all right?" Sarin cried, as she came running from the house.

She could not reach Huy before Bill intercepted and threw her roughly to the ground.

"Don't you remember our chat last time I was here? Are you two that dense? I told you to let me know if there was anything happening out at the site."

Huy just sat in the dirt cradling his bruised arm, which was starting to ache, his heart racing. Sarin crawled over to her husband with tears streaming down her face. *Why is this happening to us? Why does he think we can tell him anything about what's happening in the desert?* She finally reached him as Bill stood over her, raining a tirade of curses at them, not even thinking about what they could or couldn't tell him, just wanting answers. Huy's heart could not take much more of this physical and verbal abuse so he raised his hands in submission.

"Please, please stop. I'm sorry I can't give you any answers. Please don't hurt my wife," he begged.

Conniving thoughts swirled in Bill's head. *Maybe I'll use their place to set up a monitoring hub so I can get the info I need, because I will get it one way or another. I'll bet this old man knows more than he's telling me. I just have to scare him a little.*

"Tell you what old-timer, I'm going to set up a small device here to keep an eye on what they are up to out at the pyramid site. If you value you or your wife's safety, never ever mention meeting me or what I will put here. And next time I come, I would strongly advise you not to withhold any information you have from me. You got that?"

Huy sat there trembling, not meeting Bill's cruel gaze. In pain and fear he nodded in agreement.

18

SUNDIAL

Early in the morning, a small red helicopter landed just outside the little settlement that had been built for the workers. Anik, Sitaya, and Dendree greeted the helicopter pilot just as the blades stopped. The pilot stood in front of them, glancing at the pyramid in the distance. He was a tall man, with short dirty-blonde hair, six foot two inches and thirty-seven years old by Anik's deduction.

"So you guys want to take a trip? Where are we off to?" Shaaban, the pilot, wanted to know.

Dendree and Anik had discussed this trip extensively over the last several days, and they had calculated that the distance should be measured one hundred-fifty kilometers from the original spot where the statue was found. Dendree and Anik took Shaaban to the spot where the statue of Amenemope had once stood.

"We want to go one hundred-fifty kilometers due west from this location," Anik said with confidence.

"That's in the middle of the western desert! What the hell do you want in that barren place?" Shaaban retorted. "I hope you are bringing lots of water. That is the most miserable, God-forsaken place on Earth. Are we going there just for a look? This 'copter can only do 350 kilometers per tank, so there won't be any sightseeing. You know the temperature swings from freezing at night to almost boiling in the day?"

"No, we don't need to do sightseeing. We just want to land and look around," Dendree piped up.

"It's your dime. We'd better get going before it gets too hot out there for you," Shaaban said, shaking his head.

Anik stood where the statue of Amenemope once was, and took one last reading on his GPS. The helicopter refueled, and Sitaya, Anik, and Dendree piled into the small machine. The blades spun into action with a loud beating that was diminished when they put on the earphones that Shaaban supplied.

Anik kept a wary eye on his GPS, advising Shaaban of any course corrections needed. The desert they flew over was a constant ripple of yellow dunes that looked exactly the same from one spot to the next. The barren landscape was periodically dotted with ficus plants and dry weeds, but not much else. As they neared the proper coordinates, Dendree quickly typed in the location on his laptop and filled out the permission form in Anik's name to dig at that location. Stepping out of the helicopter, all four of them were surprised at the wall of heat that radiated off the burning sand.

The low, smooth sand dunes looked like small waves on a lake. The sun blazed down on the barren sand. After the helicopter's motor was shut down and the blades had stopped, the only sound was the wind blowing softly — a vast emptiness — silent, dazzling and sweltering.

Anik, the first one out of the helicopter, checked his GPS and walked the short distance to the exact location they had been seeking.

"This is exactly one hundred-fifty kilometers from the statue, Dendree" said Anik. "It looks no different from any of the surrounding terrain — just sand and more sand."

Dendree followed right behind him, surveying the barren emptiness.

"Are you sure this is the right spot, Anik?" Dendree questioned.

Anik checked his GPS for a third time and nodded his head.

"I'm positive. Let's look around and see if we can spot anything significant. Figuring the distance was a bit of a guess, but if we are correct, there should be some indication that we are in the right place."

Sitaya sat in the sand with her legs curled underneath her, lounging in the shade that the helicopter provided. Shaaban sat down beside her as she noticed a stone sliver leaning against her foot. *That's funny,* she thought. *Where did you come from?* As she looked at the ground around her, she noticed more stone chips sticking out of the sand. She picked up the biggest one and rolled it around in her hand and then stuck it in the ground as if it were a mini sundial. Sitaya stared at the shadow the stone sliver was casting. While she was lost in thought, Shaaban spoke up.

"How long have you known Anik?" he asked.

"Well, we've known each other since we were little kids. I first met him when I caught him playing 'Spacecraft' in my father's old pickup truck."

"Yes, I can see that an old truck would be a draw to a young boy's imagination."

Sitaya chuckled and remembered Anik making his rocket sounds. Such a long time ago, she thought.

Anik and Dendree walked back towards the helicopter. She smiled to herself when she noticed his T-shirt with the red and white striped knit hat and a pair of glasses with the caption "Where's Waldo?" at the bottom.

Anik squatted down, pulled out his GPS and typed in some coordinates.

"I can't understand it," he sighed. "I was so sure this trip would turn up some new clues or discovery. If we can't find something around here, I don't know what our next step will be." He sat down on the ground and his hand leaned on the spot where Sitaya had propped the stone chip into the sand.

"Yikes" he exclaimed, yanking his hand back. "What was that? Look, something has drawn blood."

Sitaya replied, "Yes, I found that sharp little stone in the sand. I wondered where it came from."

Anik brushed the sand away and exposed the needle-sharp splinter of blue granite. He picked it up and inspected it. Then he started moving more sand away and picked out several slivers of stone. Looking more closely at the desert floor, he was able to see a quantity of chips. He picked up a handful and had a closer look at them. Hope soared as he rattled them as if he were getting ready to cast them like dice.

"I think we are on to something. Dendree! Have a look at this! These definitely look as though they were cut with man-made tools."

Dendree walked over and looked at what Anik wanted to show him. Dendree noticed the stone fragments immediately and a smile spread across his face.

"I'm sure you are correct. Do you know what this means, Anik? ... We are on the right track."

"I would say so, but where do we go from here?"

"We need to get a view of this location from the sky and then maybe we can see the outlines of some buildings or something."

Shaaban, who was standing nearby and overhearing the conversation, shook his head.

"We don't have that much fuel left. When we lift off, we can circle around once and then we need to go home. We can't do multiple stops."

Dendree and Anik looked at each other and nodded.

"That will do. Once in the air, we can take some pictures and analyze them later."

The helicopter lifted into the air and Shaaban did one sweeping survey of the site. Upon closer inspection, Anik and Dendree noticed the faint outline of some oblong structures that the sand had hidden when viewed on the ground. They took as many pictures as they could on the flyover and then they headed back to the pyramid.

Anik was buzzing with excitement on the trip back. He kept scrolling through the digital pictures, trying to figure out what was hidden beneath the sand. Could it be a structure hidden underneath the odd shapes?

As the helicopter landed, Anik turned to Dendree and said "I can hardly wait to see what we find out when we hook this camera up to your computer. Let's check it out right away."

Anik, Dendree and Sitaya made their way over to the dry old hollow-sounding work trailer that was used as an office, to examine the pictures and plan the next step in their exploration. Sekani joined them to see what they had learned.

"We need to figure out what we are looking at here," Dendree said as he motioned to a table that sat in the middle of the room.

He set up his laptop and connected the cable between it and the camera. They all stood around the screen and strained to see the details of the photos.

"There are no sharp edges to these shapes right here where we found the stone chips by the helicopter, so I doubt that there are buildings there," Dendree said.

"I wonder if this was a place to dump excess material," added Sekani, who usually had little to say.

"We will not know that for sure without digging into them," Dendree replied.

"Yes, but suppose we go, dig and find that those dunes are just covering big piles of stone chips, what then? If those stone chips are from an ancient excavation, how are we possibly going to find it? That is a massive area!"

Just then they heard the roar of a vehicle coming to a halt outside. Anik stood up and walked over to the window that was covered by yellowed Venetian blinds. He parted them with his two fingers, peered out through the dirt stained window and then he gasped as he quickly pulled his hand back.

"Oh no, not him again."

The blind snapped back into place, sending a puff of dust in the air. It was Bill. Anik felt tightness clench his innards. *Why does he always show up? Can't he just leave me alone?* The big man had been invading Anik's dreams lately, giving him restless nights.

A knock on the door came shortly after, but the door opened before anyone answered. Bill Landing walked in, his size filling up the door frame. It was obvious he was out of shape by his heavy breathing.

"I heard a helicopter just a little while ago. You are on the hunt for something else, right? I told you last time that I wanted to be included in the search. I intend to help you out with this search. You got that?" He looked squarely at Anik.

Anik felt Bill's oppressive energy punch him in the chest. A few older, aggressive men that he had come into contact with seemed to have that effect on him. But this was the worst. *This guy is a real bully,* thought Anik. *Why doesn't someone say something?* Anik looked at Dendree and Sekani, who were sitting, silently observing. They did not move or help in any way. *I cannot let him steal my prospective find. I have to keep him at a distance — the more, the better.*

He took a deep breath and looked Bill in the eye with all the conviction he could muster.

"Whatever we are looking for, we are doing it on our own," Anik stated.

"So you are looking for something. Yes?" Bill's eyes lit up. "I knew it! You are not strong enough for this, kid. You're out of your depth."

"That is enough out of you, Bill. Please leave," Sekani said as he stood up.

Bill smiled menacingly as he turned and reached for the door. "See you out there, boys," he muttered under his breath. He slammed the door as he left.

"Why didn't you guys step in sooner? Now he knows we are on the hunt for something."

"Yes he does, but he doesn't know where we are looking. Besides I have already filled out the license for the dig, remember? Bill would not legally be allowed to dig at the site."

Anik felt a cold comfort at Dendree's reassurance.

"I have a bad feeling that we haven't seen the end of that guy. Somehow I don't think that not having a license is going to stop him from interfering with our search. Isn't there anything we can do to keep him away from us?" asked Anik.

"Perhaps he won't really be a problem," replied Dendree. "There are lots of wannabe treasure hunters out there, but we have the legal right to be doing these explorations. He doesn't know exactly where we are headed, and it is way out in the middle of nowhere. I can't see that we are in any real danger. He hasn't done anything illegal so we can't expect the police to take any action. We haven't found anything at the new location which would warrant hiring security. I suggest we just carry on and keep our business confidential. It should work out, and in the event that he does show up again, well, we can deal with that at the time."

"That's right, son. It's a big desert out there and how could he track you down? Maybe down the road something will need to be done, but unless you find something really valuable, it won't be a problem anyway. Try not to worry about it."

"Easier said than done," replied Anik. He sighed and thought, *those guys sure aren't much help. I've got to suck it up and carry on.*

"So what is the plan now?" Sekani asked as he drummed his fingers on the table.

Dendree rose and pointed to a relatively flat part on the picture that seemed to be surrounded by the strange oblong piles. "First we need to see what is in these dunes. If they contain stone chips, then we dig there."

"I can strap some extra tanks of fuel to the helicopter so Shaaban could fly a little more. Would that help?"

"Yes it would, Anik. You should pack a tent to use as a small shelter as well. And can you look after getting food and water and tools for digging?"

Anik pointed his hand like a gun and made a click with his tongue. "No problem, Dendree."

The next day the helicopter flew out with Anik, Dendree and Sitaya, as well as the supplies they had assembled. When they arrived at the site, they circled it a couple of times and then landed beside one of the odd looking hills. They unloaded everything and refueled. Anik picked up a red-handled spade and started attacking one of the dunes. He found the stone chips without much difficulty.

"Well, I found the chips!" he called out.

They set up the tent and took out the pictures that they had taken.

They refreshed their minds on the positioning of the oblong mounds.

"You can clearly see that they seem to radiate out from this flat section here," Dendree said as he tapped his finger on the photo.

"Yes, and that is just over there about 100 yards," Anik motioned with his head.

An hour later the men had peppered the ground with test holes in an organized search for the answer to the riddle. All of the oblong mounds yielded piles of stone chips. As they dug closer to the flat area in the center of the oblong mounds, all they found was blue granite bedrock. Then suddenly, Anik came upon a definite man-made cut that sliced into the rock and disappeared underneath the nearby sand.

"Hey, guys, come here. I found something."

The men gathered around and stared at the deep cut that ran straight along the bedrock.

"I think this what we are looking for, Anik. Let's clear the sand away and see how far this cut goes, and then we can figure out what we have here," said Dendree. "But let's stop for lunch and a rest. This heat is just too unbearable to carry on. I don't know what we will find here, but we are at the right spot and it's not going anywhere. This is going to take us a while. If we get more supplies, we can spend the night and do some more work tomorrow. Shaaban, could you fly back to the pyramid and pick up some more supplies while we have a rest? I think we'll need another tent and some sleeping bags, some sledgehammers, wedges, pickaxes and chisels. We'll also need some more food and water.

"I can get all those things for you. Just call Sekani and have him get them ready for me. I'd like to have lunch and a break before I head back, though" Shaaban said. "This heat really takes it out of you. Sitaya, you said you wanted to go back, isn't that right?"

"That's right, Shaaban," answered Sitaya. "I hate to leave you guys here to do this work by yourselves, but I have a couple of errands to do at home and they can't wait any longer. But I'll be glad to have lunch and a bit of a rest before we head back. I can't believe how exhausting it is to work in this heat. If anything is buried under the ground, I've got to say that there couldn't be a better or more remote hiding place."

Within the hour, Shaaban and Sitaya climbed into the helicopter and headed back to the pyramid, while Dendree and Anik lay down in the tent for a rest. Dendree quickly fell into an exhausted sleep, but

Anik's mind was racing with the many possibilities of what they might find, once they uncovered the rest of the deep cut into the bedrock.

As the worst of the noonday heat began to subside, Anik got up, picked up his shovel and continued to remove the sand concealing the deep cut which ran straight along the bedrock. He couldn't see anything in the cut, which was only about two inches wide. But as he continued to clear the sand away, his curiosity deepened. Why was this cut here? Was there some access to the area below? What was located beneath the stone? His questions energized him.

A while later, the familiar thump, thump, thump of the helicopter's blades sounded in the distance. Dendree emerged from the tent, still a bit groggy with sleep. Shaaban landed the bird and hopped out of the cabin. He made his way over to Anik, who had exposed two grooved straight lines at right angles carved deep into the bedrock.

"I see you've been busy while I was gone," said Shaaban. You should see what your discovery looks like from the sky. I bet when you are finished, you will see a good sized square or rectangle that certainly didn't occur naturally. If there is no entrance to whatever is beneath it, it's going to be a mighty heavy stone to lift."

"That's what the pickaxes and sledgehammers are for, my friend," replied Anik.

"If you and Dendree would like to carry on with your shovelling, I can unload the supplies," said Shaaban. "I'll set up the tents too."

Shaaban readied the camp and put together another meal for them and by that time, sure enough, the entire outline of two rectangles side by side forming a large square was clearly exposed, but no entrance was anywhere to be seen.

"Man, I am really bushed now," said Anik. "Thanks for setting things up, Shaaban. Now we can see what the surface is showing us, but that doesn't really tell us very much. It looks as though this is not going to be made easy for us. Getting beneath that stone is going to be hard work."

"Let's stop for supper," said Dendree. "And Anik, just relax. We can't get this done in a day. It has occurred to me though, that since there are all these mounds of stone chips, they likely have been cut out of the space beneath this rock slab, so the chances of finding something down there are good. Wouldn't you agree?"

"I think that is what will keep me going," said Anik. "I'm just going to take a walk around the circumference and see where the best spot might be to create an opening. I'll meet you back at the tent in a couple of minutes."

As the sun began to settle a little lower in the western sky, the rich warmth of the rays embracing the dunes cast longer shadows that gave a whole new feel to the desert environment. The gentle breeze freshened the air and the men sat relaxing in their chairs drinking a cool beer, and enjoying the setting.

"Now this is the desert at its very best," said Shaaban. "Of all the places I fly, I can't say there's any place I enjoy more than here at this time of day. It just doesn't get any better than this."

Even though a thorough fatigue had set in on Anik, he grew restless as Dendree and Shaaban sat back in their chairs.

"I'm going to spend some time with a sledgehammer," said Anik. "I think I found a place that might be a good spot to make a hole. The edges of the rock over in that corner seem a little worn, and maybe that was where people went in and out."

As the eloquent silence of the early evening was broken by the sound of metal striking stone, Dendree turned around to watch Anik pour even more of himself into the task.

"Maybe I'll go over and give the young man a hand for a while, Shaaban. He can't be expected to do this job single-handed, and I have a feeling that there may be a lot at stake here, so I'd like to help him out the best that I can. It won't be light much longer and then we can settle in for the night."

"Sure, you go ahead. I've had a really full day, so I think I'll pass for now," said Shaaban. "I'll clear the supper things away and get the sleeping bags set up. I brought a couple of lanterns so we can have some light after the sun goes down. But with this full moon rising, the moonlight reflects off the sand. Very nice."

Anik and Dendree worked at chipping a hole at the one corner of the rectangle until the sun was completely set.

"Let's call it a day, Anik" said Dendree. "You have worked hard today and you look exhausted. All this will wait until tomorrow."

His energy fully spent, Anik made his way to the tents and collapsed into his sleeping bag. As soon as his head hit the pillow, he fell into a deep, dreamless sleep as his body relished the relief of rest. The other two wasted little time getting into their sleeping bags. The day's labor had taken its toll on all of them and sleep was a welcome respite for their weary bodies.

They woke early as the rising sun shone on their little camp-site. There was a chill in the air and Anik thought he had better enjoy it now, as the temperature would continue to rise until even he would be slowed by the force of the heat. The three of them stirred themselves awake and Shaaban got up and made a small fire.

"We can have coffee with our breakfast, guys. Let's get up and at it before the sun gets too hot."

"It's not easy getting up this morning," said Anik. "Even though I slept well, my muscles are telling me they did too much yesterday. I guess we had better try to make good use of our time here. We still have a lot to do."

Dendree rose slowly and stretched in order to work the kinks out of his back.

"I am pleased to be here to share this adventure with you, my boy, but I've got to say that I am definitely getting too old for this sort of life. Working at the museum and sleeping in my own bed at night is more my speed now. However, we are here, so hopefully we can make some good headway today."

"I think we are on the brink of a huge discovery," said Anik. "It's almost worth having to do the work ourselves to keep this whole thing secret, don't you think? I'm realizing that there's a lot more to treasure hunting than just finding the treasure."

"I don't know how you can possibly expect to break through those huge slabs of stone by yourselves, boys," said Shaaban. "I can give you some help today, but the supply of water and food is getting down. I think I had better plan to fly back to the pyramid today and load up on some more supplies."

"I think Sitaya wanted to come back. If you return tomorrow, she could meet you at the pyramid in the morning. I'll call her and let her know you are coming," said Anik. "Maybe we will have broken through the stone cover by the time you get back. I would sure love to have her here when we discover what is buried under there. And I know she really wants to share that with me."

So they all set to work, doing the hard labor of beating the rock with the sledgehammers. Progress was painfully slow, with the rock yielding little to the force of the hammers. The unrelenting sun rose higher in the sky, challenging their endurance in the blast-furnace heat of the desert. By noon they were spent and they collapsed into the faint shade offered by the tents.

Hope and enthusiasm were wrestled away from them by the force of the inhospitable climate. Conversation dwindled as their doubts and exhaustion forced them against a wall of impossibility.

"Let's break for some lunch," Anik suggested, defeatedly. "I can tell you, there had better be something worthwhile at the end of this job."

They ate their meal quietly, each of them lost in their own thoughts. Dendree entertained fears that this endeavor might cost him his life. He was not a young man, and he had rarely been exposed to such brutal labor in such a harsh environment. *I don't know if I can take it much longer*, he thought. *I would hate to disappoint Anik, but I don't think that any treasure is worth dying for.*

Anik was mulling over the toll this exercise was taking on him. *I thought finding a treasure would fulfil my dreams, but I don't know whether or not I have the strength to do this myself. And what if we don't find anything? It's no wonder the ancients picked this horrible place to conceal whatever is beneath us. Who could possibly find it and access it?*

Shaaban observed the two men as they ate disconsolately. *Well, it's been a nasty morning's work, but I do feel sorry for those buggers. I'm getting paid for flying whether or not they find anything. They are in for the long haul, if they can stand it. I'd hate to come back tomorrow and find that they didn't survive. At any rate, I have to have a rest before I fly back to the pyramid. I'll do what they hired me for. The rest is up to them.*

They slept fitfully through the hottest part of the afternoon, their exhaustion competing against the heat for a balance between rest and discomfort. After 3:00 pm they stirred and woke up.

"Guess it's time to set off," said Shaaban as he gathered his things together. "I've made a list of what I should bring back with me. Do you think you will be okay here by yourselves until tomorrow morning?"

Anik got up and checked the supplies that were left — water, beer, bread, cheese, some dried meat, and some dates and figs. The ice in the cooler had melted, but it was tolerable. There was also a tin of mixed nuts — unsalted. The quantity was going down, but it would be enough. He looked forlornly at Shaaban and shook his head.

"Yeah, it looks okay."

Shaaban climbed into the cab of the helicopter and lifted off, heading east.

Anik and Dendree looked at each other, each of them understanding that more of the same was required of them.

Anik, noticing Dendree's exhaustion, said, "Why don't you just relax here and let me work by myself for a while? The heat has let up a bit, and I think I'll just take my time more now. The stone is starting to weaken and maybe I can break through by myself. We have several hours of work time available before the helicopter comes back."

"Thanks Anik, I appreciate that. I don't know that I have much left to give you on the work front. Maybe if I have more time to recover, I can take a turn in a while."

Anik made his way over to the spot where they had been hammering and kicked the surface of the stone with his shoe. There was a substantial layer of stone chips on the surface.

"We are making headway here. If we knew how thick the stone was, we would have a better idea of how long it will take to break it up" he called over. "It looks like we have cut through about two or three inches."

This time he moved at a slower pace, trying to beat the stone with wiser strokes and using the wedge along the original cut in the stone to increase the depth of the cut. After a couple of hours of unenthusiastic pounding, a large chip from the original cut flew away and upon observation, Anik could see that he had pierced through the stone slab.

"Dendree, Dendree, come here. I'm through the rock."

Dendree hurried over to where Anik knelt and handed him a flashlight.

"Can you see anything?"

"No, just black nothingness. The hole is only a couple of inches across. Wait — wait a minute. I think I see a step cut into the rock. This was likely a place of access to the inside. I think we're getting close now."

"Well, I know this is what we have been working towards, but let's break for some supper. Now that we know we are on the right track, we can continue working at this point knowing that we will be getting somewhere useful. We can probably open the hole enough that we can get in by the time Shaaban and Sitaya arrive tomorrow.

This time their simple meal was eaten with their hope renewed. As the food was restoring Anik's energy, reflecting on his progress with the hammer was restoring his confidence. The stress he had been feeling subsided as he and Dendree shared some easy conversation.

"I think I'll turn in early tonight," said Anik. "I'd like to get a good start in the morning. Sitaya will be coming tomorrow, and it will be great to have something positive to show her. Now that we're through the surface, I think enlarging the hole will go more quickly."

"That sounds good to me too," replied Dendree.

The sun rose early in the east, casting long shadows at the pyramid site. Shaaban arrived just shortly before Sitaya, and together they loaded the supplies aboard the helicopter. Sekani joined them and spent a few minutes listening to Shaaban tell about the situation at the site far away in the desert. Anik's father was glad to hear any news about his son, and he felt pride at Anik's vision and drive for the project.

After the chopper was refueled, the pilot and Sitaya climbed aboard and headed back into the desert. When they landed and disembarked, they were greeted by the smiles of Anik and Dendree.

"We got in," was the only thing that Anik said.

"What did you find? Tell me everything!" Sitaya insisted.

"Well, we opened up the hole and found a staircase straight down into a pit, but the entrance to a separate room is blocked by stone. We will need to chip that out as well. The bad news is that we found a few skeletons in the pit. When we break through the inner door, I sure hope we find more than just dead bodies like we found at the pyramid."

"So you are really getting somewhere," she replied. "Why don't you carry on? Shaaban and I will unload the supplies and then we'll come and check on you when we are done."

Anik and Dendree took their tools down the shaft so that they could begin their work on the doorway below. They spent nearly two hours pounding away at the door and then came up for some lunch.

"It's cooler down there that it is up here," commented Anik. "Not so exhausting. I think I would prefer to have my rest down there instead of up here in this oven."

The three men made their way down the staircase with their sleeping bags as Sitaya stayed back in order to clean up after the lunch. She heard a rumble in the distance and as it grew louder, she could see sand and dust rising from the ground.

What on earth can that be? she wondered. She climbed a dune for a better look. What she saw made her feel sick to her stomach. She raced down the dune and over to the opening which the others had so recently passed through.

"Anik, Dendree, Shaaban — come here right away. We have trouble."

19

DESERT SANDS

The three men came scrambling up the steps from the pit and ran over to where Sitaya was, their eyes following where she was pointing in the distance. They were all annoyed and distressed to see an orange SUV heading straight for them.

"Oh no," groaned Anik. "It can't be him. How could he know we were here? I am getting so sick of this Bill Landing. How can we ever get rid of him?"

Before long the SUV pulled up in front of them and came to a halt. Bill was the driver. He stepped out of the truck and was joined by three other men.

Anik noticed the light beige army fatigues, high boots and pistol belts. Two of the men held machine-guns and stood in front of the extra fuel tanks that were strapped to the back of the SUV.

"What is this, Bill? Archaeology, by force?" Dendree asked. "This is not right and you know it."

Bill glared at Dendree and then at Anik. "All I know is that I am not losing out again. You can only be turned down so many times. Not this time."

"This is wrong, Bill, very wrong. Is this how you want to be remembered as an archaeologist?" Dendree asked as Shaaban walked over to the helicopter.

Bill aimed his gun, fired off four shots at the engine and disabled the helicopter.

"What are you doing?" Anik yelled.

"I thought I told you to let me know if there was something else in the works, but here you are in the middle of a dig, and not even a call. I had to rely on an informant back at the Society to let me know that there was a new dig being started," Bill said spitefully.

"An informant? At the Society? If I didn't see you standing here, I would not have believed you," said Dendree. "And just who would this informant be?"

"This may surprise you, Yusik, but my greatest helper is John Thissen. It's amazing what the promise of finances will do to someone's loyalty when their family is sick."

"John Thissen? How can that be? He's my friend. I've known him for years," Dendree said, startled. His voice wavered. He did not want to believe John would do such a thing. The betrayal hit Dendree like a punch in the stomach, and he felt weak in the knees. But he continued.

"What would you do with the things you find, Bill?" Dendree asked, his heart aggrieved. "You know that any discoveries are the property of the Egyptian people and they need to be preserved."

"Well, it's simple. I have some people in England and the U.S. that are interested in getting their hands on some genuine artifacts. They will pay a premium price. The rest of it, I would melt down into gold bars."

"I wouldn't get my hopes up too high if I were you," said Anik, his anger barely suppressed. "We haven't found anything."

"Is that so? It sure looks like something is going on here. And John Thissen seems to think that you believe there is something very special hidden out here on the backside of the desert." Bill turned to one of the men holding a machine-gun and said, "Mazen, come on over and keep an eye on these archaeologists here. If anyone moves, shoot them. The rest of you come with me and let's take a look around."

The three of them walked over to where Anik had created an opening in the stone slab. They took a look into the pit.

"Go down there and tell me what you see," Bill ordered one of the men.

A couple of minutes later, the man returned to the surface and told Bill about the pit and the stone door.

"It sounds like it will be worthwhile to keep looking here, and so handy to even have the right tools for the job." He snickered.

"So, what will I do with you?" He paused for effect. "I think I'll let you go. You have a long way to walk, so you'd better get going. Oh, and by the way, hand over your phone. You can keep your hats, though."

"What? Are you serious? You can't do this! We'll die in the desert with no food or water. That's murder," Sitaya pleaded.

"It's not me who will kill you," Bill sneered, "It's the desert. You know, just a little accident. How unfortunate."

The shock of what he had just said was unfathomable. *Walk? walk where? We'll never make it back to the pyramid.* They all stood there in a daze.

"So, hand it over — that satellite phone — now!"

Anik handed over the phone. He reached into his double pocket and retrieved the phone, leaving the GPS concealed in the inner pocket of his cargo shorts.

Bill cocked his gun and fired off a round at their feet.

"Get moving now. You've got a long way to go."

They could hardly believe it. Bill was sending them out to die with no remorse, just selfish greed.

The men turned their guns on the helpless group and waited while they got on their way. Slowly, they started out, but before they were out of earshot they heard Bill say, "Wait until they are out of sight before we get busy. Their food and water and tools will come in handy, that's for sure." Then he laughed.

Anik and the others had been walking for about an hour before anyone said a word.

"I can't believe it. John Thissen, an informant for Bill Landing," Dendree lamented. "How could he do such a thing? I trusted him completely."

They followed the tracks through the dunes that the SUV had made. They were a helpful guide in the vast sea of sand. They knew the dangers they were facing: sunstroke, dehydration and hunger, primarily. They were careful to expend just the minimum of energy o keep them moving throughout the day, but the lack of water and food finally caused Dendree to collapse at the base of a dune. The others immediately followed suit. The hot dry wind sucked the moisture right out of them.

After a rest, they continued to follow the tracks left by the trucks, but the further they went, the fainter the tracks became, having gradually been swept away by the shifting sands. Walking in the hot desert was something they were totally unprepared for. Anik and the others knew that the temperature at night would drop a great deal, so as they walked, they kept an eye out for a place of shelter, or a source of water. They saw nothing but sand, no vegetation and no moisture. They had nothing but the clothes on their backs. Anik pulled out his GPS.

He said to Shaaban, while Sitaya and Dendree lagged behind several steps, "At least they didn't notice this. It should help us to go in the right direction." He took a reading and put it back in his pocket.

"It's a bit of a help," said Shaaban. "I would rather have a supply of water, if I had a choice. I never knew I could be this thirsty. But any way we look at it, anything we really need to survive is pretty much missing."

"The best thing we can do is to keep on walking. We can't just give up. I'm not looking forward to getting through the night with no shelter, though. I never thought Bill Landing would go so far. I'm worried about Dendree, too. Between the sunburn and thirst and hunger, I'm not sure how much he can stand. There's really no good solution for us here, is there?" Anik replied quietly.

Sitaya kept pace with Dendree. She, too, felt the desperation of their plight. *I could have avoided all this just by staying home and not coming to see how things were progressing,* she thought to herself. *I've got to try to keep up and not complain, but dammit, I am so thirsty and hungry. I wonder how long we can keep going before it's all over.*

"I can't believe it!" muttered Dendree, in a fit of frustration. "If I ever see that John Thissen again, I don't know what I will do. How could he do this to us?"

"Don't waste your energy thinking of him, Dendree. John is the least of our worries right now. Save your strength for walking," Sitaya suggested. She looked at Dendree as he shuffled along and noticed a tear running down his cheek."

This sure sucks, she thought.

A while later Anik reached into his pocket and retrieved his GPS to get another reading, but when he turned it on, nothing happened.

"Oh no, it's not working! That's just great."

A sick feeling washed over Anik as he dropped to his knees, holding in his hands his one hope of getting home, now taken away.

"What's wrong now?" Shaaban inquired sullenly.

"Sand, Shaaban, sand is what's wrong. It got into the GPS and now it doesn't work. Can this get any worse? I don't think so," Anik said in frustration.

They decided to stop for the night in a small valley between three dunes where there was some shelter from the wind. The warmth from the sand helped to stave off the cold for a while, and they huddled together to try to keep warm. They slept fitfully, their thirst and hunger gripping them at every waking moment. Hope was fading as the hours passed, each of them wondering if was any hope at all to make it back to civilization in time. The rising sun brought them all to wakefulness and they talked about what they should do.

"Well, if we stay here, we will definitely not get anywhere and we are done for. It we keep walking, we might find an oasis or something to help keep us going."

"I think we ought to keep walking, too. It's better than just waiting here to die."

Anik said, "I'll climb the dune and see if I can find anything that might help us." He slogged up through the sand to the summit, and looked around in every direction. Nothing. All he saw was yellow dunes, all the same, all seeming to stare back at him in passive uselessness.

After sliding back down the dune to the others, he pulled out his GPS and stared at the blank screen, not wanting to face the fact that it was jammed up with sand and wouldn't be working anytime soon. A shadow passed over the ground in front of him, followed by a screech. Anik and the others stared up to the sky as a large vulture flew overhead. Anik burst out in laughter at the situation.

"You've got to be kidding me!" he muttered.

Shaaban came over to Anik, and asked for the GPS.

"What could you possibly do with it now? I told you that sand got into it, just like sand gets into everything out here."

"I just realized that I still have my helicopter keys with me," the pilot said, as he produced the set of keys from his back pocket.

Anik looked at Shaaban; skin sunburned, dehydrated chapped lips and speech slowed by exhaustion. Along with the keys in his hand was a small utility knife with a bunch of attachments like a Swiss Army Knife on the key ring.

"Bill shot up the helicopter engine, but he didn't think to take my keychain."

Shaaban and Anik huddled over the small device, and proceeded to carefully open it and clean away the sand that was disrupting its functions. There was nothing that Sitaya and Dendree could do to help the two men, so they watched and waited until the warmth of the sun encouraged them lay down and were able to sleep some more. They worked on the GPS until the heat of the day removed any trace of available shade. Three times they had reassembled the small device with no luck.

"I really don't want to keep walking with the sun directly overhead. We have no directional help from the sun right now. Let's have a rest until the worst of the heat is past and we can try to get this thing working after that. I know the batteries are good," Anik said.

"That works for me," agreed the pilot.

They were all slowing down, in spite of their desire to continue.

They did all manage to get some sleep, and when they awoke, the two men carefully took the GPS apart again and meticulously cleaned it with the tip of the knife. Shaaban and Anik put the lid back on their little project for the fourth time, hoping that this time they would have the results they were seeking. Anik, careful not to re-contaminate it with sand, delicately touched the green ON button. After a second that seemed like an eternity, the screen lit up.

"Yes! All right," Anik exclaimed. He took a reading of their location. He was relieved to see that they were only slightly off course as they trekked back to the pyramid, not that this would help their general situation very much.

"Okay, it looks like we know which way to go. Let's get on our way."

The afternoon began to cool down a bit, and even though their thirst and hunger gnawed at them, the sleep they got re-energized them enough that they felt able to continue. Even when the sun went down, they still carried on. They were surprised to realize that the moonlight shimmering on the desert sands was so bright; they could easily see where they were going. They gazed into the sky and were amazed by the sparkling silver intensity of the stars. In the distance they heard the long and guttural call of a desert lion prowling the vast, empty wasteland.

Anik walked beside Sitaya and put his arm around her shoulders, both to be close to her and to pool their body warmth in the cold night air.

"I'm so sorry I got you into this terrible situation, Sitaya. I would give anything to spare you what we are going through," Anik sighed.

"Yeah, well, it's not really your fault. I could have stayed home. But I know that if I had, and we had lost track of you and the others in the desert, I would be worried sick about you. It is what it is, and even if we die out here, I think I would rather be with you," Sitaya replied.

When their strength came to an end, the group found another small valley in which to collapse for a few more hours of restless sleep.

The next morning they rose with the sun again. They looked at each other with the grim reality looming that they could not survive past today.

"Well, shall we try to continue? We're never going to make it unless we get some sort of miracle," said Anik.

Dendree was in the worst condition. He was lapsing into semi-consciousness; unable to get up without help, and so dehydrated he could no longer speak. Anik checked his GPS and realized they had traveled only forty-five kilometers in all the time they were in the desert … one hundred and five kilometers to go.

"I don't know, Anik. We are all totally exhausted, and even if the three of us could go on, there is no way Dendree can walk any more. Maybe you and Shaaban could go on, and if you can get help, you can come back for Dendree and me. I sure don't want to leave him alone. What do you think?" asked Sitaya.

"What do you think, Shaaban? Should we carry on and hope to find help?" said Anik.

"It's your call. At this point I don't know if it matters what we do. Pretty much anything we do will end us up in the same place, if you know what I mean."

"I can't say that I can make a good decision about it. I really don't want to split us up. Maybe we are better off staying together at this point. I don't know about you, Shaaban, but I don't think I can go very far myself any more. What more can we possibly do?"

They all sat in the sand, at the end of themselves, hopeless despair settling on all of them.

Time seemed to stand still as the bright sunshine filled the sky. They all lay back in the sand and waited.

A while later Anik was roused by a noise that sounded like an engine. He sat up and in the distance he saw a truck come into view driving along the dunes towards them. It was an army truck just like the ones used by the security service that Dendree had engaged. Within a couple of minutes the truck pulled up alongside the sorry group and Sekani jumped out, grabbed Anik and Sitaya and hugged them.

"Are you all right? How long have you been here? Thank God I found you. I should have come sooner," Sekani said. "Here, have some water." He handed bottles of water to the three travelers. "Dendree is looking pretty bad."

Sitaya helped to pour some water down Dendree's throat to revive him. She also got a paper towel from Sekani, poured some water on it and cooled Dendree's face.

"How did you know to come out here?" Shaaban asked.

"Well, I didn't get a call from Anik the last couple of nights, giving me an update like he usually does, so I called him — several times, I might add — but the phone was shut off. I knew something had to be wrong."

He asked them what had happened. Anik and the others told him about Bill Landing's actions, how he had an informant that told him where they were, on the promise of getting paid. They told how Bill had destroyed the helicopter's engine, taken their phone, water and food, and forced them to walk through the desert, being fully aware that it was a death sentence.

"I knew he was an unsavory character, but that is really criminal. Is he still back at the site? Who is it that gave him the information he wanted?" Sekani asked.

"John Thissen's the informant and yes, Landing and three other men are at the site. They are planning to take over the search. They have guns," Anik said.

"John was the guy who came to the pyramid the other day to check on our progress. Said he was also picking up the photos of the murals for Dendree."

"Did he get them out of the trailer?" Anik asked his dad.

"I don't think so. The trailer is right in the middle of the Army's camp, so he would have had to break into the trailer while they were standing right there."

They could hear a low rumble coming from the other side of the dunes, and the three army guards who had driven Sekani peered over the tip of the dune. They could see through the scopes of their rifles that it was John Thissen driving an orange SUV with "Egyptian Artifacts and Studies" printed on the side and large fuel tanks mounted on the back, similar to the ones on Bill's truck.

"It looks like our 'informant' is on the way there. What do you want done with him?" one of the soldiers asked.

"We've definitely got to stop him. And I want to get some answers from him. Besides, we can't let him get to the site where Bill Landing is. We've got to shut them down completely. It's getting to be life-and-death with that crew, and they cannot be allowed to continue," said Anik, with conviction.

The guards positioned themselves in a spot John wouldn't see until it was too late, screwed silencers to the ends of the muzzles, and waited.

John's SUV was almost on top of them before they opened fire. They ripped a groove along the hood, and blew out the left front tire. John slammed on the brakes, his eyes wide with surprise. He jumped out of the SUV and tried to escape on foot. The guards were on him before he knew it. They hauled him back to where the others were gathered. He looked them over and saw that Anik, Sitaya, and Shaaban were quite the worse for wear. His eyes fell on Dendree, who had been moved to the back seat of the truck. He was in grave distress, and John's face registered shock.

Anik got in his face and said, "Yes, take a good look. Because of your actions we almost died. How could you have betrayed us like this? You claimed to be Dendree's friend, and yet here he is like this. We hope he can make it, but maybe he won't. Your stupid decisions have put us all in danger. What do you have to say for yourself?

John slumped where he stood. He hung his head in shame and slowly shook it back and forth as he tried to compose himself.

"I — I'm so sorry. I had no idea that the information I was giving Bill Landing would cause such trouble. Dendree is my friend. Oh, what have I done? If he dies, I will never forgive myself. I'm sorry, Dendree! I'm so sorry."

John paused for a moment, waiting to see if anyone else would talk and then continued, "I did it for the money. I'm drowning in debt, trying to pay the medical bills for my sister and mother. When Bill approached me, he was so sympathetic, and he said he could pay me enough to more than cover all the expenses we have. He just asked me to get him copies of all the photos that were taken inside the pyramid. After that he wanted me to keep him up to date on what you were doing. It all seemed fairly harmless."

"But then this morning he called the museum and I overheard him on the phone joking with one of his other workers who has camped out at our office. He told him what he did to you, sending you on foot into the desert. I couldn't believe it. I decided right then and there that I had to make things right. I took their SUV because it has the most fuel on board. I came to rescue you. Whatever I can do to help you now, I'll do."

Anik and Sekani looked at him, considering his words.

"I believe you, John. You do have your own problems and it seems as though you didn't act out of malice. Maybe we can use your being here with us to our own advantage," Anik said. "But we need to get back to the city. Dendree needs medical attention, and we could all use a shower, a meal and a decent night's sleep. Bill Landing won't be expecting us to reappear, so his guard might be down."

The soldiers changed the tire on the SUV and they all drove back to the city in the two vehicles.

Shaaban headed home, and the rest of them gathered at Sekani's place. The soldiers took Dendree to the hospital first, and Anik and Sitaya got cleaned up. They had a dinner brought in, and spent the evening recounting their ordeal. After John and the soldiers had gone home, and Sekani had headed up to his room, Anik took Sitaya in his arms and held her close.

"I love you, Sitaya. When we were out in the desert, I was afraid we had reached the end of the line. You were great out there. I can't imagine trying to live a life without you in it. I want to always be able to hold you like this and know you are close by."

"That's what I want, too — minus desert treks and threats of death."

The next day all of them got together to figure out how they should proceed with Bill Landing.

John suggested, "Why don't I call him and offer more 'help'. He won't know what has happened with us, so he would probably think that all is going according to his plan. It would raise less suspicion than just attacking him and his crew. That way we could also learn more about what he has found."

"I think that would be our best bet. We do have some military clout to support us when we get there," said Anik.

John put the call through to Bill on his satellite phone.

"Hello, Bill?" John said nonchalantly. "Was wondering how things are going out there?"

"We're doing just fine, but I think we could use another set of hands to help. Anik and that guy from the historical society found a shaft cut in the bedrock that looks very promising. We still have to finish chipping away the opening they made and the stone door at the bottom of the shaft. It looks like we will be here for a while. Why don't you come and help out?"

"I'll be there as soon as I can," John replied, and pushed the red END button on the phone.

"Well, there you go. What do we do from here?"

They discussed strategy, gathered up supplies for the trip and refueled the vehicles.

"Let's head out right away. We don't want to waste time, in case Bill starts destroying valuable relics."

John drove the SUV into the small campsite just as Bill was coming out of the hole in the desert floor. Bill raised a hand in greeting and John returned the greeting.

"Great news, John. We just broke through the door down below that I told you about. It looks as though there are a lot of bodies lying on the floor of the chamber behind it. Kind of like the pyramid, but since this one is all underground, it looks more like an untouched tomb. I would say the chances of finding treasure down there are pretty good. As soon as we find something valuable, you won't need to worry about your finances anymore. The others are still breaking down the door. You could go down and help move the stone chunks out of the way. I'm just heading over for a generator and some lights so we can see what we're doing inside there. All they've got down there are a couple of flashlights."

Bill headed across to the tents that Anik had brought. John just stood there, looking at Bill and then turning his gaze towards the opening of the underground chamber.

While John was deciding just what to do, he heard a shout from down below.

Within a minute a man emerged from the subterranean shaft. He was holding an object aloft and laughing.

"Hey, Bill. Look what I found."

Bill came shambling over to the man, his eyes wide with curiosity. The man held the object out and Bill grabbed it. Its soft luster reflected in sunlight.

"This sure looks like gold. Is there more down there that you can see?" he asked the man.

"It looks like there are some pillars down there that are carved into the shapes of statues. I'd say there is gold covering on them. I found this one in a niche in the wall. It looks like there is a hallway that goes away from the main room, but we'll need more light before we can check that out."

"See, John? If we find more stuff down there like this, all those expenses of yours will be paid, don't you think so?" Bill said, holding the statue out to John.

John reached out and gingerly took the statue. He looked at it as he turned it around in his hands. *I am one of the first to handle this since it was buried in ancient times,* he thought. *This is Isis. How beautiful she is.* He felt the weight of the gold in his hands. *Yes, this would certainly pay all my bills. I am torn.* He held the statue close to his chest.

"Don't get too attached to that relic, John," laughed Bill. "It won't be yours until we are sure there is enough to go around. Let's just go down and have a quick look at what else we can find."

John hesitated, and glanced behind him.

"I don't think so, Bill," Sekani said as he and one of the guards stepped out from behind the helicopter.

"What are you doing here?" Bill demanded, as he reached for his gun.

"I wouldn't do that if I were you," said the guard as he pointed his own gun at Bill.

Bill scanned the area, looking for support, but the only one there was Jareel, who had brought him the statue, now standing empty-handed.

"Now there's no need to get all worked up here," said Bill. "I've always said that I just want to help you fellows. See, I'm being generous to John. He's being helpful and I'm holding up my end of the agreement with him. We've been working away, opening up this stone door. We can all do this together. There's got to be enough gold below to share all around."

"You are missing the point, Bill. These are not your treasures, they belong to Egypt."

"That young fellow is getting paid, right? Probably the 10% finder's fee. Right?"

Just then bullets whizzed by, hitting the guard in the shoulder as the other men emerged from the crypt, guns blazing. The guard groaned, clutched his shoulder and fell to the ground. Sekani dropped to the ground as well.

Bill pulled out his gun and pointed it at Sekani, who was attending to the wounded guard.

"This isn't helping anything, Bill. We need to take this man to the hospital."

"Well, I don't see one around here, do you?" Bill blurted out. "This could have all been avoided if I had been included in your digs. I said before I was sick of being second place all the time."

"Listen. Do you hear that?" Bill's man called out, holding his hand to his ear.

Bill listened to the desert, but all he could hear was the wind. The wounded man groaned again.

John felt the weight of the statue in his hand. Bill is not even paying any attention to me. *This relic can save my finances or my friends. Well, sorry to do this, Isis, but it is time for us to part ways.* With that, John smashed the statue across the back of Bill's head and he crumpled to the ground. One of Bill's men turned his gun towards John and the other levelled his at Sekani.

"Hold it right there, everyone," a voice called out.

The remaining two guards appeared from the top of a nearby dune and aimed their rifles at the group.

"Drop your guns," he ordered them.

Bill's men slowly lowered their weapons and dropped them on the ground. Sekani looked up at the army guards at the top of the hill, searching for his son. It was only a moment until Anik and Sitaya appeared.

The guards handcuffed Bill and his men, tended to their comrad's injuries and escorted them into the army truck. The men were driven to the jail in Luxor and the injured man to the hospital.

While that was happening Anik and Sitaya finally were able to breathe a sigh of relief.

"It looks as though those guys are out of our lives for good," Anik said. "And it didn't come a moment too soon. We had to see how far Bill would go before we could take action against him. Now we can concentrate on our explorations without worrying about them bothering us. Let's take a look behind that stone door. I suppose we should give the cavern a chance to air out before we go in. It's probably pretty foul in there and not safe to breathe. It looks like they brought the generator down already. I'll get the fans and lights and hook them up."

While Anik set up the equipment and started the fans, Sitaya, Sekani and John retreated to one of the tents and they all passed the time in casual conversation while the fans did their work.

After a couple of hours the little group descended the narrow stone staircase and crossed the outside pit, avoiding the skeletons that were scattered there.

"It looks like people were trapped here, just like they were at the pyramid," Sitaya said.

They entered the dark cavern, and their first sight was of hundreds of partially mummified, blackened, desiccated bodies, lying crowded together on the floor. The smell was of old, faint death, the strong stench of putrid bodies having now dispersed and penetrated into the walls.

Shock and horror struck the observers, especially Sekani and John, who hadn't been exposed to the similar sight at the pyramid. The faces of the dead were grotesque, frozen in terror. The bodies were crushed up against the stone doors between the statue of Osiris and the now chipped-out engraving of Ammit.

Signs of violence — blackened bodies with limbs yanked off, ancient blood spatters on the walls grieved them as they realized the last minutes of life in this subterranean tomb were so unspeakable.

Off to one side, young naked girls, now blackened by time and cowered together, were surrounded by guards still holding their spears to form a ring of protection — a gesture of valor.

Numerous pairs of corpses seemed to be clinging together — couples ravaged by panic. One group of four bodies left a different impression. Two men lay facing each other, calm expressions frozen on their faces, and what appeared to be their wives, clinging to them with quiet resignation.

In the middle of the room, statues of gods towered over them with vacant stares on their stone faces. The remains of offerings still hung around the idols' necks and small trinkets still littered the ground at their feet.

Behind Osiris a gilded throne lay on its side — Pharaoh's seat.

Anik panned his flashlight around the room and gazed at the bright murals decorating the walls and ceiling. Such beauty surrounding such tragedy.

Along the passageway beyond the great hall, they noticed that Bill's men had partially broken through a wooden door to reveal a chamber stacked with artifacts. Anik and John broke away the rest of it and made their way inside. As they looked closer they could see a sarcophagus surrounded by stools, beds, clothes and baskets. On one side of the room were disassembled chariots and weaponry. On the opposite side were delicately painted vases and bolts of cloth stacked together. At the far end, behind the coffin were a number of wooden chests. They crossed the room and opened the lid of one chest, then the others. They were stunned to see that they were filled with items of gold — dishes, household and ceremonial tools, and all kinds of jewelry. Even in the poor light, Anik could see that the wealth and treasure of a pharaoh was stored here. His invasion of this personal collection haunted him, and even though this was what he had hoped to find, guilt mixed with his sense of wonder.

From here, the Archeological Society took over. They set up a mobile office at the site, and established security around the perimeter. The team of workers removed the bodies from the crypt, wrapped and cataloged them.

Now it was time to open the vaults that had been filled and sealed so long ago. It was a stunning experience — each one breathtaking. Gold artifacts covered every inch of the twenty-by-fifty-foot rooms: statues, shrines, trinkets, furniture, gold bricks, jewelry, weapons, and a sarcophagus gleaming in the light. Disassembled chariots, swords, spears and shields lay stacked against the wall on one side. The visually congested array of riches and beautiful wall murals of daily life gave the room a powerful, yet serene atmosphere. A thin layer of dust coated everything and would swirl into the air when disturbed.

Each of the remaining annexed rooms was carefully opened to reveal their treasures. All items were photographed and cataloged. They soon realized that each room was dedicated to a particular pharaoh and his own valuables. The walls of each vault were painted with scenes and pictures of the pharaoh's life and loves. Each vault included a variety of canopic jars containing the pharaoh's viscera, all made of gold or stone. Chests full of silver and gold deben testified to each ones' wealth and power.

"This is extreme!" Anik said in shock. "According to what was written about these fellows here," he said motioning to the bodies that were in the main room. "This amount of wealth must have driven them mad."

Anik stepped out of the last gold-packed room and made his way to the image of Ptah, one of the original creator-gods who stood in the middle of the room.

If I could have seen with your eyes, what a story I could tell.

20

AN OLD RING

The items were all cataloged, and their value was recorded. The treasure uncovered was the largest single find in all of history, with a total estimated value of EGP 45,750,000,000.00 ($7,625,000,000.00 US), just in gold. The other priceless items such as the jewelry, furniture, personal idols and pottery added to the total. Compared to that large amount, the relics from King Tut's tomb, valued at only seven hundred fifty million US dollars in 2004, seemed to pale by comparison. The wealth of numerous pharaohs, thought to have been lost to ancient thievery, was recovered intact.

Dendree had made a good recovery from his ordeal in the desert and was now back to work. He was happy to see Egypt's treasures come to their rightful place in the museum, so they could be seen, studied, and appreciated by all. He spent time examining the various sarcophagi which were now housed at the large warehouse beside the Society's office. He marvelled at the lids of the caskets, each of which had a likeness of the deceased carved into the lid. *I am so glad I lived to see these exquisite relics and to share in their recovery*, he thought. *It's the highlight of my career.*

As he sat pondering the events of the last two years, there was one question that gnawed at his mind. In the pyramid's burial chamber that should have entombed Amenemope, just a painting of his sarcophagus decorated the cold stone floor. No large stone box to hold his body. Nothing. Dendree's mind tried to piece together the reasons. Amenemope went out of his way to gather the treasures of Egypt from the un-desecrated tombs and hide them in the Western Desert, yet where was his body? An idea occurred to him.

He tore himself away from his point of observation beside the coffin of Horemheb and made his way through the maze of ancient death to his office. Stepping inside, he opened the filing cabinet that held the pictures of the pyramid's interior. The drawer seemed locked as usual. He knew it wasn't, just a tight fit that needed a little coaxing. He slammed his fist against the side of the brown metal cabinet and pulled at the same time. The stubborn drawer gave way with a grinding creak. *Now, where is it?* Dendree thought as he walked his fingers through the tabs that labeled the files' contents.

Pyramid: Entrance; Great Room; Annex Rooms; ah yes, Burial Chamber. Here it is. There was a second cryptic poem hidden within a painting on the wall of the burial chamber. He flipped through the photo file. *There it is — among the neat drawings of palm trees in this family scene.* Dendree took the picture to his desk, sat down, picked up a pen and paper and transcribed the words:

> Heat of Isis
> Eyes closed to Re
> Hathor's breath cannot be followed
> Ammit guards on top

Dendree laughed to himself as he reread the nonsensical words. *I've got to hand it to you, Amenemope, you do know how to pose a riddle. You are telling us where you are hiding, aren't you! I guess I know who to call for some extra help on this one.*

Anik scrambled to pick up the phone before the answering machine caught it.

"Anik here."

"Anik, it's Dendree. I am planning a trip to the pyramid later this week to check up on something, and I would like you to come along. Will you be free for the trip?"

Anik could hear the smile in Dendree's voice.

"Sure!" Anik answered, his interest piqued. "What's happening?"

"Oh, I just want to look at the burial chamber again. Remember the poem we found written on the wall? There's something about it that is bothering me," Dendree said, his curiosity stirred

"What is it?"

"Amenemope built both the pyramid and the crypt to protect the previous pharaohs' treasures and sarcophagi. I would have expected that he would be buried in the pyramid. But he's not. I think that poem is the key to where Amenemope's tomb is."

Anik thought for a bit. "I'll bet you're right. I've wondered why he wasn't buried there near the statue of himself."

"While we're talking, I should mention that I have an envelope here for you. Could you come by and pick it up? We can arrange our outing to the pyramid at that time."

"Sure. I can come tomorrow morning. Would that work for you?"

"I'll expect you around ten." Dendree sat back and locked his fingers together behind his head. A broad smile spread across his face. He knew what was in the envelope from the Ministry of Antiquities. He and John had also received envelopes from the government.

Another brilliant day of sunshine welcomed Anik as he drove to the Society office. As he entered Dendree's office, he noticed that in addition to Dendree, along the wall there were five Egyptian policemen holding rifles at their sides. Anik could see that Dendree was fingering an envelope with an official seal and a security warning stamped on it.

Anik looked around and felt a surge of anxiety. His face flushed like it had when he'd been a young boy and was approached by a girl he liked.

"Is something wrong? Am I in trouble?" Anik asked, wondering why the police presence was necessary.

Dendree stood up, clutching the envelope in his right hand and approached Anik.

"No, no, Anik, these men are here for security. Nothing to worry about." Dendree handed the envelope to Anik.

The sense of apprehension gone, Anik took the envelope and shot an inquisitive look towards Dendree. He opened the envelope. There was one thin piece of paper inside, and he pulled it out. His breath caught in his throat when he turned it over. It was a checkmade out to him for the sum of seven and a half million EGP. He felt light-headed. *Seven and a half million — I can't believe it!* Anik screamed inwardly. "I can't believe it," he kept repeating, unable to fathom it. "This is amazing. It's going to change my life!" Anik tried to calm himself, but he was trembling.

"Here, I think you had better sit down," said Dendree, rising to let the young man take his seat. "Yes, it's quite overwhelming. But your discovery has meant a huge boost to the wealth of the country. Now these fine policemen will escort us to the bank of your choice so that the money can be deposited in an account. Oh, by the way, the taxes have been paid on that already. Actually, it was twelve and a half million, but there was a 40% tax on it, so that was deducted right off the top." Dendree enjoyed seeing the big smile on Anik's face.

"Thank you so much, Dendree, there are no words to describe my gratitude," Anik managed to say, still having difficulty comprehending the amount.

"Well, don't thank me, Anik, you were the one who was willing to turn over the treasures to the government, so give yourself a pat on the back."

Anik smiled to himself and his mind raced on to his next move.

"Can I ask a favor of you, Dendree?"

"Sure you can, just name it," he answered, curious as to what he wanted.

"I would like a ring from the crypt to give to Sitaya as an engagement ring."

"I think that can be arranged," said Dendree, nodding his approval. He motioned Anik to follow him to the collection of rings and necklaces that had been cataloged.

"Pick one," Dendree said as he pointed to the neatly displayed rings lined up in rows on black velvet.

Anik looked over the large assortment of shiny gold rings. One in particular stood out. It was gold, set with a lapis center and four more blue stones surrounding it.

"I think that's the one for Sitaya. What do you think?" he asked Dendree.

Dendree nodded. "Yes, I think that is an excellent choice." He opened the locked glass case, pulled out the prize and gave it to Anik.

As he reached into the case, Anik noticed another ring with two oval lapis stones mounted side by side on a diagonal slant.

"Um, say, Dendree, might I be able to have that other ring beside it? It could be made into a great pair of earrings."

Dendree turned around and looked at Anik with deep affection. He picked up the other ring and handed it over.

"Thanks so much, Dendree. These will make terrific gifts for Sitaya," said Anik as he slipped the rings into a zippered pocket on his shorts. His eyes sparkled with joy as he considered the destination of the ancient jewels.

Anik and Dendree walked into the First National Egyptian Bank surrounded by the police and deposited Anik's check. He was still reeling from the shock of the size of the payment he received.

After he was finished at the bank, he headed several blocks away to a gemologist friend's business and consulted with him on what he wanted done with the rings.

I love this, thought Anik. *I can hardly believe that they paid me for doing something that I enjoyed so much (except for that desert trek and having to deal with Bill Landing). I hope Sitaya loves the ring as much as I do.*

One year later, the court case for Bill Landing and his sidekicks convened in a courtroom in Cairo. It was an old building, but stately and gracious in its proportions on the outside. Large pillars were set across the front entrance. Inside, the design was airy — spacious rooms of polished sandstone with high ceilings and many windows that let in the sunlight.

The prosecution had done its work. In addition to having Anik, Dendree, Sitaya, Sekani and Shaaban as witnesses to the situation at the crypt, they had also constructed a damning case against Bill, with proof of sale of many stolen Egyptian artifacts to buyers in several countries.

Bill sat at the table for the defense, looking sour and forlorn as one witness after another gave testimony against him and the evidence piled up. The defense was weak and full of contradictions. Bill did not take the stand. By the end of the trial, it had become obvious that Bill Landing and his associates had made a business of stealing and selling antiquities for many years. How he had avoided capture before this was surprising. Being caught red-handed in the desert was key to bringing him to justice.

At the end of the deliberations, the chief justice declared him guilty.

"This court finds your actions against the Egyptian people and her treasures unforgivable.

You have lied to our officials, conspired to steal ancient treasures for your own profit, and caused numerous valuable artifacts to be taken out of the country. You are also guilty of attempted murder."

Bill shifted uneasily on his hard chair, looking petulant and unrepentant, his eyes shifting from side to side, not meeting anyone's gaze.

The magistrate asked Bill, "Do you have anything to say for yourself before I impose the sentence?"

Bill's head began to race. *How can they put me in prison? I'm just a businessman. They are picking on me because I'm not an Egyptian citizen. It's not fair.*

"Well?" the judge asked again with eyebrows raised.

Bill closed his eyes and shook his head. *We'll see how long they can keep me in jail. Bribes have helped me before. Maybe they can help me again.*

The magistrate declared, "I hereby sentence all of you to five years of hard labor in the El-Fayoum Prison, to be carried out immediately with no chance of parole.

After the stress of Bill Landing's trial, Anik felt relieved and relaxed. It seemed as though Bill had doggedly pursued him ever since he had discovered the statue. He had always been looking over his shoulder, wondering when Bill would show up next. The episode in the desert had been the worst, and the sentence handed down to Bill and his cronies had resonated with justice for Anik.

All that has happened in the last three years has been more than I could possibly have dreamed of, thought Anik. *Solving the riddles, finding the treasures, becoming so well known in the country and receiving such wealth for turning it over to the government, as well as knowing Dendree, and so many dignitaries — it has been terrific. I think it's time to move into a new phase of life. I can buy my own house now, and since I can offer her a real home, I think it's time to propose to Sitaya. Maybe I'm getting the cart before the horse, but I think the proposal is at the top of my list.*

He wanted to make the occasion special, so he planned a romantic dinner at The Nile Crossing, an elegant outdoor restaurant in the heart of Luxor that they had always wanted to try. The evening was warm, with a light breeze. The white clothed tables were arranged in small, recessed areas for privacy, with palm trees, large potted plants and colorful mosaic screens dividing between the eating areas on the flagstone floor. The light posts cast a warm glow on the tables in the darkness of the early evening and soft music floated through the air.

Sitaya wore a white peasant dress with a three tiered skirt and neutral colored sandals. Around her neck she wore the lapis pendant on a gold chain which Anik had given her. Her dark hair hung loose around her shoulders. Anik was casually dressed in a turquoise shirt with tan slacks, a taupe-colored sports jacket and tan loafers.

"You look beautiful tonight, Sitaya," said Anik.

"You look pretty good yourself," she replied. "I'm glad we're finally having dinner here. Isn't the ambiance wonderful?"

In spite of the fact that they had spent so much time together, Anik found that he was a bit nervous. Tonight was the night he had waited for and he wanted everything to go just right. The larger ring he had acquired from the treasure in the crypt had been polished and it now glistened like new. The other ring had been refashioned to make earrings which would match the necklace Sitaya was wearing tonight.

I don't think I can wait until the meal is over before I ask her, he thought. He fingered the two tiny boxes in the pocket of his jacket.

They ordered a bottle of wine to begin, and as they settled into the gentle atmosphere of their beautiful surroundings, and enjoyed the fragrance and flavor of their fruity red merlot, they leaned forward in their chairs and smiled into each other's eyes. The love between them was palpable. Sitaya laughed lightly as she saw the earnest desire in Anik's face.

"I love you, Anik. You are a wonderful man."

"I'm glad you think so, my darling, because I have something for you." With that, he took one of the boxes from his pocket, and presented it to her.

Her eyes widened with happy surprise.

"Is this what I think it is?" she asked.

"Why don't you open it and see," he replied.

She took the box and slowly opened it and there they were — a pair of lapis earrings to match her necklace. She blinked a few times and looked at Anik. His eyes danced with merriment. He was enjoying her confusion and he watched her to see what she would say.

"Well, aren't these lovely. They match my necklace. Umm, thanks, Anik. Shall I put them on?"

"I think that's a great idea. They really bring out the blue in your eyes."

He took another sip of wine and looked at her fondly. She looked disappointed, but she didn't say anything as she took them from the box and fastened them on her ears.

"You know, Sitaya, the gold jewelry and stones of royal lapis suit you so well. I think you are the most beautiful woman I know. You are so very special to me. I think I have something else here for you."

With that he slowly drew the second box from his pocket and placed it on the table before her.

Sitaya reached for the box and looked up at Anik with hope in her eyes. She turned the box around in her fingers before opening it and searched Anik's face for a sign. When she saw his smile of adoration, her heart swelled and she looked down as she opened the tiny blue velvet box. And there she saw it. A beautiful ring of gold filigree, inset with one large and four smaller lapis stones — all a stunning royal blue and shot through with flecks of gold. Elegant and unique.

"Is that what you are looking for, my lovely Sitaya? Do you like it?"

"It's so beautiful, Anik. This is from the treasure in the crypt, isn't it? Does this mean what I think it means?"

"What it means is that I love you with all my heart and I want to spend the rest of my life with you. Will you marry me? I promise to always be there for you and be the best husband for you that I can possibly be."

"I can give you an answer right away, because I have been looking forward to this for a long time. Of course I will marry you, Anik."

He slipped the ring on her finger, and they sat there holding hands across the table. The promise made, their wordless gaze conveyed their commitment to each other and their joy in the realization of a shared future. Their dinner was served, but it seemed inconsequential in view of the other reality surging into their evening and their lives.

After they finished their dinner, they drove back to Sekani's place to give him the good news. He was watching television and having a beer. As soon as he saw them, he could tell from the smiles on their faces that something wonderful had happened. Sitaya held out her left hand to show him the ring.

"Well, look what you have there. I guess that means that there will be a wedding in the future," said Sekani. Then he looked up at Anik. "And I've got to say, it's about time. I'm very happy for you both, and I'm sure that you will be happy together."

As they were talking, they were interrupted by the ringing phone. Sekani picked it up and it soon became obvious from the expression on his face that this was not a welcome call.

"Yes, Neema, it has been a while." He did the listening, Neema, the talking. After a few minutes, he started shaking his head and rolling his eyes.

"There has been a lot going on, for sure. Anik and I are both doing well. Things have changed in lots of ways. You were always welcome to keep in touch with Anik. Yes, I know."

As the one sided conversation continued, Anik could see the color rising in his father's face.

"It's always the same with you, isn't it? Always out for what you can get for yourself. I'm surprised that you have the nerve to call here, after all we've been through. I'll let you know here and now — all the discoveries have been Anik's. He's the one who has benefited. And he doesn't owe you anything. You've got everything you're going to get from us already, and that has been substantial. Besides that, you are perfectly capable of earning your own living, so don't come crying to me for more."

After a few more minutes, Sekani simply hung up. He looked at the newly engaged couple.

"Speaking of happily ever after, that was not it for me," he muttered.

"It sounds as though mom hasn't changed much," Anik commented.

"I don't think so," replied Sekani. "But don't let that put you off. You two are much better suited to each other, and you have each other's interests at heart. That makes a huge difference. It won't always be easy, but you are both strong and supportive of each other. I expect you will have a successful and happy marriage and I love you both very much."

"That calls for a group hug," said Sitaya, and they all gathered together in mutual goodwill and affection.

A couple of days later, Anik said to Sitaya, "Do you know who I would like to visit? Let's go and see Huy and Sarin and give them the good news. I'm sure they would love to know that we're getting married."

"I'd really like to invite them to the wedding," said Sitaya. "They were always so kind and welcoming to us, and at such a special time of our lives, when all the excitement was happening. I think they'd love to come."

"We have that appointment with the realtor this morning to talk about what we are looking for in a house, but we could go this afternoon."

When the hottest part of the day had passed, they hopped into the Jeep and headed down the familiar road to the edge of the desert. They parked on the side of the road by the ramshackle house and headed into the yard, expecting to see Huy at his small table with his chess set in front of him. Although the leaves on the trees fluttered in the light breeze, the yard seemed deserted. The flowers in Sarin's garden were wilted. There was an uneasy calm about the whole area that made them feel nervous. Anik walked into the yard and up to the table where Huy usually sat. He noticed that half of the chess men had been swept away and Huy's pipe lay on the board by a burn mark on the table where the burning tobacco had spilled out.

The couple stepped on to the decrepit porch and knocked on the door. When no one answered, they knocked again and waited. Nothing.

"I wonder where they are," said Anik, "and if they are okay."

He tried the door and found that it was unlocked. He slowly opened it and called out, "Huy? Sarin? Is anybody home?" Still no answer. They entered and looked around. No one was there and it was not in its usual state of order. There were dirty dishes on the table, and the kitchen chairs were scattered on their sides.

"This doesn't look good," said Anik. "I sure wonder what happened here. Is there any way we can find out?"

"I don't think so," replied Sitaya. We don't know if they have any other family around. I've got to say that this worries me, too. Do you still want to go out to the pyramid?"

"Not really. It bothers me that they aren't here. They are so kind and harmless. I'd hate to think that anything bad has happened to them. But it's troubling, all the same. Let's go home.

I'll make some inquiries and see if I can find out anything."

With that, they headed back.

21

DARK ROLLER-COASTER RIDE

Following up on Dendree's interest in locating Amenemope's tomb, he and Anik headed for the pyramid, hoping to find a key to locating the mysteriously absent resting place of this intriguing pharaoh.

"I know just where I want to look," said Dendree as they pulled up to the pyramid in the Society's SUV. "I brought copies of the photos where the poem was hidden within the painting."   The pyramid had been opened as a tourist attraction the previous year, although it catered mainly to tour groups, rather than individual sight-seers. It was closed to the public today, as Dendree didn't want there to be any curious tourists around who might overhear anything that they were talking about.

"I'm glad we've been able to secure this site. The main attraction here is the pyramid itself, and the beautiful artwork on the walls. But who would guess that there are still valuable secrets to be found here?"

Dendree unlocked that gate into the pyramid area. They made their way inside, turned on the lights and the fans, and took a few moments to admire the ornate murals that covered the walls, continuing from one area to another as though the whole interior was one complete, non-stop photograph.

"These murals are as breath-taking now as they were when I first saw them," said Anik. "The colors, the detail, the scenes, the gardens, the buildings: it's as though we can imagine what life was like when Amenemope was alive."

As they entered the burial chamber, they stood behind the cordon of blue and white rope suspended between brass posts which separated the observation area from the beautiful painting of Amenemope's sarcophagus on the floor.

"I'll never get used to seeing that," Dendree said as he motioned to the three dimensional picture in the center of the room.

"I feel the same, Dendree. It's really amazing how the artist managed that special effect so many years ago," Anik said as he gazed at it hypnotically.

The almost translucent picture painted on the floor popped out at them. Gold-colored highlights shaded the sarcophagus's 3D outlines, making it appear as though it was resting below the floor under a sheet of glass. The death-mask of Amenemope painted on the top of the tomb was like King Tut's — pure gold. The thick black lining around his eyes enhanced his piercing gaze. The body boasted blue chevrons, outlined in bright gold that flowed down his torso as though he were wearing a body suit. Black and green accents filled the remaining areas as his crossed arms held the crook and flail across his chest.

Anik stepped back and looked at the wall, scanning the vibrant garden scene that flourished before him — a feast for the eyes. Dendree headed for the other side of the room, slowly but carefully scanning the hieroglyphs painted on the wall, searching for the cryptic poem.

"Anik, I found it. The poem. Look at this!" Dendree called, his voice echoing off the walls in the hollow, unfurnished room.

"See, here is the poem that's in the photograph."

Anik hustled across to the other side to see Dendree crouched beside a section of the mural that boasted a forest of palm trees and flying ducks. He scanned the area to see if there might be any further clues. Suddenly he saw something else.

"Look at this part!" Anik said as he pointed to the wing of a quail hidden behind some ground foliage.

"The detail is astonishing," Dendree said as he bent down and squinted.

"Look at the lines. Forget the quail. Look at what makes up the lines and feathers!" Anik said, the excitement in his voice unmistakeable.

Dendree stopped looking at the quail as a whole and focused on the lines of the feathers. The shock of what he saw nearly knocked him over. The entire drawing that appeared to be a quail was made up of tiny writing, but it was not Egyptian. It changed colors as the feathers of the quail blended together over the fowl's body. "What do you think the language is, Dendree?" Anik asked curiously.

Dendree moved in to take a closer look.

"I think it's Libyan, but I'm not sure. I'll get my camera and get a close-up so that I can study it later," Dendree said as he went into the other room to retrieve his camera from his knapsack.

As Anik waited for Dendree to return with the camera, he continued to closely inspect the elements of the art on the wall to see if he could discover any other clues or secrets. The complete Book of the Dead, the instructions for the deceased when meeting Osiris in the Hall of Judgment, were inscribed on the wall. Included were prayers and spells for Amenemope to take along with him to help make his judgment favorable.

It's surprising what you can see right before your eyes if you look carefully, thought Anik.

Dendree set up the tripod and focused the camera on the poem, this time zooming in to enhance the detail. He snapped the picture and a little whine from the charging flash signaled it was ready again.

The lines were still confusing and made no sense. Anik slowly read the words of the poem:

"Heat of Isis
Eyes closed to Re
Hathor's breath cannot be followed
Ammit guards on top"

"Dendree, there are no extra clues that I can see. Maybe the writing on the quail might give us some more information to help solve the poem."

"I want to take some pictures of that quail. With the zoom, we can enlarge the writing so it will be easier to see what is written." Dendree snapped some more shots and the clicks and flashes filled the room, giving the burial chamber a haunted-house effect of eerie strobe-lights. It made Anik feel as though the ghosts of the dead they had found previously would somehow come out of the shadows, pleading for, or perhaps revealing, answers. Dendree got up from his kneeling position, straightened his stiff legs and walked to the corner where Anik was staring at the wall of writing.

"Dendree, I think maybe there is something here. Take a really close look."

Dendree focused again on the words, but still could not see anything peculiar about the verse. He squeezed his eyes shut and opened them again, blinking several times.

"Do you mean that slightly brown tinge and the symbol of a cooking pot at the line 'Heat of Isis'?"

"Yes," replied Anik. "Do you think that might be significant?"

"It could be," said Dendree. These latest pictures I have taken were with the maximum zoom, so when I print the enlargements, we can examine the details more carefully.

In the corner, hidden from sight, a digital recording device clicked off as the men left the room and the movement ceased. It had picked up all that was said in the stone room and had sent an audio/video feed of the conversation to a receiver at Huy's old home on the edge of town. Every room in the pyramid had a motion sensing recording device that "listened" to all conversations — courtesy of Bill Landing and "Egyptian Artifacts and Studies."

Outside, Dendree shaded his eyes against the glare of the sun and the bright reflection bouncing off the glossy pyramid sides. Anik had already framed his face with some sporty sunglasses and Dendree hurried to the Society's SUV to retrieve his own, to start the engine and turn on the A/C. Anik jumped inside also, and they waited for the welcome cool air to refresh them. Dendree turned the truck around and went up to the security stop that had been erected right after the pyramid had been found. They were dismayed to see the guard asleep in his booth. Dendree woke him so that he would raise the gate and warned him that he was expected to remain alert and that anyone could have walked in undetected. The deadly heat from the sun baked the desert sand and turned the whole Western Desert into an outdoor oven. The security job was often a harsh and lonely one, but competence was still expected.

The ripples on the sand flew by as Dendree's SUV sped along the road. The barren landscape had become familiar to them and the trip seemed shorter than it had at first. As they neared the edge of the desert, sparse vegetation appeared beside the road of harder packed sand. Then they reached the cracked pavement that led into the outskirts of town. The small buildings along this road soon changed to large sprawling estates and then the light industrial part of Luxor. As they turned down the main street, Dendree headed into the parking lot at the Egyptian Archaeological Society's office building. The drive back had been light on conversation, as they mulled over in their minds what they had seen and what they might discover.

Anik sat across from Dendree at the desk as he printed the photos they had just taken. He examined the close-up of the poem and tapped his finger on it.

"You can clearly see it here. What do you make of the cooking pot following the reference to Isis, and why is it brown instead of black?" Anik questioned.

"In ancient texts, a large geyser shot up in the Mediterranean by the north eastern side of the Nile delta fan. The brown sediment muddied the waters for a year. I think maybe that is what is being referred to in that particular line, 'Heat of Isis'."

"I think you are full of it, Dendree," laughed Anik. "I have never heard of that before. What about the Isis part?"

"The Isis Mud Volcano is a deep-sea mud volcano at a depth of thirty-one hundred feet, and it is still active and bubbling to this day. The desert cliffs reach right out to the Nile's edge at that location."

"Why have I never heard of this before?" Anik asked, with a raised eyebrow.

Dendree sat reclining behind his desk, arms crossed and feeling immensely pleased with himself.

"Probably because there has only been one large eruption ever recorded and even then it was quite a stretch for the imagination," Dendree replied. "I'm thinking that Amenemope's tomb is somewhere in those cliffs, if we go by his apparent love for cryptic poems. Re's eyes being closed might mean the sun cannot shine where he is, ergo, his resting place is buried. Maybe that place is in the cliff face."

Anik nodded his head and stared once again at the verse.

"Why can't 'Hathor's breath be followed?'" Anik questioned. "Isn't Hathor the cow goddess of love, and what about Ammit guarding on top?"

"Not a clue, Anik, not a clue. You know that Hathor wasn't always a love goddess. According to the story of Hathor, her father Re, created her as Sekhmet, The-Destroyer-of-Men, and he couldn't stop her from killing. He then disguised beer as blood and when Sekhmet got drunk on beer, thinking it was blood, she could no longer kill and was then known as Hathor, goddess of love," Dendree said. "I can't imagine how that figures into the puzzle."

After stopping for lunch, Dendree pulled out the pictures he had taken of the quail hidden in the brush. Anik leaned over his shoulder and gazed at the fine detail that could only have been done by a master painter.

"Isn't that amazing?" exclaimed Anik. "I have never seen anything like that before. Those close-ups show each individual feather is made up of colored miniature text that you can hardly see with the naked eye. It all flows together with color, shape and size so it just looks like the quail's feathered flank. Very impressive."

"You're right, Anik. It's a real work of art in every way. And in these enlargements, the Libyan writing can be clearly seen, so it can be translated now."

"I know this Libyan dialect is ancient and unused nowadays. Do you know anybody who can read it?" asked Anik.

"Yes, as a matter of fact, I believe that John Thissen can," Dendree replied. "I'll drop these photos off at his desk."

Dendree gathered up the photos, stuck them in a folder, and marked it with John's name and set it aside.

"How is John doing, Dendree?" Anik probed. "Can you trust him after what happened at the crypt with Bill?"

Dendree thought for a little, then replied, "I think so. He redeemed himself in the end. I don't think we could have nabbed Bill so easily if it hadn't been for his co-operation. He has been a model employee ever since. I haven't entrusted him with anything confidential. He has shown consistent dedication to the Society. I think we will be able to trust him with this little interpretation assignment. Besides, after all, he received some payment from the Ministry of Antiquities, so he was able to get his debt paid. I would say that those worries are behind him now, especially since his mother and sister are greatly improved in their recovery."

"That's good to hear," Anik said, relieved.

Dendree got out several topographical maps of the north-eastern Nile where it flowed into the Mediterranean. He pointed to where the cliffs reached out to the Nile's edge. Anik rested his forearms on the large worktable, littered with maps, and gave his full attention to the information Dendree was passing on to him.

"Look at this, Anik," Dendree said, as he traced his finger about an inch up into the Mediterranean to a small mound on the sea floor. "Read that, please."

Dendree's finger was pointing to a miniature inscription written beside the small mound.

"I can't believe it," Anik said as he shook his head. "Isis Mud Volcano."

"Do you want to take a trip, Anik?"

"Sure! I'm up for a bit of travel."

Just then, John walked in, carrying his laptop computer. Dendree handed him the file of photographs that were taken of the quail.

"I have something for you to work on, John. Can you translate this for us?" Dendree inquired.

John looked at the tiny, immaculate writing, and tapped his index finger on his cheek as he thought.

"Looks like ancient Libyan. Where did you get these, may I ask?"

"They were in the pyramid's burial chamber," Dendree answered. "Can you do it?"

"Ancient Libyan is very close to today's Libyan spelling except for some characters relying on more than one sound," John said casually. "Yes, just give me a couple of hours."

"Thanks, John! The sooner, the better," Dendree replied as he stood up.

He gathered up the maps, folded them and placed them in his brief-case.

"It's getting too late to start out today," he said to Anik. "Why don't we assemble the supplies we will need and then get an early start in the morning? We'll have to plan to be away for at least three days. Does that work for you?"

"Where are you going?" John asked.

"About thirteen hours north from here," Dendree replied.

"Does it have something to do with what is written on these photos?" John asked.

"I suppose we will need you to tell us that when you finish the translation, won't we?" teased Dendree. "Actually, would you be interested in coming with us? I think you would find it worthwhile. We're heading for the coast of the Mediterranean at the edge of the delta."

"Yes, I think I can get away for a few days. It would be pleasant to have a change of scenery, too." he replied.

"Then I guess we are all set," Anik added, excited to go.

"I can have the translation ready for you in the morning," John said, smiling.

They set out at 8:00 in the morning in the Society's SUV with Dendree driving. They had loaded all the supplies they thought they might need on their venture — ropes, harnesses, sledge hammers, crowbars, lights, camera — all the things that had come in handy at the crypt, as well as a substantial supply of water and food.

John was excited to share the translation of the Libyan writing they had found on the wing of the quail.

"This tells us about the woman who was in charge of all the painting done in the pyramid. It's truly fascinating. Knowing this information fills in some important details about why the pyramid was built and also about some of the people responsible for its construction. Let me read it to you," said John.

"What does it say?" the two men asked in unison.

"Akila, Chief Artist for this mighty temple to Amenemope, Giver of Life. I proclaim my love for my husband, Wijin, Chief Architect under Khnum, Architect under Pharaoh Living Forever. We have robbed Pharaohs' tombs. Along with all thieves, we have been sentenced to work here as slaves to pay for our crimes. I have taught all the wives to paint, but I have painted this room, personally. Amenemope, God Forever, will be pleased with my skill. Wijin treats me with respect, he is a good husband. My crimes are an embarrassment to me, they fill me with guilt. I do not know if I will be expunged from my grievous deeds. Since I have helped teach the art of painting to all the women working here, maybe they will be given jobs when our work is done. I am the chief instructor and will continue my labor out in the desert. I will work until I pay for my sins."

"That's all there is," John finished.

"Pretty short and to the point, isn't it?" Dendree commented. "I'm really impressed that all that incredible art was done by women. And this Akila sounds like a high achiever in that time and culture."

"I'll never understand how women were so limited in their options, and generally banned from reading and writing. I'll tell you one thing. Sitaya wouldn't put up with that! It seems as though someone made good use of the women's talents at the pyramid," Anik exclaimed.

"The women didn't have much opportunity in that culture and time, Anik, and in many ways that is still the case in these middle-eastern countries. But women in Egypt sometimes did have it better than they did in neighboring countries. They could own property and had some legal rights. And remember Cleopatra? She ruled the country. It wasn't easy for them, though. Thanks for that work, John. That commentary adds to our knowledge of the pyramid, but it doesn't shed any light on our current undertaking," Dendree added.

Night had fallen by the time they reached their general destination. They found a small hotel in Damietta, a town a few miles west of the spot they were looking for, so they stopped for the night, planning to get an early start the next day.

Morning dawned bright and clear, the sun brilliant in the sky as they headed for the Mediterranean after sharing a full breakfast at a small restaurant. The beauty of the azure water sparkling in the sunshine evoked feelings of delight in all three men and the coolness of the morning refreshed them as they made their way along the seaside road towards their destination.

"Thanks for inviting me along, Dendree," said John. "It's a real treat to get out of the city, out here where the air is fresh and clear and the breeze from the sea is so pleasant."

Anik had been following the map carefully and when it looked as though they were close to the spot they were looking for, he said, "I think this is where we want to start looking, Dendree. You could stop anywhere along here."

There was a wayside area between the road and the cliff they were driving along, so Dendree pulled over and turned off the engine. They climbed out of the vehicle, stretched and took some deep breaths, then headed to the edge of the cliff.

Seagulls squawked and bickered among themselves as they swooped and jockeyed for position, waiting for a handout that they would not receive. Dendree strolled over to the cliff's precipice and cautiously looked over the edge. A hundred feet or so below him, waves crashed into the sharp rocks at the cliff's base. John leaned his arm on a granite sign, watching Anik and Dendree, lying face down with their heads over the cliff, peering into the crashing surf. Dendree got up and walked over to the truck, giving John a quick nod as he strolled by. The air blowing off the blue Mediterranean Sea smelled of seaweed and salt water. The gulls kept screaming their warnings to each other, filling the air with a never ending cacophony of high pitched squawks and squeals, set to the constant beat of the waves.

John looked at the plaque he had been leaning against. Crusted bird droppings covered the message, so John reached into his pocket, retrieved an old hanky, poured some water from his water bottle on it and proceeded to scrub off the contamination. As Dendree returned from the truck with the maps he had retrieved, he looked at the sign, now legible.

"What do you have there, John?" Dendree asked, peering over his shoulder.

In bold letters the sign read:

ISIS MUD VOLCANO
300 METERS NORTH

The sign had an arrow pointing out into the Mediterranean.

"Anik," Dendree called.

Anik got up from where he was lying at the cliff edge and jogged over to Dendree and John. Dendree started to unfold the large topographical map in front of the granite post that held the informative plaque.

"This is where we are," he said pointing to a spot on the map. "And right there is the volcano."

"Am I missing something? What are we doing here?" John asked, feeling as if he had been left in the dark.

Dendree looked at John and smiled. "What we are looking for is Amenemope's tomb."

"What?" John exclaimed, his eyes wide with surprise. "So that's what all this secrecy is about. I'm thrilled that you have invited me along. Are we close, do you know?"

"I think so," replied Dendree. "We may be a little off, though. I'll check our position with the compass." He stood with his back to the marker and held the compass out in front of him. He pointed his finger straight north and marched towards the edge of the cliff where he dropped to his knees and peered over the side.

"John, bring the truck over here, please!"

Anik ran to Dendree's side, and John climbed into the SUV and drove it over to where Dendree was kneeling.

"John, park the truck parallel with the drop-off, like this," Dendree said, motioning directions with his hands.

"Do you see something?"

"Yes, Anik, Yes I do," Dendree said, beaming.

They attached two ropes to the truck's frame and threw the coiled remainder over the cliff. Anik and Dendree got into their harnesses and prepared to rappel down the rock face.

"Will I be able to come down there with you?" John asked eagerly.

"You could, yes," Dendree replied. "Right now, though, I need you to stay up here until Anik and I check it out first. We'll probably need some things from the truck when we get down there. There is an extra harness for you behind the seat, along with the rest of the equipment. We will have to see what it looks like and what we need. After you pass down the items we need, then you can make your way down and help us with the opening."

The two men stood facing the edge of the cliff and slowly rappelled down the face. At forty feet, they came to a ledge that they could comfortably stand on. They could tell that a cave entrance had been plastered over so that the surface was flush with the cliff wall. The protruding ledge was the only thing that had revealed the location. Dendree ran his hands over the rough surface. Picking off some of the flaking plaster, he wrapped his knuckles on the entrance, listening for a hollow sound.

"I think we've got it. John, we need a sledgehammer and a crowbar," Dendree called up.

"Okay!" John's voice came back from above them.

John tied the tools to a rope which he lowered to the ledge and the men went to work smashing through the hidden door.

"This is sure a lot easier than breaking through that heavy stone cover at the crypt," Anik said. "The location is way more precarious, though. Watch your step, Dendree. Back up carefully."

"They must have had some kind of scaffolding coming down here from the top of the cliff," said Dendree. "There would have been a great deal of coming and going to prepare and complete this project. And a lot of material to transport out of the cave, as well as all the things they would have stored inside."

Within three-quarters of an hour, the hammer finally pierced through the doorway. They enlarged the opening and noticed that foul air escaped from the deep cavern as from a closed-up locker room that had never been cleaned and was breathing a sigh of relief.

Dendree called up, "We're though the doorway, John. You can come down now if you like. Bring the flashlights and the camera with you. Oh, and some bottles of water."

Anik continued to break through the opening as John made his way down the cliff face. The entrance was now totally opened and the three men stood at the doorway peering into the black void.

"It looks as though this was a natural cave at one time. So the builders had some place to start," Anik commented. "Let's take a break and have some water before we enter. I think we need to wait for the air to clear first. We also need watch out for traps. The warnings seemed to be pretty explicit towards anyone who enters."

John peered into the cave, wondering what they would find, and not really paying attention.

"This will be another huge find for the Society," John said. "I can hardly imagine all that we will discover here."

As they entered the tomb, a strange smell filled the air — hard to identify but not unfamiliar. After the first ten meters things changed and the tunnel became perfectly square — two and a half meters wide by two and a half meters high, gradually sloping upwards. After the first ten meters, the tunnel levelled out and the wall murals began, revealing Amenemope's commitment to the cult of Osiris. Two lines of hieroglyphics ran tandem on each side of the subterranean hallway, one convincing the reader of his accomplishments on behalf of Osiris and the other sending out a warning to turn back. Anik started to read out loud:

"I have fulfilled the task given to me by the great god, Osiris.
I have sealed up the destroyers of Ma'at up for all time.
I have brought peace to my forefathers' sleep.
I have brought order.
I have lived by the laws of Ma'at.
I am blameless before the gods.
I have lived by truth before the gods."

"Will you look at that? This goes on and on like he is trying to convince us and the gods of his purity."

Dendree stopped walking and thought for a minute. Then he explained.

"In ancient Egyptian culture, if something was written down, the gods accepted it as truth. That's why so many times a pharaoh boasted that he built this or that, or won a battle, but in reality, he didn't. After a while, the distinction between truth and reality became blurred."

As they walked, the floor took a downward slant then abruptly flattened out for about ten meters and then the path took another climb for ten meters and flattened out again. This pattern repeated itself like an ancient roller coaster. Anik noticed a picture of Ammit, an Egyptian demon, carved into the floor at every incline, and at every level he grew more vicious-looking.

"He's getting angrier all the time," Anik said, pointing to the engraved pictures.

"Yes, the warning seems to be clear," Dendree replied.

They all turned back in the direction from which they had come. Natural daylight no longer reached them. They stopped for a couple of minutes to catch their breath and have some more water.

They had traveled up and down five level areas, hills, plateaus, and drops, each at ten meter increments. Anik felt lightheaded every time he was at the top of a rise, but he didn't give it much thought. He knew that being so deep in the ground there wasn't as much fresh air circulating.

"Look there, Anik. Can you read that inscription?" Dendree asked. Anik looked at the writing on the wall and began to read it aloud as Dendree looked on while John continued to move forward:

"Cursed is he foolish enough to come into Hathor's depths.
Hathor will rip out your lungs.
Be warned, foolish ones.
Hathor's breath shows mercy to none."

As Anik walked, he noticed dirt, half a meter deep, was everywhere along the edges and it looked like the bodies of blackened desiccated cows chained to the floor were lying on the piles of dirt. *What a mess. What are these corpses doing here?* Along with being light-headed he slowed as confusion settled on his mind. *Something may not be right here,* he thought vaguely. Up ahead, John stopped dead in his tracks and shouted down at them, since he was at the top of a rise.

"Th-there are some dead-d cows up here," John stammered as he shook his head several times, trying to concentrate on what he was saying.

"Are you okay up there, John?" Dendree called, wondering why John's speech was slurred.

"I'mmm ... ," he replied and disappeared from sight.

Anik and Dendree looked at each other, trying to figure out what was happening and what they should do. Their feet seemed like lead as they tried to step forward. They looked upwards, their gaze following the next incline. They struggled to focus and think, to understand. Then it came to them as they looked at each other and cried in unison, "Methane! John — there's methane!"

Methane from the cows had collected in the high areas at the top of the hills, making a perfect death trap. The lack of fresh air to dissipate the deadly gas had them in its clutches.

"John!" Dendree called desperately. He thought he saw John's head and arms dangling from the top of the plateau in the unsteady beam from his flashlight.

"We have got to get out of here, now!" Anik uttered in horror. "We have to leave him."

They slowly made their way back to the last slope they had descended. *We are in big trouble*, Dendree thought, panic rising. *We are trapped. We will all die.* Dendree looked again at the incline and tried to scramble up the forty-five degree angle. Part way up, the methane and lack of oxygen took their toll and sent his head into a spin. He lost his feeble grip and slid back down. Anik was still sitting, cross-legged on the floor, watching Dendree unsuccessfully trying to climb up the hill. Dendree collapsed unconscious in a heap near Anik after the failed attempt. The floor trembled under them as if Ammit was making a point about disregarding his warnings.

Anik scanned the wall in front of him through unfocused eyes. Just the same dirt that had lined the walls for the past hills and valleys. *This isn't dirt*, Anik thought. *It's decomposed cow manure.* He reached out and ran his hand through the loose soil, feeling defeated. As he did so the tips of his fingers came against a square rock that jutted out of the corner. *What is this?* he thought as he scooped the soil away. The four-inch-square stone that stuck out of the wall looked more like a plug. *An air vent for the workers!* Anik cleaned the decomposed manure away and started trying to jar the plug loose from the stone wall. The stone would not budge. Anik sat with his thigh against the wall. He positioned the heel of his foot against the stone and readied himself. After pulling his foot back he drove it forward, slamming his heel into the stone plug. Nothing. He drove his foot repeatedly against the square block, hoping that it would pop out from the wall. Anik felt another wave of delirium and nausea strike him as he collapsed on his side. Dendree had now regained consciousness and crawled on his stomach towards Anik. After reaching him, he grabbed Anik's leg to pull himself closer. If he was going to die, he wanted to be with a friend. The minute Dendree grabbed his leg, Anik woke from his stupor. He blinked and squeezed his eyes shut and then open again. With the last ounce of strength in his being he placed the heel of his shoe on the stone block, pulled his foot back and thrust it forward, knocking the plug out of the wall. Anik scrambled around, flopping on the floor so his face was in front of the square opening. Sucking in any air he could, through his mouth, he reached behind him and pulled at Dendree. Dendree felt the tug on his shirt and slowly crawled beside Anik. They lay there together, breathing the oxygen, lying face down, chins on the ground and cheeks touching. Slowly, their heads began to clear, the poison in their lungs being replaced with the meager amount of oxygen supplied by the ancient air vent.

Fifteen minutes later, the fog was lifting from their minds and their strength was improving. They still hovered close to the opening, figuring out what they would do next.

"We need to run out of here, no stopping," Anik croaked, his lungs still recovering. "Do you think you can do that, Dendree?"

"I hope so. One thing in our favor is that the closer we get to the main opening, the more the methane will have disbursed," Dendree replied, as he rose to his feet.

As they stood, they both collapsed to the ground as the feeling of "head rush" overwhelmed them, upsetting their balance.

"Slowly, this time. Take a big breath from the vent and hold it as long as you can," Anik cautioned, as he gradually stood up.

Dendree was now standing beside him and ready to attempt to climb the incline that had thwarted his previous attempt. They took a running start and with their strength renewed the incline was easily conquered. Holding their breath, they hurried past the pile of cow dung that lined the walls. There was no time to examine anything, they just ran. By the time they had reached the second plateau, light from the outside was illuminating the interior ahead of them. They slowed and tested the air. It was good. The crisis was past. They would live.

They wasted no time making their way to the cave's opening. They looked at each other, expressions of relief on their faces and then regret as they remembered that John had not been so fortunate. They sat down on the ledge to rest and recover from their exploration.

"That was too close," said Anik. "Even though we anticipated danger, it came on us so quietly, we didn't know what hit us. We will be more prepared for that when we come back."

"I can't believe that John is gone. What a tragedy!" he said swallowing the lump in his throat and shaking his head. "I guess that there was no way to save him," he paused. "The ancient trap was primitive, but no less deadly. No way to save him." Dendree repeated, his words trailing off. "It was fortunate that you found that air vent, or we would all be gone now. Even so, I am going to need a few more minutes rest and get my mind under control before we attempt that climb back to the surface."

"No problem," said Anik. "Take your time."

As they stared out at the Mediterranean Sea, they noticed a bubbling ring about three hundred meters out from the base of the cliff. In the midst of the waves, the outside of the ring appeared to be perfectly calm and became more disturbed closer to the middle. The slow crash of the waves did not stop, the air still smelled the same, but there was something different.

"What is that?" Anik asked, pointing at the frothing disturbance.

"That is right where the Isis Mud volcano is. I guess it's letting off some gases," Dendree answered. "I wonder if we will get to see it being active."

"No seagulls," Anik said with a start. "The place was swarming with them when we got here. I wonder where they are."

They felt a low rumble through their bodies as they rested against the wall, watching the water. The bubbling disturbance started getting more extreme as the center of the ring became a definite brown color and was swelling half a meter above the waves. They felt another shudder through the stone escarpment and the boiling ring exploded before their eyes. A twelve meter column of brown mud shot up out of the middle of the sea like a high-powered fountain. Steam rose high into the air, resembling a boiling, whistling kettle on the stove. Mud quickly turned the area around the dirty geyser from beautiful blue to rapidly-expanding brown-black sludge. The loud hiss that came from the fountain was terrifying, sounding like a viper. They sat, eyes glued to what they were seeing, unable to avert their gaze. The column quickly dropped to nothingness and all they were left with was the heavy stench of sulfur that wafted in, irritating their nostrils. As quickly as the eruption had started, it was over. The steaming ring of boiling mud had disappeared below the waves, leaving the Mediterranean looking like a dirty mud-puddle. Anik and Dendree looked at each other with shock in their faces, each waiting for the other to speak.

"You don't see that every day," Anik commented, trying to lighten the mood. "That was amazing."

"Timing is everything," Dendree added, a smile creasing his wrinkled face.

Anik and Dendree strapped on their safety harnesses, attached themselves to the dangling ropes they had used previously and scaled the side of the cliff. At the top they pulled up the ropes and the tools and packed them in the SUV.

"Would you like me to drive back?" Anik asked.

"Yes, I'd appreciate that. Let's stay at the hotel overnight and head back in the morning. I'll have to call the society and let them know about John."

Just saying his name, Dendree stopped talking, choked back a sob, and laid his head against the back of the seat. He sighed deeply, closed his eyes and shook his head. *Why were you so careless, John?* Dendree asked the question in his mind as if John could hear him. Of course no answer came, and suddenly he was left with an overwhelming guilt for not preparing John better. *That won't happen again when I come back here with the team.* People are depending on me, Dendree thought. *I've got to take every precaution in the future.*

22

CONFIDENCE

Within a week, Dendree and Anik had assembled the supplies they figured would allow them to safely explore the tomb in the side of the cliff, and had returned to the Mediterranean along with two other younger men from the Society — Alex Jins and Max Reeves. They were hopeful that this time they would all be able to complete the journey and discover the remains of Pharaoh Amenemope and the treasures buried with him. As they pulled into the wayside turnoff, they were surprised to see three SUVs already parked there.

Anik and Dendree exited the Society SUV, alarm quickly rising, as they had been very careful not to reveal their plans to anyone. Who could they be, these men carrying ropes and flashlights, scurrying back and forth to the edge of the cliff? Someone was issuing orders, the sound lost to the screaming of the flock of seagulls that were flying up and around at the cliff's edge and swooping down to the brown mud-mixed sea. Then the men, seven in all, turned to watch Anik and his companions make their way towards them. They parted slightly, and there at the cliff edge was Bill Landing, hands on hips, a smug smile on his face, his contempt obvious.

"Bill Landing! What are you doing here? You are supposed to be in jail," Anik exclaimed. "I don't believe this!"

"Well, hello to you too," Bill replied. "You didn't expect me to rot in prison and let all this treasure just pass me by, did you, you little piss-ant? I can tell you, I've got my ways. And this time, I'm letting you know that I'm in charge."

Dendree and Anik looked at each other, dismay and suppressed anger visible in their expressions. Dendree heaved a big sigh and cast his eyes to the ground, while Anik threw his arms in to the air and turned around to Alex and Max, and then back to Bill.

Bill snapped his fingers and pointed at the arriving men. His crew produced weapons from their belt holsters.

"Last time you got away from me, but this time I intend to keep you close by so I can keep an eye on you. You won't be running home to tell your daddy. You can wait here while I clean out this tomb for myself."

"It might not be as easy as you think, *Bill*," Anik shot back, feeling reckless.

Bill shook his head and laughed.

"Boy, I've been doing this longer than you've been alive. Just watch me," he replied smugly.

"Maybe you should listen to him, Bill. He knows what he's talking about," Dendree retorted.

Bill turned away from Dendree dismissively. He waved to his men and said, "Get some more rope from my truck and tie these guys up."

As two of the men jogged over to the SUV, Bill turned to the oldest man on his crew and said, "Mazen, I'm going to leave you up top here to guard these pests. We'll go below and check things out. We should probably be back within half an hour to let you know how things look down there. Then we'll decide how to proceed."

A small concession was made to Dendree. After he was tied up, he was leaned against the granite post holding the Mud Volcano plaque. The others were left lying on their sides, scattered across the small clearing.

Bill and the other five men put on their harnesses and dropped over the cliff's edge in turn, three at a time. The prisoners lay there passively as they heard the men unhitch their harnesses from the drop rope and make their way into the tomb's shaft.

The setting wasn't so inviting to Anik this time. Besides being tied up, the sea was no longer a sparkling blue. The eruption of the mud volcano had left the water brown, with a slight yellow haze that floated on the sea — sulfur — it smelled like rotten eggs. The fouled water had suffocated many fish, who lay dead on the rocks of the shore below, stinking up the air and making a feast for the indiscriminate gulls.

"Do you think we should have warned Bill about the methane traps?" Max asked quietly.

Anik and Dendree looked at each other and shook their heads in unison.

"Like he said, 'he has his ways'," said Anik bitterly. "He can figure it out for himself."

Mazen, the man guarding the four bound men, sat in the front seat of the SUV closest to them, holding a semiautomatic handgun on them. As time passed, he became restless. He got out and walked around, then wandered to the edge of the cliff and looked over. *Where were they?* While he was distracted, Anik managed to move closer to Max.

He whispered, "I've got a pen knife in my back pocket. Can you reach it?"

Max managed to find the knife and passed it to Anik.

Alex said to the guard, "It's been quite a while since your friends went in the tomb. How long has it been?"

The guard looked at his watch and glared at Alex. He returned to the truck and got a drink of something from a canteen. Then he walked to the cliff edge. He was becoming agitated. It had been nearly an hour since the others had disappeared into the tomb and there was no sign of them.

"They're not coming back, you know," Anik spoke out loud, aiming his words at the gun-toting guard.

"You shut up," said the guard, waving his gun in Anik's face. "They'll be back. Bill knows what he's doing. Just shut up."

"We'll wait, and you'll see that he's not," Anik taunted.

The five men waited for another half hour and still there was no sign of any of the men that had entered the shaft in the side of the cliff. The guard tried unsuccessfully to reach Bill on his walkie-talkie. Walking over to where the ropes hung down the cliff wall, the guard peered over the side and called to Bill.

"Bill, are you there? Can you hear me?"

No answer. After a few minutes, he tried again. Nothing.

All the while that the guard was pacing and fretting, Anik cut at the rope with his pen knife. When he had finally cut through the rope binding his hands, he rolled back and spoke again to the guard.

"He really isn't coming," Anik said with amused conviction.

"How do you know?" the guard asked, lowering his weapon, looking worried.

Dendree raised his face to look squarely at the troubled guard.

"I know, because Anik and I almost died in there. That tomb is a death trap," Dendree exclaimed. "If you don't believe me, check it out for yourself."

The guard stared at Dendree and then looked back at the cliff edge. He turned towards Anik, who nodded vigorously, then spent a few moments considering his options, his modest intellect working hard. He came to a decision. He packed his pistol back in the holster, walked over to the SUV that he had driven in, turned on the engine and drove away.

"There goes a wise man," said Anik as he turned and untied the ropes which bound his feet, and then loosed his companions.

"One thing is for certain. Those guys can't have survived in that cave with just ropes and flashlights. Let's get the scuba air tanks over to the cliff edge. We should be able to continue our venture undisturbed."

Anik and Max assembled the supplies they wanted in the cave and located their own harnesses.

Dendree had his harness in hand, and as he put it on, he said to Alex, "You stay up top here so you can pass down the other equipment, and in case of any emergency. I'd like you to do one more thing. I'm not sure whether or not that fellow is coming back, but I think you should call the police on your cell phone. I don't want to take any chances here and I think we'd all feel safer if we had reinforcements. Those men have guns and if they're not dead, we could have more trouble."

"Okay, Dendree. I can do that. Are you sure you want to go back in the cave? You could stay up here and I could go with the other guys, if you'd like," replied Alex.

"No. I want to do this one last trek. I've been dreaming about this discovery for a long time. I think I can manage it and it will be a crowning achievement to my career. Maybe I'm an old fool, but I just have to go for it. But thanks for the offer."

Anik, Dendree and Max stood on the ledge, each carrying two scuba air tanks to take into the tunnel. Alex stayed at the top of the cliff, bringing over the rest of equipment from their SUV.

"Okay, send the other things down," Max called up.

Alex tied a shovel and a sledgehammer to a rope and lowered it down, followed by two more filled air tanks, then a basket containing halogen flashlights and bottles of water. Inside the cave, the men set off with a tank in each hand and a halogen light. Anik had the hammer strapped to his back. Dendree came next, two air tanks at hand and the backpack containing the water bottles, then Max brought up the rear with two tanks and the shovel strapped to his back.

At the bottom past the first hill, dirt lined the edges, making Anik think that there were probably air vents buried in the corners at the base of every hill. He used his shoe to move the decomposed manure aside as he searched for a stone plug. He found one and then put the air tank down and used the sledgehammer to dislodge the plug with a quick smack on the left side. He discovered one vent in each corner of the lower plateaus and one on each side, halfway between either end — six in all. He opened each one.

At the top of the second hill, Anik set down one air-tank and opened the valve, releasing the pressurized oxygen into the methane pocket.

At the top of the third hill Anik started to experience the familiar lightheaded feeling that he had ignored the last time he was at the exact same spot. He placed his second tank on the floor and opened the valve. He went ahead, descending the slope, and opened the six vents on the plateau. Dendree and Max followed behind Anik and stared up at the third incline rising before them.

"I can't carry these up there, Anik, they're too heavy," Dendree said, feeling the arm strain.

"You're not going to play the old man card, are you?" Anik joked.

Anik grabbed one of Dendree's tanks and raced up the hill. As he placed the tank to one side and opened it, questions flashed through his mind. *How in the world did I not feel the effects of the methane right away like I do now? I guess I slowly got used to it, like a frog in a pot of water on the stove,* Anik answered himself.

The men finally reached the fifth incline where the first of the chained cows were, and there they found the first two guards face down in the soil beside the flattened, black and withered beasts. Anik stared at the chains holding the cows by their necks. The collars were adjustable, so they could also be used to tie their legs, and they were made of pure gold, something Anik hadn't noticed before. He also observed the coating of dust that had settled out of the air over the thousands of years, the only disturbance being the footprints of the people that had walked by. He placed an air tank on the floor and turned on the valve. Oxygen hissed out of the valve — too late for the deceased men that Max had turned over on their backs. Their silent faces mirrored the hopelessness of the situation that Anik and Dendree remembered so clearly from their last trip here. *We were luckier or smarter than these guys. But I wonder where Bill and the other guard are?*

Anik checked his watch and realized the time agreed upon for them to check in with Alex was fast approaching and they needed more air tanks to continue.

"Can you go back and get the other two tanks? I don't know how much further we have to go. And tell Alex to send down the backpack with the face masks for the tanks. That way we can wear the tanks and get more time of safe breathing while we explore."

Dendree and Max made their way back to the ledge to ask Alex for the tanks and masks.

"How are you guys doing down there?" Alex asked.

"Just fine, but the guards we found aren't," Dendree answered. "Did you get through to the police? They can deal with the bodies."

"Yeah. They said they would send a couple of cops out right away."

Anik peered over the edge of the fifth rise to the plateau below where he and Dendree had been trapped, and there he saw five more bodies sprawled haphazardly across the expanse. Anik slid down the hill and shone his light on them. Right in front of him were the other three guards that Bill had brought along. At the other end of the plateau John Thissen lay crumpled from his tumble back down from the sixth incline. In the far corner Bill Landing lay face down, and Anik realized he had found the air vent that had saved Dendree and him. Anik shone his light on Bill. Suddenly time stood still and Anik watched in horror as his nemesis turned around, eyes glazed, pulled his gun from its holster and fired off a shot, totally missing Anik. The loud report echoed through the shaft, temporarily deafening Anik as he sprinted back up the incline. *Holy crap! I can't believe he is still alive*, Anik thought to himself as he sat in the dirt between the cows, armed only with a shovel.

The gun shot reverberated through the tunnel, startling Dendree and Max, who were on their way back from the mouth of the cave with the other two air tanks. As soon as they heard the sound they ran towards Anik. They scaled the incline and hopped over the guards' bodies to where they found him crouched on the floor between the chained cows, holding the shovel.

Anik beat them to the question. "Bill is still alive." He found the air vent that we had opened when we were stuck down there. He is pretty dazed. I am sure we can rush him and get the advantage if we work quickly," Anik whispered.

Anik, Dendree and Max perched at the edge of the slope ready to slide down and surprise Bill. Anik, armed with the shovel stood on the right, Dendree was in the middle and Max was on the left flank. Anik held up his hand and with his fingers silently counted to three.

One, Two, Three, GO!

The three of them slid down the embankment and charged Bill, who was still lying in front of the air hole. Anik, the closest, was on Bill in a flash and kicked the gun out of his hand. Max knelt on Bill's shoulders, pinning him to the floor. Dendree used flexible straps that had been used to carry the air tanks and tied his hands behind his back. Bill offered no resistance to the quick assault and lay on the dirt in utter defeat. The three men dragged Bill up the incline, pulled one of the cows apart and fastened its gold chain around Bill's neck. Bill was left in the dirt, chained to the floor in the midst of the dead cows, with Max guarding him.

The three men discussed what they should do next.

Anik suggested, "Since we don't know how much further we have to go, let's just wear the tanks to ensure that we have enough oxygen. This is as far as we got last time."

"That's a good idea," replied Dendree. "I'm glad you had the foresight to bring the face masks along. It seems as though there is more contamination of the air as we go deeper into the tunnel."

Anik and Dendree got outfitted with the tanks and set off.

"We'll be back within half an hour," Anik said to Max. "Take good care of our prisoner."

They set out, climbing the sixth rise. Along the floor were even more dry, putrefied cows and even deeper mounds of decomposed manure. The two explorers panned their flashlights ahead and were surprised to see that things were changing. Directly before them the tunnel opened up to a large room with mounds of decomposed cow feces piled in baskets lining the walls. There was a concentration of cattle chained up, dozens of them.

Anik turned to Dendree, pointed to his air tank and gave him a 'thumbs up' signal. Dendree nodded vigorously, reassured that they could breathe safely.

As they made their way through this last obstacle, their lights caught color in the distance. They continued walking and searching for more details in the beams of their flashlights. Suddenly they saw it. A wall directly ahead of them covered with a large mural showing Osiris himself leading Amenemope into Aaru.

The two men looked at each other, expressions of delight and expectancy on their faces. They hurried forward in order to get a better look. The progression of Amenemope's journey was illustrated. Each scene was different — one showed Osiris touching Amenemope's mouth with the ankh, the symbol of life. Another showed Osiris leading him past the scales at the Hall of Judgment and into the loving arms of Isis. The last one illustrated Amenemope seated on a throne, surrounded by gifts, food and bowing worshippers.

The two men took a couple of minutes to observe the details of the art more closely.

We are almost there, thought Dendree. *I can hardly believe it.*

As they shone their lights back and forth across the painted wall, they noticed a wooden door, closed and secured with ropes tied in intricate knots, painted with a picture that appeared to be Amenemope's wife. They approached and Dendree cut the cord and opened the door.

When they stepped inside and shone their lights around the room, all they could see was the lustrous reflection of large quantities of gold. Directly ahead of them a golden statue of Osiris seemed to come alive as it glittered in the light, encrusted with jewels. Here was the treasure of Amenemope's tomb — what Dendree had been searching for.

The room was stacked from floor to ceiling with every imaginable treasure. On one side of the room were dozens of cedar wood chests bearing pictures of the Pharaoh in everyday life — getting dressed, being shaved, lining his eyes with kohl. Each chest was emblazoned with Pharaoh's cartouche. Other chests had pictures of Pharaoh wearing different pieces of jewelry — rings, pectoral medallions, arm bands and bracelets, and one bearing the double crown of the two kingdoms.

"I'm sure that the chests and boxes contain the items that are displayed on the outside," said Dendree. "That is the way they would have been stored so that the selected items for wear could easily be located."

They opened a couple of the boxes and admired the finely worked gold items inlaid with jewels and semi-precious stones of all kinds — a profusion of color and splendor.

In another part of the room was the collection of furniture — various chairs, stools, beds and divans — mostly all overlaid with gold. Some of it was dismantled and stacked so that it couldn't be clearly identified, but it all shone with warm richness in the beam of the flashlights. The most striking item in the collection was Amenemope's golden throne. It stood slightly apart from the bulk of the furniture and included the three steps up to the chair. The arms were composed of intertwining serpents of bronze and lapis lazuli. The legs were like those of lions, with gold paws. A war scene was carved into the back of the chair and there were golden rays fanning out from the circle of the sun located across the top of the back.

Beyond that was the weaponry. Amenemope's golden chariot, imbedded with jewels and bearing his cartouche on the sides, sat at the front of the bulk of the weapons. There were quivers attached to the side panels just behind the wheels which were filled with arrows and javelins. Behind the chariot stood piles of shields and helmets, breastplates and war bows. There were racks of swords and spears, and a large array of daggers of all kinds.

They also noticed piles of plates and goblets, bowls of alabaster or bronze as well as pitchers and ornately painted pottery.

The centerpiece of the display was the large statue of Osiris, and they made their way through the collection to see whatever was located on the other side of the statue, now concealed from their view. As they crowded past the statue, their eyes fell on the large, majestic sarcophagus made of blue granite standing alone on the far side of the statue.

"Wow! There it is," Anik and Dendree said in unison.

The granite outer sarcophagus stood four feet off the floor on a plinth. They expected that there would be other inner anthropoid sarcophagi nested inside each other before they came upon the actual mummified remains of Pharaoh Amenemope. The detail that presented itself in front of them was astounding. Amenemope's carved likeness on the lid was an exact copy of the statue that they had found in the dunes and the picture on the floor of the pyramid.

"I wonder, Dendree, how did they get this coffin in here? It's so large and heavy. I can't imagine how they were able to take it down the side of the cliff. And all those cows — how did they get them in here?" Anik asked, feeling overwhelmed, not expecting an answer.

"It's really quite amazing, isn't it," replied Dendree.

They looked around at the far end of the burial chamber and saw a sealed opening in the wall. Across the gold-beaten door, two names were delicately inscribed. The one on the left was that of the chief architect, Khnum, and the second one was of a man named Wijin. Dendree quickly broke the seal and walked in. Before them, two golden sarcophagi sat, and a third smaller plain wooden casket lay between them, piled high with dried flowers. Dendree and Anik walked tentatively to the middle of the room, inspecting the three ancient coffins. On each sarcophagus, in beautiful hieroglyphs, were the names that they had read on the door.

Anik said, "See that name — Wijin? His name was carved in small figures on the capstone of the pyramid I found in the desert. He must have been a builder and Khnum was an architect, as it says here."

After seeing Khnum and Wijin's titles, they turned their attention to the plain wooden casket that seemed so out of place in this royal tomb. Anik pointed to the name that was painted on the side. In beautiful stylized script was Akila's name. A finely crafted picture of her, holding paintbrushes and taking the honorary spot at Wijin's feet, showed that she was his wife.

"This is welcome detail about Akila," said Dendree. "I'm glad to see a picture of her after realizing what a skillful artist she was. I wonder how true to life the likeness is."

The sarcophagi were surrounded with gold shrines, statues, bolts of the finest linens, now blackened shreds, and beautiful painted pottery stacked against the wall, along with chests overlaid with gold.

The wall itself was like one massive story board recounting the life of each man.

"Anik, I'm going to need your help," Dendree said as he motioned towards the hieroglyphic-covered wall.

Anik stared at the lines of hieroglyphs. There was no blank spot anywhere on the wall.

"I'm really glad you invited me on this search, Dendree. It looks as though in addition to finding the tomb of Amenemope, we will find many answers to the story of these other people. I'm looking forward to helping you decipher these symbols. We had probably better head back. We want to make sure that the air in these tanks lasts for as long as we need it."

Dendree and Anik arrived back at the place where they had left Max holding a gun on Bill, who was still chained to the floor.

"We found the treasure! It is spectacular!" Dendree said, his face beaming. "Would you like to see it, Max?"

"Absolutely!" Max replied, his anticipation spiking.

As Anik took the gun from Max, he said, "Don't take too long."

"No problem," Dendree replied as they headed up the hill towards the burial chamber.

Anik sat in the soil with his back against the far wall and kept the gun trained on Bill. *What if this gun "accidentally" fires? Here I am alone with this bastard. I could put him out of his misery with one well-placed shot. I'm starting to think that putting him down is the only way we are going to keep him out of our lives. They couldn't even keep him in jail for attempted murder. Bill surely deserves it for all that he has done!*

In the dim light, Anik didn't notice that Bill had managed to free himself from his restraints. He remained quite still, waiting for his chance to make an escape.

Anik started to get a sore butt sitting so awkwardly, so he decided to stand up and stretch his legs. He sauntered over to where Bill was curled up on the floor and squatted down and looked at him. *Right here, I could do it,* he thought, feeling the gun in his hand. *I can't. That will make me no better than him.* Not thinking about his safety, Anik switched the safety to the 'ON' position. He looked at Bill's face, close enough to monitor his breathing. Anik could see Bill's eyes moving behind his eyelids, which startled him. One second later, Bill, sensing his chance, rose up and tackled him. Anik managed to slip out of Bill's grasp, aimed the gun in Bill's direction and pulled the trigger. The safety was on! Bill seized the moment, drove his body into Anik and wrestled the gun out of his hand. In one fluid motion, Bill switched off the safety and shot Anik. The bullet, like a hot dagger, pierced Anik's right shoulder. He spun around like a top and crumpled to the floor in agony, blood running down his arm and into the dirt. Bill knelt down beside Anik lying on the floor, feeling triumphant, and snorted into his face.

"You're pathetic, do you know that? You know … that old man, Huy said you were a tough competitor. I guess he was talking about your chess game and not your physical skills," Bill said with a smirk and a chuckle.

Bill slammed his fist into Anik's face, knocking him out.

"What's going on here?" Dendree asked.

Dendree had returned to see how Anik was doing guarding Bill and had just appeared on the top of the sixth rise. Bill stared at Dendree and said nothing. He picked up the gun, raised it methodically and fired one shot. It caught Dendree just below the collarbone on the right side. Dendree dropped like a stone. The loud reverberating shot rattled

Anik's head just enough to wake him. His head was swimming from Bill's blow and his ears were ringing from the gunshot. Through bleary eyes he could see Bill crouching next to him.

Anik moaned as he put his hand on his head and squeezed his eyes shut in pain. Bill saw his discomfort and rapped his gun barrel across the hand that cradled his temple, breaking two of his fingers. Anik cried out in pain.

"Huy was a tough, stubborn old fool himself, but it didn't do him much good," Bill said as he rose, turned, and shambled back towards the entrance of the cave.

Hearing the shots that were fired, Max hustled back to the spot where Bill had been tied, but now Bill was gone and Anik and Dendree were both wounded. They were both conscious, still alive.

Dendree stammered, "It should be okay, Max. Alex called the police and they were sending reinforcements. Bill does have a gun, though."

Max replied, "I'll head back and see if I can help. I'll bring someone back with me to help get you two out of here."

After he was out of sight, Anik's head began to clear somewhat. Bill had still retained the upper hand and it sure sounded as though he had done harm to Huy. *I can't believe I was so stupid as to let him take me like that*, thought Anik. *And why does he keep mentioning Huy? If he killed that gentle old man, he really needs to be destroyed.* Frustration and fury seethed within him.

Bill slowed to a walk as he neared the entrance to the cave. He was surprised when he came upon two police officers. They were all caught off-guard, but Bill was the first to aim and fire, injuring one of the officers. Shots were returned, one bullet grazing Bill's thigh. Bill limped over to the wall of the cave and knelt down to get out of the line of fire. It took him some time to refocus and deal with the pain in his leg.

He looked up to see the other policeman make his way back to the entrance of the cave.

Hearing the shots, Max picked up his pace, staying close to the wall to try to remain unnoticed. However, he inadvertently came right up alongside Bill, who heard him coming and shot him in the heart when he was just a few steps away from him.

"Maybe I'll manage to get through this mess after all," mumbled Bill to himself as he moved forward, leaving Max's body in his wake.

Back in the cave, shots that rang out filled Anik with dread.

I wonder what has happened out there, he thought. *I can't just wait here and hope for someone to rescue us. I've got to get out there myself. If Bill has survived all that shooting, we're still as good as dead in here.*

He turned to Dendree.

"I'm going back out there, Dendree. My eyes are used to the darkness now. I'm worried that Max might not have made it. Just waiting here may not be the best idea. Will you be okay?"

"I've got my wits about me, my boy, but I'm afraid that I couldn't make it back to the entrance without some assistance. Are you sure you want to venture back into such danger?"

"I'll be careful. This might be our only chance to escape. I can't let Bill keep doing this to us. I've got to stop him, or die trying."

With that, he got up, mustered all his strength, set his face like flint, and trudged back towards the entrance, denying his pain, determination churning within him. By the time he reached the far side of the third rise, the light from outside was filtering into the cave. Anik looked down on the plateau ahead of him and there he spotted Max's body and the badly injured policeman. He leaned against the wall of the cave to consider his options and try to locate Bill when another shot rang out at the entrance of the cave. Anik made his way to the top of the first rise. When he got to the edge nearest the entrance he looked down and there was another policeman's body sprawled on the floor about seven meters from the cliff edge.

Bill was there on the ledge fumbling with the harness, trying to get into it. Anik could tell from the way he was moving that he was injured and that it was hindering his progress. He seemed preoccupied and oblivious to the prospect that anyone else could be a threat to him.

It's now or never, thought Anik. He moved as quietly as he could along the wall, down the last incline and along the last stretch towards the entrance.

All at once Bill looked up and saw Anik staring at him grimly from just a few meters away. A look of surprise and shock crossed his face, then quickly passed, replaced by an expression of contempt.

"Ah! The little boy is back to save the day, is that what you think?" Bill sneered at him. "Well I'm stopping this right now!"

Bill pulled out his gun and pointed it at Anik

"Say your prayers, kid."

Anik raised his hands and said, "Wait a minute, wait a minute, Bill!"

"Wait! Wait for what?" Bill asked. "You're just like that old man and his wife, always wanting to take time. Well, time's up."

Bill reached into his pocket with his free hand and after finding what he was looking for, pulled out a clenched fist and held it at his side.

"Your friend was a poor excuse for a man, don't you think, living with his wife in that run-down dump. Did you say good-bye to him the last time you saw him? I hope so."

Anik burned with a rage he had never known as Bill continued to taunt him.

"All he seemed to do was sit with his fancy chess set and smoke that pipe. Nothing to do but just sit and wait for you. Pretty sad if you ask me …"

"What did you do to him, Bill? If you touched him … I'll …"

"What? You'll do what, boy? Ooh, I almost forgot. I have something for you." Bill tossed something at him. "Checkmate … I win."

Anik caught it in mid-air and looked at it. It was the white King from the set that he had given to Huy. Anik glared at Bill, fear gone, pain suppressed, all resolve focused on stopping this evil man who didn't know when to quit.

Bill raised his eyebrows with a smug expression, aimed his gun and pulled the trigger. "Click." Miss-fire. Bill looked at the gun with disgust. Anik charged Bill in a state of rage and slammed his good shoulder into his broad chest, pushing him back towards the opening of the shaft. Bill was thrown off-balance, but partially steadied himself by grasping onto the wall. Anik charged him again and knocked his considerable bulk closer to the edge. Bill dropped the gun, still grasping onto the wall for support. He swung his free hand at Anik, hitting him in the face. The strike dazed him temporarily, but Anik, not to be deterred, stood up to Bill, eye to eye, and shoved him again — hard. Bill still held onto wall with his left hand to steady himself. Anik repositioned the chess piece in his hand, and jabbed it into Bill's hand with all his might. Bill jerked his hand away with a scream, losing his grip on the wall. Time slowed to a crawl as Bill frantically tried to regain his balance. His luck had finally run out. He stumbled over the edge, arms flailing desperately as he plunged down the cliff face to the rocks and churning surf far below.

Anik rushed to the cliff edge and stared down at Bill. No longer a dangerous interloper and opponent, he was now a flaccid piece of flotsam, tossed about helplessly by the tumultuous water. Bill was gone for good.

The screaming gulls swooped past the entrance to the tomb, diving and soaring, impervious to the magnitude of what had just happened.

Anik couldn't take his eyes off the sight at the base of the cliff. As the adrenalin subsided, his strength ebbed, pain and weakness enfolded him like a cloak and he fell backwards against the entrance to the tomb, totally spent.

From the top of the cliff he heard Alex Jin's voice calling him.

"Is that you, Anik? Are you okay? What happened down there?"

"We need some help, Alex," he managed to reply.

"That second policeman came back to tell me to call for reinforcements. They should be here soon. Is everyone okay? I heard guns."

"No, Alex, we are not okay. Just Dendree and I are still alive, and maybe the policemen. Max is gone, and so is Bill Landing. There's no way we can get ourselves back up the cliff."

"Max is gone? Oh no! Wait … here come the reinforcements. Don't worry. The danger is past. They will look after things," Alex called down.

You said one true thing, Alex. The danger is past, thought Anik. *Finally.* Even though he had not one ounce of strength left, it seemed as though a great weight that he had carried for a long time had lifted. A realization of justice rendered surged through him and even in his weakness and pain, he was satisfied.

In time the two wounded archeologists were rescued. One of the policemen managed to survive, but Max, the other policeman, Bill and his five cohorts were dead, along with John Thissen. The locating of Amenemope's tomb was considered another major find in the country's cultural heritage, and Dendree Yusik received a great deal more prominence as he oversaw the retrieval of the treasures of the tomb. Of special interest was the blue granite sarcophagus that held the mummified remains of Pharaoh Amenemope. They found three coffins inside the large stone one: two made of wood and the final one of pure hammered gold.

All items were cataloged and photographed. A major display at the Luxor museum drew visitors from all over, and two traveling displays appeared at major museums throughout the world. The value of the collection was estimated at two hundred million dollars — giving a significant boost to the wealth of Egypt. Dendree was well rewarded for his discovery.

The hieroglyphs covering the far wall of the treasure chamber were thoroughly photographed. Anik went to work at the Egyptian Archeological Society and he and Dendree spent three years deciphering the story of Egypt's Pharaoh Amenemope and his most trusted staff. In time, they had assembled all the information that they had accumulated about this period in Egypt's history.

Dendree's debt of gratitude towards Anik for his help and valiant protection sealed the unique friendship between the two men, enriching both of their lives. At last, mysteries were solved, questions were answered, and a life's work completed except for one last endeavor — sharing the fascinating story with others who might not get to Egypt. *Maybe I will write a book*, Dendree mused.

BIBLIOGRAPHY

The History of Ancient Egypt Course
   –Professor Bob Brier Ph.D.

Egyptian Mythology
   –Aude Gros de Beler

Daily Life in Ancient Egypt
   –Lionel Casson

Ancient Egypt
   –Karl W. Butzler
   –Virginia Lee Davis
   –I. E. S. Edwards
   –Barbara Mertz
   –William H. Peck
   –Edna R. Russmann
   –William Kelly Simpson
   –Anthony J. Spalinger

Egypt
   –The World of the Pharaohs
   –Könemann

Pyramid
   –David Macaulay

Egypt of the Pharaohs
   –Brian Fagan

The Egyptian Book of the Dead
   –The Papyrus of Ani
   –Translated by Dr. Raymond O. Faulkner, Dr. Ogden Goelet Jr.

The Realm of the Pharaohs
   –Zahi Hawass

Conversations With Mummies
   –Rosalie David
   –Rick Achbold

Secrets From the Past
   –Gene S. Stuart

Ancient Egypt
   –David P. Silverman (General Editor)

The Ancient Egyptians
   –Religious Beliefs and Practices
   –A. Rosalie David

Daughters of Isis
   –Women of Ancient Egypt
   –Joyce Tyldesley

Wisdom of Amenemope
   –http://egypt.thetao.info/amenemope.htm   (1)
   –http://www.maat.sofiatopia.org/amen_em_apt.htm
   –http://www.humanistictexts.org/amenope.htm

Ancient Egyptian Songs
   –http://www.ancientegyptonline.co.uk/harper-song.html (2)
   –http://news.nationalgeographic.com/news/2004/04/0416_040416_
pyramidsongs.html (3)

QUICK ORDER FORM
for Bulk Orders

Satisfaction guaranteed

E-mail orders: books@BrightHorizonBooks.com

Postal orders:
Bright Horizon Books
520 Thorndale Drive,
Waterloo, ON
N2T 2A8

Book Title: Secret Destruction

Quantity: _____

Name: _____

Address:

_____

_____

_____

City, State/Province, Zip/Postal Code

Tel: _____

Email: _____

You will be contacted with a quote including shipping